Madam's Jewels

A Novel

Nicole Leena

1

For my mother, Margaret Klouw-Petrauskas. You have been my lighthouse, as I was a ship lost at sea my entire life. Without you, I could not have accomplished this. I would still be tossing around at sea with no guidance to pull me back home to you and our family.

For Professor Robert Andrew Zbeeb, also known as Pop Pop. Without you, I wouldn't have been given a new name from a wonderful, loving father. I never would have known what I was truly made of by watching and learning from you.

ISBN: 9798732100464

Chapter 1

"Gia, it's going to be fine! Dr. Lee is one of the most experienced fertility doctors in New York. I bet we have at *least* 4 viable embryos!"

Gia sighed out her concerns and worries. She tried to smile, but she had a gut instinct that they would be let down once again. Poor Charlotte. Her loving and beautiful wife had wanted to become pregnant so severely that she had undergone all of the horrors that befall a woman who simply wants to have what nature intended. Charlotte endured the shots, the raging hormones, the painful procedure to have her eggs removed. Gia was always the tough one. She experienced daily hatred, not just because she was an open lesbian, but also because she was the top detective in her New York precinct. She'd observed some gruesome murders, but nothing had ever made her feel so utterly incompetent as dealing with Charlotte's pain. She wasn't built to stand back and let these so-called "specialists" hurt her sweet Charlotte. Nothing could have prepared her for the bruises from the injections, and the toll the hormones were taking on a once very calm Charlotte, only to have an emotional wreck meet her at the door each morning after working nights. Gia was beat up; her love for Charlotte was something she had never wanted.

Thinking back to her life before Charlotte, all Gia wanted to do was have her standard, easy affairs that she'd meet at the gay bars. No communication, just lust, and then, it was back to work. Work was her identity. She had her freedom to do whatever and whoever she wanted.

Her face, which had once been free of lines in her 20's, now constantly looked like she was smelling something putrid. Gia was ugly. Physically, she knew how dull her brown hair was that she always had cut into a boring straight bob, just long enough for her to put up her hair at crime scenes. Her brown eyes not only looked like the color of dark shit, but they were also dull; there was no sparkle in her eyes. Her face had a constant pinched look. She looked older than 47. Her emotions were kept in captivity, but they had to be because Gia was the lead homicide detective in her precinct. That was all she wanted in life: work, affairs, and more work. That is until two years ago, when she saw Charlotte across from her at the one and only gay bar she called her home away from home.

Gia had been heavily drinking that entire day. The gruesome part of picking up pieces of a body chopped up was vomit-inducing enough, only to find out that it was a hate crime. De'Shawn, her victim, was an openly gay man. He dressed in drag, but the world was cruel, and De'Shawn paid the price for delusional sickos. She had seen De'Shawn perform his drag queen acts at her frequent hangout. He did a superb Diana Ross. The two of them would often get drunk together and laugh until it was closing time. De'Shawn had become her friend. He never judged her for being in the gay club and drinking way too much, way too often.

To say Gia was drinking to get drunk was an understatement. She was drinking to numb and forget, yet she knew the hangover the next day would only make her feel worse. She didn't care. De'Shawn was dead. Arms severed… legs chainsawed off… and the decapitated head showed De'Shawn's eyes open in a look of such pain and dread, Gia found herself wishing, not for the first time in her life, that she had chosen a different career. But she'd find the son of a bitch or the gang of racist/homophobic bastards that cut up De'Shawn as a butcher takes to slicing up meat.

As she swallowed her fifteenth straight whiskey, she saw a beautiful, tall blonde enter the room. Gia was just drab, plain and dreary in every possible way, and in walks this supermodel. She had to be close to six feet tall. She was a goddess strolling through the restaurant area to make her way to the massive bar, Gia's only place she resided in at the club. Gia didn't know what to look at first because there was so much beauty before her. The woman was literally glowing and had a lightness around her. Her eyes sparkled like a bright sapphire diamond. Gia just watched her, and she found herself glaring at this goddess on earth. She wasn't jealous by her beauty and joy that seemed to exude from her like a waft of perfume. No, Gia cringed angrily because she knew she had found the most lovely woman in the world, and there was no way in hell she would ever look at Gia's dowdy and grumpy demeanor that never left her.

As the goddess ordered her cranberry and vodka drink, Gia couldn't help but notice the way her blonde hair was wavy and cascaded over her petite shoulders. This woman was the essence of Aphrodite. Gia could not take her eyes away from the goddess as she watched her scan the room, smiling. Smiling about what, Gia couldn't comprehend. She hadn't smiled since she had made head detective.

Gia was still staring at her when the bedazzled sapphire eyes landed on her shit brown ones. She almost coughed up the whiskey she was sipping. Right then, she knew the goddess, now Charlotte, would be her wife. In fact, it was Charlotte who stared intently at Gia. She was the one who made her way to Gia and sat down next to her. Charlotte was the one who spoke first.

"You look burdened. Please, feel free to talk about it."

What shocked Gia the most, outside of this 30 year old coming up to her, was that she found herself sharing. She could see that Charlotte was only interested in her and what she had to say. Charlotte would cringe throughout her story, considering she taught preschool and was not used to the horrors and tragedy of police work, but Charlotte was stronger than she appeared. Within six months, they were engaged and married. Again, it was Charlotte who had asked dull, short, frumpy, grumpy Gia to marry her.

As Gia reflected on how their lives had changed in the past two years, she still couldn't believe Charlotte was her wife. Gia wanted to protect her, and damn it, if she hadn't had early menopause at thirty-five, she would be the one going through the pain and agony that poor, sweet Charlotte was struggling through. Gia had to hold back another sigh. Charlotte was such a fighter, and Gia was in awe of how much getting pregnant via in vitro fertilization was such a massive abuse on the body and spirit. Charlotte's life revolved around children. She was a single child and wanted to have twins, triplets, quadruplets… the number didn't matter to her. Charlotte wanted a family, and she was a stubborn Taurus who would not back down.

Charlotte was the only person who could soften Gia. Perhaps, having a baby or babies would be good for Gia's soul. She was feeling the negative energy constantly. Gia knew she drank too much, and this definitely didn't lend itself to making her a happier person. If anything, she didn't want to drink alone, so she would often get Charlotte to drink with her. Unfortunately, Gia would become belligerent, and the fights they had when drinking had caused a strain on their marriage. Maybe Charlotte thought having a child would fix Gia's dependency on alcohol. There were times, Gia admitted to herself and only herself, that she resented being married. If she wanted to go on a drinking bender, she had to deal with someone else's questions and admonishments. Life was so much easier when Gia was alone, yet for some reason, she found herself unable to separate her life and love from Charlotte.

Actually, the whole process of trying to get Charlotte pregnant was arduous and took an even larger toll on their marriage. The stress, hormones, anxiety and fear were impacting their relationship, and Gia often said she had to "work" when she'd just need a night to go and get drunk at her usual hangout. Luckily, Charlotte would be gone to work when Gia stumbled home drunk after she'd hung out at her best friend Riley's place, who also worked at the precinct with her on midnights. Riley wasn't gay, and Gia found their friendship from high school her longest and most successful relationship. When Riley had married that idiot Tim, Gia was the maid of honor. When Riley had divorced the cheating bastard, Gia had been there too.

Now, Gia felt the strain, but she knew if Charlotte could just get pregnant, they'd be back to their somewhat solid and grounded relationship. She'd been praying, but she wasn't an actual believer. This was their second round. Charlotte had gotten pregnant, but the miscarriage occurred at exactly 12 weeks. That was a pain Charlotte and Gia shared that no one else would ever understand. The setback was for a month, and then Charlotte was in full swing, ready to try again. Her parents were wealthy, so they were happy to pay because they wanted a grandchild so badly; they said they would pay a million dollars just to see their little princess become a mother.

Unfortunately, Gia had a feeling they might be paying a hell of a lot more than that. Her gut instinct was telling her this was not going to go well. Perhaps it was the sperm donor? But Charlotte was ridiculously healthy, and since she was only thirty-two, she was not considered a risk because her pregnancy would not fall under the geriatric category. Her eggs were all in great shape, but the only concern was her one ovary didn't produce any eggs. Gia knew this bothered Charlotte because she had once said she didn't understand why her body couldn't function like other women her age, who had at least two or three children by 32.

It was Charlotte who reached across to hold Gia's hand as they sat in Dr. Lee's office, waiting to see how many embryos they could implant into Charlotte's uterus this time. Charlotte's younger and smoother looking hands squeezed Gia's thicker and raw hands. Gia used the same expensive creams as Charlotte before she went to bed to no avail. Gia was alarmed at how old she appeared next to Charlotte. Her hand was thin and smooth, without a trace of an age spot; Gia felt self-conscious being fifteen years older. How would Charlotte feel when she was in her forties, while Gia was in her sixties? Gia could see from her genetics that she wasn't aging well. Too puffy, well, everywhere, while Charlotte's parents both looked younger than Gia. She still never understood what Charlotte saw in her.

The only thing Charlotte ever said was, "You looked so sad. I wanted to see if I could make you smile. And once I did, I knew I wanted to do that for the rest of my life."

Gia squeezed Charlotte's hand to offer her quiet support. Yes, this was about their baby, but in actuality, Gia was just doing this to make Charlotte happy. She didn't really want kids. Actually, she could not stand them, but if it would make Charlotte feel like their family was complete, she'd do it. Gia knew she put Charlotte through a lot with her grumpiness and, some might say, verbal abuse, but Gia was simply harsh with her words; she didn't know how to be sweet and soften her heart.

"Charlotte… it's going to be fine," Gia lied through her teeth and tried to swallow the guilt of hoping there would be no baby.

Charlotte's sapphire eyes sparkled with unshed tears as she whispered, "I know. It's just… what if it didn't work this time?"

"Well, maybe we'll just take a break to give your body time to heal and-"

Charlotte's usually large, blue eyes were now slits of rage. She reminded Gia of a menacing cat.

"I will never take a break! We will have a goddamn baby! I don't care how many times I have to be poked and prodded and endure this personal hell. I know I'm on a time limit here, since I only have one functioning ovary! I need this more than you could possibly understand."

"I do understand. I'm sorry. I know this has been terrible for you."

Charlotte immediately became her old, sweet self.

"No, I'm sorry. My hormones are all out of whack. I didn't mean to snap at you like a rabid dog."

"Eh, more like a menacing cobra," Gia teased.

Charlotte smiled, as she said sweetly, "You are my rock, and I love you so much." Charlotte's eyes started to pool over with tears, which of course never ruined her eye makeup. "I just can't wait for the day when we hold our baby, or I hear mommy for the first time."

Gia reached over Dr. Lee's dark, cherrywood desk to the box of tissues. Charlotte swiped a few out in exasperation.

"Damn hormones," she mumbled.

In a much more reassuring tone, Gia said, "You will have this dream come true. You're going to hear mommy screamed constantly! You're beautiful and strong; never forget that."

Charlotte sniffled a little and gave a wry smile.

"You know, with the sperm donor being over six feet tall and me just at six feet, our baby will come out taller than you!"

Gia rolled her dull brown eyes and replied, "Ugh, so mean!"

"You're my little elf. A perfect 5.0!"

"Being five foot is perfect."

"Yup, for a hobbit."

This is when Gia knew Charlotte, her Charlotte, minus the hormones, was back. She always found it hilarious to tease Gia about how short she was. The nicknames Charlotte came up with were dorky, beyond belief, but Charlotte's laugh made Gia smile.

They heard the door open behind them, and Gia felt impending doom for Charlotte as Dr. Lee, a short man, but taller than Gia, came into the room and took his seat behind his large desk.

"Hello Mrs. Carter," he nodded towards Gia and then towards Charlotte, as he added, "Mrs. Carter."

Dr. Lee was highly intelligent, and he carried himself that way. One could almost see the multiple degrees at Big Ten schools rolling through his body when he made his entrance into a room. He wasn't necessarily arrogant, but he was definitely lacking the social warmth one would think a doctor would have when dealing with such a life-changing course of treatment. Gia wondered if she came across to others as cold and aloof, like their doctor, and she feared it was probably much worse than her perception of Dr. Lee. Even Charlotte, who liked everyone, didn't appreciate his standoffish nature. They dealt with him because he was allegedly the best fertility doctor in New York.

As they waited to hear what Dr. Lee had in store for their fate, Gia sat back and crossed her arms over her chest. She clenched her jaw, feeling the nerves zapping her insides. Charlotte, on the other hand, couldn't keep still. She kept moving her hands and arms in a weird, puppet-like way. Her crossed leg was swaying back and forth so much, it looked like she was trying to remove something from her leg. Charlotte's once calm face was now etched with worry lines. Her blonde eyebrows furrowed, and her anxiety could be felt by Gia as Charlotte watched the doctor flip through some notes in her file, and he sometimes would glance at his computer screen with no expression at all. His circular glasses made him seem even more adept and intelligent as he scrutinized some notes.

Gia wanted to punch him as she thought, *Fuck, Doc! Give us the results already! What the hell are you waiting for?*

As Gia's mind swirled with ways she could beat the hell out of Dr. Lee, Charlotte's thoughts were pure. *Please, please, please let us implant the four embryos and let at least one take. Please, God, help me get the baby I know you want me to have.*

Dr. Lee adjusted his gold-rimmed spectacles and cleared his throat, an annoying habit both Gia and Charlotte made fun of after they would leave his office, but there was no smiling now.

He simply stated, "Mrs. Carter, there are no viable embryos for implantation."

Charlotte's face fell as though her puppet master had released her strings.

She gasped, "What? Why?"

Dr. Lee looked at Charlotte as though she were an idiot. He definitely did not have the bedside manner for such a difficult situation, but he was the best.

He cleared his throat again and stated plainly, "Mrs. Carter, none of the embryos were viable. We inserted the sperm into the four eggs, but there was no cellular development. They have been discarded."

Charlotte stood up, looming over Dr. Lee's desk.

"Discarded? Discarded! How dare you say something so blase about what could have been a potential baby or babies! Discarded as though they were nothing? Like common trash? You are a harsh, little man! Shame on you for speaking of my potential babies as nothing more than a science experiment to you! You promised us results! You promised this would be the month when we could implant new embryos! You made a fucking promise, you annoying piece of shit little man!"

Charlotte's redness was almost purple at her chest and neck, then a scarlett hue from her chin to her forehead, and finally her forehead was a shade of red that aligned more with the color of a poinsettia. Gia's mouth fell open, for she had never heard Charlotte speak like this to anyone.

Charlotte looked possessed as she began to try to catch her breath after the barrage of verbal bullets she'd just fired at Dr. Lee. She just couldn't breathe. Charlotte's fingers were numb, yet they had needles in them. She felt like a massive boulder was on her chest. She began to hyperventilate as she tried to catch her breath. She couldn't swallow. Charlotte feared she was having a heart attack.

Dr. Lee rushed over to her and helped her sit down. He hit a button on his phone that went directly to his nurse, Alice. When she responded, Dr. Lee hurriedly told her to get in his office now with some water.

Soothingly, he said, "Mrs. Carter, you are having an anxiety attack. Please place her head between your knees, breathe in for six seconds and release your breath for six seconds. This will pass. You are safe. We just need to calm your breathing."

Charlotte did as she was told. She felt Gia rubbing her back. She heard Alice enter, and heard the doctor demand what took her so long. She felt a cold bottle of water being handed to her. She breathed in and she breathed out. Although she was shaking like it was twenty degrees below zero in the room, she was finally able to control her breathing. The agonizing terror of the panic attack had her reeling. She feared it would happen again. With shaky hands, she took a sip of water.

Through her muffled ears she heard Gia ask if she was okay. Charlotte couldn't respond. How could she be okay? She was directly back at square one. In her mind, those were 4 babies he had tossed down the toilet like pieces of shit. Why was she a failure at being a woman? The thought of God punishing her for being gay flew through her mind, but only for a moment. She knew better. The God she loved and prayed to loved her because she was His child. Charlotte hated how that thought would go through her head every now and then when things looked bleak and dark in her life.

Charlotte let another thought pass through her mind. *I would sell my soul to the devil to become a mother.*

She had never thought such a thing in her life, but the scary thing was, she actually meant it. Some people craved money, power, fame, but Charlotte ached to become a mother. She recalled always putting a pillow under her shirt and gazing at herself in the mirror as she fantasized about a baby kicking her. Charlotte would have that dream. She would do whatever it took.

With calmness Charlotte had never felt before, she asked, "Who else is one of the best fertility doctors in the state?"

Dr. Lee, for the first time, showed emotion, as he looked aghast.

"Excuse me? I'm the best."

"No. No, you most certainly are not. Who is your biggest competitor?"

Now Dr. Lee's face grew red as he responded, "If you no longer require my care, then I will ask you both to leave."

Charlotte stood up and hovered over the little man, gritting out angrily, "I want all of my records… now. For my new doctor."

Dr. Lee escaped to safety behind his massive desk.

"Alice will help you with that," he nodded at Alice who was still in the room.

Alice had bold red hair, and she was the sweetest nurse Charlotte had ever encountered. Her blue eyes seemed to match her own.

"Absolutely, Charlotte. Let's go get that paperwork for you."

Before leaving, Charlotte leaned over Dr. Lee's desk. She had fire in her eyes.

She hissed, "I will find your competitor, and since my parents are well-acquainted with every politician and celebrity in New York, I will make certain you lose your business. Have a blessed day."

Charlotte stormed out with Gia on her heels.

Gia simply replied, "Yeah, what she said!"

As soon as Gia slammed the door behind her, she heard Charlotte release the breath she had been holding. Charlotte hated confrontation, but when it came to tossing her potential babies out like medical sludge, she turned almost demonic. Charlotte's shaking had eased somewhat as she went to Alice's desk to sign the release letter for all of her medical records.

Alice looked somber and sympathetic as she whispered, "Charlotte, I am so sorry. He's really an ass. I… Oh. it just breaks my heart."

Charlotte gave a pained smile.

"Thanks, Alice."

As Alice was putting the documents together, she waved Gia over to where Charlotte stood.

Again, she whispered, "I too had trouble getting pregnant. I now have a daughter and a son. She's a unique fertility doctor, surgeon, OBGYN… I mean she has so many degrees, I can't even list them all."

Charlotte's eyebrows flew up as she immediately pounced with, "Who is she? Why haven't I heard about her before on the Internet?"

Alice shrugged as she replied, "Madam's business, which is booming, is spread through word of mouth. That's all she asks: if you're happy, you refer others in need to her. Two of my friends went to her. They love Madam!" Alice paused and laughed to herself. "However, she is quite unique in her methods. Crystals, sage ceremonies, Reiki, teas, acupuncture... She's big into holistic healing, and Madam insists on becoming friends with her clients. Every holiday season, she hosts a massive celebration for the women, their spouses or partners and their children over to her house in upstate New York. It looks like a castle! I swear! I feel like I enter another century when I enter Madam's house."

Gia's face scrunched up, showing her ugly lines on her face.

"Who goes by Madam?"

Alice looked at Gia like she was a child and slowly said, "Madam does."

Charlotte elbowed Gia, but her laser focus was on Alice.

"So you have a daughter and a son?"

Alice smiled and showed them a family picture of two beautiful children with her and her husband. The little girl had Alice's vibrant red hair and blue eyes, while the baby boy was already showing signs of looking like his father, with a head of white-blonde hair and big brown eyes.

"I did lose a baby the first time around, but that wasn't Madam's fault. The cord had been around his neck. She couldn't resuscitate him." Alice paused as a wave of grief hindered her words momentarily. "But after that hardship, my husband and I now have two healthy and beautiful children."

Charlotte immediately smiled as she asked, "Can I find her on the Internet?"

Alice shook her head and said, "She is extremely old school. Referrals are the only way she stays in business, and given the size of her home and the amount of floors she owns at her fertility clinic in downtown Manhattan, I'd say she's the best there is. When we're at one of her holiday parties, there are so many children running around and so many doting parents... it's the most beautiful thing I've ever seen."

Charlotte worriedly asked, "Well, how am I supposed to get in contact with her?"

Alice smiled, went through her wallet and pulled out several laminated cards in blue and pink and gave her a blue one.

Charlotte read aloud, "Madam's Jewels."

Gia rolled her eyes and annoyedly asked, "Seriously?"

Charlotte spun around on her.

"Damnit Gia! This is it! You heard Alice. Plus, she even befriends her patients and has them over to her home. Talk about having a great bedside manner!"

"Come on, it sounds like she's a hippy or a sorceress. Crystals? Acupuncture? Reiki?"

"You know what, Gia? If you don't want to go with me, that's fine. But I am going to call this number and see this, this... Madam person."

Alice smiled and replied delightedly, "You won't regret it."

Chapter 2

Madam was in her sanctuary. She had built the mansion in upstate New York to remind her of a castle she loved from the mid-1500s. When one pulled up the mile long lane to her beloved castle, they were astonished by the three large floors that prevailed with the long, narrow windows. The circle drive often went unnoticed as most people saw the massive, oversized black door with an old-fashioned knocker. The enchantment of her castle did not end there, for there were two large spires on either side of the roof, almost making her house look like a human with horns popping out of the third floor. The landscaping was impeccable. The charm of flowers and strong bushes and trees added to the feeling of stepping into a time from long ago. Little did anyone know that Madam had crafted every window, every flower, every door to remind her of a specific and special time from her past. A time she longed for. A man she longed for and would soon join.

Many wondered in awe of the mansion as to why a woman would need three floors and so many rooms. They did not know that her "sisters" lived with her, as they remained on the third floor. The second floor was devoted to her quarters and her daughter's, Ezmerelda. The main floor was where Madam housed parties and impressed the elite in New York with sizeable and gorgeous fireplaces made by hand of specific stones in each room.

The magnificent dining room, which held perfect plates and goblets reminiscent of the 1500s, could seat at least 50 people comfortably. She even had a room designated for the children when they would come over to play in. The room had every toy a child could want, not to mention five TVs with gaming consoles set up. The room made just for the children was the one room without a fireplace. She made sure the football field sized room had all the safety precautions necessary for children of all ages to play in.

Madam also had several living rooms to entertain her guests. Again, the harsh trinkets from the 1500s would be in each room, but this was barely noticed as her guests would stare at the stunning furniture, artwork, and the crystals inserted into each fireplace that would put onlookers in awe at the beauty of the stones amongst the rocks. The mirrors were massive in each room, and were also in line with the designs from the mid-1500s. Madam had 4 living rooms on the main level, and in the very back of the house was the massive kitchen. Here is where her "sisters" had insisted she make modern.

Madam hated the kitchen. It was all silver and white, with dark blue accents of this newfound thing called backsplash. There were six ovens, five stoves, three sizable refrigerators, and a view of the vast garden in the backyard.

Madam hated the damn kitchen; it was too modern, but she found her guests marveled at the amount of stoves and ovens, not to mention the crystals inserted in the marble, handpicked by her. Apparently, modern people loved boring and harsh metal things with backsplash and bright lights that made her long to put candles everywhere. She always had to go through the kitchen to get to the backroom which led to her true sanctuary in the basement.

She had the old-fashioned key, for she alone was the only one allowed into the basement, unless of course, her "sisters" needed to go down to the wine cellar area when they had guests and Madam was too busy being the perfect hostess. The massive black door was as thick as the base of an ancient, healthy oak tree. The creak of the door made her smile, for she knew she would soon ascend to her sanctuary. Madam would head down the twenty-five steps and pause to put on her black robe, but she would wait to put her hood on until she was in her oasis.

As she lit a torch she breathed in the smell of the fire and smiled, her dazzling green eyes shining. She loved the entire basement. Madam had made the walls from crystals that were all shades of red and black. In a certain light, it would look like blood coming from the walls, which made Madam grin.

She passed the enormous wine and champagne cellar. Madam only drank when she had guests. The tunnel continued on and on. It was at least a mile walk to her sanctuary. She turned right and smirked as she looked at the door. To anyone else, they would not see a door; they would only see the black and red crystals. Madam hated to admit it, but she did enjoy this technology, as she lifted the largest black stone and the keypad lit up. She entered in her three numbers, and the door opened within. She smiled and put her hood on over her long, wavy black hair. She entered her refuge and immediately imposed the shut down of the door with another keypad to lock herself in. No one was to disturb her. Only for important ceremonies would she invite her "sisters" into this special space.

Madam placed the torch in the wall's torch holder. She looked at the largest room in the entire house. It had everything to please Husband. A massive and long wall held the fireplace. It was so gigantic that three large fireplaces had once been there, before Madam made it one large fireplace.

On the massive, oak mantle rested her elegant crown. It was made of pure gold, and it had three layers of every type of jewel in it, representing her sacrifices for Husband. There was one spot left for the sapphire jewel she had already created. Madam's crown that, when finished, would bring her to her true love that she had pined for since the mid-1500s.

Sir John William Mayhew was the one who had invited her into the thrilling world of black magic to serve Husband in all ways possible. She sighed as she lovingly touched the crown, feeling its warmth as she thought of her John William.

If only it weren't for Catherine! If only he had accepted Madam back when she was Maura, she could be with him now. Well, her wait of over 500 years would soon be over as she looked again at the crown and knew it just needed one more… one more precious jewel for Husband.

On the same wall as the fireplace were the precious black magic books handed down from Wife to Wife over the centuries. These books were filled with dark magic and spells that she could never get enough of. By now, she had memorized every potion, every word in Latin,

Gaelic, Greek, French, and Arabic. On the back wall were perfectly kept chalices. The special bowls where she created and honed her craft. It was her own lab in the back section, which she loved. That was her passion, besides making Husband happy. Madam's potions were where her true magic came to life.

Then, there was the most important side of the wall, opposite of the fireplace and bookshelves, was the shrine to Husband. It lay before her, a massive stone structure with a kneeling pad and black candles that she lit after she turned the gas fireplace on. The mirror in front of her as she kneeled would allow herself to see things that Husband would share with her. She began speaking Latin and conjuring up the names of the demons to let them tell Husband she was ready to serve him.

Madam loved this feeling, even if Husband did not come through. She loved the feeling of the demons swirling around her with respect. After all, she had given Husband sacrifices to strengthen his powers, causing horrific issues on earth. Each sacrifice made him grow stronger. She just needed one more to finally join Husband and the love of her life. Madam would pass the torch onto whomever Husband chose for his new Wife. She would finally go to the most beautiful place she could imagine.

Madam felt a swirl arise around her thick, black robe. Husband had arrived. She didn't know how long she had done her incantations. Time was no issue to her in her sanctuary.

Madam kept her eyes closed. Husband would tell her when she could open them.

"Wife," came a deep growl that made her smile. Anyone else would be terrified, but her duty and service was to Husband.

"My Husband. How may I serve you today?"

Even though her eyes were closed, the energy had shifted in the room. She could feel the darkness sweeping through her. Madam loved that feeling of hatred, anger, cruelty… she relished being near Husband, for only he had this massive energy of evil that was like a tidal wave. Madam was stronger than the demons, so she barely felt their energy of suffering, anguish and the desperation to harm. She was Wife, and Madam was the closest thing to Husband on earth.

She could hear the clicking of his claws as he moved around the room. His growl penetrated her.

"It is time for another sacrifice for me."

"Yes, Husband."

"Do not screw this up, as you messed up our plans in Los Angeles."

Madam could feel her face turning red. She had made one mistake in the 1960s, and he would never let her forget that.

"Husband, I have asked you to forgive me for my error. I had to kill her because-"

The booming voice pierced her ears, "I DO NOT WANT TO HEAR YOUR EXCUSES!"

She felt herself being tossed across the room, and landed hard against the rocks in the fireplace, snapping into her spinal cord. Madam served Husband, but her one mistake caused a vicious violence that she accepted.

"You were supposed to keep her alive to establish your credibility! Instead, we had to start all over! I needed sacrifices, like your first born son to me, but due to your arrogance, you stupid swine, you had to use possessions, which were not powerful enough for me!"

Madam still had her eyes closed, since she had not been given permission to open them. She felt herself being choked by his claws. While she knew he would never kill her, his punishment for her one mistake had been a constant for over fifty years. It didn't matter how many times she made strong and proper sacrifices since she was able to get the business up and running by the late 1980s. She had screwed up, and the sacrifices required to strengthen Husband had been delayed.

"You fucking piece of rotting human meat," he snarled. "I made a deal with you! Shall I take away my promise to you when you are so close to completing your crown?"

Madam's eyes filled with tears as she thought about losing her rightful place and the promise to finally be with John William Mayhew, her only love.

"Please, no, Husband," she choked out and coughed.

"STOP BEGGING!"

Once again, Madam was thrown across the room, which right now, did not feel like a sanctuary. She realized where she was, even with her eyes closed, that from the decades of incense and potions that the wood had breathed in from her work area, that she was in the back of the room. Madam desperately hoped Husband wouldn't throw her into her sacred oils and mess up her open spellbook that was on display on her worktable.

She felt the back of her head. Madam had bashed it on the wood table. She felt blood. He was not done with her. She felt the claws around her neck as she was picked up off the floor. He crashed her down onto the kneeler that faced the mirror, and she thought, *No, not this! Anything but this!*

"Open your eyes!"

As much as she feared what he was going to show her, Madam feared the rage and torture even more if she did not follow a direct order. She opened her eyes very slowly, finding her reflection in the mirror. Her light green eyes sparkled with unshed tears and her wavy black hair was strewn about. Madam loved that she had learned how to shape-shift herself into the most beautiful woman in the world. Her beauty was something she relished. The white porcelain skin, the taut, high cheekbones, the curve of her light green eyes. Yes, she was vain, and had been since she was no longer hideous as she was in her youth. She had no fat on her elegant and perfect body. In the truest sense of the word, Madam was strikingly stunning and utterly gorgeous.

All she could see when she glanced up in the mirror was the vibrant red glow of Husband's eyes. She could barely make out his horns in the dim lighting. She always appreciated it when he shape-shifted into John William, especially when they created their daughter together. However, on this night, he was in his true form. Yes, he was horribly deformed and one of the ugliest creatures she had ever seen, with reptile-like skin that constantly seemed to be moving about, but his power surged through her. She craved that power and felt it most when she sacrificed for him.

"I'm going to show you your true form, so you remember the gift I have given you," he snarled.

His red eyes glowed with such a ferocity that Madam couldn't speak. She gulped and looked at her beautiful features. Suddenly, the face before her was without a nose. The one eyeball was hanging out of her eye, ready to snap off at any moment. The other eyeball was foggy white, with only the black pupil present. There was no nose. There was only a massive hole in the center of her face. The skin was ripped and hanging to show the insides of her mouth, which held no teeth. One ear was completely ripped off, revealing her brain. The other ear was still attached, but the lobe had been ferociously torn away. Her shiny, wavy and long black hair was gone as she saw her bald skull that had been unendurably ripped off. She hated seeing her brain because it was black with folds. Madam now saw the thick spiders coming out of the blackness of her brain. The maggots began to form around the mouth that had no lips, for her lips had been taken off her face in the most heinous way possible. Her jaw hung and flopped around. There were flies going in and out of her mouth. Her lovely, long and slim neck was slit down the middle to reveal her spinal cord. The creepiest and jelliest looking insects were swarming around her neck. She hated the centipedes the most. The insects kept coming and eating her flesh with their maniacal teeth and slimy mouths. They sucked away at her, like she was the best feast they had ever eaten. It was like being eaten alive all over again!

"Keep looking!"

This was the part Madam hated the most. The rats came and began eating her eyeballs, and what was left of her one ear. They began to dig into the darkness of her black brain as the small spiders shifted to large tarantulas. As she watched in horror, her face, neck and brain became a feeding frenzy of the things she feared most. Out of her ears came the massive and long worms, and from her eye sockets shoving out any remaining parts of her eyeballs for the rats came the snakes, hissing in delight.

"Please, Husband, no more."

Suddenly, she saw herself as the beautiful goddess she had requested. She felt her face and grinned delightfully at how young and lovely she was. Yes, Madam acknowledged once again to herself that she knew she was vain, but damn, she was more beautiful than the goddess Aphrodite.

"Thank you, Husband."

"I'm not done with your punishment, but just remember that I can switch you back to this anytime I want to!"

Once again, she was picked up as a child would carelessly pick up a doll, and tossed into the fireplace. The burning of her skin through the robe instantly made her jump out of the fire and take the robe off to put out the flames. This was one of her best ceremonial robes! It didn't bother her that she was burned. Madam would use her black magic to instantly heal herself.

She found herself being grabbed by the back of the neck. Husband forced her face into the fire. Madam was not prepared for this! She screamed and felt every nerve being burned. She smelled her flesh melting and her hair burning.

"YOU WILL NEVER ASK FOR FORGIVENESS AGAIN! I DO NOT FORGIVE YOU! I AM NOT MY FATHER! YOU ARE HERE ONLY TO PLEASE ME! NEVER FORGET THAT!"

Finally, she felt freed from his claws that had ripped into the back of her neck and penetrated her throat. She looked in the mirror and screamed in horror, only she had no voice box. She looked like a charbroiled hamburger with blood spurting out of her throat and the back of her neck.

"Now that I have your full attention, your sacrifice this time will be your last. I shall keep my promise to you. However, I have ensured this will be the most difficult and challenging sacrifice for YOU for many reasons, which you shall find out soon enough."

She could barely see his burning red eyes as the flames bounced off of them. Madam could not swallow, speak, or barely see. She was completely burned, and she feared it would take her at least a day to concoct the amount of healing potions she would need to heal herself, let alone see through burned eyes! She could only shape shift with her full energy intact or possess someone's body while in a deep state of evil saturation.

She motioned with her hands to her face.

Husband relented and said, "Fine," and all he did was touch her face.

Suddenly, the pain from the flames was gone. She could swallow, and when she looked in the mirror, she saw her beauty was back.

"Thank you, Husband."

"Never cross me again."

"Yes, Husband."

"How is Ezmerelda doing?"

Madam shifted as she smiled. Ezmerelda was a gift he gave her. It was the best night of her life when he shape-shifted into John William, and they created Ezmerelda, who was the exact spitting image of her mother.

"Ezmerelda is doing fine in her studies. The sisters are all teaching her, and as a smart child of six, she is picking up on her studies extraordinarily quickly."

"Yes, I've checked up on her. I am hoping once your final sacrifice is completed, perhaps Ezmerelda will take over. I am growing weary of wives, and I'd like my daughter to continue the business. She has stronger powers than you. They grow by the second. Soon, I shall have to shape-shift her into an adult."

Madam was shocked by this. For thousands of millennia, Husband always had a main wife, and several lower ranking wives in different countries. This was surprising that he wanted their daughter to take over the business. Madam felt the pride swell in her chest. Half of her would live on after she was taken to her home.

"I do not doubt your decision, Husband. Is there anything you would like me to do in her training before my year is over with on earth?"

"Wife, I need you to get her used to being a proper hostess. Have her join you in the gatherings you throw for the customers. Ezmerelda needs to learn the social component of being likable. She needs to be believable that she actually cares about these women and their babies. Her icy demeanor needs shaping, so you have a year to train her on faking her kindness."

"Yes, Husband."

Madam inwardly cringed. Ezmerelda was not a likable child. She was obstinate and her evil knew no bounds, which Madam loved, but in order for Ezmerelda to take over the family business, it would take a lot of time to saw off those rough edges, at least while she was in public.

"You should know, Wife, that Ezmerelda has the power to take you down."

Madam was shocked by the statement. He was talking about their daughter. The beautiful creature she bore after nine months. It seemed as though he was warning her about impending doom.

She chose her words very carefully, so as not to anger him again.

"Does that mean she has more power because you are her father?"

Husband was in the shadows, but she saw a tiny, ugly grin form on his hideous, snake-like face.

"Wife, you shall find out everything in due time. Perhaps I shall visit her, and let her know my plans for her."

Madam struggled not to widen her eyes as she slowly stood up, feeling the bruises already forming. At least when Husband healed her face, it included the back of her head, which was no longer bleeding or throbbing. She feared Ezmerelda would be frightened by the true nature of what her father looked like.

"Husband, have you ever visited Ezmerelda before?"

"Yes, once. That was last year. I found her fearless nature and pure evil flooding through her veins as something that could be used for my benefit, hence why I want her in charge once you have achieved your final jewel in the crown."

Madam looked at all of the jewels that represented the sacrifices. One stone was left. Sapphire. She looked longingly at that empty space; she simply could not wait to be done with earth and go to the one man she loved.

"Yes, Husband."

"I will deliver her the good news."

With a swift flicker of the fireplace flames, and a massive, furious wind, Husband was gone as Madam felt the evil energy leave her. She was most definitely addicted to that energy. It made her feel so powerful. She reflected on their coupling to produce Ezmerelda which was amazing because it was like being with John William; however, and this had truly bothered and tugged at the back of her mind, she almost felt another presence in her body as she coupled with Husband to create Ezmerelda. Had she been possessed? Was she simply caught up in the moment when Husband had shape-shifted into John William?

Perhaps she was lost in the moment of pretending it was her true love as they created Ezmerelda, but that lingering feeling of sharing her body with another evil force would creep up when Ezmerelda said or did certain things that no one could possibly know. Madam chalked it up to her father's genetics, since she had sacrificed her newborn son for Husband. After all, this was the first time Husband had chosen to couple with any of his wives to create a daughter.

Madam was the only Wife that he had impregnated, and the only Wife to keep the child. He had chosen to make Ezmerelda a girl, which was quite shocking to everyone. Madam would definitely be held in high esteem when she joined the other Wives.

Ezmerelda might be only six in human years, but her personality was that of a wise, evil old woman. Madam's sisters had told her she would speak a new language to someone they could not see. They believed it was possibly ancient Egyptian, which was not in her curriculum. The girl seemed to delight in the pain of others, often hurting the sisters as they would try to teach her a lesson, and she laughed delightedly as they would run off to grab one of Madam's healing potions that they each kept in their rooms.

Madam was proud of Ezmerelda's evil nature. She had done something right, but it wasn't right to harm the sisters in your own coven. These women had been hand-picked by Madam to work with her throughout the past five hundred years. They were a family, and Ezmerelda seemed to take great joy in bringing them to tears with hurtful things she knew about them from the 1500s and beyond.

As Madam settled at her table of potions and crystals, she concocted her usual one for quick healing. Husband had broken part of her spinal cord, and her bruised body made her feel old, something she despised. She said her incantation in Latin as she chugged the healing remedy from her favorite chalice that happened to belong to her true love, her handsome John William.

Instantly, she felt everything snap back into place, and the bruises were healed. Madam felt alive and youthful. She walked over to the shrine for Husband and looked in the mirror and sighed in relief, as she thought, *There I am. Beautiful. Youthful. Desirable. I am Husband's goddess.* Her smile quickly faded as she thought about Husband telling Ezmerelda about her future. She hoped her daughter had not been too terrified.

Saying a final incantation in respect to the demons and Husband, she blew out the candles and retrieved her burned cloak. Madam could definitely use Beatrice's handiwork to make the robe beautiful and not smell like smoke. Madam lifted the stone on the wall, typed in her password, and was once again outside of her sanctuary as she closed it behind her with a longing sigh. *Just one more year. One more year, and I can finally join my rightful place with the rest of Husband's Wives.*

Madam rushed through the cave of stones and crystals; she truly hoped she would not find Ezmerelda in tears. She entered the kitchen and left a note for Beatrice to fix her robe. Then, she quickly rushed up the massive stairs to the second floor to Ezmerelda's wing of the house. She saw her door was shut. Madam was pensive. She did not want to enter if Husband was still talking to their daughter. She closed her eyes and allowed herself to feel the presences in the room. There was no Husband. Madam could feel his energy even from a mile away.

She opened the door to Ezmerelda's extravagant bedroom. For some reason, Ezmerelda opted for an Egyptian theme. Gold was the main color. Paintings, done by Ezmerelda, were proudly displayed on the walls. She only painted from the time of Pharaohs. Madam knew there were no books depicting Egyptian culture because this was not something that enhanced their black magic. Her bed was made in solid gold with white accents. Lapis lazuli, a favorite of the Egyptians, was everywhere. Ezmerelda refused to take off her thick golden necklace with Lapis lazuli as the only stone on it. Madam had not bought her this, and none of the sisters knew where she had found it.

One would think that Ezmerelda was sweet and kind by the light colors she chose. This was most definitely not the case.

Madam looked around her large bedroom, wanting to delete the color scheme Ezmerelda had chosen. It was mainly because she and her sisters stuck with black and red in their bedrooms. The lightness in her daughter's room was annoying to Madam.

As she walked closer to her bed, the darkest brown cat Madam had ever seen lifted its head and opened it's sleepy golden eyes. Those gold eyes turned into slits as the cat hissed at her. Madam and the sisters had no clue where Ezmerelda had found this beast.

"Sphynx does not like you, Mother. I fear she might try to trip you on the stairs," Ezmeredla said and laughed with disturbing glee.

"Yes, your golden-eyed cat is not a fan of mine, but let's hope she does not play tricks as you do."

Ezmerelda sat up, and it was like looking into a mirror. She was stunningly gorgeous. They had the same long, jet black and wavy hair. Their face was like porcelain, not a mole or freckle to be found. Their lips were both large and pouty. Their face shapes had strong bones, and the curve of their eyes almost made them look cat-like. But what Madam loved the most was her shiny light green eyes. The beauty and shock of them against her black hair and perfect skin was striking.

"Mother, Father came and spoke to me. I am in training to replace you."

Madam went to sit on her daughter's bed, but Ezmerelda was like a cat herself, as she stated harshly, "Please do not make yourself comfortable. I just wanted to tell you that I am prepared for the training he said I must go through in order to fake being likable to keep the family business going."

"So, you were not scared?"

Ezmeralda smirked at her, and replied with snarkiness, "Unlike you, mother, I do not need Father to shape-shift. I have no fear of him. That's *your* weakness, not mine."

Madam watched as her daughter's eyes seemed to glow in delight of mocking her.

"Ezmerelda, watch how you speak to me. We are a family."

With the most disgusted face, she said, "No, *we* are not." She paused and cocked her head to the side, as though listening to someone whispering in your ear. She slowly grinned and pierced her mother with those wild green eyes. "Leave my room and go to bed... pig."

Madam was too shocked to speak as her past came roiling through her.

She finally sputtered out, "Ezmerelda! You address me as mother! Don't you dare call me-"

With a flourish of Ezmerelda's dainty hand, Madam was picked up and unceremoniously whipped out of Ezmerelda's bedroom. As she went to stand and punish the girl, Madam was greeted by the door slamming in her face as the bedroom door locked loudly.

Madam felt her heart beating in her ears. No way could a child of six have this much power. For the first time, Madam was fearful of her own daughter's power and the obvious lack of a bond Ezmerelda had, required for a successful coven. Madam shook her head as she limped to her wing of the second floor.

Chapter 3

Gia caught a reflection of herself in the Manhattan building where Charlotte was excitedly talking to security to get passes to Madam's Jewels. She sighed at the dark circles under her eyes, and the puffiness of her face and neck. She had worked a long shift overnight. Gia was not thrilled about being here, as she sleepily perused the long list of offices and names of the CEOs of each company.

She noticed that only Madam had two entire floors, numbers 66 and 67. Gia could only imagine the amount of money that in vitro would cost in such a posh Manhattan building, but Charlotte's parents had been on board. They immediately gave their princess $20,000 cash. Gia scoffed at the CEOs name listed under Madam's Jewels - it simply stated Madam. Gia glared at this and thought grumpily, *Who the fuck refers to themselves as Madam?*

Charlotte, dressed in a smart Chanel suit came rushing over. She was glowing and more beautiful than Gia had ever seen her. Charlotte's pink blouse matched the Chanel jacket and skirt she wore. Her Prada pink heels made her even taller and more modelesque than usual. Gia wore black flats, brown pants and a black t-shirt with a black leather jacket. It was the start of August, but Gia loved her black leather jacket. It had been a Christmas present from Charlotte during their first year together as a couple. While Gia never looked at designer names, as Charlotte had been trained to do since childhood, she had to admit that the Armani jacket was the most comfortable piece of clothing she owned.

Charlotte beamed as she asked, "Okay, are you ready? Her main office is on floor 66. We can head right up!"

Gia tried a tired smile.

"Yup. Let's go meet *Madam*," she said with sarcasm.

As they headed to the elevators, Charlotte ignored the bitterness in Gia's tone. She understood that Gia hadn't slept in a couple of days. Her homicide cases were taking a major toll on her, especially being lead detective. Charlotte simply ignored her grumpiness and focused on her excitement.

In her pink Chanel bag, that matched her shoes perfectly, she had the sample of the donor, the paperwork from Dr. Lee's office, and every other piece of material she thought they might need, including a list of typed out medications and vitamins Charlotte took. When she had called to make the appointment, Madam's head assistant said that Madam's holistic remedies and teas might not fit well with some of Charlotte's medications and vitamins, so she made sure to go through her entire cupboard. For some reason, Charlotte really wanted to impress Madam. She knew in her heart that this would be a completely different experience than she had encountered with that asshole Dr. Lee.

Charlotte had bought the new Chanel suit and felt very much like Jackie Kennedy. As they entered the elevator and Gia pushed 66, her excitement bubbled over as she wondered about Madam. For a moment, she totally forgot that Gia was next to her until she heard her yawn loudly.

"Gia, I appreciate you coming with me today, but you could have stayed home and finally slept."

Gia shrugged nonchalantly.

"I want to meet this famous, yet unknown Madam."

Charlotte rolled her eyes and pleadingly said, "Please, do not interrogate her. She is not one of your suspects."

"Hey, I just know there is barely a footprint of her on the Internet. The only thing I could pull up was her driver's license, so I know she lives in upstate New York."

Before Charlotte could get annoyed about Gia turning on her detective radar, she immediately asked, "What does she look like?"

Gia remembered pausing over the license photo of Madam. She had seen the most gorgeous woman ever. Charlotte was beautiful, but Madam's stunning good looks were on another stratosphere than Charlotte's. Besides her good looks, Gia knew her name was Maura McBride, along with her address.

"Well, she has long, black hair."

"Is it straight? Curly? Wavy?"

Gia rolled her eyes because Charlotte was like an annoying toddler with her questions.

"Wavy."

"Oh, how lovely," Charlotte said happily.

"Her eyes are green."

"What shade? A deep emerald, or are they more of a hazel color?"

Gia thought back to the picture that was seared into her mind.

"No, the color is more like your favorite light green Granny Smith apples. They are very light… I mean, I'm not looking because I love you, but her eyes alone are enough to make anyone turn their heads. She's stunning."

"Really? Like my Granny Smith apples? Wow, she must be gorgeous to have dark hair and such light green eyes at her old age."

"That's just the thing. She's only in her forties, but she looks like she's in her twenties."

The elevator doors opened, and Charlotte jumped. She hadn't realized how enraptured she'd been by hearing about Madam. Madam Maura McBride, Gia had told her. Charlotte already liked her.

A petite, lovely young woman of Indian descent with dark brown hair and soft brown eyes approached them as they stepped off the elevator into a large foyer. It was not an average doctor's office. It felt like they entered a home.

Chandeliers, beautiful, vibrant rugs, and crystals were embedded everywhere. The place *literally* sparkled as the candles that were lit bounced off the crystals that were in the rocks of the walls. The only thing that spoke of an office building was the large metallic desk, where women sat and answered phone calls or were busily responding to emails. All of the women wore scrubs in either baby blue or a soft pink.

The woman before them wore a black pantsuit with a black and white polka dot top underneath. Even though she was from India, there was no accent when she spoke.

"Hello, Ladies. I'm Ibetsam, but you can just call me Beth." She smiled so warmly that Charlotte wanted to hug her, but she refrained. "I am Madam's main assistant, so if you should require anything and Madam is unavailable, I will be more than happy to help you." Beth spoke calmly and sincerely. "Now, I believe I spoke to Charlotte... and that would be..."

"Me!" Charlotte yelled excitedly and raised her hand.

Gia gently pulled her arm down.

"You'll have to excuse my wife. She teaches preschool, so she likes to raise her hand to be called on."

Beth chuckled softly and replied sincerely, "Well, Charlotte, it is lovely to finally meet you in person."

"You too!"

Gia looked up at her wife as though she had grown five heads, wondering if she'd had too much caffeine that morning.

"I'm her wife, Gia Carter, by the way."

Beth gently responded, "It's wonderful to meet you as well, Gia." Everything about Beth exuded calm classiness. She paused and looked at the pink folder in her hand. "Now, I have the paperwork from Dr. Lee's office. I know you brought your own copies, but we like to get under his skin." Beth winked and continued, "He was quite reluctant to send them over, but Madam has her ways." Beth winked again, which annoyed Gia. "So, I'll just need some general forms filled out, give you our reading materials about how we work as a holistic center, and the costs for our services."

Charlotte excitedly stated, "Money is no issue!" Charlotte realized she had yelled, and she quickly brought her voice down a few octaves. "I mean, the average price for one round of in vitro is $13,000, but I brought more for Madam's remedies to help me get pregnant faster."

Beth smiled warmly at Charlotte.

"Well, we do have payment plans because some of our mommies and daddies or mommies and mommies can't afford to pay all at once. Many insurance companies won't cover the costs of the procedures, but since Madam would be your doctor, that would be covered. She's a gynecologist, OBGYN, surgeon, and the list goes on and on of her many achievements."

"So, she would be with me throughout the whole process?" Charlotte asked hopefully.

"Oh, absolutely, Charlotte. She is there from conception to birth, and even after, we maintain our close relationships with our friends. Trust me, you don't want to miss any of Madam's parties! The best one is the party she throws between Christmas and New Year's Eve; it's lovely to see how these incredible babies Madam helped create are growing into such beautiful children and charming teenagers."

Gia looked sideways at Charlotte and muttered, "That's *if* we choose to have Dr. Madam-"

"Oh no, it's just Madam."

"-as our doctor."

Beth cocked her head slightly, still smiling as she replied, "Absolutely. You should meet her first before you decide if she should be your doctor. Now, let's get you ladies settled, and if you have the list of medications and vitamins-"

"Here! I have them. I typed them out because I have awful handwriting."

"Oh, great! Do you have the semen sample from the-"

"Right here!" Charlotte pulled out the steel canister and practically heaved it into Beth's little chest.

Beth gave a hearty laugh.

"Charlotte, I think your energy is perfect for how we handle our patients on every level - mentally, physically, spiritually. It all converges. Madam is a Reiki Master, so the simple act of laying hands on one to help them heal is a huge help in releasing negative energy."

Gia bluntly asked, "Is this a cult?"

Charlotte gasped and cried out, "Gia!"

Beth shook her head with a soft laugh. Her calmness was annoying Gia. She liked to get under people's skin, but Beth maintained her perfect composure.

"No, Gia, it is not. We simply go about treating the person as a whole being and not just a pin cushion." She paused and looked up at Charlotte. "Shall we go into the seating room to get these forms filled out?"

Charlotte punched Gia on her upper arm and hissed, "I can't believe you said that!"

"Ouch." Gia rubbed her upper arm because Charlotte was freakishly strong. There'd be a bruise there tomorrow! "Well, I'm doing my due diligence as your wife, which is to protect you."

"Protect me from what? Hmm? A nice doctor who treats the person as a whole, unlike that sniveling rat, Dr. Lee?"

"Here we are, ladies. Please sit down. Fill these forms out at your leisure."

Beth left them in the most gorgeous waiting room. Not only was the sunlight shining through, but there were recliners and soft, comfy sofas. There was a sturdy coffee table laid out in between all of the beautiful furniture pieces with a tray of tea, water bottles and pens.

It was the fireplace that truly engaged Gia. It was spread out across the entire length of the opposite wall. The damn thing literally sparkled from the crystals. The sunshine made them dance and bounce onto the ceiling and furniture.

Charlotte went straight to work filling out the forms. She was on a mission to be the best patient Madam had ever had.

As she worked hurriedly to answer the questions on the standard papers she had grown accustomed to, she overheard Gia say, "Damn. She's on the top floors. In Manhattan. No one gets this much sunlight with the other skyscrapers around."

Charlotte barely registered what Gia was saying and looked at her calendar to see when her last period was.

Charlotte could hear the awe in Gia's voice, which was not good. The awe would lead to her going into detective mode.

"The view is ridiculous." She heard Gia plop down on a piece of furniture as she scribbled away. "Charlotte, have you noticed how soft this furniture is? I feel like my ass is on a cloud right now."

"Mmm hmm."

"Are you even taking in this room? Do you know how expensive this shit is?"

Charlotte had always knocked elbows with the elite in Manhattan, thanks to her parents social status and money.

"Yes, I do," Charlotte replied nonchalantly, without even looking up.

"How expensive is this couch then?"

Charlotte glanced up from the paperwork, and furrowed her brows.

"The loveseat you are sitting on is $75,000. That massive, oversized coffee table in front of you is worth close to $98,000."

"What the… how in the hell did you know that stuff?"

She shrugged and clicked the pen, placing it gently on the silver tray.

"My mother always had me memorize any wealthy pieces, especially at high-end auctions. Do you see that gigantic fireplace?"

"Uh, yeah. It's kind of hard to miss!"

"Well, each of those stones was carved by hand. The crystals," she said as she stood up to assess the fireplace's worth, "are definitely real. So, given the labor, cutting of the stones and the application of the crystals, this fireplace is close to $800,000."

"Fuck! How much does this place charge?"

Charlotte reluctantly told Gia, "The same as Dr. Lee. $13,000 for one round of in vitro."

Gia's face smushed together as she moved around the massive waiting room asking suspiciously, "How is that possible?" Gia sensed something was amiss. "She owns a place in upstate New York, not to mention the two top *floors* of a building in *Manhattan*, and she charges the same amount as that asshole doctor… It doesn't add up."

This is why Charlotte didn't want to tell Gia the cost.

"Okay, Detective. Maybe she has a lot of clients."

"Charlotte, the amount she charges and how much she *could* charge don't add up. Where is the money coming from to afford all of this?" Gia asked, eyeing the room with new eyes taking in everything.

Charlotte really regretted having Gia come with her today. Her crankiness was annoying, but it was when Gia only saw the potential negatives that really frustrated Charlotte, who was known for being positive.

"Gia, stop it. I told you to leave work at work. Get out of your damn detective mode and focus on meeting my potential new doctor!"

Gia grumbled as she walked up to the massive fireplace. She touched a crystal, one that was a foggy white and felt an odd vibration. Charlotte noticed Gia's eyes go wide in surprise.

"What is it?"

From behind them, they heard the soft and gentle voice of Madam.

"That is called Ulexite. It's a stone that has many powers."

Charlotte and Gia whirled around to find the most stunning woman standing there. Her black hair had waves down to her lower back, yet there was not a single hair out of place. She wore an Emerald green blouse with black Givenchy pants and black high heels to match. The blouse's color only enhanced the vibrancy of her eyes. They had a living, talking goddess in front of them. She made Charlotte seem… plain.

Madam paused mid-step as she looked at Charlotte. Something odd flashed across Madam's face. For a moment, Charlotte thought she looked as though she might faint.

Madam seemed to gain her innate grace back as she continued, "This amazing little stone heals and balances one's physical vision, especially helping with headaches. It reduces wrinkles, which is why I love it," she paused and smiled, her teeth as white as new fallen snow, "but it also gives you the ability to see into another's heart. Ulexite also clears the mind. If you're struggling with a scenario at work or a relationship issue that you cannot quite figure out how to solve, this is the stone for you. It clears the brain, so you can see beyond what's in front of you. It also aligns your Chakras and opens your third eye."

Both women stood there stupified by the stunning beauty in front of them who had put them in a trance with her cat-like bright green eyes. Gia still had her hand on the stone, and she slowly dropped it as they gawked at Madam.

Madam was used to this; she smiled warmly at them and continued, "I'm Madam, the founder, president and CEO of Madam's Jewels." She looked directly at Charlotte who was exactly her height in their heels. A genuine smile came through when she said, "You must be Catherine- no, sorry. I mean Charlotte. My apologies. Charlotte, correct?"

"Yes, Madam. It's so amazing to finally meet you!"

Madam extended her long, lithe hand and shook Charlotte's. She felt the energy. The hum of recognition. Yes, Husband had been right; this was going to be challenging.

Madam turned her head and looked down at the hideous troll in front of her. Her hair was mousy and the woman definitely needed some powerful crystals and incantations to even make her mildly attractive. *Beauty and the Beast*, Madam thought, as she smiled and held her hand out to Gia.

"And you must be Gia."

Gia took the hand and shook it. Madam seemed to get a wave of something that she didn't like flash over her face for a second, and then her face returned back to hiding her true feelings she already had towards Gia.

She released Gia's hand and said, "It's truly lovely to meet the both of you." Madam turned her blazing green eyes back to Charlotte's big, blue eyes. "Have you finished the paperwork?"

"Yes."

Madam smiled and clapped her hands together.

"Fantastic. Beth," she called from over her shoulder, and suddenly Beth was by Madam's side. "Could you take the paperwork? Charlotte completed it all, and I'd like to have the data input immediately, so I can see what medications and herbs won't work well in unison."

"Absolutely, Madam."

Beth rushed away, and Madam turned her attention back to Charlotte.

"Now, Charlotte my dear, which stone calls to you?"

Charlotte turned to the fireplace and immediately pointed to the light pink one.

"Ah, so I was right. Rose quartz."

"What does it do or what is it known to do?" Charlotte asked excitedly, as though waiting for her future to be told.

"The rose quartz is what I simply call, the love stone. It's the stone of universal love, which includes friendship, your love life, and even healing your inner self. It's truly just filled with love, and that's something I'm picking up on from your energy."

Charlotte smiled as Gia rolled her eyes and almost snorted.

"Shall we go to my office and get started?"

Charlotte bobbed her head as she followed the tall, gorgeous woman out of the waiting area. Gia lagged behind, wishing she didn't have such a bitter taste in her mouth about this stupid Madam and all her crystlas that had certain energies.

They walked for what seemed like a mile towards the very back of the office floor. Everything was impeccable, but Gia couldn't help noticing how every woman, dressed in their pink or blue scrubs, seemed to be youthful and gorgeous as they bounced around from their cubicles or typed hurriedly or chatted cheerfully on the phone. There was no way that all of these women were *that* happy at work!

"And here we are. I have the entire back section of this floor. Please, come in," Madam said in a welcoming tone.

Charlotte entered Madam's main office and was blown away by the style and comfort of a doctor's office, not to mention the size. She could fit their entire apartment in this one room. There was a large seating area, like a living room. There were suede couches, loveseats, and large burgundy chairs. The accents of the room were pink, but this meshed well with the tan suede and burgundy that decorated the room. The large coffee table was almost as beautiful as the one in the waiting room, but this had pink candles already lit that offered a lovely, fresh scent.

Further back in the room was Madam's massive desk. The desk itself looked like it was from a different century because Charlotte couldn't place it. The carvings made on the desk were so intricate and old-fashioned, Charlotte figured it must be an heirloom.

There were two plush seats, in front of Madam's desk, that had been reupholstered with a blend of cream as the base, and lines of burgundy and pink. There was nothing but candles and crystals on her desk, besides her computer and telephone. There was a large picture of a Madam at a young age in a crystal frame.

The one wall, to Charlotte's right when she entered, was just like the fireplace in the sitting room. The massive boulders of tan with swirls of burgundy and pink were the loveliest. There were gorgeous accents of enormous crystals, the size of her head, of burgundy and pink crystals, along with white candles, on the monstrous mantle, that were already lit.

The opposite side had a massive metal door, which perplexed Charlotte. It didn't match Madam's theme at all, and she furrowed her brow.

Madam smiled at Charlotte.

"Behind this wall is where we do examinations, a bathroom, procedures… basically, it's where we get you to become a future mommy." Madam's smile warmed even further.

"Unfortunately, I couldn't find a strong enough door in a burgundy shade with pink stripes to match my decor."

Charlotte laughed, almost too loudly.

"I must admit, I am stunned and in awe by your decorating skills. Did you plan all of these rooms?"

"Yes. I am often here and wanted it to feel like home. In fact, on the 67th floor, I've made the entire floor into a living area for myself and the young ladies that you passed by. I, of course, have a whole section that is a mini-apartment... well, it's mini in size to me. I've been told by others that they can fit their entire apartment into just my custom made living room upstairs!" Madam purred, as though she was an aristocrat.

"I was just thinking that! Gia and I could literally fit our entire apartment in your office!"

Madam smiled, knowingly as she replied, "Well, I guess we're just two peas in a pod, Charlotte."

The brash voice of Gia interrupted their bonding.

"Look this is great and all, but can we get down to business?" she asked harshly.

She was struggling to figure out where Madam had so much money coming from. Her gut was thinking maybe she was using those beautiful girls they had passed on their way to Madam's office as sex slaves, hence being a true Madam in every sense of the word. She did just say that they all had apartments upstairs. Gia was calculating everything in her fired up brain.

Madam raised a perfectly arched black eyebrow as Gia moved like a gorilla to sit in front of the desk.

"Gia, my dear, won't you join us in the seating area?"

Gia turned and noticed Charlotte had already made herself comfortable in the oversized suede couch, feeling the fabric and smiling. Madam was seated in the large, high back burgundy chair that made her look like a queen in front of peasants. Gia noticed the expression on Madam's face. Her smile was not sincere. Madam was someone she already didn't like. Too much about her business was not adding up.

Gia hoisted herself out of the chair and stalked over to the couch next to Charlotte. Without refinement, she slumped into the massive couch, feeling shorter than ever. Her damn legs were unable to touch the ground, and she crossed her arms, her face bitter.

Madam noticed everything, but what she really noticed was the lovely Charlotte. She was the reincarnation of her sister, Catherine. She would do everything she could to make sure

Charlotte was happy, but Madam felt her now mortal enemy, Gia, would get in the way of the friendship that she could have with Charlotte.

"Ladies, would you like some tea, coffee, water, cappuccino?"

Gia replied hastily, "Got any whiskey?"

Charlotte hissed, "Gia!"

Madam shook her head and grew serious. Her light green eyes bore into Gia's.

"We do not believe alcohol is good for the body. It is straight poison." Madam turned now kind and concerned eyes towards Charlotte, who looked angrily at Gia. "Charlotte, dear, you don't drink, do you?"

Charlotte turned her stunning blue eyes to Madam's light green ones and found herself blushing.

"I don't want to lie about anything. Yes, I have wine at night, and sometimes… Gia and I spend the weekends getting drunk."

Madam pursed her lips, and she sat up straighter, as she crossed her ankles and folded her hands primly.

"Charlotte, the only way I can help you is if you are healthy in your mind, your body, and of course, your spirit. Alcohol is toxic. It does nothing good for you. I fear if you cannot give up drinking, then, I'm afraid I shouldn't be your doctor."

Charlotte's light eyebrows flew up and she sat forward, her face suddenly strained and pleaded, "No, Madam. Please. I will not drink anymore. Please don't turn me away. I want a baby so badly that if you told me to, I would stop shopping at Dolce and Gabbana!"

Madam smiled and chuckled as she softly said, "I will never tell you to stop shopping there." She paused and crooked her head. "Okay, I believe you. I will have teas that you must drink daily. You will have to come in for Reiki sessions and acupuncture to keep your Chakras level. We focus on balance during pregnancy."

"Balance!" Gia cut in, rudely. "None of this balances out!"

"I do beg your pardon?"

Gia scooted up and then up even further until her ass was on the edge of the couch, so her feet could finally touch the ground. She leaned forward as was usual when she interrogated a suspect.

"How in the hell do you explain only charging the standard $13,000 that we paid at our other doctor, when you have two fucking floors in *Manhattan* and a house in upstate New York? Hmm? Are you running some kind of sex worker scheme here with all of those beautiful ladies out there?"

Charlotte was almost too stunned to speak. She was humiliated and pissed. She could only make a squawking noise.

Madam had sat there, poised as a queen sending someone to be beheaded. She maintained the frozen grin on her face, but her eyes… oh, they were a sight to behold. She felt her power rising as Gia poured herself a cup of hot tea. As she went to take a sip, Madam flicked her finger slightly, and the boiling, hot tea was in Gia's face.

Gia jumped up screaming, "Fuck! What the hell?"

Madam stood and with fake concern said, "Oh dear! You poor thing. Are you okay? Let me get Beth to get some towels and make sure you don't need medical attention. Burns on the face are horrendous!"

Madam smiled as she quickly left her office and heard Charlotte asking Gia if she was okay and what had gotten into her.

"Beth," she hissed to her most loyal and favorite sister.

Madam was walking at a furiously quick pace. The other sisters noticed and perked up. Madam was like their queen, since Husband was their king. They were all uniquely bonded, but some, who had been with Madam since the beginning, were insync with her core being.

Beth was that one, and she came rushing out of her own office and followed Madam into the waiting area.

Madam hissed, "Lily, go tend to that loathsome, turtle-faced woman in there! Theodora, come here, now! Carmella, stand guard outside of this door and alert me if that vomit-inducing woman is coming!"

Movement happened at the speed of light. Madam entered the waiting area with Beth and Theodoara. Madam paced, something she rarely did. Her fury was beautiful. Beth and Theodora could only stare at her. Her eyes were glowing and her energy was scarlett. They had not seen Madam this angry since she made a mistake in the 1960's.

Madam continued to pace and talked out loud, seething, "How dare she attack me and try to slander my good name! She is hideous! And has the ancestry of white witch blood flowing through her! Pathetic! How can Catherine… I mean Charlotte be with someone so horrendously ugly on the outside and on the inside? Her face looks like an old snapping tortoise. She is the epitome of ugly. Ugh!" Madam paced, a disgusted look on her lovely face.

Beth, who knew her better than anyone, stepped forward and spoke quietly.

"Madam, you are the strongest woman on earth. Please do not let this creature take you down."

Theodora, who was from South Africa, stood as tall as Madam; she was lithe like a cheetah. Her dark skin was the perfect shade of rich dark chocolate, making her light brown eyes pop. Theodora couldn't walk the streets of New York without being asked if she was a model or would like to be.

Theodroa pleaded, "Please Madam, don't fret. What would you like us to do?"

Madam stopped walking and looked at both of them. While they had known her for hundreds of years, Madam's always beautiful face morphed into such ugly hatred that Beth and Theodora took a shrinking step back and looked down.

Icily, Madam seared out, "She must go."

Chapter 4

At the same time Madam was working on a plan to get rid of Gia, Gia was working on a plan to take Madam down.

"I know she did this to my face! She's a fucking sorceress or some other wretched creature with powers!"

Charlotte was caught in a mix between concern for Gia's face, which looked like second degree burns were forming, and being mortified by her words towards Madam.

"Gia, she is not a sorceress. You are the one who is acting psychotic! You accused her of running a sex slave gambit here! What the hell is wrong with you?"

"I know when I'm right, and this does not make sense, Charlotte! Take out all the beauty and flourishes of this place. What do you see?"

Charlotte was still seated, rubbing her hands on the creamy suede couch.

"I see a place that is here for women who want to have a baby. That's all I see. You always see doom and gloom in everything!"

"No, I don't!"

"You know what? I'm not doing this. I'm not going into how miserable you are on a daily basis. You need to snap out of it and stop drinking so much!"

"Ah," Gia said, dabbing the tissue on her face, "because we wouldn't want to upset your new buddy, Madam, would we?"

"Shut the fu-"

"Oh, dear," Lily said as she rushed in with fake concern plastered onto her face. "Please do sit down, Miss Gia. Madam told me about the accident. Luckily, we create our own healing balms here. It will work better than anything a dermatologist could have!"

Gia glared as the youthful and petite brunette with kind hazel eyes sat her down in one of the high backed chairs.

"Who are you?" Gia asked rudely.

Lily paused midway, as she pulled the small jar and an applicator out of her scrubs front pocket.

"My apologies, Mrs. Carter. I'm Lily. Madam came out just in time to talk to one of her clients, who is struggling with some pretty severe morning sickness!"

Lily bent over to apply the cream to Gia's face, but Gia shoved her hand away.

"Gia! Let her help you, or so help me God, I will do it myself!" Charlotte angrily said.

"What's in this shit?" Gia asked, her tone growing more annoyed.

Lily kept the plaster of happiness on her face, though she could feel the boiling anger and animosity coursing through her.

"It's all natural."

With shocking strength and efficiency, little Lily shoved Gia's hand out of the way and applied the balm.

Gia felt a coolness settle over the burned skin. She breathed in what smelled like lavender and gardenia. She closed her eyes and felt thoroughly at ease.

"There! All done, Mrs. Carter! It should heal in a few minutes."

"Minutes? Don't you mean days?"

"No. Minutes. Feel free to take a look in the mirror."

There was a massive golden mirror behind the large couch. It looked older than dirt, which meant it was probably worth more than her yearly salary. She had to stand on her toes to see her face. *Dull as ever*, she thought. Then she looked more closely and saw the blisters and bumps were fading, the swelling was going down, and the redness was diminishing right in front of her!

"What the hell," she mumbled.

Charlotte was shocked too, as she breathed out, "Oh my gosh!" She turned to look at Lily with surprise etched across her face. "How is this possible?"

Lily shrugged with a broad smile.

"Madam is a genius. A literal genius. She's working on getting it patented to help burn victims. Her years of studying at Harvard and Oxford and all around the world, especially holistic remedies in China and Japan, well, as you can see, Madam created a cure for burns." Lily glanced back at Gia, whose face had returned to its usual ugliness. "See? All better!"

Lily went to leave the room, but Gia stopped her.

"Lily, could you sit down for a minute? I have a few questions I'd like to ask you."

Charlotte rolled her eyes and said, "Wow. You're actually crazy."

Lily sat down in the chair in the middle of the two women, so she had to whip her head to the left to see Charlotte or to the right to see Gia. She would have preferred to keep her head looking towards the left. No one messed with Madam and got away with it. She could feel her sisters' energies and quiet thoughts shared between them. Everyone was bitter about this oaf of a woman upsetting their leader.

Bluntly, Gia asked, "Lily, are you working for Madam because you *want* to or because you *have* to?"

Lily looked at her quizzically and replied, "That's a silly question! I'm here because I love working for Madam. She is a mother figure to me, and she brings babies to people who would otherwise be barren."

Gia squinted her face before using an accusatory tone when she responded, "So, you're not being sold to older men as a prostitute?"

Charlotte tossed her hands in the air, stood up and paced in front of the fireplace, murmuring cuss words under her breath. There was no stopping Gia when she was in detective mode.

Lily's mouth dropped open as she stood up haughtily.

"Shame on you, Ma'am. How dare you speak to me like… like, I'm some common whore! As I said before, Madam is like a mother to me! Do you realize what you have insinuated? That my mother is selling my body to rich men! Respectfully, I wish never to talk to you again," and she stormed out, slamming the door behind her.

Charlotte bitterly smiled as her arms were crossed tightly in front of her.

"Well, you did it, Detective. You really fucked this up for me!"

******

Madam's face was still terrifying as it was taking on a demonic form. Beth knew she hated when she would shapeshift into something ugly.

Tentatively and on a whisper, Beth stated, "Umm… Madam, your face."

Madam reached up and felt the craggly skin, the forehead starting to move over her eyes, and she quickly shook her head, spoke Latin to release the ugliness she desperately hated, and then she released the toxic energy.

"Am I back?"

Beth smiled in delight and relief.

"You're as beautiful as ever, Madam!"

Theodora also smiled, grateful that Madam had not lost her temper further.

"Lovely, as usual," Theodora said sweetly.

Madam grinned at Beth and Theodora. Vanity was an issue for her, but she didn't care. Given the way she had almost died, well technically she had died, working on her family's pig farm. Madam would never allow herself to be ugly again.

"Ladies, we need a plan to get rid of her."

"I can always possess someone in the street and have them shoot her," Theodora chimed in.

Madam held up a finger and insisted, "No, this needs to be a long-term torture for our dear Gia. She needs to lose everything, including Charlotte, so we can't have Charlotte mourning her or turning to her. Charlotte must put her trust in me and only me. Distancing them is the best route to go. Let Gia be her own worst enemy… Theodora, you'll just help her along."

Madam smiled wickedly with her two sisters.

Beth added, "You know, Theodora's strength is in possessing certain parts of the brain."

Madam's eyes brightened as gleefully replied, "Yes, perfect! When I shook her hand, the negative thoughts directed towards me were tumbling through her mind! Theodora, do you think you could shut down her frontal lobe and open up the amygdala? This way, she's still there, remembers everything, but the turtle face simply says everything on her mind."

"Yes, Madam! This would be pure joy for me!"

"Also, when you're in there, see about her bad habits. Drinking whiskey is one of them. She has a former smokers wrinkles above her upper lip. See if you can get that addiction going again too, hmm?"

"Absolutely, Madam. This will be fun."

"Don't go in until I send you the signal through our minds. When you do, just slowly let her truths come out. This is a game of chess, and she'll be cowering before me by the end of Charlotte's first trimester."

Madam's green eyes lit up and she felt the blazing, evil energy between her sisters and herself. They had a plan, and they were going to implement it today.

******

Charlotte sat angrily on the plush couch as Gia continued to be mesmerized by how quickly her face had healed. Gia knew she was in the dog house with Charlotte, but Gia couldn't quite make sense of how this Madam worked her business... or businesses.

"Charlotte-"

"Don't," Charlotte said on a weary, yet furious sigh.

She was utterly disgusted with Gia. She had no remorse for what she had asked Lily, who was sure to run off and tell Madam. There went her chances of finally finding a fertility doctor she felt a strong connection with.

As Gia touched her face, she replied, "I mean, come on. Who goes by one name besides Cher and Adele and-"

Madam appeared out of nowhere in the doorway, startling the two women.

"It was a title bestowed upon me by a Grandmaster I studied with for five years in Japan."

Madam nodded and smiled at Charlotte which seemed to brighten her worried face. Gia watched as Madam walked around and sat in her chair, and Gia finally sat down next to Charlotte, who moved as far away from her as possible. A glint of joy passed through Madam's eyes.

"He could not say Maura, nor could he say McBride. For a while, he just called me Bride. Then, one day while he was out in the fields picking herbs for his healing remedy, a woman came in with a breech delivery. I was the only person there who had been a midwife and Dula. I was so involved with saving the woman and the baby, that I didn't notice Grandmaster Kim had returned." Madam looked towards the fireplace and was transported back to the moment. "I delivered her daughter through a tortuous delivery. The baby was just fine, but I noticed the mother was not. Her stomach was swelling, and I knew there was a clot in an artery in her uterus. I had to save her, so without hesitation, I sliced into her stomach, reaching the uterus. I saw the clot, relieved it and clamped the artery. Before I knew what I was doing, through all of the blood, I had repaired the artery." Madam paused and looked at Gia with a force that made Gia gulp. "At that moment, my calling was apparent. I saved both mother and daughter. That was the moment when Grandmaster Kim bestowed the highest title to a woman there had ever been given. I became Madam. It was more important than achieving my doctorates from Harvard or Oxford. It meant more to me than becoming a Reiki Master. I was finally shown my path." Her eyes flashed as they bore into Gia's, "And that, Gia, is why I go by Madam. I *earned* this title."

For a moment, all that could be heard was the breathing of each woman. Gia crossed her arms as Charlotte dabbed at her eyes.

"Gia, I would kindly request that you never ask any of my staff members if they are whores working for me. Also, please never speak to young Lily again - *ever*."

Charlotte sat forward and quickly rambled, "Madam, I am so unbelievably sorry! I don't know what came over Gia. I… I don't share her perspective at all. In fact, I'm quite humiliated! Please know that she's a homicide detective, and she doesn't trust anyone. I would love it very much if you would please be my doctor."

It wasn't just an appeal, but a desperate form of begging. As Gia's mouth pursed, Madam's mouth smiled broadly as she softened her face and looked into Charlotte's eyes that were identical to Catherine's.

"So you do not share your wife's beliefs that I am some shady, inhumane-"

Charlotte's eyes widened as she rushed over to sit in the identical chair next to Madam.

"No! I think you're absolutely lovely!" Charlotte snatched one of Madam's hands and held them in hers. "I already feel a great connection to you. You're not like other doctors. I want to have a baby, and I know you will help me with your holistic approaches to my health."

Madam felt the energy of goodness rushing from Charlotte's hands to her own. She picked up on the feelings of resentment towards Gia, with whom Charlotte secretly feared did not want a baby. Madam also picked up on Charlotte's sweet and emotional nature. Yes, this is what Catherine had been like too when they were young girls in England on their pig farm. Madam was alarmed when she felt a deep emotion come through of not only wild desperation, but she sensed severe depression. She felt that Charlotte had indeed thought of killing herself on multiple occasions.

In that moment, Madam knew she would do a spell to make sure the cells split when the egg was fertilized, ensuring that Charlotte would walk away with one son, for Madam needed her other son to finally fulfill her destiny. Never before had Madam once thought of the women she treated. She would be accused of going "soft" by her sisters, but they would never understand how sure she was that Charlotte was the reincarnation of her younger sister Catherine.

Madam squeezed Charlotte's hand and brought her other hand to gently place upon Charlotte's, which was starting to squeeze Madam's other hand a bit too tightly.

Madam's smile was true and her words were coming from the love she still had for her baby sister, when she softly asked, "Charlotte… have you ever wanted to kill yourself?"

Charlotte gasped, and immediately, Gia went into protective mode.

"Whoa, whoa, whoa, whoa! That's a bit personal, Madam!"

Madam ignored the little hermit crab that she wanted to torture.

"Charlotte, I need to know your mental state. I have elixirs and special teas to help with depression."

"Charlotte, let's go. This is getting weird," Gia demanded

Charlotte's eyes had never left Madam's, as they began to brim with tears.

She whispered, "Yes, Madam. I have suffered from depression since I was a teenager."

"And the suicidal thoughts… do they often come about when you are drunk?"

"Seriously, Charlotte, let's-"

"Yes."

"Mmmhmm. I suspected as much. First off, we're going to do an intense session of Reiki. You will most likely cry because the energy movement and release of toxins is so powerful. You will feel refreshed, yet exhausted. Then, I shall prepare a special antidepressant tea for you that will not harm your body as pharmaceutical drugs do. Those, I do not approve of."

Gia stood up in revulsion, and her yelling startled both of the seated women.

"You know what I don't approve of? You! This shit you're talking about is nonsense!"

Madam flicked her index finger, her strong intentions directed only at Gia, who was now pacing back and forth, in her hideous shoes, on Madam's expensive rug in front of the couch. Gia could have sworn that she suddenly felt a shove on her back as she tripped and flew down onto the ground, barely missing bashing her head into the massive coffee table. Gia landed extremely hard, and Charlotte jumped up in shock, releasing Madam's hands.

Charlotte rushed to help Gia up, and as she did this, Madam smiled and sent Theodoara the message. *The chess game begins now, you hideous oaf!*

"I'm fine. I'm fine!" Gia yelled into Charlotte's face as she unceremoniously picked herself up from the floor.

Madam made her face look concerned and in a mocking tone asked, "Gia, are you not feeling well this morning? Would you like some coffee or tea?"

Madam sat back in her chair in revulsion as Gia literally snorted before responding, "I wouldn't drink a damn thing from you. You and your concoctions! How in the hell did that cream work on my burns so quickly? Huh? Are you a witch or something?"

Charlotte simply retreated into herself. She plopped down onto the suede couch. This was the side of Gia she hated. Gia was definitely verbally abusive. Truth be told, Charlotte's suicidal thoughts truly picked up after she and Gia moved in together, but then again, so did her drinking.

Madam's voice was cool and calm as she knew Theodora was already in.

"I am not a witch. The cream is made with all natural ingredients. Studying with Grandmaster Kim, I learned that every plant, piece of bark, flower, and fungus had special ways of naturally healing people. I'm glad the balm worked. I am actually working on getting it patented to help burn victims. Unfortunately, the FDA won't even consider using this in hospitals where they have burn units. It's quite a shame."

Gia's eyes were in slits as she responded, "What's with the name of your business? Madam's Jewels?"

Madam could feel Theodora ramping up and couldn't wait until Gia reached her breaking point and left her and Charlotte alone.

In a calm voice, Madam simply stated, "I think of babies as jewels. They are precious, unique and exquisitely beautiful. All you want to do is stare at a fine piece of jewelry, the same way you would stare at your baby, hence the name."

Gia continued her interrogation, questioning, "Where do you make your money?"

Charlotte just held her head in her hands and shook her head back and forth slowly as she sat, slightly beaten and downtrodden. Madam felt bad for her, but this was for her benefit, in the long run.

"Through my business."

Madam wasn't about to say that Husband made sure Madam had trillions of dollars in her bank account.

"How many businesses do you have?"

"Just this one, Gia."

"Are you a trust fund baby, like Charlotte over here?"

Madam grinned as she responded jovially, "Well, I don't know about baby, but, yes, I am lucky enough to have a trust fund."

"How much are you worth?"

"Gia!"

Madam's response seethed out of her mouth, "None of your business, Detective Carter."

"That explains it then. The two trust fund babies bonding over material possessions. I bet you both have never had to work a hard day in your life or suffer to get where you are now like I have!"

Madam thought about her past love. She felt the heat rising and sent a message to Theodora to focus on the part of the amygdala to really hurt Madam, get Charlotte to defend her, and have that pinched face hag leave.

"I guarantee you, Detective Carter, I have worked hard and suffered very much to get where I am today."

"Bullshit."

Gia paused and Madam knew it was coming. Theodora was working hard to get into the meanest part of the amygdala.

"I don't appreciate your crass language."

"Alice, from Dr. Lee's office, told us how you couldn't save her son. I'd think that someone with all of these fucking degrees and studying daisies and roses with a Grandmaster would be able to save a baby." She paused and accused, "So, how many babies have you murdered?"

Madam sent her appreciation to Theodora. She feigned fake tears in her eyes as she sniffled.

Charlotte's head shot up as she looked at Madam, to Gia, and then back to Madam. She rushed over to Madam and tried to hold her hands, but Madam had to play this up.

Madam delicately brushed Charlotte's hand away, as she rose and went to grab a tissue from her desk. She sniffled loudly and dabbed at her eyes, smiling broadly, since her back was to her audience.

She walked slowly to the fireplace, pretending she was in deep thought.

When she turned, she had tears leaking out of her light green eyes and whispered, "I tried to save him… the cord had been around his neck for too long." Madam added in a hiccup for impact. "I did… I did try to save him! I carry around his death with me every single day of my life!" Madam had kicked it up to sobbing, but not hysterically. After all, she didn't want to mess up her makeup *that* badly! "That poor baby. They named him Joshua. As I held him in the blue blanket they were supposed to take him home in, I prayed for the soul of Joshua," a nice pause for effect, and then, "but I couldn't save him!"

Madam was now bawling and Charlotte came over and wrapped her arms around Madam's hysterically shaking body. Charlotte was quaking with rage towards Gia. She swiveled and glared menacingly at Gia.

"Get the fuck out, now! You are such a bitch!"

Gia shrugged.

"Whatever. I'm over this shit. Let me know when she plans to knock you up."

Charlotte gasped and was shocked by Gia's swift exit out of Madam's office, as she thought, *What the hell just happened?*

Charlotte immediately turned her attention to Madam, whose back was turned towards her. She was by her desk reaching for tissue after tissue. Charlotte could see her thin shoulders shaking up and down lightly, and she heard the sad sniffles. Charlotte did not know what to do. It was her own wife who had caused such a painful response from Madam. Charlotte raged between furiousness at Gia and sympathy for Madam.

"Do you want me to get Beth?" she asked softly.

Madam was getting bored pretending to cry, so she made it seem like she was trying to clear her throat and get her composure back. Madam turned and Charlotte's heart melted for the pain she saw in the woman's eyes.

"Oh, Madam. I'm so sorry about Gia. I don't know what got into her."

"Please Charlotte. You have nothing to apologize for." She dabbed gingerly at her eyes. "Would you mind if I used the restroom to clean up my face?"

"Not at all."

Madam gave a half-hearted smile, before barely whispering, "Thank you. I'll have Beth bring us in some Chamomile tea."

She gently closed the door behind her. Madam saw her sisters perk up, and that's when Madam's smile flashed brightly. She nodded her head and sent a loving message to them mentally. She headed towards the bathroom with Beth on her heels.

Once inside, Beth handed over all of Madam's makeup.

As she beautified herself even more, she asked, "What happened with that little piece of mouse shit?"

"Madam, Theodora had her storm out of here. She still has her frontal lobe open and is inside the amygdala, awaiting orders from you."

Madam smiled, her cat-like eyes shining.

She laughed and said, "I have just the plan!"

*****

Gia burst out of the Manhattan building, smiling. She had never felt so amazing! For once in her life, she said everything she wanted to say to that freaky woman. If she heard any more fucking sob stories, she would have puked.

Fuck Charlotte for taking Madam's side. That was total bullshit. She was done with not telling people what she really thought.

In fact, she had something she wanted to say to her in-laws. She took out her phone as she walked hurriedly to get rid of her excess energy.

"Hello?"

"Hey Marty! Is Diane there with you? It's Gia."

"Oh, hey there, Gia. Yeah, I'll put you on speakerphone."

She heard the old man struggling with the phone and finally heard Diane say, "Gia? Are you okay? Is Charlotte okay?"

"You know, I just wanted to tell you both that you raised a spoiled little bitch who only cares about designer labels and how much shit costs. You both ruined her with your money. That's all. Peace out, motherfuckers!"

Gia clicked the end button and smiled as she waved down a cab. She was fueled with power. It felt great! She was finally being true to herself and her feelings.

As the cab driver pulled down her street, she motioned for him to drop her off on the corner. She paid him and headed into the liquor store.

As she grabbed a cart, she put in her favorite whiskey bottle… and then another… and yet another. By the time she approached the checkout, she had five bottles of whiskey and a smile. Suddenly, she felt the urge to smoke. Gia had quit after Charlotte had begged her to stop smoking, but Gia was her own woman, so fuck it all! She requested a carton of her former favorite brand.

Gia walked home whistling. As soon as she entered their apartment, out came the whiskey glass, the whiskey and the cigarettes that she would smoke in the apartment because she wanted to! She was tired of answering to little miss perfect Charlotte.

Before Charlotte would arrive home later on that day, an entire whiskey bottle would be flowing through Gia's body before she passed out on the couch, drink still in her hand, and two packs of cigarette smoke clouding their apartment.

******

It had been at least two hours since Gia's departure, and Madam and Charlotte were still talking and laughing about fashion, travel, and their goals in life. There had not been one moment of awkward silence. Madam felt like she had her sister, Catherine, back; Charlotte felt like she had found a kindred soul. Madam had done Reiki on Charlotte, and as promised, she had cried, but she had also felt lighter than cotton candy.

Madam had focused a lot on Charlotte's uterus, sending in incantations. She now felt it was time. Her spell had been completed and would now get the lovely Charlotte pregnant with twin boys.

Madam glanced at her watch and asked, "Charlotte, would you like to see if you're ovulating?"

Charlotte widened her eyes in surprise.

"I don't think I am. I have one ovary that doesn't work."

Madam smiled and stood to open the metal door. As the door opened, Charlotte's mouth fell open. She immediately followed Madam into the room. It definitely did not compare to any gynecologist's office she had ever been to. The amount of devices in the room must have cost Madam a fortune.

"As you can see, I have the latest equipment to help women get pregnant. I feel the Reiki helped open you up. I think, if everything looks good, I can simply insert the sperm into your egg to be fertilized. The procedure is a bit uncomfortable, but it's nothing like the pain from the shots you've gone through. I can get you pregnant today, Charlotte, if there's enough mucus in your uterus to get the embryo to latch onto."

Charlotte nodded, unable to speak. *Pregnant? Today?* She had so many thoughts whirling through her mind. For some reason, she wanted to focus on the one that had really knocked her for a loop earlier in the day.

"I have to ask… are you psychic? I mean, how did you know about my depression and suicidal thoughts?"

Madam nodded her head and grinned warmly at Charlotte.

"I think being open to energy allows me to read people. You're a lovely person. I see nothing wrong with your past, but I do strongly feel that your depression is a medical issue with the receptors in your brain. I guarantee you that the antidepressant tea will help you more than any pharmaceutical drug. We don't want you putting anything in your body that might harm your child."

Charlotte hesitantly asked, "So… what energy did you pick up from Gia?"

Madam ignored the question as she handed a plush, soft pink robe to Charlotte to change into as Madam turned her back to give Charlotte privacy.

This was the first awkward pause they had, but Madam waited until Charlotte was in the robe before she turned around with kindness in her eyes.

"Now if you'll sit up here and put your feet in the stirrups, we'll see what we can find. Just in case, I'll call Beth to bring in the sperm sample you brought with you."

As Madam called Beth, Charlotte eased into the chair and put her feet into the stirrups. She was astonished that the table was more like a heated lounge chair. Even the stirrups were heated and pillow-like! This was definitely no ordinary doctor. She made sure every minute detail was to bring comfort for her patients.

Madam grabbed for her plastic gloves, but before she put them on, she asked Charlotte, "Do you believe in reincarnation?"

Charlotte looked dumbfounded.

"Umm, I don't think so. I feel like once you die, you either go to heaven or hell."

"Mmm, interesting."

"Why do you ask?"

"I had a younger sister, Catherine, who looked just like you. She had the same laugh and mannerisms. The same great energy. She was my best friend... when she died, I literally felt my heart crack in two."

"Oh, I'm so sorry."

"As am I."

Madam put the gloves on and set up the machine that would give her an internal view with the wand. Gel was used on it, and it didn't bother Charlotte at all. In fact, no procedure she'd ever been through had been this simple.

Madam looked hard at the screen. Charlotte wished she knew what she was looking for. She looked back at Madam who was now grinning from ear to ear at the screen.

"What is it?"

Madam circled a spot on the screen and magnified it with a tap of the computer.

"You see that white spot?"

Charlotte didn't, but she nodded her head dumbly.

"That is your egg, and the mucus is thick. The fertilized egg will attach perfectly!"

"Seriously?"

Madam gently took the wand out.

Grinning broadly, she asked, "Charlotte, would you like to get pregnant today?"

Charlotte's eyes were already brimming with tears that just kept flowing.

She ecstatically whispered, "Yes."

Madam patted her knee.

"Fantastic! You'll have an Easter baby!"

Charlotte couldn't respond. She laid her head back, letting the tears fall towards her hairline and ears. She didn't want to hope, but something about Madam made her believe that this miracle of life was about to actually happen!

Suddenly, the room began filling up with Beth and Lily. They buzzed around, grabbing supplies and neatly laying them on the sterile tray. The large needle made Charlotte's eyes widen.

Madam saw this and said, "Not to worry, my dear. We'll put anesthetic on your stomach as we place the sperm directly into the egg."

Lily came up with a petri dish.

"This was the strongest and fastest swimmer."

"Fantastic," Madam murmured.

Beth put a gauze cape over Madam and Lily.

The women got to work and within no time, Charlotte felt slight discomfort, but watched as Madam intently focused on inserting the sperm into her egg. Her hands never wavered or shook. Her eyes were amazingly astute. The procedure was done in less than 10 minutes.

"Beth and Lily, thank you for your excellent work. I'm going to sit with Charlotte for a few minutes, just to make sure she doesn't move."

"Yes, Madam," they said in unison as they cleaned up the mess and discarded the sanitary gauze capes and gloves.

Once they left the room, and after Madam washed and dried her hands, she pulled up a chair and sat next to Charlotte.

"You must take it easy for the next few days. Cramping is normal. I'll get you some tea for that. No over the counter medication, okay?"

Charlotte nodded her head and asked, "Is this where I come for all of my appointments?"

"Yes. It'll be your home away from home for the next 40 weeks."

"Don't you have an apartment on the floor above us?"

"Yes. This is where I need to be for my friends. We deliver here. We keep an eye on you after the birth. I'm lucky that I have a fantastic support system to look after and homeschool my daughter, Ezmerelda."

"Is that the picture I saw behind your desk?"

Madam smiled, but it seemed strained. Her Ezmerelda was growing in strength, so she often stayed upstairs on the 67th floor to be away from the increasingly powerful girl who had no fear and all evil pumping speedily through her veins.

The problem was, the evil was never to be directed at her mother or the sisters in the coven, but Ezmerelda seemed to be on her own unbreakable path. This was extremely worrisome to Madam, but she'd work on getting the girl in line.

"I thought that was you as a child!"

With a soft laugh, Madam replied, "No, she's like a mini-version of me. It's like looking in a mirror."

"I hope my baby has my eyes."

"I'm certain he or she will."

Madam stood and asked if she could do some additional Reiki over Charlotte's stomach, which she agreed to excitedly.

As Madam lay her hands on Charlotte, she closed her eyes, so Charlotte wouldn't see her trance state. Having one's eyes roll back in their head is not a good look. As Madam went into her trance, she said the Latin phrase and felt the fertilized egg split into two. She added in another Latin phrase to ensure they were both males.

Charlotte watched Madam's face harden and her eyelids flutter. Her lips were moving, but there was no sound coming out.

For a moment, Charlotte was a little freaked out, but suddenly, Madam opened her eyes and said, "It's done."

After waiting fifteen minutes, Charlotte gingerly retrieved her purse and Madam handed her a business card.

"This has my cell phone number; never be afraid to use it. Remember, I am here most of the time. Oh," she paused and went behind her desk to retrieve a long, velvet box, "and... I have a special gift for you."

Charlotte laughed, shaking her head.

"If you were able to get me pregnant with that procedure, that's a gift for a lifetime."

Madam gave Charlotte the lovely box.

"I want you to wear this throughout your entire pregnancy."

Charlotte opened the box and found the most gorgeous single sapphire stone she had ever seen. The strong silver chain was even more elegant!

"Madam, I can't! This is too much!"

"My dear, Charlotte, this sapphire represents the restoration of balance within the mind, body and soul. It brings forth peace of mind and serenity. And finally, it is called the stone of prosperity." Madam paused as she placed the necklace around her throat and clasped the strong necklace together. "Prosperity does not have to be just money... it means you can be prosperous in the amount of children you have."

Charlotte was overwhelmed and hugged Madam.

"Thank you. You're too kind. I will wear this every single day." She paused and added, "I hate to ask you this, and if you don't want to answer, I completely understand."

Madam nodded.

Very softly, she asked, "How did Catherine die?"

Madam's face plummeted into sadness. She had to pause before she could actually answer, for her mind tossed her back to that horrific day.

"It was in the worst way. She died being burned alive. I watched it happen, but I couldn't get to her."

Madam's head spun through time as she remembered Catherine being burned at the stake in London during the reign of Bloody Mary, as she was so fondly known as. She remembered her sister's screams, the hoots and hollers from the crowd to burn the witch... and then the smell of burning flesh. Madam had stayed the whole time and kept eye contact with her sister. She felt the pain through her eyes.

"I'm so sorry," Charlotte brought her back to the present. "I cannot imagine how awful that must have been for you."

"Yes… I am the older sister. It was my job to protect her, and I failed. Fate can be quite cruel."

Before Charlotte could speak again, Madam quickly whisked her out of her office and called for Lily to get Charlotte the two herbal teas. Madam waved at Charlotte, reminding her to call her about anything.

Madam shut the door to her office, took the matching sapphire stone out of her pocket that now connected her to Charlotte, and then she fainted.

******

"Oh good… I think she's coming around. Thanks everyone. I'll take care of Madam from here."

Madam opened her eyes to find herself lying on the large couch in her office. She saw the haze of her sisters leave the room and felt Beth's presence.

"Beth? What happened? Where's the sapphire?"

Beth shook her head with worry.

"You fainted, Madam. Here," Beth put the sapphire stone into Madam's shaky ones, "I fear this new sacrifice might be too much for you."

Madam sat up slowly and brushed away Beth's hand that was offering to help.

"There is nothing I cannot handle."

Beth sat quietly and then looked into Madam's eyes.

"She looks just like Catherine."

"I know."

"Husband said this would be challenging."

"Yes."

"This is your last stone for the crown, and then you can move forward into the life that has John William in it."

"I know, Beth."

"You did something different this time. I felt you pulling up an incantation I had never before heard."

Madam swallowed, hard.

"I have changed things slightly."

Beth's eyebrows furrowed as she whispered, "What did you do?"

Madam cleared her throat, knowing she technically didn't have permission from Husband to let a woman leave with a baby, while the other was sacrificed, but she saw Catherine when she looked at Charlotte. She could not deny her the child she so desperately craved.

"It will be twin boys."

Beth's mouth dropped to her chest.

She practically hissed, "What? Are you mad? The coven, and more importantly, Husband, will think you have gone soft! What if you lose the sapphire to complete the crown?"

Madam had the same fears.

"I am not going soft. I'm trying something different for a change."

"With all due respect, I call bullshit on that!"

"Shut up, Beth! I have not gone soft! They both have 9 letters in their names. They both have the same eyes, hair color, mannerisms…"

"I know, but this is against protocol."

Madam blew out a breath, replying, "Husband will still get his sacrifice. I will earn my last stone for my crown."

Beth eyed her as Madam stood up and left her office. Madam knew the coven would be forced to tell Husband if asked. This was not good.

Chapter 5

Charlotte was smiling as the cab took her out of Manhattan. She looked at the bag beside her that contained the two types of teas that Madam insisted she take. Charlotte would make herself the tea as soon as she was home.

The thought of home had her feeling heavier, for she knew there would undoubtedly be a huge fight between herself and Gia. She clasped the sapphire stone around her neck for comfort. The Reiki Madam had done for Charlotte had indeed made her feel lighter, but now she felt the anxiety of having to confront Gia, and she hated confrontation. However, accusing Madam of murdering a baby was inexcusable, no matter how exhausted Gia was from work. It sickened Charlotte to the core to see the impact it had had on Madam.

As Charlotte was holding the sapphire, she thought about how it was the stone of prosperity. She moved her hand to her stomach hoping that she would be prosperous in the children she could bear and raise. A soft smile appeared on her lips at the strong feeling that this was definitely different. She could indeed have her baby around Easter. Charlotte looked at the skyline and wondered if there were cute Easter-themed names for a boy or a girl.

She glanced down at her watch, amazed that she'd spent the whole day with Madam. It felt like she had known her for years. Perhaps there was something to reincarnation. Could it be possible that she was the reincarnation of Madam's sister, Catherine? Charlotte shook her head and knew that was a ridiculous thought.

As she looked outside at the sun lowering in the distance, she wondered if Gia had already called to apologize to her. Perhaps she wouldn't have to have an all out drag out fight that would drain her.

Charlotte unlocked her phone that had been on silent, and she saw ten missed calls from her parents.

"What the-" she mumbled.

She talked to her parents each morning, so now she began to panic. They had also texted her.

Mom: *Charlotte, is everything okay? Your father and I are worried about Gia's behavior. Has she hurt you? Are you safe?*

Dad: *Charlotte, can you call us back? We need to make sure you're okay.*

Mom: *Seriously, I'm getting VERY worried! Call me!!!*

Dad: *We just need to know if you're okay! I'm ready to call the police!*

Mom: ***CALL ME!!!***

Dad: ***CALL YOUR MOTHER!!!*** *I can't handle her freaking out like this!*

Charlotte wasted no time and immediately called her mom, who picked up on the first ring.

"Charlotte? Marty! It's Charlotte!"

"Mom? What's going on?"

"Charlotte, are you okay?"

"I'm fine. I was with my new doctor."

"This whole time?"

"Yes, why? What's going on?"

"You didn't listen to your voicemails?"

"Mom, no. I saw the texts, and I immediately called you. Are you and dad okay?"

She heard her mother click the phone to speakerphone, and she heard her father's deep voice.

"Charlotte, are you okay? Did Gia hurt you?"

"What? Dad… Mom, just tell me what the hell is going on."

"Please don't curse, dear," her mother stated in her usual calm voice.

"Diane, who cares about her damn cursing? She's an adult!"

"Don't encourage her potty mouth, Marty!"

"I'll encourage it! Shit! Damn! Hell!"

"Oh, stop it! Now you're just trying to piss me off, you old shithead!"

"Mom! Dad! Focus! What is going on?"

Her mother replied before her father could, as they both almost talked over each other.

 "Well, Gia called us and her behavior was quite reprehensible."

"What did she say?"

Her father won the contest in this round as he quickly replied, "She said we raised a spoiled bitch-"

"Marty!"

"I'm quoting! Anyway, she said that we raised a spoiled bitch who only cares about money and designer labels."

"Oh," her mother added, "and that you only cared about the cost of things."

"Yup. And that we ruined you with our money."

"Honey, did you tell Gia this? Do you feel like we raised you poorly?"

"For fuck sake, Diane, she's the best daughter anyone could ask for! We didn't raise her poorly!"

"Don't you fucking swear at me, you old shithead!"

"MOM! DAD! I never said anything like that. What else did Gia say to you guys?"

There was a pause as the two were probably looking at each other.

Her dad's voice piped up, "Oh, that was it. Then she said something about peacing out motherfuckers."

"Yes, that's right, Marty. I don't know what peacing out means, but I derived a very negative connotation from the phrase."

Charlotte rolled her eyes and felt herself begin to fume.

"Mom, dad… I am so sorry for Gia calling you. She worked a long shift, and we went straight to the doctor's office afterwards. She was rude to the doctor, and Gia left before I even had the procedure done."

Suddenly both of her parents were talking over each other, but Charlotte could pick up on their excitement, knowing they were both beginning to yell over each other to ask about the procedure.

"Okay, okay. Relax, please. Madam was able to insert the donor sperm into my egg. I saw it. I have a fertilized egg!"

"Darling, that's wonderful news!" her mother exclaimed through a sniffle.

"How do you feel?"

"The needle was as long as your arm, dad. So, I'm a little sore. She put the needle in through my stomach, and I'm a bit crampy, but Madam said that was to be expected. I just need to take it easy for the next few days."

Her mother turned overprotective and resolutely said, "I demand you come here to the Hamptons and stay with us! You should not be around Gia when she's like this. I swear, it was like talking to a different person! I don't know why you ever married her! You could have married Bonnie. She has the bloodline-"

"Mom, stop! Bonnie isn't gay!"

"She is too! Her mother told me that she saw Bonnie with a pretty, lanky blonde, and they were kissing."

"That's a man, mom. His name is Buster."

"Buster? What the hell kind of name is that?" her mother asked in revulsion.

"See! You're the potty mouth."

"Oh, shut up, Marty!"

"You guys, I'm sorry about Gia-"

Her father interrupted her, and firmly said, "No. You don't apologize for her words or actions. You need to take care of yourself. I'm in agreement with your mother. You should come to the Hamptons while you are starting the process of growing a little grandbaby for us. We'll send you a car."

Charlotte saw she was on her street and quickly said, "I'm home. I'll let you guys know, okay? I just want to check on Gia."

Her father sounded somber.

"You call us, Charlotte. I'll have Mack standing by with the towncar for you."

Charlotte smiled at the love she was grateful to have from both of her parents.

"Thanks, dad. I love you guys."

"Love you too," they shouted over the phone in unison.

As Charlotte made her way up to their fourth floor apartment, she was seething. It was one thing to pick on her, but it was quite another to contact her parents, who had been nothing but supportive and caring.

Charlotte was ready for a fight. Her anxiety was gone, and now she was filled with pure protective instincts for her parents. As she opened the door, the smell of cigarettes pummeled her nose and lungs. The entire apartment looked cloudy with cigarette smoke. She saw Gia passed out on the couch, drooling, as she held a whiskey glass in her hand.

On the coffee table stood an empty whiskey bottle, and it looked like Gia had tried to start on a second one. Charlotte knew she could bang pots and pans over the drunken woman, and she'd remain passed out, still holding the whiskey glass like a baby clutches their favorite blanket or stuffed animal.

She took out her phone.

Her mother picked up on the first half of the ring, "Yes, Charlotte?"

"Have dad send the towncar."

"He already did."

******

On Madam's way to the bathroom, she saw Theodora in her trance and mentally called her out of it.

Smiling with pure adoration, Madam said, "You did a great job. Are you okay?"

Theodora grinned back at Madam, as she tried to hide her yawn.

"Yes, Madam."

"I think you should work with Victoria on this Gia situation."

"But, Madam, I can handle it."

"I know you can. However, I also know this is going to be an almost year-long process. It's a lot. Plus, we can't constantly have Gia's frontal lobe shut off… we don't want to draw too much suspicion about her change in behavior."

Theodora lowered her head, and replied sadly, "Yes, Madam."

Madam gently touched Theodora's shoulder and told her in a message only she could hear in her mind, *You are the best at mental possession. Never forget that. You must learn to rely on your sisters, as I rely on you. We are a coven. I cannot have you losing your strength. Just know, I am proud of you and how far you have come in your training since you joined us two hundred years ago.*

Theodora smiled brightly, and nodded. Madam patted her back and quickly went to the restroom.

As she was washing her hands, she felt the heat of the sapphire in her pants pocket. She took it out and held it, going into the view of Charlotte. It was like watching a video on fast forward. She heard the conversation with her parents, saw Gia and even smelled the cigarette smoke. She saw her sitting in an expensive town car with her Madam's Jewels bag next to her, along with luggage, knowing she was heading to the Hamptons to stay with her parents.

Madam smiled and looked up at her reflection. She shared the good news with her sisters in her mind and heard triumphant yells from them, with special congratulations going to Theodora.

As the wife of Husband, she enjoyed the ability to specify whom she would communicate with, but she was also able to shut that down and have thoughts none of the sisters would ever hear. Not even Theodora could penetrate her brain. Madam was the strongest. She looked at her reflection in the mirror and smirked at how beautiful it would be when she was finally back with her true love in less than a year.

As she was about to bid a goodnight to her sisters after a long day, and head upstairs to her second home, she suddenly heard her sisters talking to her worriedly. In her head, they were all talking over each other, nervously.

Madam couldn't figure out what was being said. It was like trying to hear a message through a crackling walkie-talkie. She covered her ears and screamed at them to shut up and clarify the message.

Madam walked out into the front office to see her sisters there. Beth held her purse and light trench coat.

Madam was now frustrated by the silence.

"What is happening!"

Beth stepped forward and said purposefully, "You are needed at home, Madam."

"Why?"

"It's Ezmerelda."

Panic went through her blood as she asked anxiously, "Is she okay?"

The sisters looked at the ground.

"I asked a question!"

Beth sighed, and as her second in command, told her, "Ezmerelda is wreaking havoc on the sisters at your home, Madam."

"They can control her with one of their binding spells! Don't waste my time with-"

"Madam, the sisters say her eyes have shifted to gold, and her hair is now straight and dark brown."

Madam's eyes widened.

"She's being possessed?"

Beth helped her put her coat on as she replied, "If she is, then the demon is very powerful. None of the sisters can control her. She's harming them with spells she was never taught. Maybe it is Ezmerelda and she's simply a shapeshifter?"

Madam snatched her purse and hit the down button for the elevator.

"No. She doesn't know how to shapeshift yet. There is an unwelcome entity in our coven. As long as we make sure we never complete the spell on Ezmerelda, she won't know our thoughts. We have the advantage over this demon."

As Madam stepped onto the elevator, Beth stopped the doors from closing.

"One more thing… we figured out the language she is speaking. It's ancient Egyptian."

******

It was a little over an hour when Madam sped through the long path to her house and screeched her Land Rover to a stop. Several of her sisters were waiting for her outside. Many of them had ice packs over their eyes, lips, or cheeks. Several of them had bandages from wounds that were already bleeding through the thick gauze.

Madam didn't stop to ask. She knew exactly where the rest of her sisters were as she raced up to the third floor, dropping her purse and removing her coat.

She paused at the classroom door, seeing the couches, chairs, and desks flipped over.

She heard the voice of a woman with a heavy accent demand, "What is her secret! I know she did something, and you stupid witches know! Tell me what that lead witch did, or I shall torture you until I kill you!"

Madam hadn't entered the classroom yet. She heard the accent as this demon, who might or might not be female, struggled with English. The Egyptian accent was in its voice. The demon shifted back to speak Egyptian as Madam saw Elizabeth, Franny, and Nora being thrown against the wall at the front of the classroom. Now, they hung there. Their faces were unrecognizable from the battering they took from this demon. Deep cuts, bruised faces and eyes swollen shut. They were limp, as Madam watched them being thrown to the other side of the room.

Madam entered, and demanded, "Enough, demon!"

The body of Ezmerelda was there, but the eyes were golden and fiery. The hair that used to be black and wavy was definitely dark brown and bone straight. Her usually porcelain white skin was now beautifully bronzed, as though she had been kissed by the sun itself.

"YOU! I demand to know what you have done!"

"Release my sisters and go back to hell. No one in our coven has welcomed you!"

"I will torture you all until I know what you did today. Something is amiss, and when I find out, Husband will know your disloyalty. You shall suffer, pig."

So, Ezmerelda had been communicating with this demon in her bedroom, which explained her newfound love for ancient Egyptian culture and the language.

"No male demon is allowed into a witches' coven unless invited! You have not been invited!"

"I AM NOT A MALE!!! I AM MUCH STRONGER THAN ANY MALE! I AM A GODDESS!!!"

Madam was firing up the protection spells in her head. If this was a demonic goddess from ancient Egyptian times who was using her daughter as her own personal pawn, she would definitely need to brush up on Egyptian curses.

"RELEASE MY SISTERS AT ONCE AND LEAVE MY HOME!"

"FUCK YOU, YOU FILTHY, ROTTING PIG CARCASS!"

With that, the demon goddess went to throw Elizabeth, Franny and Nora again, but this time, Madam was ready for it. She shot up her hand to protect her sisters. They didn't move, which was good.

Madam revved up her energy even more, trying to pull them down to the ground.

She saw the demon goddess glare at her, and Madam anticipated the demon goddess' next move was to take her down. Madam shot up her left hand and released a burst of energy at the same time the demon goddess did the same thing. Their spells bounced off of each other and canceled each other out.

The demon goddess laughed.

"You cannot defeat me, pig!"

Madam knew what she had to do, but it would cause much pain to everyone in the room. She brought forth every strength spell she could think of between her hands, and watched as the ball of energy grew and changed into a deep blood red.

"A ball, pig? You want to play catch?"

In her head, she told everyone to hit the ground and cover themselves. With a curse said in Latin, she threw the energy ball at the demon goddess, and in slow motion, the entire room was crashing. The sisters dropped to the ground, not moving. The glass in the windows shattered, as the walls splintered down the middle. The body of Ezmerelda was thrown so hard into the back wall, that her head left an indentation.

Madam ran to Ezmerelda as she cast a spell to stop the walls from crumbling with a flick of her wrist. The other sisters came rushing in to help their own.

Madam peeled open Ezmerelda's eyelids. She audibly sighed when she saw her matching green eyes. The girl was back, and breathing, but she'd been knocked out cold.

"Sisters, take care of the wounded. We shall heal each other in the sacred place, but I need to take care of her," she said as she picked up Ezmerelda and carried her to the second floor.

Madam swiftly walked into the girl's bedroom, which she now hated, realizing the changes in it had come to Ezmerelda from that demon goddess bitch.

Madam wished Beth were here. Beth was her second in command, and she would be barking orders and taking care of the wounded sisters. This was their coven and war had been brought into their home. She couldn't help but feel mild guilt that perhaps getting Charlotte pregnant with twins had been the catalyst.

Madam flicked on the switch for the fireplace in the girls' bedroom, looking at all the Lapis crystals on the mantel. She picked them all up and with a fierce curse on that bitch who declared war on her coven, she threw them into the fire. She turned the flames up as high as they would go. Her adrenaline was through the roof after using so much energy. She felt the force of her strength and the evil intentions behind them at war with the kindness she brought to Charlotte. NO! She would not go soft!

Madam grabbed some healing supplies from Ezmerelda's attached bathroom and tended to the gash on the back of her head. She changed her into her pajamas and cast a spell to heal her brain from the concussion and to cleanse her of the demon that had possessed her.

Madam pulled up a chair and collapsed into it. She knew this was not over. She also knew that the secret of her helping Charlotte have one baby to take home must never be told to Ezmerelda. The secret must remain within the sisters' minds.

Madam put her chin on her hand as she looked at Ezmerelda sleeping. When had these shifts in her behavior started? As though hearing her question, Sphynx hopped up onto Ezmerelda's bed and stared with the same golden eyes she had seen in the demon goddess. The cat's hair was dark, but not dark enough to black.

She couldn't believe it. The cat had been the one possessed by the demon goddess.

Madam leaned forward and stared at the cat, who was staring right back at her.

"You little bitch."

The cat hissed at Madam.

"You've made a huge mistake entering my coven and taking over my daughter."

The cat's hair rose and on the largest hiss she'd ever heard, the cat lunged at her and began ripping off her skin on her cheek, nose, and neck. The cat kept trying to go for the arteries in her throat!

Ezmerelda stirred as Madam fought to grab the neck of the annoying creature. As the cat took a chunk out of Madam's hand, Madam, with the ferociousness of every demon united, hooked the cat under her arm and snapped its neck in two. For extra fun, she snapped the cat's spinal cord as she cursed the demon goddess inside.

Ezmerelda screamed, "MY MOTHER!!! YOU'VE KILLED MY MOTHER!!!"

Madam dumped the cat's body into the fireplace, and watched the flames engulf the little monster. Madam smiled, her evilness at the surface of her skin and pounding blood.

Ezmerelda kept screaming, but Madam was done with the girl. She had invited this demon goddess into their sacred coven. She flicked her wrist and put a binding spell over Ezmerelda's voice box. At the same time, she put a binding spell around the girl's bed, so she could not leave her bed and lash out. Finally, she put an extra protection spell over herself. Madam was worn out, and she feared the power of Ezmerelda from whatever that damn Egyptian demon had taught her daughter, would be too much for her to fight back against in her lowered energy state.

Ezmerelda grabbed her throat as she realized nothing she was saying was being allowed out. Her eyes filled with rage, as she threw back the covers to attack her mother who now sat in the chair next to her bed. Ezmerelda was met by an invisible brick wall. The girl jumped up and down screaming. Madam smiled as she thoroughly enjoyed this.

She had let this thing in, and now Ezmerelda was going to be punished, severely. As the girl looked like a mime trying to find a way outside of the invisible walls, she finally sat down, pulled her covers up and pouted as she crossed her arms over her chest. She glared at her mother as Madam simply maintained her calm demeanor.

"You've done something bad, Ezmerelda. You are going to be punished. Brutally."

Ezmerelda continued to glare at Madam.

Madam leaned forward, her voice eerily calm.

"You are going to be punished by every witch in this coven, and you will accept the burns, the drownings, the beatings, the starvation, the sleeping in the large ice room next to all of the hanging meat. You will endure every possible pain and then some. You risked our coven by bringing in this Egyptian demon bitch."

Madam watched as Ezmerelda began screaming again. It was lovely not to hear her, but she saw the strained vocal cords almost ripping through her pale skin.

"ENOUGH! You know you did something reprehensible. Our coven is supposed to protect each other. No more conjuring up your Egyptian buddy. All of this Egyptian shit is going in the fire. In fact," Madam got up and ripped down the artwork, "let's start now, shall we?"

Madam saw Ezmerelda jumping and banging on the invisible wall, but Madam was on a mission. Her job was to protect her sisters. She tossed the books about Egypt in the fire, grabbed every piece of gold and Lapis jewelry she could find and tossed it into the massive, hungry fire. When Madam was finally done, she looked back at Ezmerelda who stood there with her arms crossed.

Madam walked directly up to her mirror-like image.

"Never fuck with your mother, dear. I always win, and you're going to learn that the hard way," Madam said with an evil grin.

Ezmerelda's face pursed up as she plopped onto her bed, appearing to accept defeat, but Madam knew better. The girl had been in the process of being trained by a demon goddess. She most definitely wasn't going down without a fight. This time, Madam and her coven would be prepared. As Madam went to make her departure, she could see out of the corner of her eye that Ezmerelda was motioning to her voice box.

She turned to look at Ezmerelda and stated, "I shall allow you to speak if this is going to be a productive discussion."

Madam remained by the door, as she flicked her wrist. Ezmerelda coughed loudly and glared at her mother.

"Madam Maura McBride…" Ezmerelda said as she stood up, "I know you did something Father would not like today, and it will be your downfall because YOU shouldn't fuck with me. My parents are much stronger than you."

"Why do you keep saying that, child? I carried you in my body, nourished you, and then gave birth to you. I was *there.*"

Ezmerelda's eyes glowed as her face grew more severe.

"Were you there though?"

"That's a stupid question. I was there, you fool! I am your mother!"

Ezmerelda's eyebrows shot up as she continued to grin.

"Oh… little piggy girl. Go have one of your pigs fuck you, since that's the only way you'll ever be fucked. Oink, oink… YOU FUCKING PIG!"

Madam waved her hand to shut the little bitch up again, while at the same time, she was somersaulting back into her past when she was working on her father's pig farm. The boys and meaner girls around the neighborhood would say those exact same words to her, as she worked in the slop and carried the odor of pigs, pig blood, and pig parts that she had to hack off to sell to nearby families.

She had been an ugly girl, unlike Catherine. Even though Catherine was stunningly gorgeous, getting the genetics from her mother's side, Madam was never jealous; instead, she was proud to have a little sister of such beauty. When they walked together, no one ever bothered Maura McBride because Catherine McBride might not like them. Catherine didn't have to work on the pig farm and inside the slaughterhouse. Her mother hated young Maura from the start, mainly because she looked just as bland and ugly as her toothless father.

Catherine, on the other hand, stayed by her mother's side constantly. She learned how to properly cook, clean, sew, entertain guests, and be an important ambassador for the family business by being out and about in public. While Catherine and her mother worked at sales, using their looks and flirtatious skills, Maura and her father worked at butchering pigs.

Madam quickly brought herself to the present, smelling that awful pig scent that was always a part of her. No pork products were ever allowed in the house or in her office. Deer, duck, chicken, cow, and pheasants all made the cut into her diet, but there would never be a pig product anywhere near her.

Madam looked at Ezmerelda and realized her daughter was evil, but on a different level. To her, the coven was nothing. Working together as a team was beneath her. She had obviously inherited her Father's traits more than Madam's. She would break her forcefully.

Madam smiled at Ezmerelda who felt like she had won that round. The poor, misguided girl had no idea who she was messing with.

"You think being around pigs is disgusting, huh?"

Ezmerelda nodded and smiled.

"Do you think the smell of freshly cut pig, with blood and intestines spewing everywhere is gross?"

Again, the wicked smile from her lovely daughter.

"Well, my dear Ezmerelda, here is your first punishment."

Madam smiled menacingly as pig parts, especially the intestines and hooves and bloody throats landed on Ezmerelda.

The girl looked around at the pieces of pig meat, some with maggots on it that Madam added just for fun, and screamed silently. She stood up and kicked the parts away from her, but Madam just kept replacing more parts, adding in a sliced open brain with worms coming out of it. She added a pigs' heart that was still pumping and spraying blood all over Ezmerelda.

No matter how much Ezmerelda tried to get out, she finally realized she couldn't. She began to vomit all over herself. She made begging hands towards Madam and mouthed the words "please" and "I'm sorry."

Madam walked over to the invisible barrier, enjoying her handiwork. She smiled lovingly at Ezmerelda as she decided there needed to be more pig's blood, so she stole from one of her favorite movies, *Carrie*, and dropped buckets of pig's blood over her daughters head. She could see her screaming and vomit once again.

Madam breathed in fully and released a calm breath. She walked towards the door and turned to see her bratty daughter crying and screaming.

"Good night, my dear Ezmerelda. Sweet dreams."

Madam blew her a kiss and closed the bedroom door.

******

In the sanctuary, usually the sisters wore their ceremonial robes, but there was too much injury to tend to. Madam worked hard at creating balms, setting broken bones, healing each woman who had been harmed by Ezmerelda and the demon goddess. It took them nearly three hours to patch up everyone, including Madam from that hideous cat's attack. By the time they were done, everyone was mentally beat up. Physically, Madam healed them with her expertise, but the feeling of having an entity that had *not* been personally invited by Madam was upsetting to everyone. It felt like a violation to their safety.

Nora, with her light brown hair and gentle blue eyes, shared her thought with everyone that she was thinking about leaving the coven.

"Ladies. Let's not get ahead of ourselves. We've been through worse, especially being burned at the stake or those damn gallows. This is something that is like nothing we have ever encountered before. Now is the time when we must be bold and pull together." Here, Madam paused with a smile."And, I give you all full permission to torture Ezmerelda into submission."

All of the sisters were shocked. This was His daughter, but their leader was giving them permission to torture her? This was too good to be true!

Madam shared the image of Ezmerelda in the invisible pig cage she had created for her. All of the witches began to laugh. This was something they needed. The girl had taken their sacred bond and basically shit on it. Now, it was time for revenge, which made Nora cackle.

"I'll stay, Madam!"

"Good! Now, let's get down to business. First and foremost, has anyone invited her to join our coven's thoughts?" Everyone shook their heads. "Okay, we must absolutely keep that from happening. If she gets inside our thoughts, then so does the demon goddess, and we lose our edge."

All women nodded in agreement, as did the sisters who were in Manhattan, but were listening and chiming in when necessary.

"Next up, we have to hone our skills and strengthen them. I fear I have let our strength fall to the wayside as I have been focusing so much on finally joining Husband where I belong. So, I'm going to demand that every single one of you wake up at 3AM, and work on your spells, communing with my Husband, and strengthening your power through sacrifices. Keep low profiles. Find a human sacrifice that is evil, and we'll drain them and strengthen ourselves."

Franny, with almost an orange hue to her hair and bright brown eyes, delightedly squealed, "Madam! It's been so long since we've been on the hunt and tasted the blood of true evil."

Madam nodded her head and smiled.

"Franny, we have a battle coming our way, so the first hunt will be on the full moon. I see him. He's a serial killer in Connecticut. By his size, there should be at least four of you to take him down. I will keep Ezmerelda in her box. We cannot have her ever know about this sanctuary we have devoted to Husband."

They all bowed their heads and spoke their loyalty to him in Latin.

"Finally, I have created a concoction with some blood left over from a previous sacrifice. I have used the strengthening spell. We will all drink from our designated chalices."

As the women drank the blood, the strength built between them all. They set their chalices down, held hands, and went into a strength and bonding trance together.

******

Madam finally dropped her head onto her satin pillow and closed her eyes. She could feel the wind coming through her open windows, and she pulled the covers up to her chin.

She had felt like a strong leader, especially after their trance. Then, the coven relished going into Ezmerelda's bedroom to see her covered in pig's blood. She was crouched in the furthest corner, holding her pillow up to her face. It appeared she had finally fallen asleep, but she swiftly took the pillow away from her face and screamed, her light green eyes terrifying as the blood had dried on her forehead and cheeks. Madam couldn't help thinking that if her eyes were changed to red or black, she would look more like her father.

Elizabeth, who was born in Japan and had joined Madam after leaving Grandmaster Kim, had suffered the most and the longest under Ezmerelda's siege of the coven. Elizabeth glared at the girl who had beat her, choked her, threw her into everything until she passed out, only to revive her and torture her over and over again. Madam felt the hatred and malice pooling off of Elizabeth.

"Elizabeth?"

She didn't take her black eyes off the girl she had grown to hate.

"Yes, Madam?"

"Would you like to add in a final touch of torture for our lovely, sweet Ezmerelda?

Elizabeth's eyes widened as she looked excitedly at Madam.

"Really? Anything?"

With a wan smile, Madam gestured towards her filthy, despicable daughter and said, "Please, be my guest. Don't even think about holding back, Elizabeth. She's been hurting you a lot lately as her head teacher. Do your worst."

Ezmerelda finally had a look of fear cross her blood-stained face as she shook her head, looking back and forth between Madam and Elizabeth.

"Oh come on," Madam encouraged her young recruit, "I can read your mind! Do it! We can heal her tomorrow. Plus, you know how much she hates bugs."

Elizabeth smiled broadly as she stared at a now worried little demon child in front of her. She said the spell in her head, and suddenly, fire ants ascended and were on every part of Ezmerelda. They began to chew through her skin. The sisters watched in delight and laughed as she screamed and ran to the edge of her bed, putting the rotting meat with maggots on top of her to protect her skin from being torn apart.

Madam was pleased with Elizabeth's choice of torture.

"Well done, Elizabeth… How long did she have you hanging in the air and beating the shit out of you?"

"I had it from the start, so about 3 hours."

Madam nodded.

"Then for 3 hours, you will sit here and torture her however you like. I only ask that you keep the pig parts and blood in there for… sentimental reasons."

Madam sighed in bed. She had shown more strength today than she had in decades, maybe even a century!

She silently closed off her brain from her sisters, who were enjoying themselves over Ezmerelda's much-deserved torture.

In her private thoughts, she knew the demon goddess wasn't done. If she continued to use Ezmerelda as her own personal possession doll, Madam would take it upon herself to kill Ezmerelda in a way Husband would never suspect that it was Madam who did it. Perhaps an accident… in a fire.

Madam smiled as she thought of all the ways she could kill her daughter. There was no way that little bitch was going to keep her from John William and her rightful place along the thrones of Husband's other wives.

Madam snuggled into the pillow with a gleeful smile, thinking of ways to murder her daughter.

Chapter 6

At 4 AM, Madam felt the vibration from the sapphire on her nightstand, even before she opened her eyes and saw the blue glowing like a beating heart. She picked up the stone that was cut from the same large sapphire that Charlotte now had. They were bonded together; Charlotte just didn't know how deeply they were bonded.

Madam could see the large bedroom and heard waves in the distance. She could feel the pain and depression washing through her as she felt everything Charlotte did. Madam felt tears on her face, and then she heard Charlotte's thoughts, wishing she could have someone to talk to.

Madam, who had already programmed Charlotte's number into her phone, called her immediately. She could feel the startled shock as Charlotte looked at Madam's number, and the hesitation to pick it up. Madam held the stone and urged her to click the accept button on her phone, which she did.

"Madam?" Charlotte asked through a clogged nose and trembling voice.

"Charlotte, my dear. I apologize for the early hour. I just felt this need to call you and check to see if you were okay."

Charlotte blew out a shaky breath with a somber reply, "I'm fine." She paused to blow her nose. "Just some mild cramping as you said. I've been drinking my tea, and that really has helped."

"Charlotte, I mean how are you doing emotionally?"

Here, Madam had to wait as Charlotte began to sob uncontrollably. Madam sent calming and soothing emotions through the sapphire. Within a minute, the energy had reached Charlotte. She heard her blow her nose again.

"I'm sorry," she whispered, "it's just… I've been through a seesaw of emotions. I'm sure you don't want to hear about it."

"I absolutely do. Every detail, Charlotte."

Madam listened patiently as Charlotte went on a rambling rampage about Gia calling her parents, her drunk and passed out, the smoking habit she promised to stop for her, and how she was now in her parents' home in the Hamptons to get away from Gia's negativity.

"Oh Charlotte. I'm so sorry." Here, Madam knew she had to pretend that Gia wasn't someone she wanted to feed to hungry pigs and watch as they ripped her apart as she was still alive. Instead, she had to play the part of a kind friend who offered support of their relationship, even though her main goal was to tear them apart. "Perhaps Gia simply had a bad day, and she took it out on your parents and then on herself with alcohol."

"Madam, please don't stick up for her, especially after the awful things she said to you."

"We all have bad days, and we all say and do things that we regret. Have you heard from Gia?"

Charlotte laughed, a very icy and bitter laugh.

"Oh, I've heard from her. She called and figured I was staying with my parents. Gia apologized for saying all of those horrible things to my parents about me, but then she immediately turned her apology into an accusation, telling me that I run home to mommy and daddy when things get too difficult between us." Charlotte paused and Madam felt the sadness shift into anger. "But the worst part was, she said she didn't regret a single thing she said to you. I even told her how you lost your sister Catherine in a horrible house fire, and how you only wanted to help me."

Madam's left eyebrow went up. If only the girl knew it was most definitely not a house fire.

"I then explained how my uterus had an actual egg, and that you did the implantation procedure, right there in the office. Do you know what she said?" Charlotte asked in anger. "Why the fuck did you go and do that?" Charlotte made a growling noise of frustration. "I swear, Madam, it's like she doesn't even want a baby with me. Which is fine, but tell me the truth! I am fine raising a baby on my own. I have amazing parents and a great group of friends from school. If she continues down this road of verbal abuse, alcoholism and smoking, I don't want her around my baby!"

Madam wanted to rip Gia's ugly turtle face to shreds, but she knew that she had to be a calming resource for Charlotte to rely upon.

"I know you can raise a child on your own. And it sounds like your parents would be there every step of the way… but sometimes, it takes a partner time to come around. When Gia sees the baby," Madam almost slipped and said babies, "on the sonogram, sees your beautiful, round belly, and feels your baby kick, I have no doubt that she will come around."

Charlotte said in a shocked voice, "How can you even try to stick up for her after the terrible things she said to you? She made you cry! Gia can be verbally abusive, and she took it out on you!"

"Well, you told me she's a lead homicide detective, and that she had just come off from working a midnight shift. I cannot imagine the horrific things she sees on a daily basis. So, I'm cutting her some slack. Plus, I hope she does come around, for your sake. I know you love your wife, and she loves you… she may not show it sometimes, but she's a bit, umm… rough around the edges."

Charlotte finally burst out laughing and responded, "That's the understatement of the year!"

Madam smiled as she soothingly said, "Charlotte, I just want you to take care of yourself over these next few days. Please know it will work out. Sometimes, time is all we need. Enjoy being taken care of by your parents. Relax in the sun and let the waves sooth you. Drink your tea, and call me whenever you need to talk, okay?"

Madam saw the sapphire in her hand go dark. Charlotte's emotions were finally under control now. She had done her job as her friend and confidant.

"Thank you, Madam. I feel so much better." She paused and sighed. "But, I mean, how did you know to call me when I was so upset?"

Madam tightened her grip on the stone and sent love and serenity to Charlotte.

"Well, I guess I'm an empath with people I connect to. I just felt something was wrong. I think we truly connected as friends."

Charlotte smiled, and Madam knew the love and serenity had reached her stone.

"I'm holding the sapphire right now, and I just feel so much love and calmness after talking to you. Madam, you are a saint!"

Madam grimaced at that comparison, finding it revolting.

"Thank you, but I'm just your friend. Now, get some rest. We'll have to get you in to see how you're progressing. In about four weeks, so the beginning of September?"

Charlotte didn't speak for a moment.

"How can you be so sure I'm pregnant?"

Madam grinned and responded, "Because, I just know."

******

Madam hung up with Charlotte, and decided to check on Ezmerelda. She threw on her satin emerald green robe and her matching satin slippers. Yesterday had been the longest day of her life, well, at least in this decade.

As Madam walked to Ezmerelda's bedroom, she thought about the punishments the girl would receive from each sister she had harmed. They would break her. She would learn the ways of their coven.

She entered the bedroom and found Ezmerelda's body limp against the headboard. As she walked closer, Madam couldn't tell if her eyes were open, or if she even had any eyes left. The skin on her face was so swollen and eaten up, she could see some teeth through her cheek that the fire ants had burrowed through. Her nose had been eaten clear off, along with her ears and her bottom lip was hanging by a single piece of skin.

Ezmerelda's arms had been chewed, so it looked like little openings in her skin had been burrowed through by the fire ants. Madam smiled as she looked at how well the fire ants had attacked Ezmerelda's exposed skin, leaving either deep wounds to her bones or just a hole, after Elizabeth had ended her three hours of torturing the girl.

Madam looked Ezmerelda up and down. There was no sense of pity, as she now realized there were no eyeballs left, or that certain sections of her brain were visible from the torturous insects. No, she felt nothing for this child in front of her. She was the head witch, and Ezmerelda had brought an unwelcome and very powerful demon into their sanctuary. This was the price she had to pay, and the sisters would make sure Ezmerelda paid severely.

As Madam looked upon the chewed up girl, something she knew a lot about from her own past, she couldn't help but notice a light glow beneath the girls' shirt. It was a quick flashing glow of light blue. Madam's face turned into anger as she realized it was the last remaining Lapis stone she had not gotten rid of.

"Son of a bitch," she hissed.

Madam gasped and jumped at the same time as she felt a light hand touch her shoulder. She turned to see Elizabeth standing there sheepishly, with bags under her eyes.

"Elizabeth! Why did you startle me so?"

She spoke softly as she replied, "I called your name several times and even knocked on the door. I apologize."

Madam released her hand from her chest and patted Elizabeth's shoulder.

"It's fine, dear. I was just realizing that the Lapis stone on Ezmerelda's necklace is the binding type to that damn demon! It's even glowing right now. Damn!"

Elizabeth chimed in, "I did notice her eyes, before the fire ants chewed through them… the one seemed gold."

"Damn!" Madam hissed again. "That Egyptain demon is still here. We need to do the binding breakage ceremony."

"Madam, before I get the sisters ready… umm, I just…"

Madam glared at her. She had no patience for a sister without a strong backbone.

She sighed in exasperation and bit out, "What, Elizabeth?"

"Well… it's just… I feared all night that you would be furious with me for your daughter's punishment. I haven't slept at all. I hope I didn't go too far."

Madam's face looked quizzically at her.

"Too far? My dear, Elizabeth! You were tortured for three hours! Ezmerelda deserved the same fate. You did nothing wrong. I'm very impressed with your choice! We need to break her and build her back up into the ways of our coven. Ezmerelda invited this Egyptian demon into our sanctuary and allowed it to possess her body. Every sister here is going to punish her. I think the stronger the pain she endures, the faster we shall get her to be a part of us. Never doubt your powers and strength. These are practices we've had to implement for centuries! We are carrying on the traditions of our mothers, sisters, aunts, and grandmothers of the past. You did your duty, and I'm proud of you."

Elizabeth blushed brightly as she said, "Thank you, Madam."

Madam nodded and looked back at Ezmerelda with anger.

"Now, it's time to break the damn binding spell between the girl and that bitch. Get the sisters ready in our sanctuary."

"But Madam-"

"Do not worry. I shall cover her head and face with a black cloth, so even if she can see, she won't know where we're going. I'll then bind a black blanket around her, so she cannot move. She's a shifty little shit. We must be careful."

Elizabeth bowed her head in acknowledgement and raced out of the room to gather the sisters. She could hear Elizabeth in her mind calling to the sisters at the downtown office to join them in their sanctuary that was on the 67th floor. She heard Beth barking out orders, and smiled. Now, it was time to focus on this little brat in front of her.

With a swift flick of her hand, the entire bed disappeared with all of its ugly contents. She held Ezmerelda up in the air as she flicked her index finger and there was a new bed, with a black comforter and blood red accents.

The girl would no longer have this Egyptian-themed bedroom. As Ezmerelda hung limply in the air, Madam went throughout the room, getting rid of gold or anything related to Egyptian colors from the past. She threw her hand at the fireplace and made it black onyx. Rubies and garnets sparkled as accents. The large curtains were made blood red. Madam threw her hand, and the entire bathroom was made black with only blood red accents. She had thoroughly had enough of this tan, gold, and Lapis bullshit; the girl would become a part of their coven through whatever torture was necessary. And, in that secret spot of Madam's brain, she remembered that killing her daughter was still on the table if this ceremony to break the binding spell didn't work.

Madam did not want to touch the girl, since the demon could easily jump to her. With her daughter hanging in the air, she had a thick black cloth bag go over the girls' head. She then brought forth a thick, black blanket. She rolled the girl in it over and over and over, her wrist manipulating the rolls. Her hands were pinned at her sides as Madam made sure the girl was tightly sealed inside the massive black blanket. Madam saw the irony that Ezmerelda looked like a mummy, but she needed to make sure she didn't touch her until she severed the connection. Madam had no clue about the power the Egyptian demon wielded. She had to be careful.

As she made her way with Ezmerelda hovering limply above her to the sanctuary, the sisters paused to help each other with their robes. No one wanted to hold Ezmerelda up with their powers while Madam had to focus on her robes. Madam understood and dropped the girl as she tended to her robes.

She picked her back up with her hand, the girl hanging limply in the air, as they all made their way into their sacred room. The girl was laid down atop a metal table. With a flick of her finger, Madam cleared the black hood and blanket, tossing it in the fire just as Nora had lit it. She poured the healing remedy into several spray bottles and gave them to the sisters. No one wanted to heal the girl.

"Sisters, we cannot release her from the binding with the Egyptian demon unless she is awake. Get to it!"

Beth was in her head letting her know they were all in their sanctuary, and they could see what was happening from Franny's eyes.

Madam had just completed the remedy for dissolving the binding between Ezmerelda and the Egyptian demon, when she heard the screeching of Ezmerelda's voice.

"YOU BITCHES ARE ALL GOING TO PAY FOR THIS!"

Madam turned around and found Ezmerelda sitting up and glaring at the entire coven.

"There's my little shit! Awake and ready to go!" Madam's face began to contort into vile evil as she stood next to her daughter. "You've been a naughty girl, haven't you?"

Ezmerelda's eyes pierced into Madam's.

"Fuck you, pig."

Madam loved a good fight.

"Well, I see your Egyptian friend has taught you some colorful language!" Madam flicked her finger, and the girl was slapped by an unseen force, extremely hard in the face, shocking Ezmerelda. "Mommy's going to put a stop to that right now!"

Madam ripped the chain necklace with the Lapis from Ezmerelda's neck. Again, Madam didn't touch it; she kept it hanging suspended in the air.

"NNNNNNOOOOOOOOO," Ezmerelda screamed and howled with such ferociousness that some of the sisters covered their ears.

The girl went to reach for it, but Madam shoved her down, hard, on the metal slab with a simple movement of her index finger. Ropes immediately appeared as she made sure her daughter was tied to the metal table and couldn't move.

Madam came closer to Ezmerelda's eyes and hissed, "You are part of *this* coven! *My* coven. I am the leader, and you will abide by our rules of the sacred bond of sisters."

"I am not ever going to be part of *your* coven! You are all old, dried up hags! I'm better and stronger than all of you combined!"

Ezmerlda tried to spit in Madam's face, but she moved in time and the spit ended up back on Ezmerelda's cheek.

With bitterness, Madam stated, "That's a lovely look for you, daughter."

"I AM NOT YOUR DAUGHTER!"

"You've been possessed to believe that."

"No! It's true! My mother is an ancient Egyptian demonic goddess. My Father is your king! I have the strongest bloodline of any creation on this earth! And you shall all pay! Once my mother is fully released from her punishment from Father, there will be no stopping my power! AND YOU WILL ALL ANSWER TO ME!"

Madam kept a fake smile pasted onto her lips, but concern gnawed away at the back of her mind.

That's impossible! I coupled with Husband; I carried her for nine months, and I gave birth to this little creature. There is no way I am not her mother... Madam grew sick to her stomach. *No, I couldn't have been possessed by this Egyptian demon! No one can possess the leader of a coven! I am the leader.*

Madam felt the heavy worry, which she used to fuel her rage.

"ENOUGH! SISTERS! THE BREAKING OF THE BINDING SPELL BEGINS NOW!"

As Ezmerelda screamed and shouted, Madam held the cup up and sent the Lapis into it. Ezmerelda was crying and shouting, but the spell was being chanted by every sister as Madam performed the ritual.

With the strength searing through Madam, she threw the contents from the goblet, including that wretched Lapis stone, into the fireplace. The fire roared and almost reached the metal table. They were reaching the pinnacle of the breakage. Ezmerelda was crying and screaming out for her mother, which only pissed off Madam even more. She brought a new ferociousness to the spell and she could see the thick bindings on Ezmerelda's Chakras finally start to sever. Seeing it made the chanting louder and stronger. The energy of the sisters was on a new, powerful level.

A gust of fury overcame the room, as the sisters were shot backwards against the walls. The only one to remain standing was Madam.

Husband was here.

The growl came first, and then loud screeching that broke the glass mirror. The sisters covered their ears, but some of them already had blood oozing out of their ears and down their necks.

Madam was in her zone. She did not experience anything from Husband. She was furious that the ceremony had been interrupted. For the first time, she didn't bow her head or close her eyes. She looked him dead on his ugly, reptilian face. His red eyes glowing, his lips in a snarl, the horns on his head reminding her of the bulls she saw in Spain. She studied Husband and he seemed to have grown more spikes out of his back and shoulders. His snake-like skin was constantly shifting, as though there were actual snakes under his skin. His claws looked longer and his hands and hooves larger. The damn tail was disgusting; it reminded her of the rings around an opossum's tail. Husband was the most hideous creature she had ever seen, yet she loved the evil energy that permeated off of him like a thick fog she could get high from.

Those chaotic lizard-like eyes bore directly into hers, but Madam did not blink. He had ruined everything. His voice was low and menacing.

"What is the meaning of this?"

Madam's voice met his as she stared wickedly into the red depths of hell: his eyes.

"Husband," she said through gritted teeth, "Ezmerelda has been possessed by a demon of ancient Egyptian heritage. She harmed our coven. We were just finishing the ceremony to break the binding spell."

"This is unacceptable!"

Madam flashed a grin at a very depressed looking Ezmerelda. The little brat would get her comeuppance from her Father.

"HOW DARE YOU TRY TO SEPARATE MY DAUGHTER FROM HER RIGHTFUL MOTHER!!!"

Madam's eyes widened as Husband released the ropes that tied Ezmerelda down with a swipe of his claw. Ezmerelda quickly stumbled from the table to stand next to Husband, with a delighted grin on her face.

"I am her mother!"

Madam flew back against the wall and found herself on the floor with the rest of her sisters. She wasn't done. For once, she stood back up.

"You are just a witch," he snarled.

"I am your Wife!"

His response was immediate and menacing.

"One of hundreds."

Madam watched in horror as Husband took Ezmerelda's hand and gently embraced it into his own claw.

"Daughter, would you like to join your Father in his home? Perhaps I shall have you meet your mother, my one true queen, face-to face."

Madam was aghast as she mumbled, "What the hell is going on?"

Again, Husband bashed her up against the wall.

"Do not speak of my home in a derogatory manner!"

Madam stood up again, but this time a little slower as she watched Ezmerelda's delight in joining Husband.

"Husband, she cannot go. She needs training with our coven, and she needs to be here to keep up appearances. I have started the sacrifice that will occur on Easter."

Husband eyed Madam's face, searching for something.

"You have started the sacrifice… Easter." She could see he was impressed since it was an insult to the holiest season. He scratched his jaw, the reptilian skin moving askew. "First of all, my daughter will never belong to your coven. She is from royalty and once you have completed your final sacrifice, you shall join me, as promised. I am going to take Ezmerelda with me for training. None of you witches are on par with her level of powers. You'll just hold her back. However, I will send her back up when you host your parties to keep the pretense going."

Madam was reassured that after her final sacrifice was completed, she would be able to join John William, who had been waiting for her since 1556.

Husband wasn't done, as he snarled, "As for you witches, my daughter will be in charge. She shall decide if she even wants a coven or not, for she'll be strong enough on her own after her training."

The silence was deafening as Husband and Ezmerelda vanished with a torrential tornado of air into the flames.

The sisters all began speaking at once. Some said they would leave the coven, while others questioned how it was possible that Madam was not Ezmerelda's true mother.

Madam spoke aloud to talk over them. She felt their worry, frustration, anger, and fear.

"Sisters, if you choose to leave the coven, that is your choice. You are free to go at any time. I hope most of you will stay on with me as I ascend to my seat among Husbands' wives. You may let me know if you wish to leave the coven to start a new life, but I simply request that you think about it for a few days."

Madam breezed out of their sanctuary and hung up her robe. She raced upstairs to her bedroom and looked out the window. She saw Ezmerelda's favorite tree. It was a monstrous Weeping Willow, and it was where they had set up her swing. With both hands, Madam ripped the tree from the ground and crumpled it into a massive pile of ashes.

In the private part of her mind, Madam was sure Husband was going to ask if she had done anything different with the sacrifice, like create twins; luckily, knowing the sacrifice would occur on Easter had excited him enough. Madam also worried that she had indeed been possessed during her coupling with Husband, which horrified her to her inner core, but nothing terrified her more than the idea of Ezmerleda returning to earth and running her own coven, if she so chose. Luckily, she would not be here when that happened.

Chapter 7

"Marty, come on. Would you please just put Charlotte on the phone?"

Gia was trying hard not to slur her words. It had been two weeks since Gia had stormed out of the fertility office. She had been on a drinking bender since then. When she returned home from working midnights, it was the same routine: drink, smoke, drink some more, and pass out on the couch. She would wake up, hungover and force herself to shower, go to work, deal with death and paperwork, and then come home to start her routine all over again.

She was in a bad place and missed Charlotte, who refused to speak to her when she was drunk, which was every single day since she left Charlotte with Madam. Gia was lucky if Charlotte responded to a text message just asking how she was. They were mostly one word responses. She missed her wife.

"Gia, are you drunk already at ten in the morning?"

Concern and annoyance were prevalent in his voice.

Gia lit another cigarette and blew out the smoke with a sigh of sadness. She couldn't lie to Marty. He was like a father to her. When Gia came out as a lesbian at the age of 22, her parents and two brothers, all devout Catholics, disowned her. Gia's heart had shattered that day, and it had never fully fused back together. She had sadly been on her own for over twenty years because she preferred the company of women. Marty and Diane had accepted her into the loving embrace of their family.

"Marty, you know I won't lie to you."

"And I won't lie to you. Get your shit together Gia, or you're going to lose my daughter forever."

Gia heard a click, and she stared at the phone, willing Charlotte to call her. Gia was in a dark hole. She was spiraling into her best friend: whiskey. She knew she needed help. Gia needed to stop this reliance on alcohol, but it had become her balm; it soothed her loneliness and pain. It never judged her. It numbed her past traumas. It numbed her life that she didn't realize she hated because the hatred was directly pointed at herself. No one but an alcoholic could understand the torturous love affair with the bottle. The drink is a cruel and menacing companion that sucks out who you could be and replaces you into someone you hate.

While she was always angry at work, and she fought constantly with Dean Marziatti, her partner who was a stubborn, purebred Italian, she was still great at her job. At least that was the one thing she could count on… that and the bottle of whiskey in front of her.

Gia tried to clear her head. She went to the bathroom and decided she needed to get out and walk around in the fresh air. August would be over in another two weeks. She needed some sunshine; she lived like a vampire.

Glancing in the mirror, she grimaced. Her face was puffy from the booze. Her eyes were red and glassy. She was never attractive, but now she looked haggard. She wiped away the tears before she began weeping again, something she had become extraordinarily good at in the past two weeks. She feared that Charlotte hated her as much as Gia hated the person she stared at angrily and bitterly in the mirror.

She forced herself to get her somewhat drunk ass outside. She paused and wanted to hiss at the sun, but she needed to get out without having a place to rush off to. Gia needed to simply walk. She forced one foot in front of the other and slowly began to find a rhythm through her buzz. She looked at storefront windows around her neighborhood that she had never noticed before. There were a lot of dry cleaners and old mom and pop shops. It was an old, established neighborhood, and the crime rate around her apartment wasn't as bad as it was in other precincts.

As she looked at the stores, she jerked back and saw a small sign that said *Witches Brew*. She peered in and saw there were a few people inside. For some crazy reason, she entered the store.

The smell of incense hit her first, making it hard to breathe. The older woman at the cash register was helping another customer, but she made sure to wish her a good morning as Gia nodded and offered a tired smile.

Jesus, she thought, *I'm going to vomit or pass out from this fucking incense!*

The store was narrow, but it went further back than Gia expected. She saw so many candles and crystals that she was instantly brought back to Madam's office, wondering if this was where the woman bought her abundance of crap.

As Gia kept walking further back, she saw sage. An entire section was literally devoted to sage. They all had different names, but to Gia, they looked the same. She continued her pilgrimage through the store, and she saw there were even more crystals, but these were massive and locked in a glass case. They were beautiful, until Gia noticed the prices. One large blue crystal was $550! She shook her head and noticed the walls on the opposite side lined with books.

She strolled over, passing more incense and crystals and candles. The books ranged from spells to white magic, then grey magic, and then black magic. There were so many books on crazy topics she had never heard of, like seances, Wicca and building your own coven. On the bottom shelf were tarot cards and Ouija boards.

Gia shook her head at the ridiculous nonsense people actually bought! Then, she noticed the back metal staircase that led to an upstairs balcony. Part of the upper half could not be seen, as though someone had created a half wall. There was a black chain hanging at the bottom stairs that said: READINGS ONLY BEYOND THIS POINT.

Gia looked at the front cashier, noticing she was busy with the same customer who seemed to have every possible sage she had seen in the store. With a quick move, she climbed over the chain and quietly ascended the stairs. She was still buzzed, so she had to hold onto the railing to keep from tripping.

As soon as she was at the top, Gia gasped and almost fell backwards. There was an enormous woman sitting in a large chair staring at her. She had been covered by the half wall. Her hair was crazy wild, like she hadn't combed the fiery, red curls in weeks. The woman wore so much makeup, she looked like a clown from the 1960s, with blue eyeshadow and bright pink lipstick. Her pale blue eyes showed no emotion. They simply stared at Gia as she realized the fake eyelashes the woman wore reminded her of tarantula legs. Even Gia knew this woman was in desperate need of a makeover.

She spoke in a deep voice, saying, "Welcome, Gia. I've been expecting you."

What the fuck!

"Would you care to sit down? I know working midnights and then drinking whiskey to knock yourself out is exhausting." She paused and her eyes narrowed. "Yes, you should definitely sit down."

Again, what the fuck!

Gia didn't know what to do. She slowly stepped forward into the half room, noticing the white lights, usually seen only at Christmas, decorating the curtained walls all around the woman's space. The table in front of the woman was covered in a deep purple that looked like velvet, with little silver moons and stars sewn into them. Gia found herself sitting on the cushioned fold up chair across from the unusual woman.

Again, her husky voice reached Gia's ears quietly, as she calmly said, "Since you're getting used to a clairvoyant, I'll let you process this. Plus, you're a little drunk right now. My name is Miss Sophie. This is my business." She paused and moved slightly in her large chair. When she moved, her numerous necklaces jangled on her large chest, like a bunch of wind chimes during a hurricane. "I was told by my spirit guide that you'd be coming for a visit today. I understand your wife has distanced herself from you, and you're too much of a stubborn fool to go get her and apologize for being an idiot. Am I correct?"

Gia's mouth felt like cotton was growing at an astronomical pace inside of her mouth, as she nodded, wishing she had water. Sophie stood up, all of her necklaces clanging together on her oversized chest, and limped over to the mini fridge. She wore a long skirt with crazy swirls, and orthopedic-type shoes. Gia could see her swollen ankles and wondered if she suffered from diabetes. Sophie placed the water bottle in front of Gia and sat back down very slowly and sighed as she sat in her comfortable, large chair.

"We're not here to talk about my medical problems, Gia. We're here to talk about the darkness that is surrounding you. I fear that the alcohol is bringing you to such a low vibration that an evil entity could easily possess you."

Gia guzzled the water and eyed the woman over the water bottle. She had yet to say anything. Was she a mind reader?

"Gia, I have the ability to go into your thoughts because my spirit guide is talking to your spirit guide. He is concerned about you, and tells me there has been an unwelcome entity in your mind. Now, I don't know if that's the alcoholism and your depression, but my readings aren't free."

Gia had chugged the entire water bottle and set it down on the circular table. She touched the purple table cover and realized it was velvet. Charlotte would have been proud of her for knowing that.

She finally found her voice and asked, "How much?"

"Every minute is a dollar."

Gia went into her pocket and pulled out a ten dollar bill and handed it Sophie. Their fingers touched and Sophie flew backwards, toppling her massive frame over the chair and landing on the cheap, thin rug on the floor. Gia stood up, but she was terrified to touch her again.

"Oh no… no, no, no," she whispered, completely horrified.

As she watched the terror ascend over Sophie's face, she realized the woman was truly afraid. She eventually used the strength of her chair to help heave herself off from the floor.

"Miss Sophie? What is it?"

Her grainy voice was shaky as she replied nervously, "I can't read you right now. The darkness isn't just the alcohol; you have a possession occurring in your brain."

"What?"

Sophie was shaking her head and holding her cross, one of the many on her chest.

"You need help, and you need it now."

Gia tossed her hands out in front of her and said, "Okay, so help me. I'm possessed?"

For some insane reason, Gia was drawn to Sophie, and she firmly believed what the older woman was saying.

Sophie shook her head, the crazy, wild hair matching the look in her eyes.

"This is dark magic at play. You need to stop drinking at once. You're too easy to possess, but it's just two parts of your... wait, have you been saying things you normally wouldn't?"

Gia snorted loudly, "Uhh, yeah. That's why my wife left me."

Sophie's eyes widened as she whispered, "You need the evil eye."

Gia leaned forward and asked, "The evil eye?"

"It's to protect you, but there is more you need to do, and then don't come back here for two weeks. They cannot know I'm helping you. Miss Sophie likes being alive."

Gia watched as the now very nervous and upset woman went behind the wall and came out with a large necklace. It was a gorgeous blue, like a blue bird. Inside, it had an eye. Sophie placed it on the table and snatchd her hand away, fearing touching Gia again. Gia picked it up and looked at it. Blue and silver and black for the pupil. It was hefty, but the chain was strong.

Sophie sat back down, blowing out a breath at either the effort or trying to calm herself down or from the evil she had experienced from touching Gia.

"It's long enough to hang at your heart."

Gia went to put the necklace on, but Sophie gasped as she hissed, "No! Not yet! You MUST follow my rules to get rid of this darkness."

Gia nodded at the woman. It was truly odd that Gia felt such a kindred connection to someone she barely knew. Sophie looked up at her and smiled warmly.

"That connection between us you're feeling is not surprising. You, just like me, come from a very long line of white witches. That's why you were urged to enter my store. That's why you feel bonded to me."

Gia nodded her head, slightly doubtful, as she clung to the necklace in her hands, finally feeling sober and a bit of anxiety. She watched as Sophie took out a pad of yellow, legal paper and a black pen from the small drawers next to her.

As Sophie wrote, she spoke slowly, "Get sea salt and fill a bowl halfway. Then, place the evil eye in it, and then cover it completely, including the chain with sea salt. Make sure it stays in there for 24 hours. After, you must keep this in the sunlight and moonlight for a full day."

"I have a patio outside of my living room. Will that work?"

"Does it get sunlight and moonlight?"

Gia worriedly said, "Yes, but not all day!"

"That's fine. The energy is there from the sun and moon. After that, you wear this every single day. You do not ever remove it, even in the shower. This is going to break the parts of your brain with darkness in it."

Gia replied with a bit of fear and reluctance, "Okay."

Sophie wasn't done.

"Next up, you're going to stop drinking immediately. Anytime you want to drink, you hold the evil eye in your hand and say the "Our Father," as many times as you need to. You can also add in the "Hail Mary" too."

Gia's bland brown eyes widened as she asked in a stunned tone, "Wait, you want me to pray?"

Sophie stopped writing and looked at her like Gia was the stupidest person she had ever encountered.

"I want you praying morning, noon and night, and I want you to go to church every day. It doesn't have to be a mass, but the evil entities cannot hear or do anything while you're in a sacred place. Splash yourself with holy water, especially your forehead and the back of your head."

"Do you know how many people put their hands in those bowls?" she asked disgustedly.

Without an ounce of hesitation, Sophie replied sternly, "Do you want to be a sacrifice to the devil?"

That stopped Gia's smartass retort in its tracks.

"Now, you're also going to open every window and door, and use white sage to purify your home. As you do this, you need to say prayers and commands… like, only good, pure spirits are allowed in this home. Anything negative or evil, I demand you must leave. Sage yourself too saying the same commands." Sophie paused and looked down at her chest filled with necklaces. She saw the smallest of the massive crosses and took it off. She laid it on the table. "Put that on now. Never take it off either."

Gia looked at the tiny cross lying on the purple, velvet cover as though it was something she had never seen before. She carefully took it into her right hand.

"Do I have to do the purifying thing with sea salt?"

Sophie shook her head, her fiery red curls dancing.

"That has been dipped in holy water every single day. You should do that when you go to church. I might see you there sometime if you go to the one that's just four blocks from here."

Gia was overwhelmed. This was more than she had bargained for when walking into this small store she never knew existed in her neighborhood.

"I know you are overwhelmed. I'll see you in two weeks. By then, the demonic entity should be gone." Sophie tore off the paper from the legal pad and handed it shakily to Gia, careful not to touch her. "You have to promise me that you won't come back for two weeks. I am intervening on something evil at play that could harm the both of us. As a practicing white witch without a coven for protection, I am more at risk for helping you than you can imagine."

Gia saw sadness pool around Sophie… sadness and fear with a massive force of reluctance to get herself involved. Sophie was right: Gia had no idea what she had gotten this kind, gentle woman into. While she had never been a believer, Gia now found herself at odds with her old, closed-mindedness and this wave of new knowledge that was blooming in her freshly fertilized mind. Without rhyme or reason, she believed everything Sophie had told her.

Gia cleared her throat and asked, "How will I know when this thing is out of my brain?"

Sophie looked down wearily. Gia's visit seemed to have zapped her of her strength.

"It won't be pretty. It's going to hurt. You just hold the evil eye and my cross… and you pray to God because, Gia, your life truly does depend on it."

******

For the next two days, Gia followed Sophie's advice. She watched the evil eye on her patio table, like she was starving and waiting for the pizza to finish baking in the oven. When it was finally time, she put the evil eye on. She never wore jewelry, but now she wore the cross and the evil eye under her shirt.

She had researched Sophie at the station. She found her full name was Sophie Turner, and her residence was the shop. There were no restraining orders on her, and she had never been arrested. By all accounts, she seemed like a good woman, to a homicide detective.

As the days unfolded, Gia found herself more at peace with the evil eye fixed near her heart. She found joy and utter serenity simply sitting in the local church, and even filled up an empty water bottle with the available holy water at the church. She made sure to put this on her head daily.

Gia amazingly found herself not wanting to drink or smoke. She was feeling and looking better. People at work, especially her poor partner, Dean, were finally joking around with her again. She felt stronger than she had in years. She even texted Charlotte daily with updates about her sobriety and sitting in church every single day as her own form of AA. Charlotte would text back her encouragement, but Gia knew it would take time to win back her trust.

On the third day of wearing the evil eye, Gia had just finished her ritual of placing holy water on the back of her head and on her forehead. She said her prayers and went to sleep, grateful for another day of sobriety.

Then, she was dreaming. She didn't even remember closing her eyes as she had just rested her head on the pillow. She could only see dark shadows with pinks and blues attached to them moving around her, ready to pounce. She felt her head slicing open and could hear shrieking, not realizing that it was her shrill screaming.

Gia was conscious but also in a state of something she could only describe as a trance. She felt around for the evil eye, and she immediately said prayers from her Catholic childhood, even begging Archangel Michael to help her fight. This was it; this was exactly what Sophie had warned her about.

Gia held onto the evil eye and the cross with two hands. She continued her prayers and saw two separate pairs of red eyes glaring at her, swiping at her with claws. She felt the energy of females, evil females, all around her.

With a final push, she sat up and screamed, "GET OUT THEODORA, AND STAY OUT!"

With screeching in her head and coming from herself as well, due to the unfathomable pain, she felt the back of her head being ripped open and her forehead was dealt the same severe tearing sensation.

As Gia fainted from the astronomical severing of evil from her, over on the 67th floor, Theodora and Victoria were both whipped from their chairs and found themselves on the ground.

They looked at each other with horror on their faces, and in shaky unison said, "She knows."

******

Gia awoke to pain. Severe pain that made her want to vomit. While she felt like her head had been hammered with spikes, she realized, however, that she felt lighter.

Her first thought was, *Who the fuck is Theodora?*

As she went to sit up, she felt blood drip down her face and then more blood dripped down from her neck to her upper back. Gia wanted desperately to lie back down, but she had to see for herself what was left after kicking out a demonic entity. As a once non-believer, this event had made Gia truly understand that there was good and evil. Heaven and hell. It terrified her to have experienced this, but it also gave her hope.

She stood up slowly, almost fainting, but took a deep breath and slowly maneuvered her way to the bathroom. It was a mere fifteen steps, but each one caused waves of nausea; Gia had been shot in the leg before, and that was like a pinch from a child compared to this pain.

The lights in the bathroom were too bright. She couldn't quite make her eyes look into the mirror. She was the epitome of being blinded by pain.

It must have taken her five minutes to finally look up with pinched eyes. Now she saw it. There was a massive bruise on her forehead, the size of a softball. It had three claw marks through it, hence the bleeding. She tenderly touched the back of her head to feel the same thing. Gia smiled and realized that she had fought and won back her mind.

She instinctively knew to say the "Our Father" over and over again as she poured holy water on the back of her head and on the forehead. There was no stinging, only a coolness and soothing aloe feeling after a bad burn. She continued reciting the "Our Father" as she slowly walked back to bed and gingerly laid her head back down. For the first time since childhood, she slept soundly without any nightmares.

Chapter 8

As Gia slept soothingly, Charlotte tossed and turned. Madam had been in constant contact with her, but she missed Gia. She was shocked that Gia was going to church each day. Her text messages were caring and apologetic, always wanting to know how Charlotte was doing.

Well, Charlotte was missing her wife, and her parents were definitely suffocating her. She adored them, of course, but there was nothing like being in the home you created with your wife.

The daily routines of Charlotte making coffee for herself as she prepared a dinner for Gia. The way they could talk during a movie, and then have to go back a few scenes because they missed an important part. Gia was her best friend. They were the opposite of each other, but it was in the best possible way for them, but this was only true when Gia wasn't drunk. Charlotte could not allow herself to forget the alcohol binges, anger, and verbal abuse though. She hoped Gia was starting to realize how much she needed to change for their marriage to work.

Charlotte went downstairs, close to noon. She had been sleeping a lot because she was ridiculously depressed without her best friend. She had missed a period, but Charlotte didn't want to take a pregnancy test without Gia there. And right there on the kitchen counter, next to the prepared coffee, were three different types of pregnancy tests. She saw her parents peak in from the living room.

"I see them, you guys."

Marty and Diane rushed in with glowing smiles.

"Your mother couldn't wait anymore."

Diane hit Marty's shoulder.

"You're the one who picked out the digital test that cost more than my expensive eye makeup!"

"Well, Charlotte deserves the best!"

"Mom... Dad... I just really don't want to get your hopes up. It's only been two weeks-"

"Going on three," her mom chimed in.

Charlotte tried to smile.

"I don't want you guys to be disappointed."

"We won't!" they yelled together.

"Honey," her father was going to talk her into it, she already knew this. "We know it's still early, but that's why we bought you all of these tests. IF they're all positive, then we can celebrate!"

"Dad-"

"Please, Charlotte. We want grandkids so much."

Charlotte looked at her father. She was the mini-version of him, given that he was 6'7 to her 6'0. He was so handsome and kind, yet stubborn and definitely a little shit when he didn't get his way. She glanced down at her petite mother, with her perfectly highlighted blonde hair and hazel eyes. She smiled inwardly because these two should not have been married for almost forty years, but here they were, showing that opposites truly can work if there is love.

Charlotte looked at her parents pleading eyes, and of course, she relented to an ecstatic burst of joy from them. She was ushered back upstairs with the three pregnancy tests. Charlotte had them all prepared in her hand.

She was a pro at taking pregnancy tests by now. She luckily hadn't gone to the bathroom when she first woke up. She had plenty of urine and then some. She laid them on the toilet paper she had already set up on the sink, and cleaned herself up. Men would never understand the splash effect when peeing on pregnancy sticks.

She washed her hands and used a hand towel to wipe all the pee that had sprayed onto her legs and butt. Charlotte felt gross, so she hopped in the shower just to rinse off her body with soap and water. No need to wash her hair. She had no plans for the day. That's what dry shampoo was for.

As she dried off, Charlotte glanced down. It hadn't been ten minutes, but already she saw three pregnant words on each of the three different types of pregnancy tests.

"Well I'll be damned," she smiled. "I'm pregnant."

She heard yelling outside of her bathroom door and immediately wrapped the towel tighter around herself in case her parents burst in through the door!

"She's pregnant!!!"

"I heard, Diane!"

"She's pregnant!"

"Diane, I'm not deaf! Stop yelling and jumping. You're going to break your damn hip if you keep dancing around like a hipster!"

"Don't you cuss at me, Marty, you old shithead!"

She heard them kiss and then her dad say softly, "We're going to have a grandbaby."

Charlotte's eyes welled up with grateful and sad tears. She was grateful she was pregnant and her parents were here to share in the moment, but Charlotte's sadness for Gia missing this moment would haunt her for the rest of her life.

******

When Gia woke up, there was no more pain. She gingerly stood up, and was delighted to find she felt fine. She rushed to the bathroom mirror and couldn't believe it as she looked at her forehead.

Besides the dried blood, there was no sign of the bruise or cuts. She felt the back of her head, and there was nothing there! Gia held the cross and the evil eye, saying a prayer of gratitude.

Now that she was fine, she had to jump in the shower and run to Sophie's store to figure out what to do next.

******

"What do you mean she knows, Theodora?"

Theodora and Victoria, a small young girl from Poland with icy blonde hair and beady blue eyes, had their heads bowed in Madam's office as they sat together on the massive couch. Madam was standing and gripped the back of her tall chair, her knuckles turning whiter and whiter, until the bones were almost popping through her skin.

"Madam," Theodora choked out, "she has to know because of the evil eye and cross… the prayers and church."

Madam gritted out, "Didn't you see anything?"

"Madam, everything was blurry. Victoria was with her when she was window shopping, and then she said she couldn't see anything, so I jumped in. Even with my powers honed to their levels, I could only see shapes; the voices were muffled."

Madam glared as she seethed out, "And you didn't think to tell me about this problem earlier?"

Victoria sputtered, "It was just a few days, and then…"

"WHAT!"

Theodora chimed in to help the younger sister.

"We were kicked out," Theodora said, her head bowed in guilt.

Madam's eyes flew open in shock and then they turned into slits.

"You two have let me and the entire coven down! She must have some protection around her! Find it! Where is she getting this advice from? It must be from a white witch."

Victoria stuttered, "But... but… how?"

Madam reached her on half a breath and slapped the idiotic girl.

"RETRACE HER STEPS AND FIND THE STORE SHE WENT INTO!"

Victoria clutched her face and cried.

"Theodora! Get your ass up and go with her! Everything is going wrong! This sacrifice must not be stopped by that hideous turtle faced woman and a white witch!"

Theodora and Victoria scurried out of Madam's office. She was most terrifying when her sisters of her own coven let her down.

Once they found that meddling white witch, Madam would be the one to take care of her, while making sure she sent a message to that disgusting, little pinched faced woman!

******

Gia happily marched into *Witch's Brew* with a renewed sense of energy and hope. She entered and, this time, she enjoyed the scents of incense wafting around her. She saw Sophie at the cash register ringing up a customer, and Gia smiled and waved at her.

Sophie's face fell.

"Louise? Louise, would you come out of the stock room and help this kind customer?"

Louise, a woman in her 60s with grey hair and thick glasses, came out from the door behind the cash register, closing it and locking it behind her.

With the grace of a buffalo, Sophie grabbed Gia by the arm and practically dragged her up the stairs.

"Ouch, okay! Miss Sophie, what's wrong? The negative entity is gone!"

They both sat in the same chairs as the last time.

Sophie was fuming, yet there was absolute terror in her light blue eyes, as she angrily said, "I told you two weeks! I can still feel them milling about you, trying to figure out the meddling white witch that helped you. They're hunters. They're coming for me, and it won't be pretty. I need to leave town tonight."

Gia's face screwed into a quizzical look as she asked, "What are you saying? She's gone."

Sophie looked startled.

"Female energy? Great! She's part of the coven in New York."

Gia was completely frustrated by this lack of conversation as she almost yelled, "What coven?"

Sophie shushed her and leaned in.

"Legend has it that there is a woman who has been alive since the 1500s. She never ages and has a coven full of followers. She is the current "wife" of the devil and to appease him, she makes sacrifices to him to increase his powers."

Gia shook her head, not understanding Sophie at all, who was talking at warp speed.

"What kind of sacrifices?'

"Human," she hissed. "I'm going to be next on their list because there's something about you! Maybe it was someone you arrested. I don't know. Curses and hexes can be placed by any witch in the black coven."

"But you're a white witch. You're good. Good trumps evil, Miss Sophie!"

"Yes, but I don't have a coven to protect me!"

"I'm a detective. I'll take you into protective custody."

Sophie laughed bitterly.

"You don't understand, Gia. I have a target on my back, and the only place I can go and be safe with other white witches is Vatican City. The dark witches cannot enter such a holy space. They would be burned if they tried to enter the city."

"Wait," thoughts were forming like a hurricane building in Gia's head, "if this coven has been around since the 1500s, then there must be records I could find about sacrificial murders in New York."

Sophie sighed and smoothed her hands over the purple velvet cover on her small table.

"Gia, the devil can control anything, including keeping things out of the newspaper. I know there was one investigation in the 1960s… it was a sacrifice that went wrong. The head witch was called to trial, but she vanished. No one knows where she ended up for certain, but by the negative vibrations I feel in the city, she and her coven are here."

Gia shook her head in disbelief.

"So, you're really going to Vatican City?"

"Tonight. I'm going to book a flight as soon as you leave. But before you go, it was a good call to pray for the help of Archangel Michael in battle. I know it hurt like hell, literally, but you healed nicely. Always keep that bottle of holy water with you."

"I will," and she meant it. "Miss Sophie, before you go, can you at least point out the spell books, well, any kind of book that can help me keep me and my wife safe?"

Sophie nodded, knowing she was risking her life, but she desperately wanted to help Gia.

"Let's get to work."

******

Gia rushed to get to work on time, but she had to find new places for all of the books, protection crystals, especially the black tourmaline and black kyanite, Sophie had told her, and the sage, candles… her home now looked like Sophie's store. Gia had to put the black tourmaline and black kyanite through the same cleansing process as her evil eye necklace.

The one thing Sophie told her that really stood out was, "Legend has it that Archangel Michael's sword was made of black kyanite. That's going to be your stone. The fact that you called on him was no coincidence."

Gia looked at the time. She rushed out of the door and ran the two blocks to her precinct, yet another advantage of where she lived. She could walk to work, and she knew the people and criminals well. It's better to know what's going on around your own neighborhood than keep your head in the sand.

At eleven, Gia was still finishing reports from last night that she hadn't been able to complete. Dean was eating his breakfast: tuna with grape jelly and peanut butter. Gia rolled her eyes at the smell and clicked save on her last report. She wanted to research the arrest files for someone named Theodora when she was interrupted by her cell phone ringing.

It was Riley, their Harvard graduate forensics leader, and Gia's best friend since high school. Riley knew *everything*; literally, her IQ was tied to the current highest holder, Ainan Celeste Cawley, at a staggering 263. While Riley was pissed off that she didn't carry the title on her own, at least there was another female on the list next to her.

Riley never said so, but Gia knew it meant a lot to her to be the only African-American/Hispanic female who was tied at the top of the prestigious list. Riley could have been a model or an actress, only known for her beauty. She always called herself the color of caramel. Perhaps Riley didn't know how rare her beauty was, or she simply didn't care. Her deep green eyes were always turning glassy when she was bored with people, which happened often. That's why she never married. While Riley had the beauty and the brains, due to her high IQ, she simply could not find a man that was her equal. However, she was a tried and true friend for life, so when Riley took over the forensics department, as the first woman, Gia knew the turnover in cases would increase ten fold.

"What's up, Ri?"

"Hey, Carter. We have a pretty wicked homicide near your home."

Alarm bells went off, and she instinctively pleaded, "Please tell me it's not at Witch's Brew!"

"Shit, how'd you know?"

Gia jumped out of her chair and screamed for Dean, who was munching on his gross breakfast.

"I'm eating!" he yelled.

Gia ran over, snatched the disgusting sandwich from him and threw it across the room, where it landed on the Chief's window and slowly slid down it. Luckily for Gia, the Chief wasn't there.

Dean's Brooklyn accent came out as he yelled, "What the hell, Carter!"

"Move your ass, now!"

She bolted and Dean soon followed as he looked back wistfully at his sandwich, which had now plummeted to the floor. He began his usual tirade of cursing in Italian, but Gia took no notice. She needed to see if Miss Sophie was okay.

Within two minutes, Gia had the squad car in front of the building. She walked in, pulling her dull hair into a ponytail and was handed the blue booties and purple gloves to avoid contaminating the crime scene. She observed everything as though she were a machine. To her right, there was Louise who had been locked in the back door and was released after everything happened. She was shaking and had already been vomiting. The cheap blanket around her shoulders would do nothing to stop the shivering.

Scanning the first half of the room, there had been nothing toppled over. It looked like the same store Gia had left that same afternoon. She walked forward slowly, eyeing every piece of crystal and sage she had ever seen. Something seemed off with the crystal display.

"Dean, check that display case and make sure we get any fingerprints off of it. There are two crystals missing."

"On it."

She looked at the books with a fine tooth comb, and remembered exactly how it looked before she left.

"I want another dusting for prints over here! There's a couple of books missing."

Gia didn't have to say Dean's name; he simply nodded. They had worked together for five years. Yin and yang. They knew Gia was the head detective, but without her feisty Italian partner, Gia wouldn't have solved half of the cases she'd been through.

Riley shouted over the balcony where she paused from taking pictures of the crime scene to say, "I think those missing books are up here, Carter!"

"Still, get any print or spec of DNA, Dean!"

Again, the nod from Dean as he began taking the lead around the downstairs level.

Gia looked up and saw Riley had already gone back to work. Gia and Riley often talked about being in a precinct full of men, and Gia never admitted it, but she felt more comfortable not being the only female on a crime scene. There were certain male cops that were just assholes, but one in particular would always haunt Gia.

Gia came up the stairs and immediately wished she had never met Sophie Turner.

She even sighed and whispered, "Poor Sophie."

Riley heard her and nodded at the dead body.

"You knew her?"

"Yeah," Gia replied somberly.

"Then maybe you should remove yourself from this case."

Gia glared at her because she felt like it was her fault Sophie was murdered.

"No fucking way, Ri," Gia hissed as she glared at her best friend.

She shrugged her shoulders, and matter-of-factly stated, "Okay. Just don't start crying when I go into the gory details."

"Fuck you."

"Fuck you back."

Their predictable friendship and camaraderie was the only soothing thing Gia had at the moment, and she silently gave gratitude for having Riley there.

"So, what'd you find?" Gia asked, not really wanting to know.

Riley pointed first at the eyeballs that had been ripped out, leaving just the thick red veins that had held them in place.

"The eyeballs were ripped out when the vic was still alive." Gia crossed her arms in front of her chest, which Riley immediately noticed. "Hey, I told you, I'm not fucking holding back on this shit scene."

"Did I fucking ask you to?"

"Bitch, you look like a toddler about to cry."

"Fuck off. You look like a mix between a Chihuahua and a pit bull."

"Nice stereotype burns from my cultures."

"Eh, I've been working on it."

Riley lasered in her intense focus back to the dead woman seated in her chair.

"So the eyeballs were placed in front of two books. Spells to Reverse Black Magic and the other eyeball was set in front of a book named White Witches: A Guide for Developing Your Talents. They were set up right over there by the-"

"Vatican City poster," Gia softly muttered.

That had most definitely *not* been on the wall before. Nailed into the poster with a thick, ancient-looking metal spike was Sophie's heart, still dripping blood down the poster and onto the wall beneath it.

A wave of ferocious anger swept over Gia. Those were two of the books she had purchased today, and she already knew about Sophie's plan to leave for Vatican City that night.

Riley moved closer to Sophie's body and continued her analysis.

"Her throat was slit to the point of decapitation. It's only hanging on by the spinal cord. The unusual thing is, the amount of blood we usually see was not there... almost as if the blood had been drained into something."

Gia looked down at the purple velvet cover over the table. She could see circular rims in the velvet with spots of blood.

"What do you think? Glasses to catch the blood and then drink from them? There's a small blood ring the shape of the bottom of a wine glass or something larger," Gia said as she looked harder at the dark purple cover, trying to find droplets of blood.

Riley immediately snapped pictures from every angle, as she stated with no emotion, "A sacrificial kill."

"What?" Gia asked, unable to tear her eyes away from the force of nature known as Sophie who was now known only as the victim.

"Dude, my research on black magic is staring me in the face right now," Riley said thoughtfully as she took in the whole scene with her dark green eyes, seeing what others couldn't.

"You know about that stuff?"

Riley nodded.

"Hey, my brain is photographic, and I read everything. You know how bored I get." She paused and continued her microscopic scanning of the scene. "There should be an upside down cross somewhere…"

Gia touched her own and looked at the crosses on Sophie's bloody and ripped apart chest. She saw her largest cross had been turned upside down and taped to remain in that direction. It was hard to see with all the blood, but Gia saw it and so did Riley.

"Shit. I hate being right all the time," she said angrily as she got up close and snapped more pictures.

Garrett came running in from the back. He was Riley's overworked assistant, but he was like a puppy dog when it came to Riley.

"Detective Carter - oh shit!"

He paused and stepped back clicking his flashlight to stare intently at the back of Sophie's head.

"What?" Riley demanded as she shoved him out of the way and snatched his flashlight. "Fuck."

Now Gia was shoving Garret out of the way to see what Riley was so shocked by. The hair and scalp had been ripped and pulled down from the back of Sophie's head to the top of her neck, revealing her brain. Hammered inside were two black stones. The same black stones that Gia had at home in sea salt.

"The top one that's been hammered into the skull is black tourmaline and the other," Gia firmly said, trying to keep it together, "is black kyanite."

Riley snapped pictures, nodding her head.

"Yup. Archangel Michael had black kyanite in his sword."

"Riley, you've got to find some prints, anything!" Gia paused and looked at Sophie's wrists and then at her ankles. "Why aren't there marks on her arms or legs? They would have tied her up to keep her still. She would have fought back! You said she was still alive when they removed her eyes. Where's the bruising from ropes or handcuffs!"

"Gia, I think she was alive until they finally removed her heart or slit her throat." She paused and whispered, "As for no present lacerations on her wrists or ankles as signs of a struggle, well," Riley paused to ensure no one else was listening, "I think they did a binding spell, where they use their minds to keep her in place."

Gia was about to be sick.

"This is fucking ridiculous! Where was Louise?"

Riley looked concerned as she saw the impact this was having on her usually tough as steel best friend.

"Locked in the storage room downstairs. She said she heard chanting in a foreign language and… umm, Miss Turner screaming."

Gia moved away from Sophie, sending a prayer of apology to her.

Garrett walked up and stood next to Gia as he quietly said, "This was left for you. I found it in Miss Turner's bedroom next to her luggage. I'm so sorry, Detective."

Gia looked at the handwriting and wished she had never met Sophie; she'd still be alive if it hadn't been for her. She opened the envelope, which felt like it had things in it besides a letter.

There was, indeed. Another evil eye necklace that matched her own, and the two black stones for protection. The same two that were now nailed into the back of Miss Sophie's brain. She opened the letter and hoped she wouldn't cry.

Dear Gia,

I'm preparing for my journey, but you need to prepare for yours as well. These are for your wife. There is no doubt in my mind that she needs protection too, along with the twin boys that are now growing inside of her.

Take my advice: everything you would usually say or do in a situation with your wife… do the opposite. Happy Wife, Happy Life!

Keep the prayers, saging, and going to church a new daily norm for you. Avoid that alcohol; it's too easy for negative energies to possess you. Read the books, and place the protective stones with prayers of protection on your wife's ever-growing bump.

I don't know which one of you the coven of black witches is after, but you must protect each other. Also, the less your wife knows, the better.

With prayers of gratitude, love, and protection,

Miss Sophie

Gia reeled from the letter. Pregnant? Twins? Boys? Black witches after Charlotte or herself?

"GIA!"

Gia gasped in shock at Riley screaming at her.

"What the fuck, Riley?"

"I've said your name at least ten times, you fucking psycho! Where'd you go?"

Gia shook her head and put the envelope on the inside pocket of her black, leather jacket.

"Nowhere, you lunatic. What's up?"

Riley was standing in front of the heart that had been driven through with a stake.

"Do you see this metal stake in the heart?"

"Yeah, dumbass. It's kind of hard to miss."

Riley elbowed Gia, but she knew sarcasm was Gia's defense mechanism.

"You're such a little bitch. Anyway, this is crazy, but I *know* this is not from recent centuries."

"What do you mean?"

Gia prepared herself to really pay attention, because when Riley recited exciting things from books, she spoke extremely fast.

"Back in England, in the 1500s, this was a popular stake to use to stab people through the hands, like crucifying them, or through the heart if they were accused of being an adultress." Riley paused flipping through the stored files in her amazing brain. "This type of stake was most often used on women through the heart who were accused of untrustworthiness or being an alleged whore, usually by the husband who claimed she had cheated, so he could get a younger, more fertile wife."

"So what you're saying is..."

Riley whispered excitedly, "We have a coven who came from England, and now they're here!"

Gia intensely whispered right back, "To do what?"

Riley eyed the spike again with absolute assuredness in her response.

"To sacrifice humans for the devil."

Chapter 9

Madam was with Beth, Theodora, Elizabeth, Nora and Lily in Madam's home away from home on the 67th floor. They lounged in Madam's massive living room suite, relaxing and fitfull after the brutal sacrifice of Sophie Turner.

They all felt like they were high, and the smiles that passed between them were ones of pure ecstasy. To drink a white witch's blood had empowered them and soothed their nerves after realizing that she was the one who had been talking and helping Gia to unceremoniously kick Theodora out of her brain.

They laid around languid, as though they had dipped themselves in a bath of relaxation and evil. Their blood pulsed with the kill, the torture, and bubbled in their bellies.

Lily was the baby of the group, and she grinned like an idiot.

"Madam, I cannot thank you enough. I've never felt this satisfied. I feel like my body is on a cloud. My blood is like a river of evil. I have never felt this alive, yet relaxed."

Madam nodded slowly, enjoying the white witch's blood in her body.

"It is truly wonderful, isn't it? But the sacrifice was extra special because it was from the blood of a white witch. You are all to be applauded for your work. I know we couldn't get everything out of her, but we knew the stones and books she gave that pinch-faced, Gia. I think we definitely sent a message to her to back off. Without Sophie's help, Gia is no longer a threat to us. Plus, Charlotte is still with her parents, and our sacrifice is on track for Easter. I think it's safe to say that Gia won't be bothering us anytime soon."

******

Gia scoured everything she could. Riley was over at her place after the horrific crime scene. It was nice to have someone with a photographic memory. As Gia took notes on special protection spells from one book, Riley had already read four books, requesting another.

"Damn, Riley! Now you're just showing off!"

"Dude, you need me in this, okay? Not only was this a human sacrifice of a white witch, as you told me Sophie said she allegedly was, but I can tell it's a warning to you too after you kicked out the demon named Theodora." Riley was on hyperdrive with her speech. "The three scratch marks you talked about are definitely demonic. You and Charlotte are not safe." She paused and then smiled, "Plus, I love reading about this stuff."

"You are such a fucking dork! Who reads for fun?"

"Shut up, asshole. I do!"

Gia paused their bantering and picked up her cell phone. It was past noon, but she had to know.

"Who are you calling?"

Gia clicked the speaker on her phone and said, "I'm calling Charlotte. I think I might have an idea about this Theodora."

Riley's eyebrows picked up as she took another sip of her heavily dosed sugary coffee.

Gia was shocked when Charlotte picked up and asked quizzically, "Hello?"

"Hi Charlotte. I… umm, I hope I'm not bothering you."

"No. I was just going to take a nap." There was a pause from her. "Speaking of sleep, shouldn't you be in dreamland by now?"

That was Charlotte, always worried about her, even when she was angry and disappointed in Gia.

"I will, but I was thinking about you. I just miss you. I know I've been asking for your forgiveness every day, and I know it'll take some time for you to trust that I'm truly no longer drinking or smoking."

Riley cocked her head and nodded, finally registering her friend's improved behavior at work. She extended her long arms and lifted both thumbs up.

"I was just wondering if I could come with you and your parents to the next appointment with," she had to bite out the next word and remain positive, "Madam? I have a feeling you're pregnant, and I want to be there for you and the babies-"

"Babies?" Charlotte laughed and then happily said, "I am pregnant."

Riley threw up her fist and pumped it as she guzzled more coffee.

Gia smiled as she looked at the phone.

"Oh Charlotte! I'm so happy! This is the best news! I've been praying."

Charlotte's silence seemed to say everything she was feeling: doubt, joy, worry, frustration, and fear.

"It does sound like you're happy," Charlotte relented.

"I am! I'm ecstatic! I'm going to scream out the window right now that my wife is pregnant!"

Charlotte giggled.

"Let's wait until we get through the first trimester."

"You're going to be fine. This pregnancy will bring healthy and adorable babies!"

"You keep saying babies. How many do you think we'll have?"

Gia's heart fluttered when she said *we.*

"I have a feeling it'll be twins. I don't know why… maybe wishful thinking, so I can hold one and you can hold one at all times."

"Aww, that's a lovely thought. Yes, I definitely want you there. It's at 1 o'clock on September 2nd."

"That's amazing. Thank you for letting me come with you." Sophie's words in her letter came through in Gia's brain. "Would you mind if you and your parents met me for brunch beforehand? I would really like to apologize to them in person."

Charlotte's silence was filled with hope, as she said, "Yes. I… wow, Gia. I love this new you. Going to church, not drinking, making amends… I would love that, and I know my parents would really appreciate it too."

"Oh. I'm just starting to make amends. I want to apologize to Madam and that young girl… was her name Theodora?"

Gia knew it was Lily, but she pointed to the phone, and Riley perked up.

"Oh… I think it was Lily. Theodora is the neonatal nurse."

Riley and Gia both stared at each other, their eyes wide, as Riley whispered, "Fuck!"

"I forgot. There were so many people there. Well, I probably smashed into her on my way out too. I'd like to apologize to Theodora as well."

"Gia, I have to say, in less than a month, you've turned into the best version of you. I'm so proud of you for staying sober, and going to church daily. I hesitate to move back in with you though…"

Riley gave her a thumbs up, since this would give them the time they needed to research together how to stop Theodora and investigate the heart of this coven that was alive and beating in New York.

"Absolutely. I agree with you completely. I want to keep building a solid foundation for myself too. I don't want to let you or those babies down - ever."

She could hear the smile on Charlotte's lips.

"Twins. Wouldn't that be nice?"

Gia looked over at Riley who was signaling with her index finger in a circular motion to wrap it up. Gia nodded. They finally had a lead.

"Charlotte, I want you to go take your nap and dream about two babies cradled in your arms… I love you, and I miss you."

Riley rolled her eyes and pretended to vomit. Gia gave her the middle finger in response.

"I love you too."

Gia clicked off the phone, and for a moment, they just sat there in stunned silence. Immediately though, they were jumping to their feet, pacing past each other in the small living room.

Riley was almost screaming, "What the fuck! What is going on!"

"I know! How is this a thing! How in the hell do we have a dark witch after me?"

"Dude, this is some fucked up shit. I don't know. My brain is swirling."

"What do we do now?"

Riley paused midstep.

"We research, and we learn how to fight back."

"If Theodora is the head of the coven-"

"Seriously? You know the head of a coven is the devil's wife, right?" Riley put on her most disgusted look as she eyed Gia up and down. "I don't think the wife of the devil would waste her time in your brain. Offense meant."

Gia rolled her eyes and continued to pace.

"Well, how will we know who the leader is?"

"We can tail her. See where she goes."

"Yes! An old fashioned stakeout!"

Riley grinned as she rubbed her hands together.

"Hell no! This is an old fashioned witch hunt!"

******

Gia sat at the table that was a block away from Madam's office. She had a massive bouquet of flowers for Charlotte. She also felt inside of her leather jacket and felt the two stones zipped up safe, and the small vial of holy water. She had on her cross, which just this morning she'd dipped in holy water while she was at church. Gia had also put out her evil eye necklace yesterday in the sun, just because she felt it couldn't hurt.

Riley, a drill sergeant when it came to anything related to studying, had grilled her on the specific spells to say to ward off evil. Gia had been a Catholic growing up, and she now knew ten different spells and prayers from the white witch's book. Riley had been a force to be reckoned with as her teacher, well, more like an insane drill sergeant.

She was the one who pushed Gia to constantly memorize spells about white witches being able to defend and defeat the dark witches. Riley had pointed out that they were at a major loss though without their own strong coven, since it was just the two of them.

There was power in numbers, but there was also power in faith and God. While Gia had the thought breeze through her mind before, she really focused on the realities that were jumping up and down in front of her face, like an annoying mime in Central Park, while she was seated in church. If the devil existed, then God, too, existed. It made her feel utter joy inside to know she was on the good and righteous side of this fight.

Gia saw Charlotte and her parents enter the diner. Gia smiled at the beauty that was Charlotte. She had taken her for granted. That stopped now.

She immediately hopped up and hugged Charlotte. Gia then stood on her tippy toes, and kissed Charlotte on the side of the cheek and practically stuffed the flowers under her nose.

Charlotte laughed.

"Thank you, Gia! My favorite flowers all together."

Gia looked at Diane and Marty with shame drenched all over her face.

"Hi Mr. Avery and Mrs. Avery. I would like to sincerely apologize to the both of you for my behavior. There's absolutely no excuse for the awful, cruel things I said... I-"

She was cut off when Diane grabbed her face, almost knocking Gia backwards.

"You, little Gia, are forgiven!" She kissed her on the forehead and embraced her tightly. "And no more of that Mrs. Avery nonsense. I'm mom!"

Gia craned her neck and looked up at the male version of Charlotte.

"Mr. Avery, I umm, I-"

"Shut up, Gia. And stop that Mr. Avery bullshit. It's dad, damnit!"

He picked her up and hugged her tightly. Gia felt her back crack, and smiled in relief when she was able to breathe again once he put her down.

"Oh Marty, don't you start with that damn potty mouth in public!"

Marty and Diane sat in the chairs as Gia scooted into the booth next to Charlotte.

"Diane, I can say whatever the hell I want to."

"I swear, you piss me off on purpose just to get a rise out of me!"

As Gia smiled at the usual squabbling of Marty and Diane, she felt Charlotte squeeze her hand.

"I like your cross."

Gia reached down and held it, thinking of Sophie. She made sure to wear a v-neck sweater under her leather jacket to make certain Theodora saw it today.

"I like it too. It reminds me of who I was… and how I never want to go back there again."

Charlotte smiled and kissed Gia on the cheek.

"You won't. I can see it and feel it. You're a lighter person."

Gia smiled, a blush on her cheeks, as she whispered, "I'm sorry I took you for granted."

The waitress came up and waited for Marty and Diane to stop bickering about what was healthiest for him, as Diane explained to the bored waitress about Marty's high cholesterol and being on the cusp of diabetes.

Gia smiled and squeezed Charlotte's hand. It felt incredible to have her family back. She felt her nerves ablaze at the thought of seeing the evil witch who had possessed her. She had to protect herself, Charlotte, the babies, and crazy old Marty and know-it-all Diane.

Gia ordered toast, but her nerves were like haptic electricity. She felt like she could vomit at any moment, and she wished Riley were going into battle with her.

The vile of holy water awaited her hands. She knew it would burn the demonic, so anyone who was singed by her hands that had been drenched in holy water and then air dried, would prove to be part of the coven.

Madam perused her office, fluffing pillows and making sure the tea tray had the best China for Charlotte's parents. She had to impress them, since Gia was out of the picture now.

As Madam heard the elevator ding, she rushed out into the foyer with Beth, while Theodora and Lily remained behind the large front desk. As the doors opened, Madam felt a wave of nausea. The smell and feel of something pure was making her and the rest of the sisters feel feverish and nauseous.

Then, with severe and biting bitterness, she saw Gia amongst the group, and the closer she came, the more Madam and the others wanted to step back.

There was a forcefield of purity around that damned turtle faced, ugly woman. She told the sisters to remain calm inside her head. Poor Lily was not accustomed to this, and Madam saw her shakily sit down out of the corner of her eye.

Madam plastered a smile to her face as she embraced Charlotte.

"Hello, Charlotte! I'm so excited to see how your pregnancy is progressing!"

Charlotte was glowing with pure love and energy.

"I just want to make it through the first trimester. Then, I'll feel more at ease."

Madam nodded and smiled warmly at Charlotte's parents.

"Hello, I'm Madam, Charlotte's doctor."

Her mother, Diane, spoke quickly, "It's so nice to meet you! Thank you for helping our Charlotte. That last doctor was simply awful!"

Behind Diane was Marty, the father. It always amazed Madam when a daughter looked just like her father. The blue eyes, the cheekbones, the height… It's as though Diane had just been an incubator for Marty's daughter.

Madam internally shook at that thought, remembering how painfully clear Husband had told her that she was simply the same thing: an incubator for some demon's child.

Marty stuck out his hand, saying, "It's a pleasure to meet you. I was wondering if you have another name I could call you by? It's a bit unusual to call a much younger woman than me Madam."

Madam went to respond, but that horrid little woman stepped out from behind her father-in-law and replied, "Now dad, Madam earned that title after studying with a Grandmaster in Japan for five years. Women don't ordinarily receive such an honor, especially in a culture that is male dominated in the origins of healing. Calling Madam, Madam, is the highest honor you can bestow upon her."

Gia grinned and held out her hand.

"It's lovely to see you again, Madam. I do hope I can talk to you, Lily and Theodora about my previous behavior. I feel I really need to make amends to all three of you who have been nothing but kind to me," Gia grinned knowingly about how truly "kind" they were.

As Gia said this, Madam noticed the cross at her throat, and she wanted to strangle her with it. As she shook Gia's hand, she felt like her hand was in a fire. She immediately ripped it away, noticing the redness from where Gia's freakishly small hand had gripped hers.

Mother fucker! She hissed to her sisters in her mind. *This little bitch came prepared. She's got the cross, the protection stones, and I think holy water on her hands! Watch yourselves, sisters!*

Everyone was startled by how swiftly Madam had pulled her hand away from Gia's.

"I apologize. My hand acts up from playing too much golf," Madam swiftly lied.

Gia kept a straight face, but she was in awe of how much she was enjoying realizing Madam was part of the coven! She couldn't wait to tell Riley! Then, she noticed two women behind the desk, looking sickly.

The smaller one was Lily, who looked like she was smelling burning hair with shit mixed in with it. Next to Lily was a very tall African-American woman who was still standing and smiling, although the smile seemed forced.

Gia eyed her with malice, but sweetly asked, "Theodora, I presume?"

She nodded, finally looking down at Gia.

"Yes, Mrs. Carter."

They eyed each other and Gia held out her hand. Theodora looked between the hand, Gia's confident gaze and to Madam. Madam's lips tightened, as she gave a slight nod.

As Gia took Theodora's slender hand in hers, she saw her eyes widen in pain as Gia gripped her hard for trying to fuck with her mind. Gia's strength in her hand was pulsating as she said the spell about punishing the wicked.

Although no one else could see it, there was literally smoke coming from Theodora's hand, and she felt a horrible sickness coursing through her veins as though she was being attacked by an unknown virus.

Gia finally released her hand, and Theodora excused herself to the restroom, trying to walk straight, even though she was so dizzy, she could barely see straight.

Gia watched her walk away in her pink scrubs. She had never felt so wonderful before. It felt amazing to get back at this wicked coven who were coming for her or Charlotte or both of them.

Finally, she eyed sweet, little Lily who was bracing the arms of the chair so tightly, there was no blood left around her knuckles.

"Lily, I just want to apologize for the awful things I said to you. I feel terrible, and I hope you can someday find it in your heart to forgive me."

Lily stood up, and in a timid voice said, "All is forgiven."

Gia wanted to see if this little monster was part of the coven too, so she held out her hand, but Madam quickly said, "Ah, Lily is a bit of a germaphobe. She doesn't like shaking hands."

Gia was smiling broadly, as she looked at how Charlotte, Marty and Diane were nodding and whispering with proud smiles about Gia really turning over a new leaf. She swiftly went behind the counter, and gave the girl a sideways hug, making sure her hands touched Lily's exposed arms.

"I'm so glad you forgive me!"

Lily was being burned. Unlike Madam and Theodora, she was a youngster at this, and she didn't understand that the holy water only burned momentarily. She quickly shoved Gia off, lost her balance, and fell to the ground.

Everyone gasped, and rushed around to help her, but Gia was there first, picking Lily up by the bare part of her arms with her hands. She heard Lily whimper and pull away as fast as possible.

Madam's nose was twitching angrily. Her sisters were making Madam look like a fool in front of Charlotte's parents! This was not how this day was supposed to go.

She glared menacingly at Gia, who cocked her head and looked directly at Madam. Gia held the cross in her hand and she could see the turtle faced woman chanting something. The forcefield she had up around her only strengthened, making any black witch around her ill if they were inside of it.

So, Sophie taught you a thing or two, hmm? That's just fine. I like an intelligent fighter.

Madam looked around at the curious and perplexed faces of Charlotte and her parents.

"I sincerely apologize. This has been an utterly terrible day for us. We ate something last night, and I fear it caused us horrible food poisoning. Do not fear. We are not contagious," Madam said on a light laugh. This was her home court; she had the advantage of one white witch wannabe. "Shall we go into my office, so Charlotte can change and we can see how she's progressing?"

All of them rushed forward and Marty and Diane oohed and aahed at Madam's massive office, as Charlotte followed Madam into the open metal entranceway. Gia saw the tea set and then noticed how preoccupied everyone was. While Riley had just told her about the holy water on her hands, she never told her what would happen if a black witch unknowingly drank it.

With swift and steady hands, Gia lifted the top of the silver tea holder and dumped in the holy water, placing the top back efficiently. She quickly joined Marty and Diane as they were touching all of the stones on the gigantic fireplace.

"Mom, dad, could you imagine having a fireplace this large at your place in the Hamptons?"

"Hell no! I'd have to add on at least another 50 yards to fit this sucker into one of our rooms!"

"Oh, for fuck sake, Marty, you and your damn cursing!"

"I'm not cursing! Hell is not a cuss word! Gia, tell mom that's not a cuss word."

Gia smiled and threw her hands up.

"I know better than to pick sides because you'll both kick my ass if I don't agree with you."

Diane's eyes widened as she pointed at Gia.

"Do you see? Do you see what you do, Marty? Your potty mouth is rubbing off on little Gia!"

Gia laughed out loud. If they only knew how she really talked at the precinct. They used cuss words as nouns, verbs, pronouns, adjectives, adverbs… Gia always had to be careful about cussing in front of Diane, even though she was the worst when it came to swearing, especially when they played board games.

Gia realized how much she had missed them. They took her in without judgment.

"Hey, mom and dad," Gia interjected. They both looked at her like she was interrupting an important verbal tennis match. "You know how you guys want us to move closer to your place in the city? You know, get a place with 3 bedrooms and 2 bathrooms?"

Diane's eyes grew hopeful and excited, as she hurriedly responded, "Yes!"

Gia shrugged as she quietly said, "Well, I was thinking with the baby coming, Charlotte and I could get a place closer to you?"

Diane clapped her hands and grinned, and, as usual, she embraced Gia's face, smooshing her lips together like a little fish.

"I am so damn happy! What about the same building? There's a place just listed with 4 bedrooms and 4 bathrooms!"

Marty showed concern on his face.

"What about being so far from the precinct? Won't that bother you?"

Gia shook her head and genuinely smiled at her adopted family.

"Mom, dad, I love you guys both so much. I love Charlotte more than anyone. I have truly realized the importance of family. I get it now, and our kid or kids deserve to be close," she paused, "maybe not in the same building close, but maybe a few blocks down, from the two best people I know who created the most amazing wife I could have ever been blessed with."

Marty blew out a breath and looked up at the ceiling, willing himself not to tear up, as he whispered, "Son of a bitch." He picked up Gia in a tight bear hug and told her, "You have just made me the happiest father in the world!"

Gia felt her back being smushed into as Diane hugged her from behind. There was laughter from Charlotte as she had her arms crossed in the pink robe.

"Did I miss something, or did dad finally get Gia to agree to be his real life teddy bear for Halloween?"

Marty put Gia down as Diane rushed over to Charlotte.

"It's even better than that. Gia wants to get a place closer to us in the city… maybe even the same building!"

Charlotte's mouth dropped to the floor.

"What?"

Gia shrugged and stated, "We need more room, and our baby or babies need to have these pretty awesome grandparents around them as much as possible."

"Everyday!" Diane exclaimed.

Charlotte rushed to give Gia a hug and a kiss.

"You really have changed for the better."

"Yes. I know what's important now. Our family."

Charlotte bent down to embrace Gia, and soon, Marty and Diane joined in the hug. Gia had never felt happier, but she sensed evil and glanced over at Madam who was glaring at her, only to quickly catch herself and smile.

"Well, who wants to see how Charlotte and the baby are doing?"

Swiftly, everyone rushed into the room and stood at the head of Charlotte, since this was an internal exam. Gia stood to her left and held her hand.

Madam was completely professional, even though being so near Gia made her physically ill.

"There we are. This little spot… well, wait."

Everyone was anxious, except Gia. She knew there were twin boys growing in Charlotte.

"Folks, I do believe we have a split embryo here. You're going to have identical twins!"

The uproar of delight and tears was overwhelmingly beautiful. Gia watched as Madam looked at Charlotte and she saw that Madam had true joy and happiness on her face towards her wife.

Charlotte had said she reminded Madam of her younger sister who died in a fire. As Gia was about to ask, she instinctively felt Sophie telling her to do the exact opposite, so she kept her mouth shut and let everyone enjoy the moment.

******

As Charlotte cleaned up in the privacy of the other room, Madam sat down in her usual high-backed chair. Gia, noting her forced smile, sat down in the identical chair next to her.

Marty and Diane were enjoying the comfort of the plush, suede couch, and quickly patted in between them as Charlotte entered the room, smiling in disbelief.

As Charlotte said, "I can't believe you were right, Gia! Twins," Madam paused in her pouring of the tea.

"My goodness, do we have a psychic on our hands?"

Gia laughed and responded, "Nah. Or else I would have already won the lottery! No more work for me!"

Everyone laughed, but Madam simply smiled as she held out teacups served on matching tea saucers to everyone. Madam was sure not to touch Gia, but the damn turtle face still managed to burn her with her finger.

Madam smiled graciously at everyone as she held up her tea cup and said, "Here's to two of the most beautiful babies that I'll have the joy of delivering on Easter."

As Madam went to sip her tea, Gia prodded her more.

"Maybe, if they're both girls, we could name one of them *Sophie*?"

Gia was smiling at Charlotte, but she was watching Madam out of the corner of her eye as she gulped back her tea.

Charlotte made a face.

"Mmm, I don't know. It sounds a little too old-fashioned."

As Marty and Diane threw in names of their grandparents and favorite aunt or uncle, Gia saw something happening from the corner of her eye.

Madam shakily put the tea down and coughed. She kept coughing and spit up blood into her hands. She excused herself, but Gia went to follow her.

"Don't worry, you guys. I'll make sure she's okay," Gia said in a reassuring tone.

Gia closed the door behind her and saw Madam look like she was having a seizure while standing up. Beth and Lily were on either side of her, bringing her to the elevator to take her up to the 67th floor.

Gia watched in horrified revulsion as the shiny metal doors showed Madam's face turning into wrinkles, then it was shifting to a gnarled, cramped version of what used to be a long, beautiful face. Her twitching was getting worse, as was the curve in her back. The dress she wore was now hanging on the floor, barely able to stay on her morphed, decomposing body.

As the doors opened, Gia couldn't stop staring at the hideous creature that was once gorgeous.

When the doors closed, she caught sight of Madam's eyes, which were completely black. Her skin looked like it was being ripped apart. As the doors closed, Gia was certain she saw a snake popping her left eyeball out.

"What the fuck," she whispered.

She watched the doors close, but Gia couldn't look away. She instantly picked up her cross and said the "Our Father" over and over again in her mind.

Gia saw the women in their pink and blue scrubs staring at her. This was part of her nightmare. Blue and pink smothering her to death. It was beyond creepy. She knew this was the coven. Madam had to be the leader… and Gia had just won the first round.

She jumped as Charlotte gently touched her shoulder.

"Whoa, are you okay?"

Gia was still staring at the other women, but they immediately went back to work.

"Huh? Yeah. Yeah. Madam was, uhh, really sick. Like… revoltingly sick."

"Oh no. That food poisoning. We need to find out where they ordered from, so we stay away from that place."

Theodora, who had been standing and staring at Gia in a mix of anger and fear, finally found her voice after Charlotte whispered, "Why is she staring at you?"

Theodora cleared her throat and strongly said, "Sorry. Umm… Madam will be out for the rest of the day. She'd like to see you in a month from now, if that's okay? Perhaps the beginning of October?"

Charlotte called over to her parents to let them know they'd be leaving and if the beginning of October suited their schedules.

As they were checking their calendars on their phones, Gia was definitely shaken to her core. She immediately said a spell of protection, now that the coven knew she was onto them.

Shit, why did I put holy water in the tea? Riley is going to kick my ass… this was not part of the plan!

******

Madam was writhing in pain, feeling the death she had experienced over 500 years ago, when the mean, neighboring boys had picked her up and fed her to her family's pigs.

There was no way a white witch could cause this much damage. She was growling as she felt more teeth being ripped out of her mouth.

Beth stayed back, but told her the healing potion was on its way from Madam's house in upstate New York.

She screamed and howled, but it was barely audible. She knew that would be at least an hour away. A torturous hour of suffering that would never give her the release of death she so terribly wanted!

Madam knew this was Gia's fault. Maybe Madam was right when she first met Gia and sensed ancestors from a grey or white witch coven. But whatever she was, she would pay dearly for this. Sophie's suffering would look like a paradise vacation after Madam was through torturing and finally killing Gia.

Chapter 10

"YOU DID WHAT!"

Gia hurriedly raced to Riley's office door and shut it. Riley was looking at her in stunned shock. Gia noticed how swiftly Riley clutched her own evil eye and cross that Gia had bought for her.

"Ri, keep your voice down!"

Riley shook her head and sat on the stool in her lab. She had almost knocked her favorite microscope over when Gia told her about the incident with Madam drinking the holy water.

"Dude, what the fuck? This was not part of our plan."

Gia grabbed another lab stool and pulled it in front of Riley.

"I know, but something told me to do it, and even though I'm freaked out by what I saw, I'm glad I did it. I think Madam is the leader of the coven. She rules the roost. Everyone jumps for her. She *has* to be the so-called "wife" of the devil."

"Gia, this is… insane! Shit!" she yelled as she brought her hands to her face in exasperation.

Riley kept shaking her head. She picked up the evil eye and cross again to hold in her shaking hand.

"You don't have to do this with me," Gia said, trying to calm her best friend down. "I know I jumped in, but now we know who we're up against."

Riley stood up, completely flustered, almost knocking back her stool as she began to pace her lab.

"I'm not bailing on you. This is a bit premature. We were supposed to play the long game… and now…"

"Now I've shortened it."

Riley blew out a nervous breath.

"Yeah. And I don't know if we're prepared for the consequences of the head of a black witch coven coming for you... Charlotte... Us!" Riley stopped pacing and stared hard at Gia. "So she was really changing into some haggard old beast?"

Gia shivered, yet she smiled through her response, "Yeah. It was fucking scary but amazing at the same time."

Riley was still working on controlling her breathing.

"I still can't believe the holy water burned their hands. It was a hypothesis I wanted you to test out for me. It's pretty awesome that it worked."

"It looked like it singed them. They were all in pain and grimacing. It was amazing payback for what they did to Miss Sophie." Gia paused, recalling the way poor Sophie was brutally murdered, and her only role in this tragic series of events was helping Gia. "I want more revenge."

"Well, something tells me that this has only just started. We need to read about the black magic side to see what they can do. We need to play offense and really throw them off their game."

A knock sounded on the door. It was one of the night shift officers at the front desk. He came in after Gia signaled for him.

"Hey Carter. What's up Riley."

"Hey Fink, what's up? I'm guessing you're not here for me," Riley said in a snarky tone.

Fink had been one of Riley's sexual conquests, and now it was awkward between them.

"Sorry, Riley, I'm not." His tone didn't match his words. Fink had fallen hard for Riley who tossed him away after using him for sex. "Carter, there's a woman who wants to speak to you about the Sophie Turner case. I put her in interrogation room 2."

"Thanks, Fink." As he left, Gia looked at Riley. "Are you ready to *maybe* meet another witch?"

Riley grinned before responding, "Hell yeah. Let's meet this bitch and cast a spell on her crazy ass!"

It turned out, as they closed the door behind them that Gia and Riley were coming across a much younger version of Sophie Turner. It took Gia's breath away as the young woman had the same amount of necklaces and crosses on her large chest. She wasn't at the level of obesity Sophie had been, but she was definitely on the same path as her mother in the weight department.

The woman cocked her head to the right, her wild red hair moving haphazardly across her forehead. She brushed it out of the way and smiled with Sophie's same light blue eyes. She looked directly at Gia.

"So, you're Detective Gia Carter."

Gia finally made her feet move to sit down at the table across from the woman, and Riley followed.

"Yes, Ma'am. And you are…"

"Ziggy Turner. Sophie's daughter."

Gia couldn't stop staring at the young woman. She looked so much like Sophie that her heart ached.

"My mother wants me to tell you she enjoyed the holy water in the tea. She was the one who gave you the idea," Ziggy said with a soft smile.

Gia and Riley looked at each other, eyes wide in shock.

Gia sputtered, "How-"

"Detective, I am my mother's daughter. We share the same gift. She's here with us now. I never wanted this gift or curse, whatever you want to call it, but mom wouldn't leave me alone until I talked to you." Ziggy shrugged. "So, here I am."

Gia was speechless, and Riley sat back in her chair, almost tumbling backward, but she caught herself on the table.

Ziggy laughed, and Gia realized she had never heard Sophie laugh. Not once.

"I was told you'd be surprised, but I didn't think you'd almost fall out of your chair."

Riley blushed before replying oddly, "It's just… I never met Miss Sophie like Gia did. So, umm, I… uhh, never knew… I mean, the gift… it's, wow."

Ziggy smiled and leaned back.

"For someone who is matched with another woman who has the highest IQ in the world, you don't do too well speaking to a real life white witch."

Gia looked hard at Ziggy.

"You say she's here with us now?"

"Yup."

Gia leaned in and bore her eyes into Ziggy's.

"Does she know who killed her?"

Ziggy's response was nonchalant when she replied, "Oh, yes. The black coven of Madam."

Gia's head whipped to face Riley.

"See? I told you she was the highest one in the rank!"

Riley was spooked. Fully spooked.

Her response was a simple, "Uh-huh."

Gia turned her attention back to Ziggy.

"Sorry. This is all new to us."

Ziggy shook her head before saying, "No, it's not. In your lineages, you both have had white witches. Riley, your maternal aunts were part of a coven. Gia, your grandmother on your mother's side was a white witch, which is why your mother became a psychotic Christian… No offense."

"Yeah, that's true… well, about my mother, I mean. I never knew my grandmother."

"That's because your mother kept you away from her. She only died a few years ago, but she's in heaven with my mom, watching out for you."

Gia sat back and folded her arms, feeling unnerved. She felt tragedy inside when she thought about her mother, and now Sophie's daughter shows up saying her mom was there, in the room with them, and talking to her. Gia was out of her mind; she had no clue how to handle *any* of this.

In the truest and most confused tone, Gia said, "Ziggy, I don't know why you're here."

"Well, like I said, it was my mother's doing. She had nothing but high praise for you, and she wanted to thank you for getting some revenge on what that Madam bitch did to her. But there's a lot more at play here. Someone as evil as Madam and her entire coven are going to be hard to fight and win against. They sacrifice humans in the name of the devil to grow their strength and to please him. It's like a fucking cult. Remember Charles Manson?"

"Oh yeah," Riley said. "I researched him and other cults around this century."

"Well, my mother believes anyone who goes against Madam's last official sacrifice for her husband will receive the same fate as my mother… And, no, Detective, she doesn't blame you. She's glad she was able to help start the chain of events to stop these devil worshippers. She went into this business to help others, knowing there was something really big she would do one day. This was it. Helping you get sober and getting your life back." Ziggy paused and swiped away the tears. "Sorry. She's still in my head, but I wish she was here, in person."

Gia winced and mumbled, "I'm so sorry, Ziggy. Miss Sophie was wonderful to me."

Ziggy batted her hand in front of her.

"Nah, it's okay. Anyway, you've been on their radar because you were an annoyance. That's why… who was it, Mom?" Ziggy paused and nodded before she continued, "Theodora was in your mind. She was going to keep having you fuck up your relatinship with Charlotte, so you couldn't protect her or the babies."

Gia's eyes widened in terror.

"I'm not the target? Charlotte is? The twins are?"

Ziggy leaned forward and abruptly said, "You are the target *now*, but not for Madam's last sacrifice before she finally goes to hell as one of the devil's hundreds of wives… No, there's some sacrifices to the devil of first born sons. They symbolize the jewels in her crown. All jewels need to be in the crown in order for Madam to finally achieve her goal." Ziggy stared hard at Gia. "And guess who's getting in the way of that?"

Gia gulped as Riley whispered, "Shit."

Ziggy continued, "Now, besides you being in the danger zone, Charlotte is the one you need to protect. If you happen to see a piece of jewelry given to her by Madam, that's the sign… that tells you she's looking to sacrifice the baby or babies, since they're both boys. I'm not sure about that one… it's a bit hazy."

Gia smashed her hand onto the table, making Riley and Ziggy jump.

"Can't I just find the damn stone and crush it?"

Ziggy's eyes widened in horror as she cried out, "No! Then you will most definitely lose your family. No, no, no! The only thing you can do is say protection spells over your wife and do the same on the twins, including placing the two stones on her stomach that my mother made you buy."

Gia was livid as she cried out, "I need to tell Charlotte that her doctor is a fucking sacrifical demon that's going to kill one or both of our sons!"

"You do that," Ziggy replied calmly, "and you're going to be in a mental institution. I'm literally being told this by my mother. What you need is evidence."

Gia threw up her hands in helplessness as Riley leaned forward.

Riley began talking fast as she started, "There was one mistake… one mistake that occurred in the 1960's in Los Angeles. It wasn't the murder done by Manson cult. This was another actress… Betty Chapel. Her husband went on record, saying his wife's doctor had sedated him and Betty, but he was still awake, just paralyzed. Apparently, he watched as the doctor slit their son's throat open and drained the blood into an old-fashioned looking cup, like from King Arthur's time… his words, not mine. Betty awoke, saw this, and got up to grab her baby. According to the husband, the doctor looked like the devil as it did some weird hand gesture and Betty bled out her entire uterus, dying from the blood loss, as the doctor or witch drank their son's blood."

Gia glared at Riley.

"Are you fucking kidding me? You're just telling me this now? This witch bitch wants to slit my son's throat?"

Riley held up her hands and innocently replied, "Hey, I just thought it was the ramblings of a crazy man. I didn't know this shit was true!"

Gia crossed her arms and asked anxiously,"So what happened?"

"Like I said, poor Betty bleeds out in front of him. She's dead. The baby is given some cream to put on the neck, covering up the slicing. The husband, Richard, he sees it all, but can't do anything, right? The devil arrives, grabbing the ruby necklace from the carcass of his dead wife. The last thing the husband remembers is his wife's doctor taking her own ruby out. He said it was glowing so brightly with so much evil that he passed out from the energy it radiated… or so he says."

Gia and Ziggy stared at Riley open-mouthed.

Riley nodded, and added, "So I do my research because, of course, Richard Chapel wants to take the doctor to court. Any pictures I found of the doctor, who went by Mademoiselle Murphy, were all blurred… like, even my digital enhancement couldn't change the swirled blurriness."

"Damnit," Gia whispered.

Ziggy wasn't so deterred.

"You need to go to the psychiatric hospital and do a sketch. See if it matches Madam."

Gia shook her head.

"This isn't going to be enough proof for Charlotte, trust me."

Ziggy's response was blunt: "You're not going to prove anything to Charlotte! You're going into battle, and you need to know everything about her. Research her past. See about witches being burned at the stake in the 1500s. Mom is telling me there's someone even more evil than this Madam bitch. And… while she's more dangerous and powerful, she hates Madam more than you. She doesn't want to see her ascend to her throne in hell."

"Who?" Riley and Gia asked excitedly.

Ziggy paused and closed her eyes. She was literally having a conversation with Sophie in her head.

"Really? Okay." Ziggy opened her eyes. "It's her daughter but not her daughter." Two pairs of eyes squinted at Ziggy. "All I know is my mother said when you're invited to a party at Madam's, you must go, and there you'll meet... a 6-year-old girl who just might be the one to stop Madam."

Gia scratched her head, and Riley scrunched up her face.

It took awhile for Gia to hesitantly reply, "I'm sorry, but a 6-year-old girl is going to possibly help us take down the devil's wife?"

Ziggy shrugged her shoulders as she took a card out of her wallet and placed it before Gia.

"This is where I'll be. I changed the name of mom's store to Sophie's Coven. She always wanted one." Ziggy stood up and before leaving, added, "The devil has hundreds of wives, but he only has one daughter... I'd think one daughter trumps one wife out of hundreds, don't you?"

Ziggy walked out, just as Riley leaned back and finally fell to the ground and Gia began to lightly smash her head onto the metal table to stop the overwhelming thoughts swirling around in her overworked mind.

******

"The elixir is almost here, Madam. I'm going to wait for it downstairs," Beth said nervously as she scurried out of the room.

Madam was writhing in an endless stream of pain. It felt like she was being ripped apart by those damn pigs again, but this time, she wouldn't die! She felt the creepy, slithering bugs and ripping from the rats and the creepy snakes entering in and out of her eye sockets. She felt *everything*! Madam couldn't think straight. She couldn't see, and could barely hear with worms making their way through her ears, but she still sensed a powerful evil had joined her.

Ezmerelda stood by the fireplace and walked around the entire bed. Her grin was hideous in the same way a crocodile appears to grin before it gobbles up its live meal.

"Well, well, well, *Madam*. So this is your true beauty!" She paused and poked a long fingernail into Madam's open flesh on her arm. Madam writhed in pain even more, but due to her voice box having been eaten by the hungry insects swarming around in her throat, with maggots tumbling over each other to get to the fleshiest parts of her, she couldn't talk or see, since the wretched snakes were enjoying slithering in and out of her eye sockets.

"I like you like this," Ezmerelda said as she put another finger into Madam's open wound on her leg, and dug it in deep. She laughed maniacally as Madam could only try to wither away from the pain. "How does it feel not to speak? Hmm? It must be torture to have these open wounds with rats eating your brain and maggots feeding on your flesh... almost as awful as red ants eating into your fleshy body, hmm?"

Ezmerelda went by Madam's ear and pulled out one of the wriggling worms. She put it into her mouth and ate it.

She went to Madam's ear and said, "Mmm... worms from the 1550s definitely have a saltier taste to them." Ezmerelda moved in closer to Madam's ear. "To think this was how you died, slowly and painfully until your lovely Sir John William Mayhew took pity on you and saved you, bringing you into his world of dark magic." Ezmerelda paused and said, "I have been learning a lot from him. I think he might be the man for me when I take over."

Madam tried to screw her body away from Ezmerelda, only causing the girl to let out a loud cackle.

"Oh yes. He's quite fond of me because, you see, Maura, I am beautiful naturally. You, on the other hand, have always been a filthy, ugly pig."

Ezmerelda cackled some more before she made loud pig noises in Madam's ear.

The door whipped open as Beth rushed in and said, "Madam, I have- oh!" She stopped dead in her tracks, almost tripping herself. "Ezmerelda. Hello. You startled me."

Ezmerelda smiled and hopped on the foot of the bed, bouncing purposefully to cause more misery for Madam.

Beth hurriedly put the elixir into the open wound on Madam's throat, hoping it would seep down to her brutally busted body to begin the healing process.

"When I take over this weak coven, you shall call me by the name my mother, Isfet, has given me. It is Apopis. Egyptian for evil, of course. Until then, I shall allow you to call me Ezmerelda."

"Yes. Thank you, Ezmerelda," Beth said in a shaky voice, alerting the other witches to be on guard in her mind.

Ezmerelda eyed the terrified woman as wounds started to heal on Madam.

"Who did this to her?" Ezmerelda asked with joyous curiosity.

Beth just watched Madam, as an eye socket was finally filled with a light green eyeball. The elixir was working.

"Beth, I asked you a question," Ezmerelda stated viciously.

Beth looked at Ezmerelda and shrugged her shoulders.

With a cock of her head to the side, Ezmerelda had Beth smashing into the rigid rocks on the fireplace. Then, she threw her across the room, breaking the annoying witch's nose on the wall, and then flung her back over to the fireplace, holding her there. Beth's eyes were watering, but her arms were pinned, so she couldn't even stop the faucet of blood pouring out of her nose and onto her lips and chin.

"I ASKED WHO DID THIS TO HER!"

Beth stammered, "The wife of the next sacrifice."

Blood from her nose made her teeth look pink as she tried to sputter the blood out of her mouth. Beth tried to breathe through her mouth without choking and gagging on her own blood.

Beth watched with a sense of hope as Madam was finally looking like herself, but that soon turned to horror as Ezmerelda's one eye turned pure gold. Her eyes were glowing with evil mischief.

"So… a white witch did this much damage to one of Father's wives?" She nodded and grinned. "I'm impressed."

Madam glared at the girl, who had increased her powers and evil energy to significant proportions in the short time since she had been gone. Madam could barely move her neck to look at Beth, hanging on the fireplace like one would hang the head of a buck deer.

Ezmerelda thought about the white witch, and how much damage she could get her to do to Madam who thought she could control and break her. That was a huge mistake, as Ezmerelda thought about using this white witch to her advantage.

She smiled directly at Madam, who was simply lying limp on the bed. Physically, she had recovered, but this hit on her had sickened her evil heart and zapped her strength as though she were a newborn fawn, trying to find the willpower to stand up and walk.

"What's the white witch's name?"

There was no response, so Ezmerelda cocked her head again, throwing Madam's limp body up and smashing it into the ceiling.

"No!" Beth cried. "Please. Please, let Madam rest. I'll tell you, if you'll just please put her down. I beg of you!"

Ezmerelda glared at Beth as she dropped Madam onto the bed. Madam's forehead had a bruise forming so swiftly, it looked like a unicorn horn was forming from her forehead.

"Her name is Gia Carter."

"Gia Carter," Ezmerelda repeated. "And what does this Gia Carter do for a living?"

Madam couldn't even communicate through her brain to tell Beth to lie. She was powerless.

Beth quickly stuttered out through the blood that rained down on her lips, "She's a homicide detective."

"Really? How interesting."

Ezmerelda cocked her head again, this time, flinging Beth out of the room, and slamming the door behind her.

Madam whispered, "What are you doing here?"

"Didn't you miss me, *pig*?"

Madam coughed, wishing for any form of beverage. She could still feel the maggots in her throat.

"As you can see, I have more than enough to keep me occupied to miss you." Madam paused, trying to find her breath. "Why are you here?"

Ezmerelda hopped off the bed and walked around the room.

"Father wanted me to ask you when you're hosting your next stupid party, so I can be here and learn how to be the hostess with the mostess," she said sarcastically.

Madam tried to move, but she was too sore, and the energy was nonexistent.

"Between Christmas and New Year's."

Ezmerelda stared at Madam from the reflection in the mirror.

"And you'll invite the white witch?"

Madam nodded.

"Good." She turned away from fixing her hair. "Now, there's just one more question. What did you do differently this time with your last sacrifice?"

Madam simply stared at the girl.

"Oh come on! I know you did something. You're hiding it, and those damn minions aren't going to talk because of your ridiculous coven code!" She paused as the gold eye sparkled brightly. "Isfet and I *will* figure it out, pig."

Madam sighed, and whispered, "Nothing to figure out."

Ezmerelda walked over and slapped her, hard, across the cheek.

"Never lie to me, pig. Ever!"

Madam felt the sting surge through her entire body. She was too limp to even raise her hand to her pulsating cheek. The girl was stronger than she looked.

"Oh, and I do have a lovely little surprise for you. It's waiting at the house. I think you'll enjoy the irony."

Ezmerelda cackled and disappeared into the flames, leaving behind a massive gust of wind, causing Madam to shiver.

As soon as she was gone, Beth, Theodora and Lily flew into the room.

"Get my things and alert the others at the house. Ezmerelda has been there."

"Madam," Lily cried out, "you must stay in bed and rest."

"There's a bed at the house for me. Let's go."

******

It took the two strongest witches to help Madam be half carried into the house. She had slept on the ride over and was at only five percent of her strength. She needed her coven to surround her to keep her protected.

Nora came rushing down the stairs at an alarmingly fast pace.

"Madam, we checked the basement. Nothing seems out of place."

"You are certain?"

"Yes, Madam. We checked everything at least twenty times. The potions, your books, the crown… everything is there."

"The third floor? You all checked your rooms? She can get in through anywhere, but she, like her father, loves to make an entrance through the fireplace."

Again, Nora bobbed her head insisting that, "Nothing was amiss in our rooms."

"What about her bedroom?"

"We found nothing."

Madam sighed and resigned herself to sleep.

"My bed chambers, sisters."

They all took turns helping lift Madam up. She felt something was amiss. As they entered Madam's wing, she felt like she was missing an integral part of herself. She had thought it was from the brutality of living through the horrendous pre-death she experienced, but this was plaguing her deeply.

"Do any of you feel like a piece of you is missing?"

The sisters had been so focused on Ezmerelda's return and Madam's poisoning that they didn't even think to check themselves.

There were some murmurs as the lights were turned on in Madam's bedroom, and then they saw it… no, not *it*: her.

Elizabeth lay on Madam's bed with fire ants chomping away happily through her dead corpse. They were moving in such a flurry that there was smoke coming from her body.

"No," Nora gasped.

The entire bed was flooded with blood, pieces of skin that had been tossed aside to get to the meaty flesh. Elizabeth was dead.

There was something painted on the ceiling directly above what had once been Elizabeth's beautiful face, but now, it was being mutilated and shredded apart right in front of them.

Franny floated up and said, "It's a message in blood."

"What does it say?" Madam asked, trying to hold back her feelings of loss, as though the fire ants had personally ripped out a piece of her as they burrowed further and continued their feast on poor Elizabeth.

"It says: Don't fuck with the devil's daughter, pig."

Irony, indeed, Madam thought before she collapsed.

Chapter 11

Madam slowly opened her eyes. She didn't recognize this room. She tried to roll onto her side, but she could only groan from soreness. Thoughts were swirling around in her head as she remembered Elizabeth's corpse being eaten by fire ants on her bed... the warning from Ezmerelda.

Now she knew she was in a guest bedroom in her wing of the second floor. She remembered writhing in pain, and how she wished she could have died. Ezmerelda's words came pouring into her already burdened mind. She had met the love of her life, John William, in her father's home. He was assisting in her training.

What if she did, just to spite Madam, choose him as her mate to accompany her on this transition to ruling sacrifices for her father on earth? Madam felt the uncontrollable tears flow from her exhausted eyes.

Beth sat up in the chair next to Madam's bed and eyed her with concern.

"Madam, are you alright? Should I get more elixir?"

Madam sighed, wishing she could cry her fearful and bitter tears alone.

She could barely say, "No. I'm fine," without her voice shaking uncontrollably.

Beth stood up and brought water to Madam's crusty, dried lips.

"I have broth if you would like some?"

"No. Well, yes," her mind was foggy, "we need to prepare Elizabeth for her proper resting place. We have to complete the ceremony."

"Madam, we have three days to complete the ceremony, and you are nowhere near to being remotely strong enough to stand with us as we release her from our coven and this world." Beth paused and swiped a tear away. "She deserves better than that."

Madam looked at Beth, her most loyal and trusted sister.

She sighed and replied tiredly, "Yes, you're right."

"Is there anything I can do for you?"

Madam could barely smile. It was too exhausting to flex her facial muscles.

"Make sure that when I do go to my final resting place that my love is there to greet me."

Beth nodded, fully understanding who Madam's tears were for. Beth had been there on that fateful day. She knew John William was Madam's true love; the idea that Ezmerelda would take him away from Madam when she finally ascended to her throne and make him her spouse on earth, was the most wicked thing Ezmerelda could do.

"Do you have enough energy to go into your head where it's just the sisters who can hear us?"

Madam wearily perused her body.

"I'm at about twenty percent. I won't last long."

Beth sat down and went into the space of her mind that she shared with her sisters and Madam.

"Madam, can you hear me?"

"It's like I'm hearing you through water, but I can catch what you're saying."

"We must talk about Ezmerelda."

"She's going to take him away from me."

"I don't doubt it, Madam."

"She's more powerful than me. I can't fight her. I can't win."

"Ezmerelda is not more powerful than you, but I do believe she is at your level of strength… which is petrifying, for she will only grow stronger and more evil. This truly terrifies me and the rest of the sisters. How can we get rid of her?"

"I don't think we can. Our whole coven would be severely punished. You must understand, this is Husband's only daughter, and apparently, the Egyptian demon goddess was the closest thing to an equal he had, which is probably why she possessed me when we coupled."

Beth determinedly stated in her mind, "Madam, you are strong. You must find a way to get rid of her. We are a strong coven; we will help you."

"I understand. When I'm better and after Elizabeth's ceremony, I will begin looking into my old spell books."

Madam passed out, and Beth told her sisters, "She has faded to sleep." Beth heard the other sisters murmuring their fears about Ezmerelda and their anger about Elizabeth. "Sisters, please calm yourselves. Madam will figure out a way to take Ezmerelda down. She knows our futures depend on it."

******

Riley yawned as Gia drove the Sedan rental car. They had taken the earliest flight to Los Angeles after finding out where Richard Chapel was staying. He was in a psychiatric facility, Forestview Rest Home, on the outskirts of L.A. Riley looked over at Gia as she sipped her coffee. She had grown accustomed to hearing her conversations with Charlotte.

"Charlotte, I'm happy to look at places by your parents' apartment, but does it have to be in their building?"

"Gia, I know this is a huge step, but there's a place just listed, and yes, it's in their building. But, before you grimace, it has 4 bedrooms and 4 bathrooms, although I think it's more like 3 and a half bathrooms! You can finally have a home office, and the twins will eventually be able to have their own rooms."

Charlotte's excitement bubbled out of the car speakers. Riley eyed Gia and saw her hold her cross in her hand.

She breathed out slowly as she responded, "We'll take a look at it, okay? No promises."

Charlotte's thrilled squeal leapt through the speakers in the car, startling both women who were running on fumes.

"Okay! That's awesome! I'll tell mom and dad to get in touch with their realtor."

"Hey, what did the school say about you taking a sabbatical?"

"Oh," Charlotte paused, "well, they were disappointed, but of course they were delighted to hear about the twins. I didn't tell them that I might quit after the twins are born and be a stay-at-home mom once these little angels arrive!"

Gia sucked in a breath and looked at Riley. Charlotte had already said she would buy any apartment outright. She had a trust fund, and her stock portfolio was booming, according to Charlotte and her dad.

Riley hissed, "Turn right up here!"

"Okay, Charlotte. Listen, I have to run to church right now."

She shrugged at Riley who made a face at her before she stuck out her tongue. They were both sniping at each other more than usual; lack of sleep brought out their bitchy sides even more.

"Oh, yes, absolutely! You go and stay sober. Say prayers for the babies!"

Gia's face turned grim, as she responded, "Believe me, I'm always praying for them and for you."

Once Gia hung up after the "I love yous," Riley said, "It's another mile, and then there should be a slight curve to the right up ahead."

Gia chugged her hot coffee.

"Okay."

Riley eyed Gia pensively as she asked, "Are you sure this is a good idea? I mean the man could be totally gone in the head after he saw his wife and baby butchered in front of him."

"You can still sketch faces, right?"

"Duh," Riley said, insulted, motioning to her bag that carried her sketchpad and charcoals.

"Then whether he's bat shit crazy or not, all we need to do is get him to tell us what that Murphy doctor looked like."

Riley sipped her coffee, and almost choked on it as she saw the facility and said, "Whoa, that place is huge!"

Gia pulled up, and was startled by how well it had aged. Riley had researched the place on the plane, of course, and shared the details with Gia as she had *tried* to sleep.

It had been a hospital in the 1800s, but was gussied up by a bunch of doctors who bought the place and changed it to only a facility for psychiatric care. Apparently, the place was haunted by people who had been subjected to physical and mental torutre. Gia shivered, knowing there was something about this place that had a very evil vibe to it.

"Are you thinking about those stories we read about the patients who were tortured, and how they're now haunting the place now?"

"Yup."

"You know, before Miss Sophie and Ziggy came along, I didn't believe in this spiritual world, but now you've got me wishing I was wearing an adult diaper in case I shit myself."

******

Mrs. Smith had given them an unnecessary extended tour, which made Riley want to smash her over the head with her heavy charcoal holder.

They were both exhausted and just wanted to interview the crazy man, so they could get the fuck back on a plane to New York, and get home to sleep, but old bitty Mrs. Smith kept rambling on and on.

Riley couldn't take it anymore. She snapped.

"Mrs. Smith, can you just take us to Richard Chapel's room? This isn't Disneyland. I don't need a fucking guided tour of the different types of pudding you serve."

Mrs. Smith gasped and sputtered out nonsense as Gia, annoyed by her best friend's rudeness, stepped in front of Riley.

"Mrs. Smith, I sincerely apologize. We're both exhausted, and we need to get back to New York to work on the homicide case that we believe Mr. Chapel can give us some insight into."

The old woman was in a huff.

"Room 307." She glared at Riley. "I'm sure I don't need to give you a tour to his room."

The old woman stalked off as Riley swiftly took the lead and headed towards the third floor.

"That was a bit rude. Hey, why are we taking the stairs?"

"Because I need to wake the fuck up after Granny almost lulled me to sleep about how their facility is cleaned with Clorox Bleach, not just regular bleach."

As they took the stairs two at a time, Gia laughed.

"I have to admit, I was shocked *you* were the one who finally snapped. I thought it would have been me."

Breathing hard, Riley said, "Yeah, well, your constant rudeness and bitchiness is rubbing off on me after all of these years."

"You're an ass," Gia said huffily, realizing how out of shape she was from *only* three flights of stairs.

They reached the third floor and saw room 307 was down the hall, and the door was open. They were both breathing heavily, realizing how much it sucked to be in their late forties, and how winded they were from simply climbing *stairs*! They were struggling to catch their breaths as though they had just completed a triathlon.

Gia breathlessly stated, "We need to workout. We're too out of shape."

Riley was in no mood for anything other than interviewing Richard Chapel.

"I just want to get this damn interview over with. This whole building gives me the creeps."

Riley entered first and paused as she only took a few steps into the doorway. There was a bathroom in the room, a queen sized bed and a nightstand with a picture of Betty Chapel in her prime. The room had a small television set, and further back by the window was a couch and a bald man in a wheelchair, facing the window, staring out.

"Come on," Gia whispered.

Gia walked directly up to Richard Chapel's wheelchair, as Riley sat on the small, dingy couch.

"Good morning, Mr. Chapel. I'm Detective Gia Carter, and this is my associate Riley Roosome, the head of forensics," Gia held out her hand, but Richard Chapel seemed to stare directly through her.

He didn't move. As Gia saw how thin he was, she backed off, feeling like her loud, New York attitude might break the poor guy. His cheekbones literally jutted out, as though it was painful. His eyes were a dull brown, like Gia's, but there was no spirit in them. The decrepit, old man had given up on life.

Gia went and sat beside Riley, accidentally sitting on her metal box of charcoals.

"Watch it, fatty," Riley said grumpily as she took the box and placed it, along with the sketchpad onto her lap.

Gia glared at Riley and elbowed her in the side, annoying her best friend even more.

"Mr. Chapel, we were hoping we could ask you some questions that might help us in a homicide investigation in New York. We were wondering if you could describe what Madam Murphy looked like, so Miss Roosome could sketch her face."

His faded brown eyes sharpened, but he continued staring out the window.

"Her name was Mademoiselle Murphy, not Madam. Get your facts right, Detective."

Richard Chapel's voice was strong for someone who looked so frail.

"Right. Yes, I'm sorry." She paused and looked at Riley. They were both shocked by how lucid he was. "Sir, I know this is painful to bring up, but we were hoping you could give us a description of her or anything you remember from that terrible time in your life."

"No," he said with no anger or bitterness; there was no emotion, but his voice was powerful with that one word.

Gia was not one to back down.

"Mr. Chapel, we believe *Mademoiselle* Murphy is working with her coven under a new name in New York, and killing people, perhaps as a sacrifice to the devil."

There was no change in Richard's demeanor as he replied, "No."

Gia could feel her body tensing, as could Riley. She spoke up before Gia could lay into him.

"Mr. Chapel, there are lives at stake. All I need is a description of her. I can sketch it. None of the pictures of her turned out at the time of the trial. They were all… blurred," Riley stated, trying to prod the man to give her a description.

"No."

Gia stared at the man. He had his wits about him, so why wasn't he talking?

"Mr. Chapel, even the color of her hair or eyes would benefit our case."

"No."

Riley looked at Gia and shook her head.

Riley defeatedly said, "We thank you for your time, Mr, Chapel."

She stood up and gathered her things to her chest, but she was shocked that Gia was still seated on the lumpy couch.

Gia was seething. She just needed verification from this old coot if Madam had in fact been around in the 60s, killing off women and babies. She jumped up and lowered her face to Richard's.

"My wife is pregnant with twin boys. Your first born was a boy. I am not going to lose them, and you can help me!"

He looked her dead in the eyes, and replied, "No."

Gia threw up her hands and walked away from Richard, yelling, "Fuck!"

Riley's eyes flew open as she looked out the open door to his room to make sure no one heard her explosion.

"Gia! Calm down!"

"How in the hell can I calm down? This is bullshit! He's lucid and could give us a description to see if it matches Madam. He shouldn't hide inside his mind because he's too much of a chicken shit to talk about what happened to Betty!"

"Betty was a sweet girl." Gia and Riley looked at the man in shock, as he continued talking. "She was from a small town in Georgia. She had dreams of being a movie star, so she competed in the Miss Georgia pageant."

As he talked, Gia sat down slowly and Riley moved back towards the couch, only to gasp in surprise, as he ripped the sketchpad and charcoal box out of her hand with the speed of a child. Riley quickly sat down next to Gia as he chose his charcoal and opened the sketchpad.

"She won, of course. Oh Lord, her beauty was astronomical." He began sketching. "I had seen other beauties. Hell, I was the Warner Brothers head photographer. I did all of the photo shoots for these beautiful actors and actresses… but Betty. She was the ocean. Her blue eyes were light like pure water on an uncompromised beach. Her golden, wavy hair was the sand. Her makeup, always done without error, was like the colorful beach umbrellas in the sand. I met her and fell in love when, after I did her photoshoot, she asked if I knew how to sketch or paint. I told her I did. Her smile beamed up at me… I painted her first portrait, and she said she felt like the Queen of England."

Richard smiled, his brown eyes bright, as he tossed the sketch pad and charcoal box at Riley.

Gia thought it would be a sketch of Betty, but she gasped and said, "Holy shit, that's Madam!"

"No," Richard corrected her, "that's Mademoiselle Murphy, and she murdered my Betty. She had befriended her and even gave her that goddamn ruby necklace that was snatched back when she was on the floor, bleeding to death." Richard paused, his voice shaky with anger. "And that bitch murdered my newborn son right in front of me. She bled Betty dry. Her uterus had splattered on the floor as blood gushed out of her when she leapt to save our son." Once again, he paused, his eyes clearly stricken with the horrors of that day. "She bled our son dry as she slit his throat and had that damn goblet waiting under his throat for his blood. I know she was speaking Latin… She bled them dry… she bled them dry." He let the tears roll down his wrinkled face. "That day, she bled my soul from me." He stared directly at Gia, "And she'll do the same to you, your wife, and your babies. You're all going to be bled dry, even if you survive like I did." He paused and his eyes turned back to a dull, lifeless brown. "Go away."

"I'm going to leave my card if you remember anything else."

"No."

Riley asked softly, "Sir, why Betty?"

He bowed his head, softly crying.

"I don't know. I had been drugged too, but they didn't drug Betty enough. I kept hearing something about a mistake, can't kill Hollywood royalty… I still believe that Betty was never the target of their sacrifice; it was our son. Betty should have been knocked out cold, but she was a fighter… and now she's dead. And I'm just a corpse waiting to join Betty and our son. So please, leave me in peace to die alone."

He buried his face in his withered hands and his sob broke Riley and Gia's hearts. Riley left, feeling the unwelcome tears. Gia placed her card on the nightstand and looked at the picture of Betty. She couldn't help but notice how much she looked like Charlotte.

******

"You okay?"

Riley snapped, "Shut the fuck up. We just tortured that old man in there! We made him cry!" Riley swiped angrily at the tears that wouldn't stop flowing. "And I'm not crying! I'm just tired and it's my crying day before I get my period, so stop looking at me like that!"

"Okay. I know it was hard, but-"

"Shut the fuck up," Riley enunciated every syllable of every word.

Gia felt bad, but it was hard not to get emotionally attached to such a heartbreaking case. She searched the vault in her mind for anything related to Madam. Charlotte had said Madam thought she reminded Madam of her deceased sister, Caterine. She'd asked her about reincarnation.

Maybe Madam would sacrifice one boy and leave the other one alone, so her alleged reincarnated sister could leave with a baby. Gia shook her head. She couldn't let this happen to Charlotte. She deserved her twins, and Gia knew she'd never come back from the loss. No, this had to end now, but Gia had no idea how to stop a black witch.

Riley looked at the sketch. She was inspecting it very closely.

"Does Madam wear a necklace with a really large jewel on it?"

Gia thought about it.

"I don't think so."

Riley nervously realized what was happening as she sputtered out, "The ruby for Betty... the sapphire for Charlotte. Richard said she took the ruby back *after* the sacrifice of his son." Riley gulped. "Dude, I think those jewels Madam gives are to the ones who are going to be sacrificed."

Gia almost swerved the car off the road as she turned sharply to look at Riley.

Gia's mouth dropped open as she hissed bitterly, "Madam's Jewels... the name of her business."

"I think it's safe to say, Charlotte and the twins are the next sacrifice," Riley stated quietly.

The phone rang from the speakers of the car, startling both her and Riley. Riley looked at the screen.

"It's a California area code."

Gia accepted the call, and said, "Detective Carter."

There was a pause on the other line.

"I remembered something else."

Gia and Riley looked at each other in shock, mouths and eyes wide open.

Richards's voice was shaky as he muttered, "The main assistant to Mademoiselle Murphy was a woman from India… I can't recall her real name, but Mademoiselle always called her Beth."

Gia nodded, her exhausted mind spinning.

"Thank you, Mr. Chapel. Was there anything else you remembered?"

There was pause as both Riley and Gia leaned forward, looking at his phone number on the screen, as if willing him to talk.

"No."

Then, the click as the car notified them in a British accent *Call Ended.*

Chapter 12

By the third day of bed rest and her sisters working on Madam's energy constantly, she finally felt capable enough to lead the essential ceremony for Elizabeth. It was of grave importance that a black witch be sent to live with Husband, or her soul would roam the earth for all eternity. The soul would have no mouth, no ears and no eyes, and there would never be an end to the waking nightmare of their version of purgatory. The witches in their coven would never rightfully be severed from them either, causing a massive breakage in their own souls.

This was a horrible and ghastly path that black witches from every coven from the beginning of time had feared. Their goal was to find their home with Husband and shine in the light of evil after having worked for him for hundreds to thousands of years. To let a sister succumb to this wretched fate was something only for those who had turned away from the coven or released their secrets to a white or grey witch.

Elizabeth had been a loyal sister to the coven. Madam knew this painful and heinous way of sending off the soul of a sister to roam the world in anguish could not be allowed. Besides being cast out of a coven, this was the largest fear of any witch. It was this fear that kept them in line if they ever thought of conceding to another, holier power that the sisters did not serve. Once you became a black witch, you were there for this life and the one they coveted in the afterlife.

The sisters of the coven had all come in from Manhattan and were in the sanctuary, wearing their black robes. Madam, as head of this special ceremony, wore a satin and scarlet, blood red robe. Only the wife of Husband could complete this ceremony for one of her own. It was six o'clock at night when Madam entered the sanctuary that was packed with her coven. They made way for her, so she could get to Elizbeth's heart.

In the ceremony of finally ascending to live with Husband, Madam used the dagger that had been passed down from generations of black witches. The knife was sharp and the fire roaring in the massive fireplace glinted against the shiny steel. The handle was made from pure ivory. The urn was to hold Elizabeth's heart as Madam released her soul to finally find peace. This was the one thing Madam could do for her sister. They all stood around chanting the incantation of releasing Elizabeth from being doomed to walk the earth with no ears, no eyes, and no mouth.

Madam looked sadly down at Elizabeth. The sisters had done a good job of cleaning her up from Ezmerelda's destruction from the fire ants. Madam sighed, glad that she was able to give this gift to Elizabeth.

Madam moved the robe aside to reveal Elizabeth's chest. With steady hands, she plunged the blade into her chest, and cut out Elizabeth's heart. The urn that would hold her heart was next to her, but Madam had to say her verses first to release Elizabeth from the earth; some might call it a prayer, but to Madam, it was the sacred verses of black magic she had learned from John William after Catherine's death.

Madam held the heart in her hands, hearing the sisters chanting, as they felt the soul of Elizabeth in the room. It was a powerful moment; the sisters would be released from feeling her anymore. Madam began her verses in Latin. This was the most sacred finality for a black witch, and she took great care in enunciating every syllable, as she focused on how one wrong word could cause Elizabeth's soul to never leave the earth. That would be a brutal damnation for such a good sister.

As Madam was on the last verse of the transition for Elizabeth to hell, a massive wind gust made the sister's robes fly up, and many of them had to hold onto each other to keep from falling over. Some teetered, keeping themselves up by grabbing onto the metal surface of the table that held Elizabeth's body, but Madam did not move. Her focus was solid as she stared at the heart in her steady, lithe hands and continued the final verse.

Madam saw Nora being tossed backwards, as though she was a puppet and the puppeteer had grown tired of playing with her. She now looked up and saw the puppeteer was Ezmerelda. She grinned, and that's when Madam saw her one golden eye and her other light green eye. Those eyes leapt with glee as they eyed Madam. No way was Madam going to let Elizabeth's fate be so torturous. She swiftly ran through the last verse with conviction.

As she was on the last sentence, Ezmerelda cocked her head and Elizabeth's heart was now in the child's hands. Gasps were heard all around from the sisters; this was sacred! This monstrous six-year-old couldn't stop the transition ceremony!

Madam calmly stated, "Ezmerelda, please give me the heart. I need to send Elizabeth's soul to Husband. She has been a valuable member of this coven; she does not deserve to be damned to walk the earth with no mouth, eyes or ears."

Ezmerelda grinned wickedly. She was now tossing the heart from one hand to the other, like it was a softball.

"You really think I'm going to let her into my Father's house… *my* house? He gave me permission to come here and do anything I want to these sisters of yours."

Madam heard the murmurs in her head of the sisters. She agreed with them that Ezmerelda was not a true witch, but a demonic entity that did not belong in their coven, so with a flick of her wrist Madam tried to pull the heart back into her hands, but the heart only hovered two inches above Ezmerelda's hands.

She heard Nora think it before she could tell her not to do it, but Nora had already moved swiftly and put the little girl's head into a choke hold. Nora's veins were popping out of her head and hands as she used her formidable strength to choke Ezmerelda out.

Terrifyingly, the girl was unfazed by this, and was smiling as she took the heart up to her lips and bit into it like an apple.

As she chewed with her mouth open, she delightedly said, "Mmm."

The sisters felt the agony of Elizabeth. They heard her howl as she was now damned to walk the earth.

"You have no respect for the sacred coven of sisters!" Madam screamed in painful agony as she felt Elizabeth still tethered to her own soul.

Madam was shaking as much as the other sisters were. They all felt a slice of their souls entrenched with Elizabeth's.

Ezmerelda only smiled as she took another bite out of the heart and then tossed the other half into the flames of the fire behind her.

"Chewy… but now I have to take care of this atrocity trying to choke me. One moment, please."

Pure evil flashed in the girl's wild eyes while she licked her fingers and suddenly cocked her head. Nora was ripped from Ezmerelda and thrown across the room, landing hard on the concrete floor. Ezmerelda cocked her head to the side again, and swiftly brought Nora to her, pinning her hands at her sides, as she hovered in the air looking down at the girl.

"Tsk... tsk… tsk. You shouldn't have done that. Don't you know by now to never mess with the devil's daughter?" Ezmerelda paused and said thoughtfully, "I never liked you. You suck as a teacher, you stupid cow. I'm really going to enjoy this. You'll be cursed just like your friend, Elizabeth."

With shocking swiftness, Ezmerelda reached into Nora's chest and ripped out her heart. Some of the sisters fainted, while others simply vomited or began sobbing. The heart was still beating in her hand, as Ezmerelda held it up and said something in Egyptian.

Blood was pumping out of Nora's heart as Ezmerelda put the heart to her lips and smiled gleefully at the entire coven, but her eyes landed on Madam as she tore the heart apart with her teeth and chewed loudly, making sure her mouth opened ridiculously wide, so everyone could see. The blood of Nora was on her hands, running down her arm and chin.

Madam could barely breathe. She felt the torturous, burning agony from Nora as she too succumbed to the same fate as Elizabeth. Madam urgently told the sisters inside of her mind not to do anything, or they would go next.

Ezmerelda glared at Madam as she continued biting into the beating heart.

"You know," she said with chunks of heart in her blood-stained teeth as she swallowed, "I do like the live hearts better. They're nice and warm, unlike Elizabeth's... that was just chewy and cold." She paused to take the final bite of Nora's heart and began talking with her mouth full. "The warm blood really acts as an enhancer to the chewiness… it gives it more flavor."

Ezmerelda turned to face Nora, who was still straight as a board, under Ezmerelda's spell.

Nora's face would forever be etched into Madam's brain. The look of sheer terror was in her eyes, and yet there was the agony around her mouth as she was stuck in mid-scream forever.

Madam couldn't stand this little deviant anymore. That was two sisters from her coven doomed for all eternity because of this stupid, vengeful little bitch. They all felt the loss in their souls that had merged together. The pain in their hearts was real because as they had merged as one, they each felt like two parts of their hearts had been shredded by the teeth of a six-year-old.

As Ezmerelda made Nora dance in the air, Madam embraced her anger and evilness. She used both hands and pushed all of her energy at Ezmerelda with a scream. As the girl was shoved into the fireplace, Nora dropped in a heap to the ground.

Ezmerelda sat in the fire, holding her knees as she laughed maniacally. There were no burn marks on her. There was nothing… except two menacing eyes, and wicked, cruel laughter with blood and heart pieces still in her mouth that she hadn't fully swallowed yet.

Ezmerelda stood before Madam. She saw the golden glow of the eye, as though the Egyptian demon, that was allegedly her mother, was giving her some newfound idea to torture the coven with.

"You know, pig, that was possibly the dumbest thing you could have ever done." Ezmerelda paused and looked around the room, but the sisters looked down, trying to hide under their hoods from the horrible little girl. "Now, while I can't kill you, since Father needs you for his final sacrifice, and you two made a deal over five hundred years ago when you became his Wife… but I do have other options." She tapped her bloody lips thoughtfully with her little fingers. "Since I can't rip out your heart and make you walk the earth in agony, I *do* have a whole coven that I can choose from to be cursed for eternity."

There were some nervous whimpers amongst the sisters.

Madam's willful voice stated urgently, "Ezmerelda, don't. You've already banished two witches to a lifetime of horror and torture. You've made your point! You're strong; we get it. Now, that's enough!"

"I WILL TELL YOU WHEN IT'S ENOUGH, PIG!"

All Ezmerelda did was cock her head slightly, and Madam felt a hard slap across her face, and then she felt the other side get hit so severely, she was certain that her jaw bone had been cracked.

"Now… little pig, little pig… who would hurt *you* the most to see punished for all eternity? Hmm? Who has been with you since the very beginning and been your second in command?"

Madam felt her spine turn to ice. Not Beth. Not Ibetsam who had been her best friend and most loyal sister. They had learned the dark arts together. *Please, don't let her take my Beth,* she thought in the part of her brain only she had access to. Beth was her favorite sister.

"Little pig… little pig… let me into that mind of yours," Ezmerelda declared gleefully.

Never had a nursery rhyme made Madam want to vomit more.

"Could it be… Theodora?" Theodora cried out as she was flicked to the ceiling in a flash. "Nah," Ezmerelda said as she dropped her onto her fellow sisters. "Perhaps Victoria?" Victoria gasped as she, too, was thrown up to the ceiling. "Hmm… I don't think so…" she said as Victoria was thrown across the room with a minor little cock of Ezmerelda's head. "What about young Lily?" The terrified, newer witch screamed and screamed as she hung above everyone. "Oh, shut the fuck up; we know it's not you! You're an infant!" Ezmerelda hurled the girl across the room, smashing her into Madam's table of potions. "No… I think it's someone who never leaves the little pig's side… Oh Beth," Ezmerelda sang out in glee.

Madam screamed, "NO! NOT BETH! STOP IT!"

Madam tried to run to the other side of the table, but Ezmerelda stopped her in her tracks; she was a frozen statue, only able to watch in absolute terror and dread as Beth was flown directly above Ezmerelda. The girl looked at Madam and winked.

Ezmerelda saw the coven all look down, and cocked her head, making sure their heads stayed up and their eyes remained open.

"No. You're going to want to see this. See what your fearless leader, Madam, is making me do!"

Beth's eyes met Madam's. There was terror and fright in them as Madam felt tears fall down her face like a massive waterfall. She kept eye contact with Beth, just as she had done with Catherine when she was burned at the stake. She saw Beth's eyes bulge open as her screams pierced Madam's ears when Ezmerelda tore out her beating heart.

Beth was still alive and staring at Madam when Ezmerelda made a big production about eating the heart and going under Beth's body to catch the blood that was flowing like water from her open chest. Madam kept her eyes on Beth and saw the moment when the soul left her body. She felt the gigantic rip of torment as her eyes, ears and mouth were taken from her. She heard the last shrill scream of pain, and shared the agony to the depths of her own heart. They had been two peas in a pod; their bond was the strongest, so Madam felt everything her dear sister suffered through unnecessarily, and she realized this was worse than when she suffered while being eaten alive by pigs.

"Oh… someone's crying! What's the matter, pig? Did the big bad wolf kill your little buddy?"

Ezmerelda unfroze the witches, including Madam, and she swiftly wiped her tears away. She watched as Ezmerelda danced under Beth's body, pretending like the blood was rain as she opened her mouth and let the blood pour in.

Beth didn't deserve this fate. She was supposed to spend eternity with Madam. Something snapped inside of her as she relived the pain of losing Catherine. In a disgusting instant, Madam was no longer the same.

As the light went out from Beth's eyes, Madam felt herself walking hand-in-hand with Beth along the planes of the earth, bumping into things randomly, and knowing this was an endless nightmare. Madam didn't know what snapped, but she knew she wanted revenge, the likes of which she had never felt before.

Ezmerelda was certain that she had shocked the coven, as she comlpleted dancing under Beth, and tossed her carcass into the sisters, who screamed, as they were finally snapped out of their shock from watching the atrocity play out before them.

The cruelty was in her eyes as she stared at Madam and asked, "Anyone else?"

Each of the witches bowed their heads, or had already fainted once released from being frozen to watch the Ezmerelda show of death and doom, but Madam kept her head up. Her back was like iron. She eyed the girl… Beth's blood was everywhere on her.

She watched as Ezmerelda used the back of her hand to keep the blood from going into her eyes… Beth's blood that was dripping down her forehead and cheeks.

They stared at each other, and for the first time, Madam had the same demonic eyes staring back into Ezmerelda's. She had taken so much from this demonic heathen in a matter of ten minutes. Ezmerelda watched her eyes shift.

"Careful, pig. I can't kill you off, but you have a whole coven I can ruin, and I know you feel it too, being such a good leader and all."

Madam went to the quiet part of her brain and wondered if she knew about Catherine. Madam knew she needed to get this freak of nature out of her sanctuary. She gave a slight nod, admitting defeat.

Ezmerelda's eyebrows flew up as she felt the pure joy of causing the once powerful Madam to bow her head, slightly, in defeat. She smiled, and unceremoniously pulled a chunk of heart out from in between her teeth. She flicked it at Madam, and it landed on her forehead, causing Ezmerelda to cackle.

She clapped her hands together, splattering blood everywhere, and said, "Well, I'm glad I popped up for a visit. The meal was fabulous. Rave reviews, Ladies! Five stars!" Her evil grin never left her face as she looked at Madam. "And I'm glad we understand each other, pig. Let's hope, for the sake of your coven, you don't try anything sneaky to undermine my authority, or this will happen again until each one of your sisters is walking the earth as a deaf, blind mute."

Again, Madam gave a slight head nod, signaling, once again, Ezmerelda had won.

A surgeful gust of air shot throughout the sisters, but this time, their energy was unbalanced from losing three of their sisters. It was an unspeakable agony they all felt together. Many did not stand back up; they chose to weep on the ground. Those who did stand back up were sobbing or simply staring wide-eyed in shock.

Madam walked around the room, looking at her three sisters, but especially Beth. They would never find peace. She couldn't stop Ezmerelda. She didn't know how. Madam only felt the shared pain of her fellow sisters, and the pain was gut wrenching and twisting her heart.

Madam needed to be alone with her thoughts. When Beth died, she felt the massive shift inside of herself.

She swiftly went to the door, tore off the piece of heart stuck to her forehead, tossing it at the sisters, and without looking at any of them, harshly said, "Stop crying and clean up this mess!"

Chapter 13

Madam had tossed her sacred robe onto the floor of her bedroom, well guest bedroom. She had taken a hot shower to cleanse any of the blood from her, especially Beth's. She had scrubbed at her forehead so long, it was red and raw.

She couldn't stand the idea of it being Beth's heart that had been flung onto her forehead. As she finished wrapping herself in her warm bathrobe, she paced the room, barefoot, feeling the plush carpet under her feet.

Madam slipped into her inner thoughts, and she realized she no longer cared about what happened to the coven. Half a piece of her heart had been shredded to death when Beth died, and now she would only focus on herself; she only cared about ascending to her throne among Husband's other wives. She had to focus on her last sacrifice.

Oh, she would pretend to care about the sisters in the coven, only because she needed to use them to keep up the facade of her business and when she hosted parties at her home. But deep in her core, she couldn't care less what happened to them once Ezmerelda took over.

She wasn't going to waste her time looking for something that could diminish the powers the little demonic monster now had, which Madam felt had heightened when Ezmerelda deviously ate the hearts of three of the black witches. She would use the coven, and once she left, she didn't give a fuck if Ezmerelda made them all walk the earth deaf, blind and mute.

Madam's evilness and cruelty were so severe after Beth's loss that she truly felt hatred for her own coven. *Let them die. Let me focus on my last sacrifice and be done with this hellish place called earth!*

Madam picked up the sapphire on her nightstand. She needed to focus on Charlotte. She had to gain her trust, friendship and love. Luckily, she could still plan how to oust Gia, that damn, ugly woman from Charlotte's life. Her sacrifice had to be made.

She saw the time was only half past six. It was hard to believe that a mere thirty minutes ago, she was a different person. Now, she picked up her cell phone and found Charlotte's number to call. She plastered on a fake smile and tried to urge her energy to sound jovial, but Madam would be disgusted by the person who answered the phone.

******

Charlotte, her parents, Marty and Diane, Gia, and their realtor, Nancy, had been touring apartments all afternoon. They were at the last one, which happened to be in Marty and Diane's building, across from Central Park. It was a tenth floor apartment, and Charlotte's parents lived on the thirtieth floor.

As soon as they entered, Nancy hit the lights, and Charlotte was immediately in love. She placed her purse and cell phone down on the massive kitchen island. The kitchen had stainless steel appliances, and the accents, as she often saw today on their other apartment tours, were grey, black and white.

The canned lighting was bright, but Nancy immediately dimmed them a bit. The oversized refrigerator was like two fridges in one. The backsplash was a perfect blend of black and grey, with little hints of white. The cabinets were as pure white as newly fallen snow. The kitchen floors were black, which made everything pop.

Nancy said, "Now these floors are real wood. They just stained them black to mix well with the whiteness of the cabinets and the backsplash."

The entire setup of the apartment was just like Charlotte's parents apartment, but with more updates. The kitchen, attached dining room, and the massive living room were the central part of the apartment. There were two bedrooms and two bathrooms on the hallway leading from the dining room. The master bedroom with an attached bathroom would be Gia and Charlotte's bedroom, while the bedroom next to it would be for the twins.

Back in the massive living room, there was a gigantic fireplace, along with a large patio door that had a balcony with a view of Central Park. The half bathroom and separate laundry room were on the opposite side of the patio door, which was half a football field away, the living room was so expansive.

On the other side of the fireplace wall were the two other bedrooms and the last bathroom. It would be the last bedroom that would become Gia's home office, while the other bedroom would be made specifically for overnight guests, or for the nanny, if Charlotte needed extra assistance with the twins… this was all planned out by Charlotte as she scurried around the place, leaving her parents to talk to the realtor and Gia to remain in the kitchen.

Charlotte whirled back and forth throughout the apartment and smiled glowingly at her parents, who were now in the living room complaining that their own fireplace wasn't this nice. She paused and glanced at Gia, who was looking in the massive refrigerator.

"Hey! What do you think?"

"Umm, I'm pretty sure I could fit in here, along with you and your parents… not Nancy, though. That'd be pushing it."

Charlotte laughed and quickly said, "I need to go back and check the closet space."

Gia didn't get a chance to respond before her sweet and overly excited wife was off again. Gia let out a breath as she closed the refrigerator door shut. She hadn't even taken a tour of the place, but she already knew this was what Charlotte wanted, so Gia knew she would comply to keep Charlotte happy. Plus, it made her feel better knowing Marty and Diane were in the same building, so they could help Charlotte once the babies arrived.

A grim look took over Gia's face as she kept observing Charlotte fiddle with her sapphire necklace as they had toured apartment after apartment that day. Gia had asked her if the necklace was new. Charlotte had laughed and told her that it was new to her from Madam, but it seemed like it was an antique.

In that moment, Gia's heart had stopped beating and dropped to the pit of her stomach. This was like Betty with the damn ruby! Another piece of the puzzle, and Gia was not happy about it. All signs now fully pointed to Charlotte or the baby or babies being a sacrifice, as Richard Chapel had sadly observed and lived through; he was now just the shell of a man, broken forever by Madam.

Gia shook her head, listening to the soft murmurs of Nancy, Diane and Marty. She couldn't believe that this would be her new home. Hell, they even had valets for their cars! She was not accustomed to such posh living, but she knew Charlotte missed a large home.

Gia did feel a bit overwhelmed with four bedrooms and 4 bathrooms, although, as Diane clarified, it's *only* three and a half bathrooms. Yes, this was overwhelming, but as Miss Sophie's note reminded her, do the opposite of what you would do.

Right now, Gia wanted to run away from this monstrosity that they called an apartment. It was a mansion… in Manhattan… across from Central Park! Being born and raised in Brooklyn, she felt like she didn't belong here.

She yawned and looked at her watch. It was getting closer and closer to seven. She definitely wouldn't be getting in a nap before work tonight. As she was about to slowly walk around to try to warm up to the idea of this being her new forever home, Charlotte's phone rang. She walked over to the kitchen island and her eyes first popped open and then narrowed as she saw Madam calling.

What the fuck! Why was this psychotic bitch from hell calling Charlotte?

Gia *could* have let it go into voicemail. She could have, but she didn't. This was the woman who was trying to harm her family, and had used witchcraft to cause Gia to almost lose her loved ones.

She clicked accept.

With a jovial tone, she evenly said, "Good evening, Madam."

There was a pause on the other line as she quizzically replied, "Charlotte?"

Gia bit her anger back as she seethed out, "No, this is *Detective* Gia Carter."

There was a pause and Gia smiled menacingly.

"Oh… hello Gia."

"How are you feeling, Madam?" Gia asked cheerfully. Another pause. "You know, after the last time I saw you, you had severe food poisoning. You literally looked like death when I saw you by the elevators," Gia said smugly.

Yes, she was poking the bear, but she was a lioness, ready to rip her to shreds.

There was another long pause before Madam replied, curtly, "Yes. I'm much better now. Thank you for your *concern,*" and Gia heard her bite out the last word.

Gia was going to take this over the top.

"Well of course I'm concerned! You're my wife's doctor! I mean honest to God, I thought I saw your face shriveling up from the pain you were in. I prayed and prayed and prayed to God to take care of my wife's dear, sweet doctor. It's all in the power of prayer and God's amazing grace, isn't it, Madam?"

Madam sounded off as she quickly responded, "May I please talk to Charlotte?"

Again, Gia played up the act.

"Oh geez. I'm sorry, but we're in the middle of buying our new home together. Thank GOD that Charlotte is taking the reins on this deal. I'm just sitting back, saying the *Serenity Prayer*… do you know it, Madam? 'God, grant me the serenity to accept-'"

"Gia, I didn't call to pray. Could you please tell Charlotte I called to check on her?"

"Oh, praise the Lord and Jesus and Archangel Michael, aren't you a dear! I'll have to give you a big hug at our appointment next week," Gia said as though she were mimicking Joel Osteen.

"Ah, so you're coming," she replied flatly.

Gia was full of fake joy in her voice.

"You know it! I'll be there for every appointment! I think Marty and Diane will be there too. We're all just so excited! We praise the Lord everyday that Charlotte is pregnant with twins. Thank *God* for you, Madam, to help bring us such a miracle. I could start singing "Amazing Grace" right now-"

Sighing, "Please don't. Just tell her I called."

Gia grinned and replied with unabashed, fake joy, "Absolutely! And I look forward to seeing you at *every single* appointment!"

Gia heard the bitterness as Madam said, "That's grand… just.. grand."

The phone clicked and Gia smiled as she felt her heart beating quicker than she had realized. She quickly dug her phone out of her jacket pocket and made sure to put Madam's number in her phone as Bitch.

She wondered if Riley could get some tech nerd to hack Madam's phone, so Gia could see what was going on through the crystal eye on her cell phone. She shook her head as she realized it would be pretty easy to find a hacker to do that for her. Riley had already gone above and beyond for Gia.

As she put her phone back in her jacket pocket and placed Charlotte's back on the kitchen island, she heard Charlotte yell her name. Gia jumped, and hoped she hadn't been caught, but she knew Charlotte's tone; she sounded eager, not pissed. Regardless, she hustled as she moved through the dining room and glanced in the massive master bedroom.

"Charlotte?" her voice echoed.

"Next room."

Gia walked down the hallway and saw a brightly lit room with Charlotte walking out of the second walk-in closet. She was smiling.

"There are literally walk-in closets for the walk-in closets!"

Gia slowly walked in the room and turned three hundred and sixty degrees, taking in everything.

She whispered, "This should be the nursery."

Charlotte lunged at Gia and embraced her tightly as she kissed her.

She pulled back and said, "That's exactly what I thought!" Charlotte's brow furrowed, "Are you sure about moving here? In the same building as my parents?"

Gia earnestly looked up into Charlotte's blue eyes.

"Yes, because I know this would make you happy."

Charlotte squealed excitedly and hugged Gia, then she stopped.

"Are you only doing this for me? I want you to be happy too."

Gia held Charlotte's hand and looked around the room.

"I never had a forever home in Brooklyn. I mean, yeah, I'll have to get used to having a valet, but if that's my biggest concern, I think this place could be the one… plus, I do like knowing your parents are in the same building when I work midnights. I'll definitely worry less about you. Twins are a lot," Gia gulped, hoping she could make certain both babies came home.

Charlotte smacked her shoulder.

"That's what I was thinking! I wouldn't be so scared as a first-time mother if I had my parents just an elevator ride away."

Gia shrugged her shoulders.

"So buy it. You know I can't afford this place, but I'll tip the valet at Christmas."

Charlotte hugged Gia again, and Gia was actually grateful to God that she got her shit together just in time to have a family. Yes, she was older, but she was used to never getting enough sleep.

"I feel like this is a fresh start for us. You've finally embraced sobriety, and we're expanding our family. I'm just so grateful for this. For us."

Gia was not the mushy one in their relationship, but she stood on her tiptoes and gave Charlotte a kiss. She then looked around the room and saw the long wall without a window.

"The cribs should go there, along that wall. Too many infants and toddlers get choked by the cords of the blinds." She continued to scour the room for any problem areas. "The two rocking chairs, we can set up in front of the window, and the changing table can be in the back corner." Gia whirled around at the one wall she hadn't used yet in her mind. "That wall will be for the dresser, but you better believe we'll be anchoring it to the wall. Again, too many toddlers climb on dressers, and they get crushed from them. In fact, we'll anchor every piece of furniture to the walls."

"Here, here," Marty said as he walked in with Diane at his heels. "We're going to hire a professional to do it because I sure as hell don't know anything about anchoring furniture."

"Oh Marty," Diane sighed.

Marty paid no attention to his wife.

"Look here, you two. I… I have a gift for you both, and I don't want to hear one damn protest against it, or I'll ground you two."

Gia laughed and Charlotte shook her head, knowing her father was being absolutely ridiculous with this dad jokes.

He walked forward, took the hands of Gia and Charlotte and placed keys in them.

"Dad… what did you do?" Charlotte asked in shock.

Gia looked confused as she looked from Marty to the female version of Marty.

"I bought you this home. It's a gift for the twins."

"Dad! I can't let you buy this for us! It's way too expensive!"

Marty pawed his hand in front of him.

"I have so much money, little girl, you don't even know how buying this outright won't even impact my bank account in the slightest."

Charlotte threw her arms around her dad, and she began crying.

"Thank you," she whispered.

"Anything for my baby girl." Marty grabbed a stunned Gia by the jacket and pulled her into the hug. "Come on in here, shorty. This is a gift for you too!"

"Thank you," Gia mumbled through Marty's stomach in her face.

Diane yelled eagerly, "And *I'm* buying you all new furniture!"

"Dammit all to hell, Di! Couldn't I just have a damn moment to celebrate my gift to the girls? You always have to make it about you!"

"Oh shut the fuck up, Marty!"

Marty released Charlotte and Gia, and he put his arm around his wife's small shoulders.

"I love this pain in the ass woman."

Gia smiled and put her arm through Charlotte's.

"I completely get that, dad" Gia replied with joy as she looked up at Charlotte.

Chapter 14

Time seemed to whirl by in a flurry of speed. Once the apartment was officially theirs, Charlotte and her mother took shopping as seriously as a full-time job. Marty oversaw the painters for accent walls Charlotte liked. Charlotte held off on buying anything for the nursery. She was just at 12 weeks, the day of her monthly appointment with Madam. It was the beginning of October, but it still felt like summer as they all sat in the waiting room.

Gia had immediately put on her holy water, letting it air dry on the way up in the elevator. She was also carrying a vial with her, as well as her cross and the evil eye that Charlotte laughed at when she saw it. The black rocks were in the other interior pocket of Gia's jacket.

Theodora was at the waiting room door, and she kindly said Madam would see them now.

As they all walked past Theodora, Gia grabbed the woman's arm, seeing the pain on her face as she said, "Thank you so much, Theodora."

Theodora all but ripped her arm away.

"You're welcome," she muttered as she tried to hide her bitterness towards Gia.

Gia noticed that every woman looked haggard and tired in the office. They looked like… well, her. Even Madam looked beaten down. Something must have happened. As Gia went to shake her hand, Madam backed away.

"I apologize, but I'm a bit of a germaphobe during fall and winter with all of those germs. It is the start of flu season."

Gia grabbed her arm, just as she had to Theodora.

She noticed Madam wince, as Gia said, "We understand, Doc. We need you healthy to keep them healthy," she tossed her head in the direction where Charlotte stood.

Madam walked away from Gia, and retrieved a file from her desk, faking a smile.

"Yes, well, let's get started shall we? Theodora?"

Charlotte looked quizzically at Madam.

"Where's Beth? No offense to any of your other nurses, but she's my favorite."

Madam's face turned grim and the shine that was left in her eyes faded.

She cleared her throat, before responding stiffly, "Beth is no longer with us. Theodora will be my main assistant."

Something was definitely off. Luckily, Riley would be over later to talk about more books she had read and researched that were now in her photographic memory, and Ziggy might be able to help Gia figure out what might have happened.

******

Riley walked into Gia's new apartment with a bag filled with books.

"Damn, girl! I need to marry someone with money! This place is incredible!"

Her bright green eyes lit up as she took in the massive kitchen, already decorated with red accents.

Ziggy soon followed, also carrying a massive bag, her red hair as wild as ever.

"Wow! Seriously, Gia, this is the most gorgeous apartment I've ever seen!"

Charlotte came into the kitchen from the master bedroom with some candles she had bought while out shopping with her mother. She smiled joyfully.

"Hi Riley! I haven't seen you since the precinct's Christmas party! That's almost a year ago! You look great!"

Charlotte embraced her in a warm hug.

Riley was not one for affection, but she returned the hug because Charlotte was so kindhearted.

"Yeah, it's been awhile. So, how are you feeling?"

Charlotte lit up and replied, "I'm great. We're great," she said as she patted her stomach. "We're looking good, and we're past the 12 week mark." Charlotte paused and took in the large woman with wild red hair and kind light blue eyes who almost matched her height. "I'm sorry for not introducing myself sooner. I'm Charlotte."

Charlotte extended her hand to Ziggy, who shook her hand in response.

"It's nice to meet you. I'm Ziggy."

"Ziggy? That's an unusual name, but it's cute!"

"Well," Ziggy shrugged her shoulders, "my mother was unusual."

Gia felt herself cringe. She had only known Miss Sophie for a couple of weeks, yet she would never get the sight of her horrific death out of her head. Plus, if she had never met her, Miss Sophie might still be alive today.

"So, Ziggy, do you work at the precinct with Gia and Riley?"

Gia wanted to keep their unusual meeting under wraps, but Ziggy was not one to lie.

"No, we met through a… uhh, crime scene."

"Oh… so you don't work with Gia?"

"Umm… I'm hired on as a consultant with murders related to… uhh, the supernatural."

Charlotte set down the candles she would use in the sconces her dad had set up on the living room walls.

"Supernatural," she almost questioned with sincere interest.

Ziggy cleared her throat before saying, "There are some people who commit murders in the name of the devil. I have studied this my whole life, hence all of the books Riley and I have to show Gia."

"Oh, wow. I didn't even know that was something people still believed in." Charlotte furrowed her brows. "Is it like a cult? Like the Mansons?"

Gia cut in, "Something like that. Anyway, we have a lot to go over with this homicide case. We're going to head into my office."

Charlotte smiled before replying, "Mom and I had a new desk, chairs, table and a couch set up in there. I hope you like the color scheme. It's all pink."

Gia's face was frozen in disgust.

"Yeah… sure," Gia said through gritted teeth.

Charlotte punched her in the arm.

"Oh stop it! I made the colors black, white, grey, and yellow! I know you hate pink!"

Gia wiped her brow in exaggeration as she said, "Thank God! Okay, we're going to let you decorate, while we get to work."

"Sounds good. It was great to see you again, Riley, and it was nice to meet you, Ziggy."

They both smiled at her, but she had already returned to unpacking the large candles. As they walked through the living room, Riley and Ziggy both paused and looked around in awe.

"Wow," Ziggy said.

"And you all just moved in? This place is already decorated and painted! Damn, Charlotte needs to leave your short ass and marry me!" Riley paused as she looked around. "For all of this, I'll turn gay!"

Gia laughed at Riley as looked around the living room. There was plush black furniture, scarlett pops of color, and a cool, new and very expensive looking black, grey and white rug underneath the new furniture. Even the smell was new.

"Hmm… it does look good. I didn't even notice," Gia said as she shrugged her shoulders nonchalantly.

Gia continued walking as Riley rolled her dark green eyes and followed Gia to her home office.

"Of course you didn't notice! You would decorate your apartment with shit off the streets." Riley and Ziggy both paused at the entranceway of the new office. "Do you smell that?" Riley asked.

Gia sniffed.

"Smell what?"

"That smell is what expensive smells like!" Riley said shaking her hips in one of her ridiculous, excited dance moves.

"Oh shut the fuck up! It's just furniture. And stop moving your hips like that! You're going to break one, and then I'll have to take care of your old ass."

Riley paused and replied sassily, "Who the fuck are you calling old? Bitch, you're the same age as me!"

"Yeah, and I know better than to dance like a teenager when I'm middle aged, you moron!"

"Shit, you wish you could dance like me, but you don't have soul!" Riley started dancing again. "That's what you get for being pasty ass white!"

As Gia was about to respond back with a zinger, Ziggy shook her head, her fiery curls shaking back and forth, as she interrupted the banter between the two.

"Umm… no. This stuff is luxurious and probably just the matching chairs and couch are $50,000."

Gia shriveled her face looking at the furniture.

"Get the fuck out of here. There's no way-"

Charlotte walked in with a tray of lemonade and water bottles, pausing as she looked at Riley moving her hips like she was trying to keep a hula hoop from dropping to the ground.

"Make sure you use the coasters on the desk and tables. Those alone were $10,000."

Gia's mouth hit the floor as she looked at the black desk, side tables and coffee table.

"But they're black. I could have just spray painted them from cheap pine wood… How much for the grey couches and matching recliners? How much for the yellow shit? How much-"

Charlotte gave her a kiss on the cheek.

"Mom bought it all. Don't worry about a thing. Ladies, do you like the pale yellow accents?"

"Definitely," Riley replied, as stopped dancing, feeling a bit out of breath.

"Okay, we have to get to work. I can't deal with this talk about money," Gia said as she ushered Charlotte out of the room.

She yelled back before the door closed on her, "Use the coasters!"

Gia relaxed against the back of the closed door.

"Damn," she softly said, suddenly feeling uncomfortable to even sit down, knowing that this furniture was worth way more money than she had anticipated.

"I'm just going to say it… you're a bitch, Gia."

Gia rolled her eyes at Riley as she carefully sat down in one of the expensive chairs, her ass melting into the softness.

"I already knew that."

"You're living like a princess, and you don't even acknowledge it. I know it's different than where we grew up, but, dude, you need to embrace it."

Ziggy took out some books as Gia nodded her head, looking around her new office.

"Speaking of princesses," Ziggy started, "it seems these covens always have one Alpha female who will sacrifice humans for the prince of darkness, thereby becoming his princess of darkness once she has completed her required amount of sacrifices to prove herself to him."

Riley sat cross-legged in the other chair and brought out some books.

"Yeah, and I found some interesting stuff about the Egyptians during B.C. times," Riley said.

Ziggy was on the couch, already taking things out of her bag, including yellow legal pads of notes, reminding Gia of her mother.

"Apparently, a witch practicing the dark arts, who doesn't follow through with the requirements from the devil can have her soul sent to something along the lines of purgatory, but, allegedly, they are blind, deaf, and cannot speak."

Riley cried out, "Oh yeah! I read about that too! Did you see the part about the heart being the most sacred part of the ceremony?"

"And how in a coven, they all feel the pain of the loss if they don't disconnect from her?"

Gia thought back to the doctor's office, and she recalled how everyone looked beat up… and then there was Madam's missing second-in-command, Beth.

"What if a coven had one of their own taken away to this purgatory place, but they hadn't disconnected?"

Ziggy and Riley looked at her with somber faces.

Ziggy said, "If that happened, there's a darker force that had the power to do that."

"What I'm asking is, would the witches in the coven look distraught? Like… tired and haggard… umm, not as pretty as they usually look?"

"So, like you, except you never look pretty," Riley remarked with a smile.

"Shut up! You're such a little bitch!"

"Yup! My momma raised me right!"

Ziggy cleared her throat to reign them back in.

"Do you think this happened? With Madam's coven?"

Gia shrugged her shoulders.

"Her go-to assistant, Beth, is no longer there. Theodora took her place. All of the women who "work" there, well, they looked beat up, and shut up, Riley. I know what you're going to say," Gia said before Riley could make fun of her looking beat up.

"I'm getting nothing from my mother. That's not good. It means the darkness that was present was out of her realm, meaning she couldn't go near it."

Gia sighed loudly and dropped her head to her chest.

"Look, we know these are black witches. We know they are going to harm my baby or both of them and maybe even Charlotte, now that we know about the jewelry having a direct correlation to whom Madam chooses. We know that they use drugs to kind of roofie anyone in the room… what we don't know is how to stop this fucking sacrifice from happening!"

Riley and Ziggy looked at each other with worry etched across their faces. They were all stuck. How in the world do you stop the devil's princess from fulfilling her duty to him?

Ziggy looked up. She was listening intently.

"Okay, I'll ask. Riley, did you come across anything about Egyptian goddesses… good and evil working together? It's a longshot, but my mother keeps insisting that help will come to Gia after Christmas but before the new year. She's showing me a mini-version of Madam… but she can't see what choice you make. There's something about a black witch and a white witch linking together in unison that upsets the natural order and causes major chaos."

Gia shivered.

"Yeah, this whole little girl thing is creeping me out. If she's the evil that blocked what your mom could see… well, then that's pretty damn evil. And for the last time, I'm not a witch!"

"All I know is, you're going to have a choice. Work with evil against evil, or work to find the answers in your own ancestry."

Riley was flipping through pages of a decrepit and smelly book.

"If that smelly ass book leaves its' scent in here, Charlotte will murder you, Riley."

Riley was intense, her green eyes were pursuing something. Gia had seen her like this before.

"Her brain is in the zone," she told Ziggy. "There's no sense in talking to her until she finds what she's looking for."

"Is she really an actual genius?"

"Unfortunately, yes. And it's annoying to work with someone who knows how smart they are."

Ziggy nodded, watching as Riley was speed reading at a pace she had never observed before. She turned back to Gia.

"When will you accept the fact that your bloodline is filled with white witches?"

Gia plopped her head back against the chair and rocked.

"Easy - never. Because I'm not a white witch."

"You don't have to be practicing. It's in your blood."

Gia rolled her eyes and sarcastically said, "Right, Ziggy. I'm a white witch. It's in my blood."

Ziggy paused and listened.

"My mom wants you to test the theory."

"Miss Sophie is with us?"

"Always."

"Look, uh, can you tell her-"

"She said she knows how awful you feel, but mom also said to knock your crap off. She's grateful to you because it brought me back into the family business."

"I'll never forgive myself for the pain she went through."

Ziggy paused and wiped her eyes.

She whispered, "Yeah, but she's happy now. She gets to be happy for all eternity."

Gia cleared her throat, and tried to calm her flow of tears that were cropping up.

"What's the test?"

Ziggy said, "Close your eyes and only picture white energy swirling around your body."

Gia's one eyebrow went up.

"Seriously?"

"Do you want to upset your buddy, Miss Sophie?"

Gia swiftly shook her head and said, "Nope. I'll do the stupid test while Speedy Gonalez reads a thousand page book in under ten minutes."

Gia closed her eyes. She pictured the white energy swirling around her. Initially, she was looking out at herself, but soon, she was inside the white energy. She felt like she was in a massive tornado of pure, light energy. She smiled and felt lovely warmth, as though the sun's heat was shining directly onto her and through her.

She soon saw her Grandma joining her. No words were said. She just held her hand. Suddenly, there were great-aunts, great-great-great grandmothers joining in the circle of light. Gia had never met them before but she *felt* the bond of their relationship to her. She could only hear soft words from a woman with the hair the color of icy snow. *Beware the evil. The evil will be in your veins.*

Suddenly there was a large thud, and Gia gasped as she opened her eyes. She looked around her and the light had changed in the room. Riley had joined Ziggy on the couch as they were talking about… Gia couldn't even tell. She felt like she was brought out of a trance that she wasn't ready to be pulled out of. Everything felt like she was in a slow fog.

"She said evil in my veins. I'll have evil in my veins."

Riley and Ziggy looked up, forgetting she was there.

"Hey sleepyhead! You've been out for two hours," Ziggy jovially said.

"What? Two hours? It was just five minutes!"

Riley shook her head.

"Nope. I finished the book in *eight* minutes, smart ass, and you were out for the past two hours."

Ziggy smiled and asked excitedly, "Did you see your ancestors in the white energy?"

Gia nodded her head in utter bewilderment.

"Yeah… it was… cool."

"Now do you believe me?"

"I mean… it could have been a dream if I was out that long."

Ziggy, annoyed by Gia's lack of faith, threw a yellow legal pad at her.

"Stop being a cop and listening to your head; focus on your heart. Obviously, you came back with a message."

Riley stood up, the books falling from her lap as she rushed over to the massive, stinky book she had been reading before Gia went into her trance.

"Wait… wait… wait…"

Gia stretched and told Ziggy, "It's her photographic memory. Something just clicked like a picture. I said something that-"

"Found it!" Riley yelled. "It's an old folklore from ancient Egyptian times. There was a woman… she worked her status of evil from being what we would recognize as a black witch today to a demon with no desire to serve anyone. She apparently wanted to rule the empires, and her power grew so strong that she was taken to hell for her punishment by the devil… Yup! Here it is. According to legend, she was the devil's favorite, but as her power grew nearer to his level, he forbade her from studying or practicing anymore… Isfet was her name. She changed her name to this because it basically means evil in Egyptian."

"Does it say what her name was before she changed it?" Gia asked.

"No… it does say she wanted so desperately to grow in power that she worked with anyone, including what we know today as white witches and grey witches. Blood was shared. Bonds were bound. And then all it says is the devil found out, and he brought her to hell to serve her time for disobeying him… umm… oh, here it is. But she vowed to get her way 'through the daughter of a woman in darkness.' Allegedly, she can sway the devil, and she's been released a few times when he needed something horrendous done… the book went on to say when evil struck thousands, millions, that was Isfet working for the devil to win his grace back."

Ziggy shook her head, whispering,"Okay, now I'm freaking out."

Riley looked up from the book in surprise.

"Why? It's a folklore from ancient Egypt to keep kids scared of crossing the devil and working with darkness."

Ziggy bore her eyes directly into Gia's.

"Do not share your blood with evil. That's what you were warned about, and that's what that ancient Egyptian demon is going to have you do."

Gia leaned forward in the chair and asked quietly, "How do you know for sure?"

"Because I just saw it."

Chapter 15

As the weeks flew by, Gia was constantly working on going back into her trance. It was always the same message as before. She would also lay next to Charlotte when she was sleeping or napping and place the protective rocks on her growing belly, saying prayers of protection to God and her ancestors. Gia honed in her skills of picturing white, protective light around Charlotte and the babies. She would use the goodness within her to protect her loved ones.

Charlotte would sometimes be awake when Gia would place the two stones on her pregnant bump. She would keep her eyes closed and listen to Gia say prayers in soft whispers. Charlotte did feel more at peace when Gia did this, and she would quickly fall back asleep, never asking Gia why she did these things. If Gia being more spiritual with God had made her into a better person, she was not going to embarrass Gia with questions or tease her about it.

At the beginning of November, Madam was able to announce that Charlotte was pregnant with twin boys. Marty, Diane and Charlotte all cried together, as Gia smiled and kissed Charlotte's hand that clasped hers.

Gia looked at Madam, who still looked haggard, and she noticed that Madam had a newfound gleam in her eyes. Gia went within and saw a white, protective light around Charlotte and the babies. Her focus was so intense that Madam had to step back from the positive energy radiating from Charlotte. She eyed Gia suspiciously, glad that by Easter, she'd be done with these wretched humans, the weak coven, and that she'd take her rightful place with Husband, so she could finally be together again with John William.

Thanksgiving was a massive production, and when Gia found out that Charlotte was inviting teachers from her work and officers from Gia's precinct over, she immediately went out and bought a new lock for her home office door. She always made sure to close the door when she left her office and lock it with the thick key that only she had. When Charlotte had asked her for a key to her office, Gia reminded her that a lot of horrendous crime scene photos were strewn about, and she didn't want to upset Charlotte, especially in her condition. Luckily, that seemed to appease Charlotte. She knew Gia put up with Marty and Diane constantly popping in because, of course, Charlotte had given them a spare set of keys to their place.

Even during Thanksgiving, when the mood was bright and teachers and detectives had brought over adorable gifts for the baby boys, Gia was inside of her head. She was anxious and often sick to her stomach about the party she knew Madam would throw and how Gia would meet pure evil in the form of a little girl.

Without fail, each and every single day, Gia went to church. She prayed for protection from God and for her ancestors to guide her on this upcoming meeting with a demon or the spawn of a demon. The name Isfet had been seared into her brain, as her fear grew daily.

Gia put on a great act in early December, when they were with Madam for Charlotte's monthly checkup. She was 20 weeks along, and the babies were doing great. Sporadic kicking and punching occurred as Charlotte, her parents and Gia watched on the sonogram. It was pretty amazing, and Gia's protective instincts to keep them safe from Madam grew.

Gia had been practicing throwing up the white, protective forcefield, as she now saw it, over the babies. She did this again when Madam was using the device to observe the babies on the outside of Charlotte's stomach. Gia saw Madam's hand begin to shake, as she cut the session short, saying she was feeling a bit lightheaded from not eating. Gia glared at Madam and Madam only raised an eyebrow. No matter what, Gia would die to protect her boys from this psychotic woman's desire to sacrifice one or both of them.

The invite to Madam's party on December 28th arrived the following week. Charlotte immediately called Madam to RSVP a huge yes for her and Gia. Charlotte used a magnet to place the invitation on the refrigerator. Everytime Gia looked at it, she grew more worrisome and sick to her core.

Christmas was a small event, with only Charlotte's parents. Gia gave Charlotte a necklace that was a cross with two sapphires in it. Gia let her know it was to represent the boys, and it also matched nicely with the sapphire Madam had given her. Charlotte didn't know it had been dipped in holy water, and protection prayers were said over it from Gia, and then Ziggy added on some protection spells, since Charlotte would never wear the evil eye. But as soon as Gia said the two sapphires symbolized the twins, Charlotte never took it off. Definitely a win for the good side!

As Gia struggled, she too had someone she knew going through the same feelings of anxiety and fear. It was Madam. Only her anxieties were when Ezmerelda would show up again, unannounced, and terrify her. Madam didn't care if Ezmerelda wanted to keep killing off the coven.

Madam was now dead inside. She only lived to see this final sacrifice through. When Beth had been taken from her, it was like losing Catherine all over again. At least John William and Madam had taken care of Catherine's heart after she was burned at the stake. The sacred ritual was completed, and Madam still had the urn that carried her sister's heart locked away in her sanctuary.

As Madam gave orders to the sisters about decorating only with red and silver on the Christmas tree, she felt the evil wind gust through the house.

"Hello, Ezmerelda," she said, clearly annoyed.

"Hi, pig. Ahh, I see your lovely decorations are in full swing this year. Your little elves are working so hard." Ezmerelda paused as she looked up at Madam. "Why aren't you simply flicking your finger or wrist to have it done?"

Madam did not want to say that her powers had decreased substantially. With three of the sisters gone and not released from her or the other sisters, they were weighed down by the three of them walking around in helpless and hopeless forms on earth.

"It's my last Christmas on earth, so I wanted us to actually do the decorating. Anyway, I bought a beautiful green velvet dress for you. Please make sure you keep that gold eye under control for the party," she bit out with venom.

Ezmerelda eyed the woman as a predator eyes its prey.

"I shall keep it hidden because that is what father expects of me… that and to learn how to schmooze with these morons that you helped have children." She paused and asked innocently, "Will your current sacrifice and her wife be in attendance tonight?"

Madam kept her eyes focused on the Christmas tree her sisters were decorating, and she simply replied, "Yes."

"I wonder if I shall find out your secret when I meet them," Ezmerelda said while looking astutely at the woman who had given birth to her.

"There is no secret," Madam said with a dull sigh.

Ezmerelda laughed.

"Funny, pig." Ezmerelda bore her eyes into Madam, sensing her energy was dull. "You're not looking your best, Maura. Don't tell me that you're depressed and oh so very sad that I took away three of your witches?"

"I'm fine," she replied stoically.

"Mmm hmm… it seems like it. I'm just curious about something…" Ezmerelda waited until Madam finally looked down at her, and she cocked her head.

Madam had put her hand up to stop whatever was about to happen, but she was flown across the room, hitting her head on the piles of reindeer that had yet to be set up. Ezmerelda laughed with glee.

"I knew it! Your power is barely there! This is awesome! I'm so glad I made the trip back just to find that out!" Her gold eye was glimmering. "Not to fear, Mommy Dearest, I shall be on my best behavior tonight, but only because I promised father."

Another piece of Madam's strength fell from her like the last leaf on a tree, slowly, slowly falling to the ground to get trampled on.

******

"Is my ribbon tied in the back to look like a bow?" Charlotte asked worriedly.

Charlotte was definitely pregnant, with her belly popping out. She wore a red dress, with sleeves, because she felt she was getting too fat to show off her arms. The silver tie was above her bump. She made sure her purse and high heels were also sparkling silver, along with her silver jewelry.

"It's fine. I checked it five times. I just wish you would have worn flats. Why in the hell are you wearing heels?"

"Because I feel fat, okay Gia? These heels make me feel pretty," she snapped.

"Okay, okay." Gia held up her hands to admit defeat. Charlotte was a bit hormonal, and Gia just learned to keep her mouth shut. "You look beautiful, Charlotte."

"Oh shut the hell up. I look like a manatee!"

Gia scratched her head, trying to hide her smile.

"Well, look at me. I look like a lesbian."

Charlotte rolled her eyes before bitingly saying, "That's because you are a lesbian. And I bought you that nice outfit, but you refused to wear the skirt."

Gia looked down at her black ballet flats, her black pants, then up to her white turtleneck and her black leather jacket she always wore.

"Hey, I make this look good."

Charlotte smiled and in a mocking tone said, "Oh sweetie, no, you really don't."

Gia made a face at her as the front door opened. Fuck, she was not ready for this! She felt around in her leather interior pockets for the stones and holy water. She laid the cross out on top of her turtleneck, but she kept her evil eye underneath her thick turtleneck.

A maid came up and asked, "May I take your coat?"

Gia looked her up and down with her derision on full display.

"No. I'm good."

The maid did a little curtsey and went to help the next couple who were arriving.

"What the hell," Gia whispered to Charlotte, "Are we in England? She just fucking curtised at me!"

"Hush!"

Gia replied as she sighed, "Why are we in a fucking line?"

Charlotte hissed, "It's a receiving line to meet Madam and her daughter!"

Gia instantly shut her mouth. *Oh fuck, oh shit, oh dear Lord in Heaven!* Gia's heart began to beat ferociously. Her mouth felt like there was a bag of cotton in it. She could feel the sweat coming down her back to her ass crack. *Fuck, fuck, fuck.* Gia suddenly felt like she wanted to bolt. She couldn't do this. She didn't want to meet a demon or the spawn of a demon!

Instantly, when she saw Madam hug Charlotte and place her hand on Charlotte's already large stomach, she focused on the white, protection shield. Madam swiftly moved her hand away, but, as always, she maintained her smile. Now Gia remembered why she was here: to protect her loved ones from this bitch.

She heard Madam say, "Charlotte, this is my daughter, Ezmerelda."

The little girl curtised, *again with the curtsying,* in her green velvet dress and white tights with those stupid little black shoes parents thought looked cute, but only made their kid look like a live doll, like Chucky.

"It's so nice to meet you Ezmerelda. You're as beautiful as your mommy," Charlotte cooed.

Gia rolled her eyes and Madam raised a perfect eyebrow.

"Madam," Gia said tightly.

"Gia," Madam responded with bitterness.

They shook hands, the holy water burning Madam. Gia saw, from the corner of her right eye, the little girl's head had swivel incredibly fast when she heard Gia's name being said by Madam.

"Ezmerelda, please say hello to-"

"Gia. Yes, I heard," the little girl said excitedly.

The girl's green eyes were flashing super bright.

"Hey there. I'm Gia."

She felt like she was sweating bullets. *Damn leather jacket!* It didn't help to think she was looking at a demon right now. The kid was tall for six. Her head probably reached Gia's shoulder.

"I'm Ezmerelda." She flashed a massive grin. "Would you like to play Checkers with me?"

Madam cut in swiftly, "Later, Ezmerelda. We still have people to greet."

Gia could have sworn a flash of gold glimmered in the girls' left eye.

"Yes, mother," the girl bit out with a clear fake smile.

Gia cocked her head at the girl. Something told her the hatred she had for Madam was around the same level as hers.

"Yes, Ezmerelda, I would love to play Checkers with you once you are done greeting your guests."

The little girl smiled, and shockingly, Gia smiled back.

******

While Charlotte was bonding with four other pregnant women that Madam had helped get pregnant, Gia went into detective mode. As Charlotte and the women gushed about Madam, Gia quickly slinked back, something that was quite easy as such a short person among the women who all wore high heels.

She had made her rounds with Theodora and Lily, making sure to burn their hands with the fresh holy water she applied in the bathroom.

Gia moved around asking women about Madam's help with their pregnancies.

As she found Alice, the nurse from Dr. Lee's office, who had recommended Madam to them, Gia began asking her and Billy, Alice's husband, questions about their first pregnancy that had ended with their son tragically dying after her painful birth.

"Alice, did Madam ever give you a piece of jewelry? Like a diamond or an emerald necklace? Anything like that?"

"No. She's my doctor. That would be odd."

Odd it most definitely was! Damn, I'm not getting anywhere here!

Gia looked up at Billy, and asked, "Were you there for the entire birth?"

Billy nodded his head and replied, "Absolutely. I never left Alice's side."

Gia pinched her face, and continued interrogating them as she asked, "And you never saw Madam try to cut your baby's throat?"

Alice gasped and brought her hand to her mouth as Billy protectively wrapped his arm around her shoulders.

Alice's voice started to tremble as she barely wheezed out, "What the hell kind of question is that? We saw him born with the cord wrapped around his neck. God, what is wrong with you!"

Alice quickly bolted to the nearest bathroom, with Billy shaking his head at Gia in disgust as he hurriedly followed his poor wife.

Damn! She was frustrated because only Alice had lost her firstborn son, six years ago, but Madam had never given her a trinket or jewelry or drugged the couple. They were both awake and aware of what happened. Even after that terrible loss, they had a son and a daughter. Every other couple she had interviewed didn't lose a child at birth. Many of their firstborns were sons.

Gia shook her head, trying to figure out the rhyme and reason as to how Madam chose her next sacrifice.

So, Alice was alive, obviously. Madam had told her if they didn't get her son out, she'd have an emergency C-section. Alice had told Madam that she didn't want a C-section, but, later, after the tragedy, realizing that she should have listened to Madam; the damn cord had ended her son's life, even before it began. Alice said it was her fault, as Billy had told her to let it go. She remembered being given her son to hold, so she could say goodbye and mourn him properly.

While Alice went off to cry, Gia felt slightly bad about hammering away at her with so many questions, but she was on the hunt for the truth. Maybe that was a freak accident that happened with Betty Chapel in the 60's. She had to be killed because she was still cognizant of what was happening, and they couldn't have a massive celebrity like that spoiling Madam's work.

Gia glanced at Charlotte and saw her watching her. *Uh-oh, too much time away from the Queen of Hormones.* Gia rushed over and asked if Charlotte needed anything.

"No, I'm fine. I see you've been making the rounds though," Charlotte said angrily.

Gia grabbed some cashews out of a crystal bowl, replying innocently, "Yeah, just some light chitchat."

"Uh-huh." Charlotte glared down at her as she whispered, "Is that why I saw Alice excuse herself to go cry over her firstborn son, who happened to die? Gia, what is wrong with you? You don't talk about that at a Christmas party!"

Gia swallowed the cashews, quickly replying, to avoid the wrath of a very hormonal Charlotte, "Look, I'm sorry. I was just asking questions to avoid the same thing happening to us."

"Gia, I understand you're worried." Charlotte's face now showed sympathy as she looked down at her wife. "It's been etched on your face since the beginning of this pregnancy. I'm fine. The babies are healthy. Stop worrying."

If you only knew what I knew, Charlotte, you'd be running to Vatican City with me right now!

"I know… it's just, I'm here to keep you and the twins safe."

Madam and Theodora walked up, both wearing dark green velvet dresses. It seemed green velvet was a requirement if you were related to, or worked with, Madam.

"Charlotte, dear, how are you feeling? Perhaps you should sit down and rest," Madam said with the utmost sincerity and charm.

Gia looked around because seeing Madam made her want to murder her. She had kept one eye out for that Ezmerelda demon girl all night. She was always running around. Suddenly, she looked right in front of her and saw bright green eyes staring at her.

Gia gasped. Loudly.

Charlotte rubbed her back, and asked in concern, "Are you okay?"

Gia had to catch her breath as Ezmerelda stared at her and smiled creepily.

"Yeah, she… she just scared the shi-"

"Language," Charlotte hissed, as she smacked Gia lightly on her back.

"The heck out of me. You're pretty fast, Ezmerelda."

"Like a cat?" Ezmerelda asked as she smiled directly at Madam.

Gia nodded, still freaked out about what might happen with this demonic child.

"Yeah, sure. Whatever is a fast animal to a kid."

"Mommy, may I please play Checkers with Gia now?"

Madam looked at her daughter suspiciously and quietly said, "I don't think Gia-"

"I'd love to!" Gia said happily, realizing this kid was the secret to saving Charlotte and the twins.

Ezmerelda grabbed Gia's hand to pull her towards the massive playroom, when she felt her hand burning.

The little girl, in her cute green, velvet dress, ripped her hand away and shouted, "OUCH! Son of a bitch! Mother fucker! That hurt!"

Gia started laughing, but she quickly stopped when she heard, "EZMERELDA!"

Ezmerelda was still shaking her hand and blowing on it, when she angrily whipped her head around, and yelled, "WHAT!"

Gia saw the gold eye. She then saw Madam point to her own eye. Within a moment, the eye was back to light green.

"Language, please!"

Ezmerelda looked around at everyone who looked at the little girl in shock, and she whispered, "Shit," only loud enough for Gia to hear.

Gia quickly said, "Yeah, that was my bad! I shocked her by accident. It's these ballet flats on the nice rugs. Sorry about that, Kiddo," Gia said ready to reach her hand out to rub the top of Ezmerelda's head, only to see the girl cock her head, and find her own hand shoved into her jacket pocket, but not through her own volition. "What the-"

"Sorry everyone! I apologize! Mommy, I am very sorry for cussing in front of your guests. I guess I picked it up from my nanny, *Elizabeth*," Ezmerelda said soberly.

Madam plastered on a fake smile and responded sweetly, "Fine, dear. We'll talk about it later."

Ezmerelda whispered, "The hell we will." She heightened her voice so everyone could hear her as she skipped ahead. "Come on, Gia! Let's go play Checkers!"

Gia smiled and followed along. The board had been set up away from the little kids who were playing video games and throwing balls and blowing bubbles. The table and board were still child-sized, but with Gia being so short, it didn't bother her.

Ezmerelda stared at her, never blinking.

"You're white. I'm black."

Gia scrunched her face and replied quizzically, "Are you color blind? I'm red."

Ezmerelda leaned forward and whispered, "Are you *daft*? I'm black and you're white…"

Gia wasn't getting it, and Ezmerelda was growing more and more frustrated by the second.

"Umm," Gia picked up a red checker and said, "this is red." Then she pointed to her turtleneck. "This is white. Do you see the difference? If not, I think we should tell your mother to get your eyes tested."

Ezmerelda rolled her eyes and annoyingly whispered, "I am *black,* and you are *white…* from our ancestors… our energies." Ezmerelda sat back and folded her arms. "That was a nice protective shield you put around your wife's stomach. I was impressed with the speed. You've been practicing, white witch."

Gia's eyes widened. She couldn't speak or breathe. This was the demon that was staring directly into her eyes with unabandoned fascination?

"What the fuck are you?" she whispered.

Ezmerelda's golden eye came back as she winked at her and leaned forward, so only Gia could hear her say in a spine-chilling tone, "I'm the thing you've been warned about."

Chapter 16

Gia stared in horror, like she'd been caught with her pants down in front of the whole precinct, but couldn't find her damn pants to pull on.

She started saying every prayer in her head. She felt cold and hot at the same time. Fuck, she was going to have a panic attack.

"Take it easy," Ezmerelda hissed. "Just play the game." Gia couldn't move. She was a statue now, filled with terror instead of concrete. Ezmerelda kicked her under the table. "Don't freak out," she whispered, "I'm not here to hurt you, your wife, or your baby. I just need to take down Madam, and I think you can help me."

Gia couldn't speak, so she followed Ezmerelda's example and began moving her Checker pieces along the board. Her hand was shaking.

"I would touch your hand to calm you down, but I don't feel like getting burned again - nice touch with the holy water. I noticed you got Madam and the rest of her crew."

Who was this speaking to her?

Gia barely whispered, "Isfet?"

Ezmerelda's gold eye sparkled.

"She's in here with me, but I have to keep the gold eye hidden." Ezmerelda blinked, and both of her eyes were back to being a lovely shade of light green.

Ezmerelda watched Gia's face turn from astonished, to fearful, back to astonished again. She now saw why Madam often referred to her as having a pinched up turtle face. She definitely was not attractive.

"I see you've done your homework about ancient Egyptian folklore… Your move."

Gia was barely paying attention to her red pieces on the board. They both talked quietly, even though no one would be able to hear them with the kids in the background being so loud, yelling at each other or at the video games they played.

Gia still felt the need to whisper, as she said, "I don't understand."

A little, pudgy boy came up eating caramel candy and stared at them, as he asked politely, "Can I play the winner?"

Ezmerelda looked at him with such a look of disdain that Gia shrank back in her seat.

"Beat it, fatty," Ezmerelda said harshly.

The pudgy, little boy's lower lip quivered, and then he shrugged his shoulders as he walked away.

Gia scowled at Ezmerelda, "You're six!"

Ezmerelda laughed loudly as she quickly stated, "Come on, Gia. You know I'm not. I'm just stuck in this body for now. I'll be able to shapeshift into anyone I want to look like, once that damn pig is taken care of once and for all."

A *normal* person would have sprinted out of that room, away from this shapeshifting child who apparently had an Egyptian demon inside of her, but Gia's two decades of being a cop and then a detective made her want to get the answers she desperately needed to keep her family safe. She had to know who or what she was dealing with.

"I'm just… trying to make sense out of," she paused and circled her hand in Ezmerelda's direction, "all of this."

Ezmerelda nodded, as she did a double jump and snatched away Gia's two red pieces.

"I will not lie to you. I know if I lie to you that I will lose my chance at taking down that fucking pig," Ezmerelda cringed at the thought of Madam making her way to *her* home in April.

Gia stared hard at Ezmerelda. Yes, this was insane talking to a six-year-old who cussed as much as she did, but inherently, she felt the evil wafting from her like a smoker's cigarette scent comes off of them.

"Why do you call Madam pig so much? I mean, with your cussing vocabulary, I'm sure you could come up with something much worse."

Ezmerelda eyed the board as Gia double jumped her right back.

"That's because she died being eaten alive by her own pigs," Ezmerelda stated matter-of-factly.

"What?"

Ezmerelda paused and looked around, making sure none of Madam's cronies were loitering around.

"Back around 1554 or some year around then… I just know it was the reign of Bloody Mary in England, our dear *Madam*," she spit out, "was this ugly teenager. She was hideous looking, unlike her younger sister Catherine, whose beauty matches that of your wife. So, being this utterly disgusting looking thing, Madam was always picked on by the neighboring kids. My mother told me that a slew of them took her at night, shoved something in her mouth so deep, it hit her throat, and they threw her in the pig pen." She paused to smile before she continued, "Well, these pigs were hungry… so they ate her alive. No one found her until…" Ezmerelda paused, listening, "oh… until two days later." She nodded, listening to someone Gia couldn't hear. "Right, she was buried under the mud and pig shit. Anyway, Catherine found her. She'd been studying the dark arts with an older man.

"Now, Catherine was about twenty, and this Sir John William Mayhew was in his forties, but he was fucking hot, like the tall and strong man every woman wanted to fuck with salt and pepper hair to make his blue eyes pop. Every woman in the county was in heat around this man, you get what I'm saying?"

"Not really. I'm a lesbian."

Ezmerelda rolled her eyes and sighed before responding, "Right. I forgot who I was talking to. So, John William had brought Catherine into his own coven. They fell in love…so gross. And when she found her sister, she knew John William could bring her back with a sacrifice of one of the kids in the neighborhood who had done this to her sister."

"Wait… I thought covens were only run by women."

Ezmerelda made a sneering face at Gia and shook her head before scoldingly saying, "Come on, Detective. You should know that's some old sexist view." She paused as if finding her way through the story. "Catherine and her lover boy brought back Madam, sacrificing the son of a well-known and highly respected elder. According to my mother, some shit went down."

"How did they bring her back?"

Ezmerelda rolled her eyes, as she double jumped to the back of Gia's side of the board, and said, "Queen me." Gia forgot there was even a game going on. She put a black piece on top of the other one. "Look, Catherine had brought her sister, Maura, that's Madam's real name, into the dark arts with her. They made a deal with my father, sacrificing the boy to him, and Maura came back, but she was able to shapeshift into someone with beauty. They lied and said she was a visiting cousin, since no one could know she was brought back from the dead."

"Damn… this is fucked up," Gia whispered.

"Yeah, but Maura was not content playing second fiddle to her beautiful sister anymore. The investigation was underway for who killed Mr. McCallister's son. Maura had been in desperate love with John William, and she was tired of Catherine fucking the hot older dude."

Gia shook her head and wondered out loud, "Why are you telling me all of this?"

Ezmerelda sighed and leaned back, her little arms crossing in front of her ridiculous looking doll dress.

"Because you need to know who you're dealing with, and I doubt all of your white witch friends know how evil she really is. Did you find any of this in your research? No. Because only my mother knows the secrets. *She* was sent from her punishment in hell by my father to stir things up. My mother can shapeshift, and she was the voice in Bloody Mary's ear, as one one of her most trusted ladies-in-waiting. You see, anytime there is death and mayhem, that was my mother getting the privilege that my father only trusted her to do. So she was there, Gia."

Ezmerelda looked up, and quickly kicked Gia.

"Ouch," she hissed.

"So when I play with my dolls, I always name them after famous women from history," Ezmerelda said joyfully.

Gia scrunched her face as she started to ask, "Are you-" she paused and felt the evil behind her, "going to name one of your dolls after Saint Joan of Arc?"

Madam moved around the table. They both looked up as Madam looked at the board.

Haughtily, she said, "Gia, I do hope you aren't letting my daughter win. She needs to learn how to lose."

Gia felt the evil and dark energy pulsate around her.

"I'm actually not. Ezmerelda is quite the little… devil when it comes to playing games."

Ezmerelda smiled up at her mother with open hostility.

"See, Mommy? I'm quite the devil, aren't I?"

Madam's perfectly arched eyebrows went up.

"Mmm… quite. Now, Gia, I hate to interrupt, but dinner is being served in the dining room for the adults. Ezmerelda, you shall be hostess to the children in the first main living room."

"Right." Gia stood up. "I need to make sure I get some food before Charlotte eats it all."

Madam did not smile.

"That's very rude, dear. I hope you don't make fun of Charlotte's weight gain in front of her. Tsk… tsk… tsk," Madam said as she left them to round up the children currently in the playroom to the living room.

Gia looked down at Ezmerelda and angrily whispered, "I need to know how we take her down."

The gold eye came back and then quickly disappeared.

"After dinner, we'll talk in my room."

"Yeah, but won't that look suspicious… not to mention weird that I'm hanging out in a kid's bedroom?"

Ezmerelda stood up, and her smile turned wicked.

"I'll take care of it, but first, I need to torture pig a little bit… just for fun," she said as she whipped out of the room.

Gia quickly hurried after her, but was pulled into her chair next to Charlotte. Madam was at the head of the table, as the servants gently placed the polished bowls onto the silver platters. Gia saw Ezmerelda off to the side, glaring at Madam as she dug into the cream of potato soup, with melted cheese and a dollop of sour cream.

She gleefully snickered as everyone agreed that this was absolutely delicious.

Ezmerelda watched as Madam ate, and she made sure to shove one of the servants out of the way who was bringing out a gigantic silver rolling cart with a large cover over it.

Madam whispered to Ezmerelda, "Why aren't you in the living room hosting the children? And what is this?" she asked, eyeing the massive silver tray cover.

Ezmerelda loudly said, "Ladies and gentleman, I was lucky to offer my help in the kitchen today. I prepared my mother's favorite food, with the help of her chef. We used the fat from it to add a pop of flavor to the soup." She paused and grinned wickedly at Madam. "And here, mommy, is your favorite meal!"

Ezmerelda lifted the lid, and there was a massive, roasted pig, awaiting to be sliced into. Madam immediately put her satin napkin up to her mouth to hide her horror. She realized she had just eaten *that* pig's fat in her soup.

Ezmerelda smiled cheerfully as everyone clapped, and their mouths began to water at their soon-to-be delicious ham dinner.

Madam had her napkin over her mouth as she hissed, "You little cunt."

Ezmerelda giggled and said exuberantly, "Mommy, please do the honors of making the first cut."

Madam, never one to look like anything but a queen, elegantly sliced at the pig, filling plates, as her stomach roiled. Unfortunately, Ezmerelda was not done with her prank.

"Now mommy, please try a piece. Tell me if I did a good job!"

Madam plastered a smile onto her face and ever so slowly took a bite, grinning in feigned delight as Ezmerelda leaned over and said, "Pig eating a pig," as she planted a kiss on Madam's cheek, causing everyone to say, "Aww!"

Ezmerelda skipped out of the room to the first living room, but she made sure to grin devilishly at Gia who found it hard not to smile back at how uncomfortable Madam was, as she tried to keep her regal composure.

******

During dinner, Gia kept replaying the story in her head about Madam... well Maura... well pig. Ezmerelda was right; Riley, Ziggy and even her research never told them about the origins of Madam. The girl was right. She needed to know.

"Are you even here right now?" Charlotte's soft voice whispered in her ear.

"Hmm? Yeah, yeah. I was just thinking."

"About what?"

Shit, about how to have a demon girl help me kill Madam before she kills you or our babies!

"Well, it was so nice playing Checkers with Ezmerelda."

Charlotte smiled and squeezed her hand.

"I must say, that was too cute! It looked like you were really having a deep conversation with her. I had no idea you were so great with kids her age! So, what were you thinking about?"

Gia hated lying, especially to Charlotte, but she had to appease her hormonal wife somehow.

"Well, I was thinking that after the boys are born... maybe we... umm... if you're okay with it..." Gia gulped, fearful of Charlotte's crazy ass hormones. "Maybe we could try for a little girl?"

Charlotte inhaled deeply, her left hand on her protruding stomach, and she clenched Gia's hand she was holding even tighter.

"I would love that." Charlotte dabbed at her eyes with the satin napkin. "I want a large family, and I was hoping you did too. I didn't want to push you on it, but I would love a little girl."

Gia smiled as Charlotte kissed her.

Gia wiped away Charlotte's happy tears as she told her, "Well, a big family it is then! Wait until we tell your parents."

Charlotte laughed softly, shaking her head.

"Oh my gosh, they'll go insane! I've never seen them so happy in my life! They are really going overboard about being grandparents."

Gia smiled through her heartache. She wished her family hadn't shunned her for loving women instead of men. She wished that she had her genetically bound family back, but twenty years of being turned away for being true to herself was too painful.

"I'm very grateful for Marty and Diane, Charlotte. It's nice to be accepted as we are."

Charlotte squeezed her hand again and with knowing sympathy said, "I know, honey. I know."

******

After dinner, as promised, Ezmerelda announced that her mother was quite an amazing piano player, and that she should lead them all together in singing Christmas carols. And the Moms-to-be, should sit down in the comfortable lounge chairs together, and have any dessert they desired brought to them.

Once everyone was established in the massive second living room, Ezmerelda nodded her head to the side at Gia, who had been shuffled rudely to the back to let the pregnant women have seats closest to the piano, as the other children and adults all scooted around and started singing "Sleigh Ride."

Gia quickly followed the girl out of the living room, going unnoticed.

"Hurry up," Ezmerelda hissed. "We don't have much time."

Gia raced up the grand staircase after Ezmerelda and they both ran to the girl's bedroom, Gia in tow. She could have sworn she heard the girl hiss as she turned on the lights.

"Fucking pig changed my color scheme."

Ezmerelda pulled out the Lapis necklace she always wore from underneath her dress and held it in her hands. She cocked her head, and suddenly, right before Gia's eyes, the room changed from black and red to gold and white, with Lapis blue as accents. She stepped backward from the fireplace, and as the flames lit up, the entire mass of sparking black stones disappeared into gold shimmering stones with more Lapis stones as accents.

Gia was freaked out… she looked at Ezmerelda, and her gold eye was back, shining like a gorgeous diamond under a chandelier. Gia felt faint. This little girl simply had to cock her damn head, and suddenly the room was transformed? *Dear Lord, what am I messing with?*

Ezmerelda rolled her eyes and rudely said, "Don't lose it on me now. Sit down." With a cock of her head a soft, light blue chair was underneath Gia. "Do you need oxygen?" Gia nodded and her eyes bulged out of her head as a small oxygen canister was hanging, mid-air in front of her with an attached mask. "Put the mask to your face and breathe," Ezmerelda said bossily.

Gia nodded and quickly breathed in through the mask, hoping it was actually oxygen.

"Now, for the rest of the story." Ezmerelda cocked her head again, and there was a matching light blue chair from out of nowhere for her to sit down on. "So, jealous Madam finds out her sister is pregnant with John William's baby. They get married, since he's been widowed for over a decade. During this time, Madam is growing in her strength and learning new spells. She's making secret sacrifices to my father-"

Through the mask, Gia asked, "Your father?"

"Duh, the devil."

Gia nodded, and breathed even deeper into the mask. *What the fuck!*

"Anyway, she realizes her strength is growing with the younger sacrifices she does, but she's an idiot. Madam would actually get stronger by sacrificing other people who are innately evil or who are studying black magic who are not part of her coven. But, she ridiculously thinks she knows everything about black magic. Idiot," Ezmerelda says in annoyance. "So, she devises a plan. She would sacrifice Catherine's baby to the devil to be at the top of the coven.

"You see, John William and Catherine haven't even been studying the dark arts and growing in strength together because they're too busy fucking and waiting on their baby. Madam's jealousy overtakes her. She shapeshifts one night into Catherine and fucks John William... now she's addicted to him... Madam keeps doing it. She craves him like a drug, and the man is so damn fertile, he knocks up Madam too!"

"Is that where you come in?" Gia asked through the mask.

"Do I look like I would come from those two? Please, Gia. Pay attention." Gia nodded and pulled the mask down as she found herself swept up in the story of Madam betraying her own sister. "Catherine thinks her husband is disgusted by her, but she doesn't know how many times her own sister is screwing her husband. We're talking every single day, Madam finds a way to shapeshift and ride him."

Gia holds up a hand and grimaces. Hearing a six-year-old girl talk like this is way too creepy for Gia, even though she knows she's a demon.

"Okay... I get it. She's a horny little bitch."

"Right! So, as Catherine goes into labor, Madam is the only one allowed in the room. Madam's belly is swollen too, but in those empire-waisted dresses back then, no one knew she was pregnant with John William's baby. Catherine knows nothing because she hasn't *really* studied the dark arts before. No, not like Madam. She was itching for power.

"As she delivered the baby boy, and Catherine passed out from the pain, Madam slit the baby's throat, drinking his blood like a fucking vampire and saying that this is done in the name of my fa- err, the devil." Ezmerelda pauses and it is clear she is listening. "Suddenly, she's more powerful than she's ever imagined she could be. Madam heals the baby's throat. Cleans her face and mouth of the blood, and lays the dead infant in her sister's arms. She calls in John William to tell him the bad news."

Gia felt sick to her stomach, as it began roiling.

"She drank the baby's blood?" she asked disgustedly.

"Yup," Ezmerelda replied, "in the name of the devil, and she gets high off of it, and her evil grows."

"I think I'm going to be sick."

Ezmerelda cocked her head, and a trash bin appeared at Gia's feet.

"Puke in that, but you need to know the rest of the story." Gia nodded and brought the bin onto her lap. "So, as all of this is going on, Mr. McCallister is calling for the killer of his son to be found, even going to the courts of Queen Mary, where my mother has shapeshifted as one of her ladies-in-waiting. Queen Mary agrees that the killer must be found. My mother tells the Queen that it sounds like witchcraft. Once Queen Mary heard that, all the females were to be looked at and investigated, again not knowing men could be witches as well." Ezmerelda pauses to sneeze, grabbing a tissue out of thin air.

Gia doesn't even think twice as she responded with, "God bless you." She watched as Ezmerelda's face shriveled up in rage. "Shit, sorry! My bad!"

Ezmerelda adjusted herself in the seat, finally looking like she wasn't going to have her head start spinning.

"Never say that again," she whispered angrily.

"Sorry. It's just... automatic when someone sneezes."

"ENOUGH!" The flames shot out of the fireplace. "It's bad enough you are wearing the cross, the evil eye, and you have holy water and two protection stones on you..." she was seething, "but to bless me with... the 'G' word! That's just cruel!"

Ezmerelda looked like she could use the oxygen tank as she tried to calm down. Gia didn't realize she was shaking, or that she had subconsciously grabbed the cross and began praying, putting a white protective light around herself.

Ezmerelda shook her hands in front of her eyes.

"Ugh, enough! I can't deal with that brightness. I am not here to hurt you, so just calm the fuck down, Gia. Relax. Mother and I lost our tempers at that hideous blessing… I cannot and will not hurt you because by the end of the story, you'll see why I need your help so desperately, I'm willing to work with a white witch."

Gia took a few deep breaths before requesting, "Can you just… try to ease down the evilness? I won't lie to you either. You're *really* freaking me out."

Ezmerelda breathed in and out.

"Our apologies," she said calmly. "Now, back to Madam. So, she confronts John William that she's pregnant with his baby. He doesn't believe her until she shapeshifts into Catherine right in front of him. Only when she is Catherine do they go at it like rabbits, which gives Madam an idea. She decides to turn her sister in as a murdering witch because she doesn't mind shapeshifting into Catherine, just so long as John William can be hers forever.

"Poor Catherine is in mourning when the authorities come for her. She's in her nightgown when they drag her and tie her to the post. They burn her at the stake, Madam watching the entire time. She held Catherine's gaze as the fire engulfed her, and even though it breaks her heart that her younger sister is now dead because of her, she doesn't care. All she wants and hungers for is John William.

"Madam doesn't want her sister to walk the afterworld alone as a blind, deaf mute, so she and John William perform the ceremony on Catherine's heart, to ensure she has her rightful place in hell." Ezmerelda pauses and leans forward. "Huge mistake! My mother was able to show her what was going on right under her nose. Catherine has wanted revenge for over five hundred and fifty years. Thanks to my mother, she can get her revenge with your help."

"Whoa, whoa, whoa, WHOA!" Gia interjected, amazed that she was actually having a conversation with a demon girl. "What happened to Madam's baby?"

"Ah, yes. So, she goes into labor, and Madam can't shapeshift while she's in that much pain. John William demands to see Catherine, but Madam is in so much agony that she can't become the woman he truly loves. This breaks Madam's heart because she realizes she has never truly had him. It's only when she is Catherine that he pays her any notice. She's a phony, and as he went to leave her, she picked up one of the heaviest skillet pans, and with all the rage and evil inside of her, she bashed it onto the back of his head, killing him instantly.

"Madam freaks out, and quickly cuts out his heart, putting it in a cup and saying the spell to release his soul to hell. She then asks the devil to help her ascend to hell. My father comes through and tells her she *can* be his Wife and sit among his other wives, but she must first sacrifice her baby to him, and then create her own coven. Another part of the deal was Madam must then complete the crown of jewels, symbolizing the babies she would sacrifice in his name. Once she completed the entire crown of jewels, she would ascend to hell among his other wives.

"At that moment, he sends Ibetsam, you knew as Beth, to help her during the delivery. Beth helps deliver Madam's healthy baby boy. Still bleeding and weak after childbirth, Madam slices her own son's neck open to sacrifice him to the devil, as she drinks his blood to grow in her own strength. The crown appears in front of her and the first jewel, a diamond, is sealed into the crown.

"Throughout the centuries, Madam's coven and power has grown. She made an error in the 1960's, which almost cost her the crown. My father does not believe in errors, so this last sacrifice, your baby, will complete the crown and let her go to hell where she will be held in high esteem for the sacrifices and finally be reunited with her loverboy, John William.

"*But* I need to stop this from happening. She deserves the fate of walking the earth as the other witches that have been damned over the thousands of years. She fucked with me, and now she needs to pay. Plus, I'm your only way to stop her from sacrificing your son."

"Which son?" Gia asked, perplexed.

"What?"

"Charlotte is pregnant with twin boys."

Ezmerelda cackled and cackled and then cackled some more as she clapped her hands together, and the golden eye grew brighter.

"Oh, I knew she did something different. She sees Charlotte as the reincarnation of her sister Catherine. She wants to leave Charlotte with one son before she leaves the earth. What a fucking softie!"

Gia finally threw up in the bin on her lap. A napkin was waiting for her in mid-air, as she stood up and wiped her mouth.

"I'm going to kill that bitch right now!"

As Gia stomped to the door, it slammed in her face.

"What the fuck?" The door handle wouldn't work as she tried to open it. She whirled around, angrily. "Open the damn door!"

Ezmerelda smiled and asked simply, "Care to make a deal with the devil's daughter?"

Chapter 17

Gia paused mid-pull on the door and slowly turned to face the young girl who had stood up and was now gazing into the fireplace.

"You cannot defeat Madam, or protect your son on your own. I cannot defeat Madam on my own, since she's my father's wife. She's off limits… at least to me."

Confusion was etched over Gia's face as she demanded, "What are you trying to say?"

Ezmerelda sighed wearily.

"We have to join forces, which is *not* something we're supposed to do. My mother did this before, and she's still paying the price for it in hell for trying to grow stronger than my father."

Gia knew where this was going. She stepped forward hesitantly.

"You want to join our blood together."

"Yes. It goes against the natural order of a white witch to share the blood of a black witch, let alone a demon."

Gia watched the weariness etch across Ezmerelda's face, and suddenly, she appeared much older than six. She looked like a woman on the threshold of something she didn't want to endure.

"You don't want to do this either, do you?"

Ezmerelda still gazed into the fire as she responded resolutely, "I know the consequences if we unite, and I also know the consequences if we don't unite our blood. Either way, they both suck for us. I'm just trying to go for the option that is the best." She paused and looked at Gia, her eyes were sad and both were a light, dull green. "I need to tell you the truth and let you determine your own fate."

Gia kept hearing the voices of her ancestors telling her not to share her blood with this demon, but the protective part of her needed to know how she could ensure both Charlotte and both boys not being sacrificed by Madam.

She sat down in the chair, shockingly composed as she said, "Tell me."

Ezmerelda nodded.

"The easiest option is obviously not to share our blood. What would happen is one of your sons would be sacrificed, leaving your wife devastated and suicidal. She could even enter postpartum psychosis, hallucinating and perhaps harming herself or the one remaining baby.

She's very sensitive… I saw how her brain is very susceptible to pain. Her neurons aren't firing through the synapses correctly. On my end, pig would join my father and live the rest of eternity in her glories as one of the beloved and revered wives of my father. She would have the love of her life back as well."

"Why do you hate her so much?"

Ezmerelda's eyes pierced Gia's.

"Because she tried to punish me through torture to make me one of her pawns. The hatred I have for *Madam* is from my inner core especially when I was shown who she really was, and what she's done." She paused to take a deep breath and sank down into the chair across from Gia's. "I have seen the misery she has caused. I have met the people whose lives she has ruined by her own selfishness. She doesn't respect the coven; Madam is selfish and cruel."

"But, your father is the devil and your mother is an Egyptian demon goddess… I would think you would love Madam for her cruelty."

Ezmerelda barked out a laugh.

"There's evil, like me, but the source of it comes from justice. I only harm Madam and her witches because they sought to keep me away from my mother. One can sacrifice evil and gain as much power and glory for themselves and my father as they can from sacrificing a newborn baby." Ezmerelda shook her head. "Madam *chose* to sacrifice these babies, so my father continued it. He actually prefers the evil humans… the power from their evil and the sacrifice of sending them to hell is just as powerful, if not more, for my father and his wives, as it is from the sacrifice of a newborn baby."

"How many wives does… umm, your father have?"

"Madam made it an even 666."

Gia's eyebrows flew up into her hairline.

"And Madam doesn't have to sacrifice newborns?"

"Exactly. She gets off on it since she went insane back in the 1550's. It's quite revolting."

Gia crossed her arms and questioned, "So let me get this straight. You… your mother… other evil entities, don't approve of Madam sacrificing newborns?"

Ezmerelda thought for a moment before factually stating, "We don't disapprove, because it's a sacrifice to garner more power, but we're not fans of it when she could be hunting down true evil… that's where the power is. If you take someone who has murdered people, especially a sick serial killer… Gia, I swear that power when you sacrifice them and drink their blood is like electricity from lightning. A newborn is like getting a shock putting in a light bulb."

"Fuck me," Gia whispered. "I'm ready to beat the shit out of Madam or pig or whatever she is. She is *choosing* this specific sacrifice because she wants to kill *babies*! I could fucking rip her eyeballs out and shove them down her fucking throat!"

Ezmerelda smiled and nodded.

"So, I'm guessing you don't care for the first option, in which we do nothing and let Madam live her life filled with pleasure for the rest of eternity?"

"I want to make her suffer and walk the earth deaf, blind, and mute, like you said. She deserves an eternity of horror and loneliness!"

Ezmerelda watched Gia get up from her chair and pace the full length of her bedroom.

She sighed and said, "Well, since I have to be honest with you before you make your decision, option number two isn't so great either."

Gia paused her frantic pacing, and glared down at Ezmerelda.

"Will it make Madam *never* see happiness and join your father? And her true love?"

"Yes, but-"

"Then what are you waiting for? Let's do this."

Ezmerelda's left eye shifted back to gold.

"My mother said we cannot until I tell you what will happen by us sharing our blood. She's done it before, and it's not easy on the white witch or on the demon."

"I don't care! I want Madam to suffer!" Gia yelled in fury.

Ezmerelda cocked her head, and with a quick sweep, Gia landed softly on the chair she had bolted from in anger.

"We're going to need you to calm the fuck down first and listen."

Gia was still stunned that she *flew* and was now sitting in a chair!

"How did you-"

Ezmerelda waved her hand away.

"Please, that's an old parlor trick. Now, promise me that you will listen to everything that will happen to us if we share our blood to take down Madam."

Gia sat forward and relented, "Yes, I'm listening."

"First off, we do a binding ceremony. We slice open our forearms, put our open flesh onto each others' and we bind it with a ceremonial piece of satin from ancient Egypt. That's to hold us together as we endure the binding spell. As my mother told me, it will burn. It'll burn so badly you're going to wish you were dead. Naturally, we will want to rip away from each other, and fight the binding because it goes against the natural blood in our veins."

"Okay, then what?" Gia asked, ready to do the binding ceremony with their blood.

"In the spell, we will bind ourselves together from now until Easter at 11:59 PM, Easter Standard Time. You will have my blood coursing through you, and I will have your blood coursing through me. We will be able to hear each other in our minds... but the worst part is, you will have evil in you and I will have goodness in me." Ezmerelda physically shook at the thought as if she was instantly thrust into frigid temperatures. "You may find yourself unable to wear your cross or go into church without feeling like you're burning or wanting to vomit. I will feel everything you feel, and vice versa. So, if I'm torturing someone at home, you'll have a desire to harm someone as well."

"Well, don't torture anyone," Gia said with her usual pinched face.

"That's like telling you not to protect or love your wife and unborn babies. It's my instinct to torture."

Gia sat back and breathed out, saying, "Okay... so far this part is freaking me out."

"Yeah, well, it's no prize for me either. This has to be kept hidden from everyone. If I'm damned to the part of hell where my mother is for doing this same exact thing, your soul comes with me."

Gia gulped.

"And if I die... like getting shot or something?"

Ezmerelda fought the urge to vomit, as she croaked out, "I'd go with you to heaven."

They sat there staring at each other.

"This is a lot to take in." Gia had to let her mind wrap around everything Ezmerelda had just told her. Very slowly and cautiously, she said, "So, I'll have to fight the evil in my blood, and we both cannot die, or we'll be doomed together. Then, we can't have anyone find out about this-"

Ezmerelda interrupted to correct her.

"Mainly Madam and her coven. That could lead to my father sending us both to hell."

Gia shook her head, trying to ease her fear before asking, "What else? I feel like there has to be more at stake."

"Well, on the bright side, you'll have my powers and energy."

Gia actually laughed.

"Oh good! I'll be able to move things around and make furniture appear out of nowhere."

Ezmerelda leaned forward, her eyes hypnotic.

"My power is unlike any you could ever imagine. Never joke about it."

Gia's smile faded abruptly.

"Alright. We're united and then on Easter, when this is all going to go down, what happens?"

Ezmerelda shook her head, fearing Gia was not getting how serious this was.

"Gia, for the next four months, you're literally going to be tortured, just as I am. You're going to want to crawl out of your skin or kill people with such aggressiveness, you might not be able to refrain from harming someone because my blood is *that* evil. I'm going to want to rip the goodness out of me. I don't think you recognize how life-altering and brutal this is going to be." Ezmerelda sighed heavily and collapsed in a heap into the back of the chair. "And the worst part for me is, I will actually love and want to protect your family members and friends, ensuring that nothing happens to Charlotte and the twins on Easter Sunday... apparently, as my mother explains it, my devotion and... instincts of evil will shift when I'm near them. I'll feel... love. Whatever that feels like, my mother made it sound like poison," Ezmerelda visibly gagged at the thought.

Gia saw the sadness and fear weigh on her little shoulders.

"Then why do this?"

"Because if I can protect your son from being sacrificed, which I will apparently protect him with every fiber of my being, it will ensure that Madam has her heart ripped out and eaten or thrown into the flames of the fireplace Madam will most likely have on..." Ezmerelda shook her head. "The terror you feel about having evil in you is the same terror I have about having your goodness in me."

"So, will I want to protect your mother? And care about the devil?"

Ezmerelda laughed and her short legs swung back and forth as she delightedly said, "Oh, Gia. We don't have those feelings like you humans do! We just crave the hunt and kill. We live to cause misery for people and inflict torturous pain. That's what will spook you out the most."

"Great," Gia mumbled. "So tell me what happens on Easter Sunday."

"You and I will take care of the remaining witches in the coven, ensuring we're not found out about. We must be in the delivery room, and keep Madam from sacrificing your firstborn son. I'm being told you have two close friends who can help?"

"How did you know- right, your mother is an all-knowing demon. Yeah, it's Riley and Ziggy."

Ezmerelda raised an eyebrow.

"Interesting names for humans... Anyway, you will rip out Madam's heart and toss it into the fireplace."

"ME? I can't do that!" Gia cried out in disgust.

"Well, *I* can't do it because I am not allowed to rip her heart out and destroy it. She's the wife of my father, but you can. And you'll be pumping full of evil as you do it, so you're going to want to do more than just rip her heart out... trust me."

Gia put her head in her hands. She was torn. Every instinct was telling her to run away, but her morals and protective instincts to stop this insane witch and save her sons and Charlotte... well, four months of evil in her veins couldn't be that bad. She was still a white witch with powerful ancestors flowing through her veins.

"So, after Madam is taken care of-"

Ezmerelda finally smiled, saying, "She'll walk the earth for all eternity cursed!"

"The babies will be safe? And so will Charlotte?" Gia asked with a pleading look in her dull, brown eyes.

"Yup... and when the clock strikes midnight, you and I will vomit out the goodness and darkness. We'll be released from each other, and you'll never see me again. We both get what we want."

Gia was strong; she knew she could handle this.

"Okay, I'm in."

Ezmerelda shook her head, leaning forward and strongly stating, "You need to think about this. I'm not kidding. My mother was damned to the worst parts of hell after she had tried this with a white witch for a day! If we're found out-"

"We won't be."

"You have to be careful around Madam… she senses shit like a fucking bloodhound. I think you should ease back from her, and let Charlotte spend time with her alone."

"Hell no!"

"You have to trust me on this. Let them bond. Madam sees her as the reincarnation of Catherine. Plus, she's going to sniff out the fact that you're not wearing holy water or the cross and having the stones with you. I think you should back off, and let Charlotte go alone to her appointments. You'll be busy simply trying to live with the evil inside of you."

Gia didn't like this, but she understood that if Madam knew she had the blood of Ezmerelda, she could easily rat them out, and they'd both be damned to hell.

"Okay. I'll miss some appointments, but not all of them because that'll be a red flag to Mdadam."

"Okay."

A strong surge of wind came through as an Egyptian woman flowed from Ezmerelda and stepped in front of the fireplace.

"Oh shit!"

Gia couldn't tear her eyes away from someone who was as gorgeous as Cleopatra. This was definitely Ezmerelda's mother. She wore a white gown, massive gold jewelry around her neck with Lapis stones adorned everywhere. Her gold eyes were highlighted by the thick dark charcoal eyeliner. Her dark brown hair was perfectly straight, along with her posture.

The demon goddess looked at Gia and said in a strong accent stated, "I am Isfet. I shall be performing the ceremony."

Suddenly, there was a massive dagger in the demon's hands as both Gia and Ezmerelda rolled up their sleeves. The fleshy part of their forearms was sliced open, and the demon swiftly binded their forearms together as she said something in Egyptian… maybe Latin?

Gia eyed Ezmerelda and could see the fear in her eyes.

Then it happened. The searing burning through both of their bodies began swiftly. As they went to scream, the Egyptian demon flicked her index finger, and they were suddenly muted as she continued her gibberish.

Gia felt the burning etching through every cell, vein and pour in her body. She looked at Ezmerelda and saw her silently screaming. The look of terror in her eyes scared the shit out of Gia, but she probably had the same look. The burning was relentless. It felt like she was on fire on the inside of her body, and Gia, did in fact, pray for death.

191

Gia looked down at her hands and saw them smoking. The holy water! She then saw Ezmerelda's hands smoking too. She felt the burn of the evil eye and Miss Sophie's cross, as did Ezmerelda. Gia surged to strangle the Egyptian demon, but she had finished the ceremony, released the binding, and their mutism.

Wash your fucking hands, Gia!

I know, you little bitch!

She raced to the attached bathroom and moved swiftly to get the holy water off of her hands.

As she breathed out a sigh of relief, so did Ezmerelda, until she screamed, *The necklaces! Fuck Gia, my chest is on fire!*

You don't think mine is too!

Get them the fuck off of us!

Gia shakily worked to unclasp both of them and shoved them into her coat pocket.

I still feel sick, Ezmerelda said, gagging. *Throw that shit away, and the stones too.*

That's a hard no on that one! she screamed.

Gia felt the angry evil, but she also felt the lovingness throughout her towards Miss Sophie.

Alright, I get it, Ezmerelda said, but when Gia looked up in the mirror, she didn't see her lips move.

Ezmerelda stared back at Gia's reflection in the mirror.

Are you hearing my thoughts?

Gia bit back a scream, and in her mind, she replied, *Yeah... are you hearing my thoughts?*

Duh, dummy!

Wow, this is cool.

Gia suddenly felt summoned, and she and Ezmerelda moved to stand back in front of the Egyptian demon. She yanked both of their arms towards her with such severity, Gia wanted to slap her. Then, the demon tapped their open wounds, and Gia and Ezmerelda were instantly healed from the deep slash that would have needed at least one hundred stitches.

"You must go downstairs now. Make sure, Apopis, you keep Madam on her toes. Here's what you're going to do."

******

As advised by Isfet, the two left separately. Gia quickly hurried to the carolers, feeling the energy of love and also evil. She already felt like she was split in two. Since she was so short, Charlotte wouldn't have noticed her absence.

Ezmerelda was able to maneuver her way towards Madam, who was still playing at the piano.

Gia moved around the back of the room, and she caught sight of herself in the large mirror above the fireplace. She looked… refreshed. Her eyes were brighter and a lighter shade of shit brown. Everything looked brighter and shinier on her, even her mousy brown hair. Gia panicked and spoke inside of her mind.

I look pretty, Ezmerelda! What the hell is going on!

That's the nice part from being a demon or a black witch. We're all gorgeous. Haven't you noticed all of Madam's coven always looking beautiful?

Yes… but won't this be a dead giveaway to Madam that we've shared each other's blood?

She saw and felt Ezmerelda looking at her.

You just look less tired and haggard. You're fine! Stop freaking out!

Do you feel that split inside of you… like, you can pick up on the good and evil energies coursing through the crowd?

Yup, and I hate the good energy. I feel sick to my core.

Me too. There's so much evil in here!

Madam finished playing "Deck the Halls," and announced it was time for dessert, tea and coffee. There was a round of applause as Madam stood and took a bow.

"Thank you, thank you, but it was all of you carolers who really brought the songs to life!"

Man she can lay it on thick, Gia thought as she headed over to Charlotte's chair.

No shit. If I could have killed her by now, I would have.

Gia smiled and Charlotte looked up, surprise flashing over her joy-filled face.

"Gia… you look… rested!"

"What can I say, my darling Charlotte? This impromptu singing has put me in great spirits!"

"I can see that!" Charlotte asked, "Would you mind helping me out of this chair? I think my ass fell asleep," she whispered. "Where were you hiding?"

Gia shrugged.

"I was stuck in the back. It sucks to be short."

Gia winked at Charlotte as she embraced her in a tight hug. This was her goodness. This was her joy and positive energy she needed to focus on.

As they walked around the dining room table, picking and choosing desserts, Charlotte paused and smiled. She grabbed Gia's hand and placed it on her stomach.

"They're kicking like crazy!"

"Wow," Gia said in utter awe. "This is amazing!"

She went inside of her mind, and let Ezmerelda know to get the plan going, making sure Madam was nearby.

Ezmerelda was there in an instant.

Her thought back was, *I am disgusted by how much I have these emotions of love over the twins and Charlotte. This is a horrible feeling!*

"May I feel your *baby* move?" Ezmerelda asked loudly, catching the ear of Madam, whose eyes sliced through the crowd.

She's on her way, Ezmerelda, so make it good!

I'm the evil one here, not you! Shut up and let me work!

Charlotte smiled down at the beautiful young girl, hoping to have a daughter someday.

Delightedly, Charlotte announced, "Actually, we're having twins!"

Ezmerelda put on a surprised face.

"*Twins!*" she all but shouted. "That's amazing! May I feel them move?"

As she asked this she turned to face Madam, who was about five feet away. She gave her the creepiest grin, as she now let Madam know that she knew her secret.

Charlotte, not realizing what the hell was happening, happily obliged.

"They're really kicking. Probably from all of this sugar!" Charlotte said excitedly.

As Ezmerelda placed her hands on Charlotte's large bump, Madam's eyes grew wide, as she scurried over when she saw a glimpse of the gold eye shine through.

"Oh wow," Charlotte said quietly. "That's odd. They both stopped moving."

Madam tried to hide her panic.

"What's that? The babies aren't moving anymore?"

Charlotte laughed.

"I guess your daughter has the power to put babies to sleep." Charlotte paused and looked down at Ezmerelda, who was smiling up at her. "I'm going to need you to stay with us after the boys are born! You have the magic touch!"

"Boys!" Ezmerelda exclaimed. "I would love to help you!"

Madam strung her hands together in a panic.

"Perhaps I should get my stethoscope? It's quite odd for them both to suddenly stop moving."

Ezmerelda released her hands from Charlotte, and the twins began moving.

"Oh, there they go again! These boys are going to be little hellions!"

Ezmerelda smiled, and thought, *This fucking sucks. I hate this protective and loving feeling I have towards your wife and unborn boys!*

How do you think I feel? I'm literally trying not to rip out Madam's heart right now! And why do I want to eat her heart as it's still pumping?

Patience, Gia. Just keep that evil energy in check. I don't know what your powers are from me, so we can't let them show now in front of Madam!

Madam pulled Ezmerelda away and said, "Excuse us."

She swiftly moved the girl into the massive kitchen where the coven was gathering the coffee and tea to be served with the desserts.

"You little brat. What the hell did you do?"

Ezmerelda's eyes gleamed.

"I know your secret, pig. You've gone soft, trying to leave this Charlotte person with at least one son. I won't let that happen. She'll be left with no children by the time I finish my curse on her," Ezmerelda hissed with fury, even though this was part of the plan.

Madam shook Ezmerelda's shoulders in hatred and anger. She had taken enough from this demon child already.

"Don't you dare!"

Ezmerelda cocked her head to the side, flinging Madam up to the ceiling.

"Pig, you're going to watch the reincarnation of Catherine suffer… again. And they'll *both* be your fault!"

She dropped Madam to the ground and headed out towards the living room.

Madam gasped, yelling out, "What do mean by them both being my fault?"

Ezmerelda paused at the doorway and grinned at a desperate looking Madam, who was still on the ground on all fours like a dog.

"You stupid, pig. Did you really think Catherine wouldn't find out about your betrayals?"

Ezmerelda left the kitchen laughing hysterically, as Madam vomited on the floor.

Chapter 18

It had only been a few days, and already Gia felt like she wanted to rip her fucking brain out. The horrific, evil thoughts of things she was always on the verge of doing, made her hole up inside of her office. She ignored the calls and texts from Riley and Ziggy.

Ziggy's last text stated: *You did it :(My mother told me! We need to get together ASAP!*

Riley's latest text of twenty was also blunt: *I'm working with you on New Year's Eve - you can't ignore me forever!*

Gia rubbed her head. It was New Year's Eve, so she anticipated being busy at work, which would be a nice distraction. After she took a shower and got ready, she walked into the living room. Marty, Diane and Charlotte were watching the New Year's Eve celebrations occurring around the world.

Gia smiled and kissed Charlotte and her baby bump twice.

"Happy New Year, my three loves."

Charlotte stifled a yawn, replying sleepily, "Happy New Year, my little hobbit."

Gia looked at Marty and Diane and wished them each a happy new year as well. They seemed as exhausted as Charlotte, but Gia was glad they were here for her wife.

At work, Gia sat at her desk, going through the case file on Dawson Banks. He was a 22-year-old society kid. He'd also been the one Gia and Dean had been hunting for the rapes and murders of five prostitutes. His mommy and daddy were New York socialites, and Gia had to make the case airtight before she brought the kid in to formally press charges. Yes, Dawson Banks would soon feel her wrath. His calling card was leaving a massive bite mark on the inner thighs of his victims.

"Idiot," Gia murmured.

He also never wore a condom, so Riley had been working hard, once Gia and Dean received the subpoena for Dawson's dental records and medical records. Dean had called her on her cell phone to let Gia know that Riley had definitely matched Dawson's dental records to the bite marks on the prostitutes.

They also had his DNA match from a previous incident that happened when he "allegedly raped" a thirteen-year-old girl at a party when he was just fifteen. The young, hispanic girl had courageously come in after going through the horrific trials of getting the rape kit done at the hospital. The Banks family had lawyered up, and the case was never brought to court. Gia heard the family had paid off the girl with a million dollar hush hush settlement. Chump change to the

Banks family, and that poor girl would never be the same, reliving that night over and over again.

Gia felt her blood boil as she looked through every piece of evidence they had against this rich bastard. The evil was definitely searing through her as she saw Dean walking towards her, and she immediately sprang up.

"Do we have him?"

"Yep. He's in interrogation room one."

"I'm going."

"Hey, Carter, you know he's going to lawyer up. It's going to be the same as it was seven years ago."

Gia glared harshly at Dean, who shrank back, even though he was a full foot taller than her.

"No, it's not." She ruthlessly snatched her files from her desk and looked back at Dean. "Are you coming?"

Dean swiftly followed as they entered interrogation room number one. The conversation was being watched and recorded.

Gia walked in first and sat down, Dean following her lead. Gia just stared at the most disgusting piece of shit in front of her. He had on a cocky grin, with his arms crossed over his large chest. He had the look and energy of white supremacy, considering he only killed hispanic and black hookers. His blonde hair was cut perfectly, and his blue eyes were shifty. It was obvious he worked out. That would make it much easier to overpower a woman who would fight back, and many of them did with his skin underneath their fingernails.

He grinned slyly before mockingly stating, "Detectives. It's so good to see you both *again*."

Gia opened up the files with the crime scene photos.

"Cut the shit, Dawson. We have the evidence from your dental records… you see these bite marks? Huh? Your little calling card? They match your fucking dental records."

Dawson shrugged and innocently claimed, "Someone could have made a mold from my teeth," he said with a preening smile.

Gia narrowed her eyes. Oh, the evil was flowing through her so fiercely, she wanted to slash his throat.

"We also have DNA from the victims who were able to fight back, as well as the semen you left over. It's pretty stupid to not wear a condom nowadays," Gia fired back.

Again, the stupid shrug and cocky smile.

"I'm not saying anything without my lawyer."

"Fine. You've already been formally charged with the rapes and murders of five young women. You'll be held in your very own little cell downstairs until your lawyer shows up. Pleasure doing business with you… *again,*" Gia sputtered out venomously.

Gia strode away at such a swift speed, she had a feeling she might be flying. Remembering Ezmerelda's warning that she would have powers from her demon blood, Gia walked slower, with Dean on her heels.

"He's going to find a way to get away with this, Carter," Dean said softly.

"We have evidence! Literal evidence of his teeth and DNA. You can't fight that!"

"You know his parents will call in the slimiest lawyer, and he'll get off with something minor."

Gia was fuming as she yelled, "NO, HE WON'T!"

The documents on her desk fluttered, and she immediately hurried into Riley's office, hoping no one had seen some supernatural shit just then, brought on by her palpable evil that was lashing out from her insides.

"There you are! What the fuck did you do? Ziggy and I have been worried sick about you. We need-"

Gia held up a hand.

"Please, I'm begging you to just stop talking." Gia breathed out, trying to calm herself, as she paced Riley's office. "I just saw that Dawson Banks bastard. He's going to lawyer up. Fuck!"

"Hey, we've got evidence against the fucker. I'm going to testify, and he *will* pay."

Gia stormed back and forth, feeling a surging category five hurricane building within her.

"Yeah, he'll pay, but he'll pay himself right into freedom." Gia finally sat on one of the metal stools. "The thing that gets me is these women have suffered, even that thirteen-year-old girl whose innocence he stole away… Dawson will get nothing of what these women endured! I wish he could have his fucking small dick ripped off, with his stupid, wrinkled balls, and bleed out. Let him feel their pain, that son of a bitch!"

Riley sat back and stared at Gia, stating carefully, "Look, I get that this case is personal. That young girl... the five women... no one deserves that." Riley paused until Gia was looking directly into her eyes. "You didn't deserve that."

Gia swiped angrily at tears that were coming way too easily to the surface.

She whispered, "The men have no idea what they do to us... for the rest of my life, that awful night in November will fucking haunt me. Do you think that piece of shit even thinks about me? Fuck, no. Yet I'm the one who will be haunted. I'm the one who will relive that nightmare for the rest of my fucking life!"

Riley tried to offer comforting words, but all she could say is, "I know."

"NO! YOU DON'T KNOW!" Gia swiped at more angry tears. "That was over twenty years ago, and I still... fuck therapy. That never helped. Fuck it all. Do you know he made Sergeant in his precinct? I mean, who does that to one of their fellow cadets? Oh, he was going to show me what I was missing out on, being a lesbian. I wish the same fate for him as that fucking evil bastard, Dawson Banks!"

Riley cleared her throat.

"I'm sorry, Carter. I really am."

"You know what? So am I. I saw myself in that girl. I saw how she would never be the same. Maybe she would turn to drugs or alcohol, just to numb the self-hatred... wonder what she did wrong for the rest of her life. Maybe she'd-"

The door swung open, startling Gia and Riley.

"Jesus, Dean! What the fuck!" Riley yelled, more out of being startled than being angry.

"It's Banks. He's dead!"

"What?" Gia and Riley responded, but they were both on their feet, racing down the stairs to the lockup cells, refusing to wait for the elevator.

Dean was winded, before he could say, "I don't know where he got the knife!"

Riley gasped when she reached the cell, and Gia felt a warm glow filling throughout her body.

There was the once smug Dawson Banks... his pants pulled down to his ankles, and his penis and balls thrown across the room. It was clear they had hit the wall, slid down, leaving three bloody marks, and those pieces of anatomy, that had caused so much pain and destruction, now lay in a pathetic heap on the floor.

Gia looked back at Dawson, his eyes wide open, his mouth in mid-scream. The blood loss was incredible… he was dead, and yet the blood kept piling up and spilling over onto the cement floor.

Riley whispered, "Oh my God."

Gia felt herself spasm a little at the name of God. She focused now on this pathetic, dickless creature.

"Where's the knife?"

One of the patrol guys replied, "I can't find it anywhere, Carter."

"Alright, let's pull up the footage and see what the hell happened."

As Gia gave orders, she had to fight her grin. She struggled not to feel the evil sending surges of victory and strength throughout her entire being. She loved seeing this. Gia was elated inside. *So this is what Ezmerelda feels like when she tortures or kills someone. I feel so alive!*

"Detective, the footage is… black. For about a minute, there's nothing, and then it comes back on to show him lying there like he is now… I don't know how this happened."

Gia looked at everyone.

"So, what we're saying is, we have no footage of how he did this? We have no knife. What the fuck did he do, just rip it off himself?"

Riley had tip-toed her way into the crime scene and looked at the parts on the floor.

"Yup. Ripped right off."

Gia looked at Riley, avoiding the mens' responses of hurt faces as they all seemed to protect their dicks by placing their hands by their crotches.

"Did he do it, or was there someone down here?"

Riley looked at his hands, both bloody and replied somberly, "From what I can see… this was self-inflicted by Dawson ripping off his own genitalia."

Again, the men winced and said things like, "Damn!" or "I think I'm gonna be sick."

Riley and Gia were the only two who were no longer looking at the corpse. Riley stared at Gia, and Gia stared right back. The message was clear… Gia had wished for this to happen, and somehow, it came true.

******

Gia raced into the upstairs women's bathroom, checking under the stalls. No one else was in there with her. She braced her hands on either side of the white sink. Gia looked up in the mirror and it looked like her face had been dipped in the fountain of youth. Her face was glowing… her skin was perfect, with no lines or bags under her eyes… and her eyes were lit up like sparklers on the 4th of July. Gia couldn't contain her smile. It kept widening, and her eyes turned more glorious and beautiful.

Suddenly, Charlotte's face went through her mind… and her future sons. Her smile faded immediately as the good part of her was coming through.

Gia finally recognized what had happened, as if coming out of a trance.

Immediately, she whispered out loud, "Ezmerelda!" She waited and then said it louder, "Ezmerelda!"

With a massive gust of air, the girl appeared behind her in the mirror. She was clapping softly and the smile on her face was utterly wicked.

"How did that feel?"

Gia turned to face her, realizing that she had just murdered Dawson Banks.

"I didn't do anything! I just wished for-"

"Did you see it happen in your mind when you wished for it? Did you feel your blood pulsating with evil?"

Gia nodded and whispered, "Yes, I did."

Ezmerelda sighed happily.

"Well, apparently the power you have inherited is when you get all fired up and nasty thoughts swarm around, and you say your intention out loud for the person, it actually happens. Well done, my evil blood sister."

Gia shook her head, resolutely replying, "Ezmerelda, no. This is not happening!"

"Oh stop it! Didn't you feel glorious when you saw him dickless and his balls thrown across the room like two shriveled pieces of dog shit? Didn't you feel that energy of darkness delight every sense and pore in your entire being?"

Gia gulped, still feeling the rush in her body.

"Yes… and I loved it."

Ezmerelda's smile grew wider and her eyes brighter.

"Then we know what your power is. When you want revenge, when you crave it so badly that you become like a junkie looking for his next hit… you can make things happen with your mind."

"I… I can't have this… this… power. I can't do this! I want to rip my damn brain out of my head!"

"Oh shut the fuck up, and stop being such a little bitch! Do you think it's easy for me to feel these… feelings of," she choked back vomit, "love and caring and wanting to protect everyone you care about? This fucking sucks for me too! I'm a demon! I don't want these damn feelings! So, just settle your ass down. For four months, you and I can suck it up!"

"The allure of killing for justice and revenge is so… well, it's like it's vibrating in me right now. I just want to feed that craving."

Ezmerelda's smile faded swiftly as she realized Gia was taking to the evilness a little too casually.

"Gia, I need you to relax right now." Ezmerelda looked concerned. "You need to focus on the good in you. You have to focus on Charlotte, the boys, Riley, Ziggy, Marty, and Diane. Remember, don't close the door on Riley and Ziggy. They're going to help you keep your good side open. It's exceedingly too effortless to be overpowered by the evil side."

Gia looked Ezmerelda dead in the eyes as she asked her, "Did you feel what I felt?"

The girl nodded and smiled, before she left in a wake of wind that tossed Gia's hair up.

"What the hell was that?" Gia gasped and turned to see Riley enter the bathroom and shut the door.

Her dark green eyes were wide with curiosity and fear.

"Seriously, what the fuck just happened? You said it, but you never left me… how did that happen?"

Gia wished Ezmerelda had stuck around, so she could explain this crazy, demonic blood, and how it makes a strong wish and desire come to fruition.

Gia whispered, "I don't know… apparently when I want something bad enough, the evil kind of bubbles over, and… uh, makes it happen."

"This is seriously fucked up! Ziggy and I are going to be at your place tomorrow." She paused, "And don't think I didn't notice you cringe every single damn time I came close to you with my cross and evil eye!"

Riley left the bathroom in a huff, and Gia took out her cell phone. It was a little after midnight. She texted Charlotte a happy new year and how this would be the year they became parents.

Gia sighed again and looked in the mirror.

To herself, she said, "Well, you've gone and done it… how are you going to get through the next four months without letting the evil take over? You're screwed. Big time."

She looked down at the sink and heard yells outside of the bathroom door. She went over to listen to the muffled cries of shock and panic.

"He's dead! His wife found him in his bathroom."

"Who?"

"Sergeant Robby O'Connor!"

Gia's eyes widened and she looked in the mirror. Her glow was back… her eyes lightened… she felt the bubbles of evil rippling through her veins. She had exacted her revenge on that rapist piece of shit, and oh, how amazing it felt to know he received the same horrific death as dear, sweet Dawson Banks.

Gia was bathing in the feeling of revenge when suddenly her palm slapped her across the face, extremely hard!

"Ouch! What the fuck!" she yelled out to no one.

Ezmerelda was inside her brain.

Stop it, right now! Pull yourself together. Good, you killed two rapists today. Now move on, and make sure you stay as positive as possible!

Gia replied inside of her mind, *Yeah, but I wish I was in his precinct, so I could see him dickless and-*

Her hand slapped her in the face again.

Gia, knock it off!

Gia rubbed the side of her cheek that had been bitch slapped twice and replied, *Yeah, I definitely need Ziggy and Riley.*

******

Charlotte waited for Gia to come home. It was all over the news about the deaths of Dawson Banks and Sergeant Robby O'Connor. Gia had texted to say she would be home late.

Gia also never told Charlotte that it was Robby O'Connor who had brutally raped her when they were in the police academy together.

Charlotte had the news on as she began taking ornaments off of the Christmas tree. She heard Gia come in and her keys and purse hit the kitchen island.

She hurried over, as quickly as she could.

"Oh my gosh. Are you okay?"

Charlotte bent down to hug Gia, the cross Gia had bought her for Christmas singed her shoulder.

Gia pulled away and replied shortly, "Yeah, I'm fine. Just tired."

"Of course you are! Can I make you something to eat?" Charlotte asked with concern in her voice.

Gia shrugged.

"I'm not really hungry. Riley and I ate some doughnuts a couple of hours ago. I just want to go to my office and do some work before Ziggy and Riley come over."

"Wait, you need sleep," Charlotte said with worry etched across her face. "Can't you see them when you haven't worked overtime?"

Gia swiped her hand in front of herself.

"Nah, it's fine." She walked into the living room and saw Charlotte was already taking down the Christmas ornaments. "You shouldn't be taking down the decorations. I know it's your family tradition with your parents, but I don't think I can help you today."

"No worries. My dad is coming over to help. I'm just taking down the ornaments, and the extra lights I put on."

Gia looked at the garland in the box and eyed her wife.

"Charlotte, you're not supposed to be standing on ladders. Your entire balance is off with the twins."

Charlotte smiled pleasantly and rubbed Gia's back.

"Unlike you, I don't need a ladder to reach the top of the tree."

Before Charlotte could tease her about being short, Gia went into the kitchen to grab her keys and headed to her office. She went to unlock it, but she furrowed her brow when she realized it was unlocked already.

"What the hell?" she bit out.

She entered her office and looked around. Maybe she had forgotten to lock it. As she made her way to her desk, she saw a book front and center before her. It was a baby naming book. Charlotte had been in here!

The fury came so swiftly that Gia felt the need for revenge. As her anger rose, she felt the evilness course through her veins. The bookshelves toppled over, and the paining on the wall of the couch flew to the other side of the room.

"CHARLOTTE!" she screamed, not recognizing her own voice.

Gia snatched the book up and stomped into the living room, where Charlotte paused mid-air taking down an ornament.

"What the fuck is this?" she demanded, breathing heavily.

Charlotte gently placed the ornament into the box.

"I bought it for us to look through. We haven't talked about baby names yet."

Gia glared at her furiously and hissed, "I mean, why the fuck did I find this in my office?"

Charlotte cleared her throat nervously.

"I noticed you didn't lock your office door, so I put the book on your desk... I didn't go through anything," she replied with a shaky voice.

Gia came closer, feeling a desperate and hungry desire to hurt Charlotte.

Gia seethed, "So what do you do? You check my office door every fucking day when I'm not home, just to see if it's unlocked?"

The questions were harsh and more like an accusation.

Charlotte's voice trembled as she said, "Sometimes I check the door. I just want to see what your office looks like. If it needs to be cleaned or-"

"STAY THE FUCK OUT OF MY OFFICE!"

Gia picked up the massive Christmas tree and threw it across the room, ornaments falling off and crashing to the ground. The artificial tree landed in a heap against the other side of the massive living room.

Charlotte began to cry, and Gia finally felt some semblance of control, but not a lot. She was furious that Charlotte had betrayed her. Gia went over to the Christmas tree and picked it up, with one hand, carrying it back to its spot in front of the large patio door.

Gia's angry bitterness was clear as she stated, "You can cry all you want, Charlotte, but you betrayed my trust. You're a fucking snoop. Don't you ever go into my office again!"

Gia stormed off and Charlotte jumped as she heard the door slam and other raucous noises from Gia's office. She sniffled and swiped at the tears. For the first time in her relationship with Gia, Charlotte was actually frightened of her own wife because her eyes had turned black as a starless and moonless night.

Chapter 19

Charlotte welcomed Ziggy and Riley into the apartment. She had already cried, and now she was putting on her happy hostess face, as her mother had trained her to do. Never mind that she saw pure hatred pointed at her from her own wife's evil, black eyes.

"Welcome, Ladies! Happy New Year! Can I get you anything to drink or eat?"

Riley and Ziggy gave the obligatory happy new year response and declined anything.

Charlotte's happy voice sounded forced, as she said, "Well, if you need anything, please don't hesitate to let me know. I'm… uhh, not supposed to go into Gia's office, so you'll have to come out and tell me if you need anything."

Ziggy's face scrunched up, as she saw pain around Charlotte.

"Are you doing okay?"

Charlotte plastered on a fake smile.

"Absolutely! I'm great! I'm carrying on the tradition established by my parents to take down all Christmas decorations on New Year's day."

They all paused as they heard Marty raise his voice.

"Damn Christmas lights! Are these bastards glued onto the branches? How in the hell am I supposed to get them off!"

Charlotte hurried into the living room with Riley and Ziggy following behind.

"Dad, those are the lights that stay on the tree. It's a pre-lit tree. I already took off the extra lights I bought. Those don't move."

Marty's head popped out from the side of the tree.

His face was red as he replied breathlessly, "What the hell? Did I raise you to be that lazy to buy a tree that's pre-lit?"

"Dad, I put on extra lights. They're over there," Charlotte pointed at the ten rolls of Christmas tree lights on the couch.

"Oh… good. You're not lazy."

Charlotte rolled her eyes, and said, "Dad, you remember Riley from the wedding and this is Ziggy, a friend of Gia's."

Marty looked at them and nodded his head.

"Hi girls. I'm just over here helping my very pregnant daughter take down the Christmas decorations. I can't have her doing the climbing… that Madam doctor says her balance is off from carrying my grandsons."

Charlotte looked at Ziggy and Riley with an amused smile as she explained, "Mom and dad hate it when people don't immediately take down their Christmas decorations."

Marty paused and put his hand on his hip.

Huffily, Marty started his tirade, "Well, it's just pure laziness! Get your ass outside and take down the damn decorations. Hell, it's faster to take them down than it is to put them up. There's no excuse for these damn decorations to be left out until July! Damn, lazy people!"

As Marty continued on with his yearly speech that Charlotte had memorized, she urged the girls into Gia's office.

"Go ahead," she said. "Dad, you need to stop cursing so much around people and the twins."

"The hell I do, I-"

Ziggy slammed the door shut as Riley and Ziggy entered Gia's office. They looked around. Things looked... different.

"Where's the painting?" Riley asked.

"Shredded to pieces when I found out my wife has been trying to finagle her way into my office. At least I tidied up the bookshelves that I had knocked over."

Ziggy nodded as she replied, "Well that explains the sad energy I picked up on her."

Riley sat down in the chair across from Gia's desk.

"Please tell me you didn't lose it on her?"

Ziggy sat down in the other chair across from Gia, watching her cover her face with her hands.

"A little."

Ziggy and Riley eyed each other wearily.

"This is what we were afraid of," Riley quietly said.

Gia held up the book she had been reading through.

"I know. I'm trying to figure out how to contain the evil by re-reading this book about white witchcraft. Maybe there's a spell in here to help me. I can't keep reacting like this when I feel slighted in the smallest way."

There was a long pause as Ziggy stared at Gia, taking in all of the changes. Riley, on the other hand, looked past Gia to the window. It was hard to acknowledge that her best friend Gia, the white witch, now had demonic blood flowing through her. It was utterly terrifying to think your best friend of over thirty years could cause such destruction with her mind.

Ziggy spoke in a soft tone, asking, "Why'd you do it, Gia? Why did you let that demon talk you into sharing each other's blood? It is pure evil… it lies."

Gia sat back in her comfortable chair, wishing she could explain the sacrifice she made was for the good of her family, but she knew she needed to listen.

Riley cleared her throat, not comfortable talking about her feelings.

"I've known you since high school, and umm… what I saw yesterday was… well it made me sick to my stomach. You were literally in your glories when you realized how much power you had. I've never seen such a sick and twisted look of pure enjoyment on your face when we found Banks' body. You creeped me out. The evil was exuding from you… it was coming through every pore on your body, Gia."

"How are you going to retain control for the next four months?" Ziggy leaned forward, her brows furrowed in concern. "You might lose your wife if you let this evil lash out at her again. So what would have been the point of sharing this blood pact with that demon spawn if you lose Charlotte and can't protect the twins?"

Gia sighed.

"I'm trying to figure that out," she said as she held up the book again.

Ziggy crossed her arms over her chest and suspiciously asked, "Have you been able to reach your ancestors when you go into your trance?"

Gia had to hold back the bile in her throat from the holy relics both women were wearing.

She swallowed and actually felt shame as she replied softly, "Not exactly… it's grey when I go in."

Ziggy shook her head, growing angry.

"You shouldn't have done it! You were warned by everyone!"

Riley hissed, "You have evil in you now! Literally, you are half evil!"

Gia began to grow defensive.

"Look, it's done. It ends at 11:59 PM on Easter Sunday. I'll be back to my old self again. And on that day, I'm going to need you two in the delivery room to help me and Ezmerelda out."

Ziggy's eyebrows flew up as she responded sarcastically, "Oh, *IT* has a name, huh?"

Riley shook her head.

"No delivery rooms for me. Nope, I'm good just being an aunt and Godmother."

Gia was not in the mood to negotiate.

"Listen, you two are going to have to hold the babies while Ezmerelda and I deal with Madam and the other witches in her coven. They'll be destroyed once and for all."

Riley looked panic-stricken.

"What? You're serious right now? Well, I'm dead ass serious when I tell you I am not going to be in the delivery room with you, Satan's spawn and a swarm of fucking witches!"

"You've lost it, Gia," Ziggy said sadly as she shook her head.

Gia slammed her hand down on her desk, causing a massive split in the wood.

"No, I haven't! I know exactly what needs to be done! You two shitheads are going to-"

A swift wind kicked up and Ezmerelda appeared next to Gia.

"Calm down, Gia, or I'm going to need to tranquilize you like a wild animal." Ezmerelda said, smiling ruefully.

She looked at the two women who were staring at her in utter disbelief, curiosity and spine-tingling horror.

"Hi there Ziggy and Riley. I'm "Satan's spawn" as you said earlier, but you can simply call me Ezmerelda."

She smiled at them, finding herself trying to put them at ease.

"She's a kid," Ziggy whispered to no one and everyone at the same time.

Ezmerelda cocked her head and floated in the air and crossed her legs. She sat forward, her elbows on her bent knees.

"I am most definitely *not* a kid. But, here's the plan of attack that you two buddies of mine *will* be a part of on Easter Sunday."

Ezmerelda grinned and began.

******

As Marty was lugging the rest of the Christmas decorations down to the supply closet in the basement, Riley and Ziggy scurried out of Gia's office and almost ran right into Charlotte.

"Oh! Hey you two! Are you done already?"

Ziggy nodded her head up and down, replying quickly, "Yup. Definitely done."

Riley gave an odd smile and nodded her head slightly.

Charlotte looked at them oddly before asking, "Are you two okay? You guys look super pale."

Riley and Ziggy eyed each other like two young punks being caught stealing by the cops.

"Hell, yeah we are!" Riley all but yelled, startling Charlotte and Ziggy.

Ziggy glared at Riley, and calmly said to Charlotte, "It was just a really horrific case… hard to, umm, understand everything."

Charlotte brought her hand up to her lips and whispered, "Is it about that Banks kid and how he was found?"

Riley almost vomited, so she just nodded her head.

"Oh no. Maybe that's why Gia was so mean today… should I check in on her?" Charlotte asked worriedly.

"NO!" they both yelled abruptly, recalling how Ezmerelda was still in the room when they bolted after being told the master plan for Easter.

Ziggy cleared her throat.

"The pictures are… everywhere."

"Everywhere," Riley chimed in.

"It's hard for us to see, so you… you definitely shouldn't see those images."

"Bad images," Riley muttered.

"Especially in your delicate condition; you don't want to see that stuff. It'll haunt you for life."

"For life," Riley whispered.

Charlotte looked from Ziggy to Riley and then back to Ziggy as she wrapped her arms around her protruding stomach.

"I had no idea it was so bad." Charlotte was eyeing Riley's face. "And Riley, usually you have an iron stomach, but you look… well, like you could throw up right now."

Riley gulped down the vomit at the back of her throat and nodded; the two women then tore ass out of the apartment, almost crashing into Marty.

Marty came back in, and shut the door behind him.

"What the hell is wrong with those two? They all but plowed into me like linebackers!"

He shook his head and began complaining about this new generation, meaning Charlotte's.

She was lost in her own thoughts as she wished she could be part of Gia's police work. It was such an integral part of who she was. She lived and breathed for her work. Charlotte didn't realize what a massive toll it was probably taking on her, until she saw Riley and Ziggy. It was especially Riley, the head of forensics and a brilliant genius, who made Charlotte realize Gia was carrying ghosts with her daily. Charlotte ignored her father as she took out the ingredients to make Gia's favorite lasagna.

******

"You scared the shit out of them, Ezmerelda. Was all the flying around really necessary?"

Ezmerelda giggled with delight.

"Well, they weren't getting it when you tried explaining our plan, so I took care of it. They needed to know everything, and now they do," Ezmerelda said as she shrugged.

"Let's just hope Madam doesn't catch wind of our plan."

Ezmererlda glared into space.

"That pig is definitely too concerned about other things right now to worry about you or me. I made sure of that at the party. Stick with me, and we'll make it through Easter unscathed by that traitor."

Chapter 20

Madam had not had a full night of sleep for the past two months. It was March 1st, and she still had no clue as to how she was going to make up with Catherine, after her terrible betrayal. Madam had not only deceived Catherine, but she had also murdered John William, the love of her life. Madam *would* make them understand once she fulfilled her last sacrifice and ascended to the throne of Husband's many wives.

Had she turned in Catherine to keep the heat off herself? Absolutely. And yes, she had shape shifted into Catherine to have John William pleasure her in ways she fantasized about over and over again, even five hundred years later.

They had to understand Madam's predicament. She was in love and craved John William so much that she would do anything to have him, even if that meant betraying her only sister. He had literally saved her and brought Madam back to life in every possible way a soulmate and lover could. It's not her fault that Catherine was in the way. Seriously, she couldn't possibly still be angry with her after all of these centuries!

The love of her life would not shirk her when she arrived as one of Husband's wives. John William would be hers, and if Catherine couldn't forgive her, then she'd see to it that Husband put her in the furthest recesses of hell, for she had been through too much to not get the love of her life back in less than two months. Nothing would stop Madam.

She grinned as she lay in her bed thinking about how she would make him see her actions were just. If he did not give in, she would make him her own personal slave. Whether John William wanted Madam or not, she didn't care. She only cared about what she wanted, and no one, not even her sister that she still loved, would get in her way.

Madam tossed and turned, and, as always, Ezmerelda ran through her mind like an annoying mouse she couldn't catch and stomp to death. Ezmerelda knew that Madam had symbolically given a second child to Charlotte, perhaps to represent the child that Madam had sacrificed from Catherine.

Madam had initially cared at the holiday party she threw, but now, Madam didn't care one iota if Ezmerelda planned to kill the second child. Let her slaughter the newborn. Madam would be in hell, where she belonged. No more having to deal with the games of Ezmerelda and dealing with sacrificing for Husband. She'd be free. She would turn her back on the coven, Ezmerelda and, yes, Charlotte, with whom Madam was certain was partly the reincarnation of Catherine.

Yes, Madam made up her mind. This was about *her*, as it should be. She was in charge of her destiny, and there was no way that anyone or anything would get in her way.

******

It was the beginning of April, and Charlotte was tired of being tired. The twins never let her sleep, she couldn't see her feet, and she waddled like an obese penguin. Her face had grown fat. Even her nose had seemed to spread! The damn experts lied about moisturizers to stop stretch marks. Bastards! And she was constantly farting! Charlotte felt like an embarrassment to herself. She no longer felt as beautiful as she once had when she was a slim, active woman. Now, it was exercise just getting up without assistance from her parents or Gia.

And of course, Gia had been isolating herself in her office. While she enjoyed Ziggy and Riley staying after their meetings with Gia, she wished she had more alone time with her. The time they spent together was fleeting; Charlotte's parents, Ziggy and Riley were always around. She delighted in the company, but sometimes, she resented all of them for taking away this special time with her wife before the arrival of the twins.

While Charlotte often tried to cheer herself up, knowing that Ziggy and Riley would make amazing Godmothers to their sons, she couldn't help but feel that Gia was disgusted by her large size. Charlotte would often cry to Gia that she didn't love her anymore. There was no sexual life. It's as though once Charlotte became pregnant, Gia only looked at her as a human incubator and not as a woman, as her wife.

As Charlotte would cry hysterically, shoving more chocolate into her mouth, Gia would soothe her, letting Charlotte know that she was beautiful and glowing with the lives of their sons. Even though Gia constantly reassured her, it did not alleviate Charlotte's fear that her wife was no longer attracted to her. Gia even stopped attending church services with Charlotte, insisting that she had too much work to do. Charlotte sighed and tried to get up from the couch. Yeah, that wasn't working, so she did an awkward roll, and was able to eventually stand up, see her reflection in the living room mirror and start crying all over again.

******

It was Good Friday. Ziggy, Riley, Gia, and Ezmerelda were holed up in Gia's office going over the plans… Ezmerelda was obsessed with their master plan. She made sure Ziggy, Riley and even Gia knew how to take care of a newborn - getting rid of the mucus or anything in the throat and nostrils, cutting the cord, making sure Charlotte delivered the afterbirth, because once the shit went down, it would be Gia and Ezmerelda fighting to take down Madam, leaving Ziggy and Riley to take care of Charlotte and the twins.

Ezmerelda was in the chair, her little feet and short legs propped up on the coffee table. Gia was in the chair next to her, while Riley and Ziggy occupied the massive couch across from them.

Ezmerelda stated bluntly, "There's one more piece of the master plan that I haven't told you. Gia, I doubt you'll care because you're sharing my blood, but Riley and Ziggy, I don't want to hear it from you too goody goods, alright?"

Riley rolled her eyes.

"Seriously, Ezmerelda, I know everything there is to know about childbirth, unfortunately! I can't handle anymore demonstrations! It's gross!"

Ezmerelda ignored Riley. She was used to her always complaining.

"As I was saying, Madam likes to have her neonatal nurses in the birthing suite to knock out everyone, so no one can recall what she did. I need to take out both Theodora and Lily."

Ziggy scrunched her face and said with dismay, "Oh no… you don't mean-"

"Yup! I need to rip out their hearts and eat them. Send them to the land of being sightless, deaf mutes forever. This will also weaken Madam, so when she goes to sacrifice the first son, Gia and I will be able to step in and save him, while Gia sends Madam to join Theodora and Lily."

"Gross," Riley muttered.

"Hey, look at this as retribution for Theodora taking over parts of Gia's brain. That caused Charlotte to leave her… so, you're welcome," Ezmerelda said delightedly.

It was odd to see a six-year-old talking so nonchalantly about gobbling up two hearts. The weirdest thing though was not the witchcraft, black or white, or even the little girl being born of an Egyptian demon. The craziest part was how the four of them had united, and they were friends. The change from fear to friendship definitely shifted in early February.

Gia, her partner Dean, and Riley were at the crime scene of five dead well-known gang members, who were definitely not on their territory's corner. It was most assuredly that it had been a rival gang who had shot the five men. Riley could tell them from the bullets, they were looking for a gang with access to semi-automatic weapons. As Riley placed her yellow placards next to the different bodies, Gia suddenly felt danger. She looked down the street and saw a massive black Cadillac Escalade, with the windows coming down on the passenger side windows. Two massive guns were revealed as she shoved Dean behind one of the massive, metal garbage containers used by the businesses.

"Get down! We have guns hot!" Gia screamed.

Riley either didn't hear her with her thick earmuffs, or she was in shock.

"RILEY! GET DOWN!" Gia screamed, pulling out her own gun as Dean laid flat on the ground from Gia's strong shove. "RILEY!" Gia screamed again, only seeing Riley stare in the direction of the oncoming vehicle and directly in the line of fire.

As suddenly as an earthquake shakes the ground, Gia watched in awe as Ezmerelda swooped Riley into her arms and dropped her beside the safety of Gia. As the shots came pouring down on them like a monsoon in Vietnam, Ezmerelda cocked her head and the entire massive, black Cadillac Escalade flipped upside down and landed hard on the hood. As the men tried to escape, Ezmerelda cocked her head again, pinning their arms down at their sides.

The entire incident had made the news; poor Dean had been knocked out cold when Gia had thrown him into the metal garbage can, but he received a commendation from the Mayor, along with Gia, even though he had no recollection of anything.

After they returned to the precinct, Riley immediately went to the bathroom and threw up. Gia waited for her by the sink with paper towels, which Riley took gratefully.

"Are you okay?"

Riley was shaking fiercely.

"No… I just stood there. They would have killed me. I'd be dead right now."

A fierce wind blew through as Ezmerelda smiled, her hands on her hips, sassily saying, "For someone who is supposed to be a fucking genius, you sure as hell don't act like you're smart." Ezmerelda paused and her face dropped. "Hey, are you okay?"

Riley just stared at her.

"Why did you save me?"

Ezmerelda shrugged and replied matter-of-factly, "I felt Gia's panic and fear for you. We share the same blood, so I had to protect you."

Riley did something unlike her usual cold self; she ran up and embraced Ezmerelda in a tight hug, lifting her little body off the floor.

"Thank you," Riley whispered through unshed tears.

Ezmerelda's legs were kicking at nothing as she angrily said, "Your damn cross and evil eye are burning me!"

"Oh, sorry!" Riley put her down as Gia felt the same burn on her chest.

From that day forward, Riley was always happy to see Ezmerelda, and even Ziggy joined the bandwagon of adoring the little demon girl.

Ziggy lived alone, and she was eating food way too fast. She began to choke, and out of nowhere, Ezmerelda appeared to give her the Heimlich maneuver, even though it burned her hands, as well as Gia's, to touch the numerous crosses and other necklaces Ziggy wore to ward off evil.

Even though Gia wasn't there, Ezmerelda realized she was bound to the loved ones of Gia, which scared the shit out of her. Ezmerelda's protection of Gia's clan was prominent and at the forefront of her mind constantly; she hated it.

Ziggy had caught her breath and looked at Ezmerelda in awe, and she asked the same question Riley had: "Why did you save me?"

Ezmerelda sighed at herself.

"Because you're Gia's best friend, so I guess… you're my best friend too. Don't get a big head over it."

As the group wrapped up their meeting and plans for Easter Sunday, they all began laughing at Gia as they shared stories about how, even with her best intentions, the evil was allowed through. While she had done a good job of mediating and focusing on white magic and spells, there had been a few bumps in the road of keeping the evil at bay.

Riley laughed as she said, "Do you remember the guy who took the taxi from that old lady?" Riley laughed again. "You said he needs to be hit by a car… I swear, not even 5 seconds later, the guy gets out of the cab he has just stolen from Granny, and walks into oncoming traffic. He was hit by a school bus so hard that the bastard flew at least fifty feet! He was in the hospital for about eight weeks!"

Gia smiled and laughed lightly as she nonchalantly stated, "Well, at least I didn't kill him, so that's a plus!"

A sarcastic round of applause from everyone began as Gia stood up and took a bow. After Gia sat back down and the giggles stopped, the mood suddenly turned somber with the realization that this would be the last time the four of them would be together.

Come Easter Sunday, Ezmerelda would leave them for good. Ziggy, Riley and Gia all looked at Ezmerelda with undeniable and startling sadness in their eyes. They all shared the shock of how much they had come to, dare they think it, love the little demon girl.

Ezmerelda looked at all of them.

"What's happening? Gia, what is this feeling you're forcing on me? It feels… awful!"

Gia tried to smile, but it never reached her eyes.

"We're just… sad. This is the last time we'll all be together. I… I guess we're going to miss you, Ezmerelda."

Ezmerelda's eyes widened in shock, as she angrily said, "Well stop it! Stop feeling this… this sad feeling! Right now!" Ezmerelda felt the feeling deepen. "Oh, this is ridiculous! The three of you need to pull your heads out of your asses! I'm a demon! I will kill you all if I want to the day after Easter!"

Shockingly, this didn't frighten any of the three, who were still staring at Ezmerelda with sincere adoration.

"I'm sorry," Gia said quietly, "but we can't just turn off our feelings."

The little girl stood up, waving her arms as though warding off the feelings of sincerity and vulnerability.

"I am the devil's daughter! I am a demon's daughter. You guys, I'm pure evil! Stop it!"

Ziggy sighed.

"We know, but we're still going to miss you."

"Ugh!" Ezmerelda felt as though she had been punched in the gut. "You're disgusting. All of you are absolutely pathetic!"

Riley retorted, "Yeah, but we see the good side of you and it's-"

"That good side will leave me as of midnight on Monday. I will turn fully evil again, ready to fuck shit up. And if any of you three ever ends up in hell, I will be the one who tortures you!"

Ezmerelda swiveled and saw Ziggy swiping at her eyes. She sniffled, and soon Riley was joining in. Ezmerelda glared at Gia.

"DON'T YOU DARE!"

Gia felt the tears stinging her eyes.

"What?"

Ezmerelda cocked her head, and they each slapped themselves in the face.

"There. That's my departure gift!"

The wind rose up as Ezmerelda left them clasping their cheeks.

"I'm still going to miss her," Riley said.

In Gia's head she heard Ezmerelda screaming, *STOP IT! Now, don't get all sappy on Easter! I need you strong and for you to let the evil out, Gia! Don't fuck this up because of your stupid human emotions!*

Ziggy asked, "Was she talking to you?"

Gia nodded, and lied, "She said she loves us and she's going to miss-"

Her hand came up and slapped Gia's cheek.

DO NOT LIE ABOUT THAT! Now, go eat the meal your wife has prepared, and stop talking about me!

Ziggy and Riley chuckled as Gia rubbed her cheek.

"So, we're being ordered by Ezmerelda to go eat now."

It's your favorite - the taco bake.

"Thanks, buddy."

Another swift slap to Gia's face.

"I still love you!" she cried out through her laughter.

Gia now had both hands slapping her in the face, but not hard.

"Okay, okay - I give, Ezmerelda! You win!"

The three women walked out of the room, and entered the kitchen, their stomachs already rumbling from the amazing scents wafting into their noses.

They walked in to see Charlotte placing the plates on the kitchen island, humming to herself. The taco bake was steaming, and there was Chihuahua cheese, lettuce, sour cream, and tortilla chips, which added to their already rumbling stomachs.

"Wow! I was just about to text you, Gia, to tell you dinner was ready for everyone. I think one of you must be psychic!"

Riley muttered under her breath, "Something like that."

Gia, Riley, and Ziggy all sat down with Charlotte at the dining room table, thanking her profusely as they dug in.

Charlotte looked at their faces intently under the bright chandelier light.

"Why are your cheeks so red?" She eyed Gia even closer. "Jesus, Gia, it looks like your face was beat up! Don't tell me you three are doing a fight club thing in there!"

Gia smiled, wincing mildly at the pain.

"The three of us? No. I can honestly say the three of us are not slapping each other," Gia replied trying to hold in her laughter.

Riley, Ziggy and Gia began to giggle, and Charlotte rolled her eyes.

"Imbeciles," she muttered as she shoved her mouth with the delicious food.

Chapter 21

Gia dropped the bag by the door, sighing in exasperation at her in-laws.

"Marty and Diane, I need you to stay here. We've already been over this."

It was bad enough that Gia had to keep it a secret from Charlotte that Ziggy and Riley would be joining them during the birth.

"Gia, this is ridiculous! I want to be there when my grandsons are born!"

"Damnit, Marty! We were alone together when I gave birth to Charlotte. We didn't want our parents in the delivery room… it was a special time, just for us. Leave the girls alone and let them become a family without us hovering."

Gia's eyes widened. For the past few months, Diane had been the annoying, pushy grandmother. Now, she was the calm and rational one.

"Diane… we should at least be in the waiting area."

"Marty, you are the love of my life and the biggest pain in the ass." She paused to rise up on her tiptoes to kiss him on the cheek. "Now, we're going to wash all of the bedding I had specially ordered from France, and we'll make up the cribs before they come home."

"Why the hell did you go and order special bedding for babies… from France? They're just going to shit everywhere and spit up on them!"

"Shut the hell up, Marty! I wanted to do this for my grandsons! These are handwoven fabrics that allow cooling for the babies, and then the comforters are hand-"

"I'm ready to hit the road," Charlotte interrupted.

Gia smiled at her gigantic wife. She knew how uncomfortable Charlotte had been, especially in the last trimester. Charlotte was always crying and complaining about how ugly and fat she was, but Gia saw her beautiful wife and knew in her heart that she would die to protect her and their sons.

"Oh, honey!" Diane rushed over to hug her and kiss her belly, something that annoyed Charlotte to no end. "When you come back, you're going to be a mommy, and I'm going to be the best grandma in the entire world!"

"Mom, please stop crying."

"When your baby has a baby, well, babies, you'll understand!"

"Jesus," Marty muttered, "take it easy Diane." He unceremoniously removed Diane and gave Charlotte a massive bear hug. "Any chance you've decided to name one of the boys after their old grandpa?"

Charlotte hugged him back, and rolled her eyes at Gia who had to hide her smile. They would use Martin as the middle name for one of the boys and George as the middle name for the other twin, which would probably cause Diane to bawl because that was her father's name.

Diane shoved her way back in between Charlotte and her father.

"Are you okay? Do you have everything? What can I do?"

Charlotte held onto her mother's shoulders to steady the little, anxious bird-like woman in front of her.

"Mom, Gia has my bag. I'm being induced at 7 AM. I'm going for a natural childbirth. I'm nervous, but I'm also excited, okay? Gia and I have this."

Diane swiped her eyes.

"Okay. You go and become a mommy."

She hugged Charlotte again, but she wouldn't let go.

"Dad... do something!"

Marty pulled Diane away.

"You need to stop this crazy, obsessive shit. When the boys get here-"

"Oh, don't you preach to me, you son of a bitch. I'll be as crazy as I want to!"

Charlotte joined Gia at the door.

"Are you ready for this?"

Gia nodded, feeling the holy water packed up tightly in her jacket, fearful it might open and singe her.

"I've never been more ready for anything in my life."

******

Gia couldn't help but notice that Theodora and Lily, even after Gia's couple of visits, making sure to miss the majority of them to avoid Madam's scrutiny, had never regained their beautiful glow. Ezmerelda happily and greedily took credit for that in Gia's mind.

As they walked to the birthing suite, Madam looked tired. She had wrinkles around her eyes and on her forehead, again something Ezmerelda took credit for.

The birthing suite was massive. The bed in the middle, was more of a spa bed than a hospital bed. Of course, Gia noted angrily, there was a fireplace in the back corner, so Madam could easily turn away with the baby in her hands and make the sacrifice. While Madam had her own agenda, Gia, Ezmerelda, Ziggy and Riley all had theirs. And no matter what, they would achieve their goal, and finally bring down Madam, while saving the babies and Charlotte.

The IV had been administered promptly at 7 AM. Gia carefully looked at the bag to make sure it was Pitocin and nothing else. Gia watched Charlotte like a hawk, making sure her wife wasn't groggy. She'd often check her pupils, much to the annoyance of Charlotte.

"Will you stop it! I'm fine! They're just minor contractions. This could take all day."

Gia looked pensive.

"Right. Umm…" she looked at the clock… it was nearing ten, and she heard the girls. "So, I wanted backup in case I fainted or something. I hope you don't mind that I asked Riley and Ziggy to be here when I needed a break and to be in the waiting area, just for support."

Charlotte breathed through her contraction.

"I thought you said this was just for *us,* not anyone else," she hissed as she glared at Gia.

Gia gulped. She would not miss this bitchy side of Charlotte one bit.

"I just thought, they're going to be the Godmothers, and they're the closest thing to family I have… I can send them away, if you want?" Gia asked sweetly as she put on her boo-boo face, which Charlotte was always a sucker for.

Charlotte sighed and leaned her head back against the pillow and annoyingly replied, "No, they're fine. I'm just ready to walk around or use the massive ball to get these kids out of me. I hate just lying in this bed."

Riley and Ziggy had been waiting at the door. Once Gia gave them the head nod, they exuberantly joined Charlotte and Gia. As they babbled on and on, making Charlotte focus on them and not the pain, Gia excused herself.

She needed to get her bearings. There was a lot riding on the next thirteen hours. She rolled her neck and went into the waiting area, where a comfy couch welcomed her. Gia rolled her shoulders back, and even though she had her eyes closed, she felt the energy of Madam. When she opened her eyes, the very tired looking woman was staring down at her with fierce light green eyes.

"I noticed you're not wearing your cross or evil eye anymore."

Gia's hand automatically went to her neck.

"I must have forgotten them in the excitement of trying to get here on time, so we can have Easter babies," she replied nonchalantly, feeling her evil grow as she looked at this sick, maniac.

Madam grinned, but as usual, the gesture never reached her cold, calculating eyes.

"No, Gia. It's not just today. It's been on the very few visits you've been able to make. I also noticed that you haven't been wearing holy water."

Gia stood up, fueled with fury.

"Do you need some? I'd be happy to pour some in your tea, you know, release all of those toxins and wrinkles you now have on your once very youthful face."

The women stared at each other, neither blinking. There was pure hatred bubbling between them.

Madam said sweetly, "Today shall be the last day I see your smug little scrunched up turtle face. Such a pity."

Gia's anger rose throughout her body. She could feel the evil pulsating in her. Every part of her wanted to rip out that bitch's heart right then and there.

Easy does it, Gia, Ezmerelda said in her mind. *She senses something is off. Don't show your powers. You have to remain calm. You need to toss her off balance… umm… mention Catherine!*

Gia's fake smile was parked on her face as she calmed down and listened to Ezmerelda.

Matching Madam's fake sweet tone, Gia said, "You know, I'm also going to miss not having to deal with you and your pathetic attempt to make Charlotte into the reincarnation of your sister, Catherine. It's pretty pathetic, don't you think?" Madam's eyes narrowed into cat-like slits. "Actually, I did some research, and there was never an incident of a younger sister burning alive in a house with her older sister watching, not able to do anything. Strange, don't you think, *Madam*?"

Madam hissed, "It happened in England."

Gia slapped her thigh and smiled fakely.

"Well, that's good to know. While I'm waiting, I can research what happened to you in England. What was the date? You know, to narrow my search."

Madam was shaking.

"Perhaps you should join your wife now."

Gia cocked her head, just like her buddy Ezmerelda always did.

Her smile was smug as she simply replied, "Perhaps I should."

As Gia eased out of the room, she slid into an empty office right next door to the waiting room. She heard her yell for Lily; Gia also heard anger in Madam's voice as she ordered Lily to go to the nearest church and get a pitcher full of holy water.

Lily gasped, as she shakily replied, "Madam, I can't go into a church! I'll burn!"

Madam snapped, "Then pay someone to do it for you, you little twit!"

Gia quickly hurried towards the birthing suite and spoke to Ezmerelda in her mind.

Did you hear that?

Duh, dummy! I knew she sensed something was off with you. But that's fine with us. The queen of pigs will get us even more arsenal than we already have.

******

It was a little after five that evening when Madam happily announced that Charlotte was six centimeters dilated.

She lost her smile as Charlotte yelled, "That's bullshit! I've been in labor for ten hours, and I'm only six centimeters dilated? Fuck that! I want to deliver these babies now!"

Riley and Ziggy had gone out to pick up some dinner, so they missed Charlotte's tirade.

Madam left as Gia leaned down by Charlotte.

"Do you want the epidural now, honey?"

Charlotte grabbed Gia's face as her angry blue eyes bore into hers.

"I want the fucking bouncy ball! I wanted these kids! I will feel everything! Where's the fucking bouncy ball!"

Gia adjusted her jaw when Charlotte released her. She felt like a dog fetching Charlotte the ball.

"Here it is," she said lightly as Gia helped Charlotte sit on it and bounce.

For the next six hours, it was horrible. Charlotte would walk with someone by her side, and then pause and scream from the massive contractions. Poor Ziggy and Riley would come back with hands that needed to be massaged back to normal looking hands, and not something floppy looking, like a penguin's flipper.

Riley, as usual, put her foot in her mouth when she dumbly asked Charlotte about the epidural. That was a huge mistake. As Charlotte's cuss words flew into the air, so did her pillows and anything else she could grab. Lily chose this time to come into the room, carefully, as though it was porcelain, to bring in the plastic pink pitcher and put it on a table outside of Charlotte's reach.

Gia smiled, knowing that was the holy water, and then quickly felt a box of tissues slam her in the forehead.

"And what the hell are you smiling about? Huh! YOU don't have to go through this! I'm going to kill you with my bare hands if you ever smile again. You think this is funny!"

Charlotte's yelling was stopped by a contraction. Gia rubbed her forehead and then clasped Charlotte's hand, feeling bad that she was suffering, but the evil side of her, including Ezmerelda in her head, didn't feel sorry for her. She could have taken the epidural.

By 11:30 that night, after what felt like being in a war zone, Madam broke the news that Charlotte was fully dilated and it was time to push. Gia's eyes narrowed as Madam flipped the switch, and the fireplace came on full blast.

As Madam sat down in front of Charlotte, she pulled the foot rests out, so Charlotte could put her feet up to finally push.

"Let me just call for Theodora and Lily."

Right as Madam said that, Lily and Theodora gasped in shock outside of the birthing suite. Each of them carried two needles with contents that were supposed to knock out Riley, Ziggy, Charlotte, and Gia.

Ezmerelda's eyes glowed, as she felt the hatred for these two boil over her.

"Hello, bitches. It's time to join your buddies."

With that last sentiment, Ezmerelda plunged her tiny hands into both of them at the same time, and shrewdly ripped out their beating hearts. She immediately bit into each heart, to make sure they could not ever have the ceremony performed on them. The two dropped like weights to the ground as Ezmerelda laughed and chomped away happily.

Gia felt the evilness coursing through her from Ezmerelda as she felt and enjoyed the demonic blood pumping through her veins.

Yes, this is what I have missed and craved, Gia thought.

Madam roiled in pain.

"No… no. It can't be. DAMN YOU EZMERELDA!"

Charlotte was pushing and screaming, as she yelled, "What the hell is going on?"

Madam saw the little girl with bloody hands and a bloody grin as she smiled at Madam.

"Go back to hell where you belong, you little bitch!" Madam howled.

Charlotte had no clue what was going on; she only felt the burn as she felt a head being torn through her.

Madam brought her focus back to the baby boy she needed to sacrifice.

"Come on Charlotte, one more push, and he will be free from you."

As Charlotte pushed the shoulders free, Madam was able to pull him out. She quickly cut the cord, no longer caring that these damn women would see what she was about to do. Madam flicked her fingers, and the sapphire necklace Charlotte wore was ripped from her and laid in Madam's hand as she held the infant in the crook of her right arm.

Charlotte, still experiencing the desire to push, began screaming, "Give me my son! Madam! What are you doing?"

Madam had swiftly turned towards the fireplace, but Ezmerelda had grabbed the pitcher of holy water and told Ziggy to get herself ready. She then ordered Riley to take over delivering the second baby.

"Give us the baby, pig," Ezmerelda hissed.

Charlotte screamed on a contraction.

"What the fuck is Ezmerelda doing here? Riley! Do you know what you're doing?" Charlotte asked breathlessly.

Gia and Ezmerelda only focused on Madam and the baby. Their eyes were burning as they stared at Madam.

"You two are working together!" She said delightedly. "You shared blood! Ha! I'll have you kept where your mother has been kept, little demonic bitch!"

As Madam produced a knife, Ezmerelda gave the pitcher of holy water to Gia.

"Do it. I've got him."

Gia singed her hands as she opened the pitcher and holy water spilled on her. She splashed the pitcher onto Madam's face, who immediately screamed and dropped the baby. Ezmerelda caught him, and swiftly gave him to Ziggy.

"Do what I trained you to do," Ezmerelda ordered as though she were a strong drill sergeant.

Ziggy shakily nodded and got to work, carefully taking the baby away from the three disturbed females.

Riley delivered the second baby as Madam and Charlotte both screamed for different reasons. Riley quickly headed over to the other incubator and began cleaning out the mucus.

Madam's face had burned off. Her one eyeball had fallen out, and her raw, bloody flesh was seeping down her face.

"I'll have you burn for this! I have three days to complete my sacrifice! I'M THE WIFE! YOU CAN'T STOP ME!"

Gia stepped forward, filled with hatred and said, "She can't, but I can."

With such brutal force, Madam flew backwards into the fire, as Gia had blasted through Madam's chest with her right hand and now felt the beating heart. With delight she had never felt before in her entire life, she yanked out the heart of Madam.

Charlotte was screaming hysterically. Ziggy took care of the boys and had Riley take care of Charlotte, to ensure she delivered the afterbirth.

Gia looked directly into Madam's eyes as she took a chunk of the heart into her mouth and bit into it, tearing a gigantic piece away. Madam dropped into the fire as Gia continued eating the heart of this evil monster who was going to kill her son.

Ezmerelda smiled at Gia, who was ferociously consuming the still beating heart, blood dripping from her hands and mouth. They shared evil laughter as both Gia and Ezmerelda experienced the excitement and energy of evilness together. They felt like they had just taken back the world.

Ziggy and Riley gave the twins to an utterly shocked Charlotte to try to calm her down. Charlotte could not believe what she had just watched in utter horror. Gia had ripped out Madam's heart and eaten it!

"You're evil," she cried out, as she pulled her boys tighter to herself.

Gia and Ezmerelda turned to look at Charlotte. All they could see was disgust and terror on her face as she safely held the two boys.

"No, Charlotte, it's not like that. I had to save the babies. You saw what happened! Madam was going to sacrifice our first born son!"

Charlotte shook her head, still in shock and defiantly said, "MY sons. These are MY sons, not yours. You're an evil monster. Go to hell, Gia, or whatever you are."

Ezmerelda felt the energy shift, and said, "Uh-oh."

The wind of a thousand hurricanes blew in, knocking everyone backwards. Ezmerelda held Gia's hand as she glanced at the time. It was 11:50. Ten more minutes… she had to keep her father talking for ten more minutes before she was banished to the furthest recesses of hell. She couldn't have Gia still attached to her after everything they had been through to stop Madam and save the first-born son.

As the wind receded, there stood the devil in all of his evil and disgusting, hideous glory. The rage was directed between Gia and Ezmerelda, the reptilian eyes blinking creepily from black to red.

Behind her father, Ezmerelda saw her mother!

Isfet, in her strong accent, pointed at Ezmerelda and said ferociously, "You see? I told you Apopis had worked with a white witch to kill your final wife!"

Ezmerelda looked from her father to her mother in humiliation. Her mother had played her, so Ezmerelda could take her place in the depths of hell.

"Mother-"

"I AM ISFET, to you! You have deceived you father. You have had your white witch kill his wife. Now, *you* are going to pay!"

Chapter 22

As Ezmerelda and Gia picked themselves off from the floor, Ziggy and Riley instinctively went to Charlotte. They stood on either side of her, hoping they had the courage to protect her and the twins.

Charlotte was gobsmacked. That was the only word that popped in her head as she literally saw the most disgusting, reptilian creature; she held her babies closer to try to shield them from the evil energy in the room. The creepy Egyptian woman was golden-eyed, but the scariest part was the way they glowed. Charlotte gulped. She was utterly helpless, and she had no idea how to protect her newborn sons.

Ezmerelda felt the concern and love for Gia, so she had to keep her father talking. She couldn't bring Gia down with her to the depths of hell, since they were still attached.

"Father, please understand that I-"

"I UNDERSTAND THAT YOU ARE A TRAITOR! HOW DARE YOU WORK WITH A WHITE WITCH TO KILL MY WIFE!"

Isfet stood next to the massive beast, smiling with chaos in her eyes at Ezmerelda, knowing she would get to return to earth with a quick spell. She immediately eyed Riley and figured she would be the best host for her soul.

As Isfet walked between Gia and Ezmerelda, she stood by Riley, and looked back at the devil.

"Your punishment is over, Isfet. You have turned in Apopis, who did the same, horrendous and traitorous act as you did. I hope you have learned your lesson. You are free from our contract."

Isfet smiled, and bowed her head.

No one noticed Isfet grab Riley's hand as she said the spell in her head. They would become two, and eventually, Riley would no longer exist.

Ezmerelda cried out in fear, "Father, it was Isfet who told me to do this!"

"LIES! She would never turn on her own child to free herself! I damn you-"

Ezmerelda looked at the clock... 11:58.

She looked at Gia with morbid sadness as she whispered, "I'm so sorry."

"To the depths of hell!"

With a whirlwind like a category five tornado, Ezmerelda herself and Gia's soul, were both snatched out of the room, and disappeared to hell for their eternal punishment.

Charlotte began to weep as she looked at Gia's dead body on the floor beside her bed.

"That was my wife! What did you do to her?" she cried out, alarmed that she had the courage to say anything to this beast.

Isfet reached over and stroked Charlotte's hair. She tried to pull away, but the pain from childbirth made her wince.

"King, I do believe we should bring Catherine back. She will eventually nudge out this Charlotte person. I could use someone I know and trust."

The devil's reptilian skin moved as though it were alive and slithering.

He nodded his head and said, "So it shall be."

The hurricane force winds accelerated, and, instantly, he was gone.

Isfet disappeared into Riley, and Riley brought her hand up to Charlotte's head. Ziggy watched in horror as Charlotte seemed to change. Her cheekbones became more prominent and her blue eyes had a lighter tint to them.

She rapidly opened and closed her eyes, as if coming out of a trance. When she spoke, she had an English accent.

"For fuck sake, Isfet, why would you give me a bloody body that has just been through a painful childbirth?"

Isfet in Riley's body shrugged.

"I figured you didn't want *that* body," she gestured to Ziggy's overweight figure in disgust, and insane red hair. "Plus, she's a white witch."

Catherine in Charlotte's body nodded and then looked down at the twins.

"Oh my. Two boys!" She snuggled them to her and inhaled their newborn scent. "This is lovely, Isfet. Thank you." She paused thoughtfully. "Maura killing my son has been a constant, fierce pain… and now look. I have two sons." She shook her head. "Bloody hell, this Charlotte won't shut up in my head!"

"Neither will this Riley person," Isfet muttered disdainfully, "But, at least she's pretty."

Ziggy backed away slowly. The Riley she once knew eyed her. Riley's eyes were no longer dark green. They were now a bright, golden color.

"Where do you think you're going, Ziggy? We're going to need you to help us," the golden eyes seared into hers.

Ziggy shrank back, whispering, "I'm a white witch."

Riley's mouth moved, but it was Isfet who said, "Don't worry, we don't want to share your horrid blood. We need help navigating the lives of these two. If you help us, we won't punish, torture and kill you as your mother experienced." She paused and gave a hideously evil smile. "Okay, fatty?"

Ziggy nodded, and left, crying the whole way home. Sophie was in her head, but Ziggy had lost everyone she loved. She thought about killing herself, but Sophie quickly reminded her that she wouldn't be able to join her in heaven.

Once Ziggy returned home, she was burdened with the knowledge she knew would be her fate. The black witch, once Charlotte, and the demon, once her best friend Riley, would eventually slaughter her, once she was of no use to them anymore.

Ziggy shook uncontrollably, knowing she'd end up like her mother.

"I'm sorry, Mom," Ziggy whispered as she took the sharpest knife from the knife display on her kitchen counter.

She could hear Sophie telling her not to kill herself, that, yes, she would be brutally killed by the two evil entities as she had been, but afterwards, she could join her. Ziggy ignored her mother, knowing that she would end up in purgatory, but it would be better than being used by those horrendous creatures.

"Mom, I can't do it. I'm not as strong as you are. I'd rather die on my own terms than go through what you experienced at their hands," Ziggy said through uncontrollable sobs.

As Ziggy slit her throat from ear to ear, she could hear her mother scream.

It would be a week before poor Louise, who had been there in the locked storage room when Sophie was brutally tortured and murdered, would find Ziggy's decomposing body. Little and old Louise would soon find herself in a mental institution.

******

"Marty, she's not herself. She looks different," Diane whispered, her eyebrows furrowed in concern.

"Honey, her wife died of a massive heart attack after Charlotte gave birth. How is she supposed to act?"

"A mother knows. We can't leave her alone in this condition."

So, for the next few days, Marty and Diane were always with Charlotte and the twins she had named John and William. Charlotte would often sing lullabies to the children that neither Marty, nor Diane had ever taught her.

While they were excited to be grandparents and cuddle the adorable babies, there was a change in Charlotte that even Marty finally acknowledged to his wife in secret on the third day of the twins and Charlotte being home.

He whispered to Diane, "I heard her in the nursery talking to John or William, and she was speaking in a British accent."

Diane's eyes flew open.

"I heard the same thing last night! I thought it was just because I was exhausted from lack of sleep."

The doorbell rang, and Diane greeted Riley at the door who had a few bags of groceries. Diane immediately hugged Riley.

"Thank you for coming. We know how important you were to Gia, and how they both wanted you to be a Godmother to one of the boys." She paused, looking at Riley's eyes in shock. "Oh my, your eyes… I thought they were green, but they look like a light golden brown now!"

Isfet in Riley's body hugged her back swiftly. She circumvented the question about her eyes easily.

"No need to thank me. It's been three days since the twins' arrival, and I really wanted to spend time with them and Charlotte. Plus, you two look tired. I was planning on spending the night to help Charlotte."

The body of Charlotte, with Catherine in control, arrived in the kitchen smiling, a twin in each of her long arms.

"Hey Isf-Riley. Meet John and William." Riley's eyebrows flew up. "They're good names, right?" Charlotte asked.

Riley grinned, her golden eyes glowing in comprehension.

"Those are perfect names. May I hold one of them?"

"Sure. You can take William. He's the second born."

Riley took him and placed little William carefully in her arms and smiled down at him.

"Riley, are you sure you want to stay over? Marty and I would appreciate it, since it's been so overwhelming planning the funeral."

"I'd be happy to stay," the voice of Riley came out from Isfet's control.

Charlotte replied, "Mom, there's not going to be a big funeral. We'll just have it be a small memorial service. She wanted to be cremated."

"Oh, well that's the first I'm hearing about that," Diane said, looking overwhelmed and beaten down by the loss of her daughter-in-law.

"Well," Charlotte snippily replied, "it's the first time I've felt like talking about my dead wife, okay?"

Marty put his arm around Diane when he saw her lower lip start to tremble.

"Come on, Di. You're overtired. It's been a long few days. Goodnight, girls."

Once Marty had shut the door behind him, Catherine spoke in her correct British tongue.

"Bollocks! Those two simpletons would not leave me be!"

Isfet walked around, allowing her accent to flow as she said with jealousy, "Your place is a lot nicer than Riley's."

"I think Charlotte's mum and dad are rich. If I'm not in the will, I'll be forced to keep them alive for their money."

"Mmm, yes." Isfet strolled into the living room and turned on the fireplace. "I think I should move in."

"But of course," Catherine came and joined her by the fireplace. "I need my co-creator to help me. We have a lot of chaos to bring about now that we're finally back on earth."

Isfet looked down at William in her arms, stating, "They are pretty children, aren't they? I like the names you gave them," Isfet said with a knowing smile. "Yes, we have a lot of mayhem ahead of us to dispense. I'm no longer at his disposal. Our contract has been severed. Let him deal with Apopis. I shall never serve another man again," she said bitterly.

"You're quite shrewd, Isfet. Now," Catherine said looking down at John in her arms, snoring lightly as he slept, "shall we start the ceremony?"

The demonic golden eyes spewed with hatred for their targets as she replied with the most menacing tone, "Let's begin. It's time for all of them to burn."

Chapter 23

Madam was terrified. She kept bumping into things, tripping, and she couldn't hear herself breathe. Madam screamed inside of her head, cursing out Ezmerelda and Gia. Right now, she should be lavished upon as one of Husband's lovely wives. Now, her eyes were gone, as well as her ears, and her mouth was fuzed and melted together. She tried to rip it open, to no avail.

This was her fate. She screamed again and again in her mind with rage and sorrow.

Suddenly, she thought she heard something… could it be Husband was coming to get her? He found her worthy enough to be at his side of wives? Did he realize she was innocent, and that his little bitch of a daughter had been the guilty party?

Madam *knew* she heard the sound again. It sounded like a faint whisper in her head.

"Husband? Husband! I'm right here. Please, come and save me," she thought excitedly.

She finally heard within her mind, "Madam! Madam, we're coming!"

Madam turned all around her, arms out. She would recognize that voice anywhere.

"BETH!" Madam screamed in her head.

"Madam! We're all here!"

Madam would have wept if she had eyes to weep from.

"Beth! Where are you?"

She heard a mountain of calls to her. Yes, it was her coven! She could still hear them in her mind! They had never detached from her!

Elizabeth, Nora, Theodoa, Lily, and her lovely Beth! Suddenly she felt a hand on her stomach and latched onto it for dear life.

"Whose hand am I holding?"

"It's me, Beth!"

Madam felt up towards her face, and felt the same nothingness that she had when she had touched her own face. She quickly embraced her best friend. It was the most amazing moment she had experienced in a long time.

"Madam, why are you here?" Beth asked as more hands reached out to her.

"It was Ezmerelda and Gia working together. A white witch and a demon shared their blood to take me down."

She heard all of them talking at once about the evil little bitch, Ezmerelda. Madam listened and hugged each body, not sure who she was hugging, but it didn't matter. These women had suffered the same fate as her, but they could still communicate!

They formed a circle, and Madam held hands with Beth on her right and Theodora on her left. She felt their energies and told them how much she loved and missed them all.

After the greetings of joy, Nora came through with a thought.

"Now that we're all here, let's figure out a way to get back."

Madam cried out, "Get back? To what, earth?"

"Yes!" they all screamed in unison.

Madam would have smiled at her extraordinary coven, if her lips were not melted together.

"I know Husband will realize this wasn't my fault. I'm going to beg him for mercy! I know he'll help us!"

******

Gia shivered uncontrollably in her cell. She didn't know if it was from the shock of being in hell, or if it was just the horrendous bone biting cold that swirled around her. She hated being cold, so this must be her torture.

She couldn't see anything; it was pitch black. Whether she blinked or opened her eyes, there was no difference. All she could feel was fear. She had no idea what was going to happen to her.

"Don't worry, Gia. You're safe," Ezmerelda's voice came from in front of her. "The demons have others to deal with. That's why we're in the furthest part of hell. No one wants to bother with us. I'm a traitor… not deserving of even being tortured," she sighed sadly.

Gia stood up, shaking uncontrollably, and looked into the pitch black.

"Ezmerelda? Where are you?"

A flame appeared on the ground, causing Gia to shield her eyes. The flame grew larger and larger. It gave off heat she instantly felt, and as she looked across from her, not even two feet away in her own cell, was Ezmerelda at her bars.

"Is that better?" Ezmerelda asked with true concern in her voice.

"Yeah. How'd you know I was freezing?"

"Because we're still attached… forever bound by our blood."

Gia looked hard at Ezmerelda, holding onto the thick bars. She looked like a broken, little girl. Even though the small area that separated them was about two feet, Gia felt like she was miles away in her isolated cell.

"It's past midnight, Ezmerelda. How is that possible?"

Ezmerelda's tiny hands held onto her own bars.

"We came together as one. We're united through our blood forever. I felt how cold you were. This doesn't bother me. I tend to run hot," she said with a smirk.

Gia swiped at her tears.

"I've lost everything… I can't spend an eternity in hell!" she sobbed.

Ezmerelda put her head down, feeling Gia's pain, as well as her own at her Isfet's betrayal.

"Yeah… I'm… I'm sorry. I didn't see through my mother's angle. The whole time, she was playing me to get released from my father. I'm so fucking stupid!" she yelled with fury.

Ezmerelda bashed her head several times against the metal bars in frustration and the overwhelming feeling of guilt she had never felt before.

"Oww," Gia cried out, "do you mind not harming yourself? It hurts my head too!"

Ezmerelda stopped and sighed as she softly said to Gia, "I kept trying to delay them. I kept… damn! If it had reached midnight, you'd still be with your family on earth!"

She slid down and put her head to her little knees, her wavy black hair covering her face.

Gia felt the pain of her own loss, but she felt a whoosh of betrayal and hurt as Ezmerelda's feelings bopped into her own. She had been deceived by her own mother.

"Ezmerelda, it's not your fault. Your mother-"

"It is MY fault!" The fire grew wider and higher, causing Gia to sweat. Ezmerelda stood up and took the bars in her tiny hands, her green eyes flashing in the massive flames. "I should have known better! She's a fucking demon who lies! I wanted to be just like her! And now I've dragged you down to hell, and I'm so fucking pissed!"

The bars between her tiny hands moved, making a moaning sound.

Gia's eyes widened.

"Did you just-"

Ezmererlda nodded and said in shock, "I did."

Gia and Ezmerelda shared the same thought… they wouldn't be trapped in the depths of hell. As their anger, rage and determination to get revenge coursed through their shared blood, they both laughed as they ripped apart the metal bars, piece by piece.

Their united blood, anger, resentment, and every other negative feeling rose up in them through their small hands, tearing apart the cells that had once tried to contain them.

Foolishly, they had no idea this was a trap. The two of them would never know freedom. They would feel the hope, but then it would be cruelly ripped away from them over and over again. The devil enjoyed watching his traitorous daughter think she could free herself and her annoying white witch friend!

The devil smiled as he ignored the pleas from his final wife as she cried to him from purgatory. He was quite happy that she was doomed forever. He shut her voice down, never planning on hearing her whimper for mercy again.

Now, he could focus on the devastating destruction that Isfet and Catherine had planned. He snarled and knew this was only the beginning of hell being released on earth.

Chapter 24

"Miss Sophie, are you okay?" Gia asked, horrified as she was hovering above the woman who had flown backwards out of her seat.

Sophie had just witnessed everything that would happen if she helped the woman in front of her. The devil, the devastation, the cruelty of death everywhere just to save one baby.

No, Sophie would not help Gia.

She would not because her daughter, Ziggy, would end up dead and in purgatory. Sophie would be the catalyst to Gia finding her white witch roots, thereby causing Ezmerelda to share her demonic blood with her. THAT COULD NOT HAPPEN!

If Sophie helped Gia to try to save one baby from Madam's last sacrifice, she would be releasing evil into the world that she could not even begin to fathom. Sophie was innately good.

If it meant that Gia would lose a child, compared to the losses of Riley, Charlotte, Ziggy, Gia and herself, along with unleashing Isfet from hell to bring uncontrollable forces of pure evil to the earth, she would not help the forlorn woman in front of her.

Sophie stood up slowly, visibly shaken by the horrors she had just witnessed. It had been like watching a movie in fast forward inside of her mind when Gia had touched her.

Again, Sophie told herself she could not and would not help Gia.

Let the story play out as it would without her getting involved. Let the baby boy be sacrificed to save everyone else from Madam, Ezmerelda, Isfet, and even Gia's evilness.

Sophie cleared her throat, knowing she had just changed the course of destiny.

"I'm sorry, but I can't read you."

"What? Why not?" Gia asked grumpily.

"Because the only thing I'll be able to tell you is you need help for your alcoholism. It's a disease, Gia. You can overcome it, and you can have a fantastic and happy life. Don't let something that happened in your past chart your future with your wife. I strongly encourage you to get support through rehab or by joining AA. Other than that, your alcoholism is what will ruin your life."

Gia had been standing with her arms crossed in front of her, seething with anger and already wishing for her next shot of whiskey.

She angrily sputtered, "You know, Miss Sophie, you don't know shit. You're a phony… I'm *not* an alcoholic and nothing ever happened to me, so I think you should just shut the hell up."

Sophie raised an eyebrow as she sat her plump, large frame back into her chair.

"Really, detective? Well, all I know is a man with the initials of R and O, who made it to Sergeant in another precinct, hurt you terribly in the academy." Gia glared defensively at her, but Sophie continued. "I'm telling you, young lady, don't let him control your current life by the actions of one night from over twenty years ago. You are stronger than that," Sophie quietly said, "And strong people *can* ask for help."

Gia threw up her arms in frustration. As she stormed away, Sophie brought her favorite cross into her pudgy hand. She held it and prayed for the future of everyone she now knew would be tormented by her refusal to help Gia.

Sophie wiped away a few tears. She hoped she had done the right thing.

Stay tuned for what happens next in: *Madam's Jewels 2: The Reckoning!*

Made in the USA
Coppell, TX
05 April 2021